NIGHT MAGIC

EMILIE RICHARDS

COPYRIGHT

NIGHT MAGIC

By Emilie Richards
New Orleans Nights, Book Three

Copyright 2018

ISBN: 9781721166589

Cover design: Art by Karri

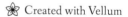 Created with Vellum

FOREWORD

New Orleans Nights

New Orleans nights are as intriguing as the lives of three friends raised together on the city's streets. Lifelong solidarity has seen each man through difficult times, but challenges still lurk in the Big Easy, where love is always complicated—but worth any struggle.

#1 *Lady of the Night*
#2 *Bayou Midnight*
#3 *Night Magic*

For the latest information and news about Emilie's books visit her website at http://emilierichards.com

CHAPTER 1

From the gardenia tucked behind her left ear to the straps of her white high-heeled sandals, Dr. Daffy Brookes was the prototype of a sacrificial virgin. The chalk-white sun dress she'd dragged from the back of her closet was unrelieved by the faintest touch of color. It was only May, but in deference to a bone-dissolving heat wave, she'd refused to wear jewelry, or even makeup. Only her wild red curls--frizzing uncontrollably in the New Orleans moisture-drenched air--gave any hint that she wasn't a candidate for the stone altar.

Daffy wasn't sure why "sacrificial virgin" had come to mind when she'd glimpsed herself in the glass door of the French Quarter shop she was about to enter. She was too old and too exuberantly alive to be either a sacrifice or a virgin. But the idea had popped out of her subconscious like a piece of morning toast, and even if the description didn't quite fit, she liked it. The idea of ruthlessly squandered innocence increased the drama of what she was about to do. And Daffy loved drama.

Assessing her reflection one more time, she threw the door open, ready for anything.

The sacrificial virgin enters the abode of evil.

She had spent too many years training to be a psychologist, and then becoming one, to believe that evil existed outside the human mind. But for just a moment, she let herself wallow in fantasy.

The room was dark and smelled of incense. The drone of muffled drumbeats filled the air, and cobweb-embossed herbs hanging from the ceiling waved back and forth in the forced breeze of an air conditioner.

Standing on the threshold of Doctor Fantôme's Sanctuary of Voodoo, surrounded by sights, smells and sounds that were guaranteed to plummet visitors back to the days of Marie Laveau, New Orleans's most famous voodoo queen, Daffy decided that the atmosphere inside the shop was like the stuffed snake hanging from a moss-draped branch behind plexiglass in the far corner. The ambience could twine around you, squeezing and constricting breath until nothing was left, except feeling and instinct, and the very beginnings of terror.

Her own response fascinated her. This was just a shop, a commercial venture playing on New Orleans' history and mystique. Doctor Fantôme probably made a fortune trading on fear and passion. But how much more frightening would the shop seem if she weren't an emotionally secure adult with a firm grip on reality? How much more frightening, if she were only sixteen and emotionally fragile to begin with?

Daffy was well-rounded and rational. Yet her skin felt clammy, and her heart was beating faster and harder. Neither was due to the long walk down Rue Saint. . . Saint Something-or-Other. Sadly, she could see how an impressionable teenager like Jewel Martinez might be taken in by the Sanctuary's carefully manipulated sensual assault. The whole package was just clever enough to affect any susceptible, suffering soul.

Now she had to figure out how much it was affecting Jewel.

"May I help you?"

The voice startled her, although it made sense someone would be in the shop to wait on customers. She closed the door behind her and turned to examine the man sitting on a stool just three feet away. She nodded to acknowledge him. "I don't think so."

Talk about drama. The man—somewhere in his early thirties—was absolutely perfect for his role as merchant of voodoo secrets. She wondered how many unsuspecting female tourists had found themselves coming back to the Sanctuary of Voodoo again and again, just to enjoy his exotic allure.

This was no boy-next-door. Looking at him, it was clear that she wasn't in a shop selling Mardi Gras T-shirts or any of the Quarter's standard souvenirs. His thick black hair was neither long nor short, waving back from a broad forehead and accenting eyes as dark as midnight. His olive skin accented white teeth. And his mouth? His mouth was best of all. She had no trouble imagining his beautifully sensual lips forming any number of incantations.

She realized she was staring, so she turned a little to give the shop the same detailed examination. As she did, something nagged at her, something about the man, other than his suitability for his chosen occupation, strummed the strings of her subconscious. But when no tune emerged she forced herself to concentrate on the task at hand.

He spoke from behind her. "This place probably has everything you need."

His voice was deep and musical, and she thought the words were tinged with humor. Humor was probably a good sign. Maybe he didn't take himself or his voodoo mission too seriously.

She turned back to smile a little. "I'll bet you do. It seems very. . . complete."

He was smiling, too, a perfectly normal smile. It was a smile you might see anywhere–if it was your lucky day. The man himself might look as if he'd feel right at home chanting and writhing, stripped down to nothing except a boa constrictor necklace, but the smile told a different story. Daffy was intrigued.

She decided to keep the conversation flowing. "I don't know anything about voodoo. I just came in to soak up the air-conditioning, and maybe the atmosphere."

"There's plenty of that."

And he was the best part. His jeans were black and just tight enough. His T-shirt was black, too, stretched across a chest that was broad, muscular and almost surely tattooed. And his hands? His hands were long-fingered and beautifully shaped, but they were also smudged and stained, calling forth visions of voodoo potions and moonlight rituals.

Strangely enough, his hands, too, seemed familiar.

Tearing her gaze away, Daffy examined the room with the same attention to detail, beginning in the farthest corner.

"Don't you think the snake is a nice touch?" he asked. "That's *Li Grande Zombi*, said to be the holder of intuitive knowledge. She's used in rituals."

His voice came from right behind her. As a psychologist she could give lectures on the principles of personal space and the ramifications of invading it, but she felt only pleasure. And although she didn't believe in repressing emotion, this was one feeling she would have to file away and investigate another time.

She stepped forward a little. "Was the snake your idea?"

"I'm pretty sure Fantôme came up with the decor."

"Oh, you're not him. Fantôme, I mean." She was relieved.

"Nope."

"But you're right. The snake does add a certain panache." She moved closer for a better look. "It looks real."

As she said the words, a narrow tongue darted out of the snake's mouth, and its head began to wave from side to side.

She jumped back and put her hand over her chest. "Holy Mother! And now I see why."

"The air conditioner probably makes her sleepy. I bet that's the first time she's moved all day."

"Turn it up."

He laughed. "She's Fantôme's darling."

"Is she used for something other than putting the fear of God into tourists?"

"Catching mice at night. When he closes he puts a sign on the front door that says. . ." He made his voice low and ominous. "'Beware the Slithering Reptile.'"

"That sure beats Beware of the Dog."

"She's all the security Fantôme needs. And besides, what burglar wants to risk a voodoo curse?"

"I'd really love to know if you're kidding." Daffy wasn't sure whether the perfumed air or the persistent recorded thrumming was affecting her, but she was beginning to sway from side to side, along with the snake.

Shaking her head to clear it, she wandered over to a set of shelves covered with apothecary jars and squinted into the gloom. The Sanctuary of Voodoo probably saved a fortune on electricity and window cleaning products. Still, the candles burning in glass jars were a nice touch. With their help she could almost see.

"So what do you think?"

"I don't know." She strained to read the labels. "John the Conqueror Root, Dragon's Blood, Love Powder, Boss-Fix Powder, Controlling Oil, Devil's Shoe Strings." She tried to think of a casual way to word a question. "I know some people actually believe in voodoo, but there can't be many, can there?"

"Judging by the people who flock through this door and leave with little brown packages, I'd say a good number."

Daffy dismissed his words. "Tourists. Tourists buying

souvenirs to take home to friends." She waited just a fraction of a second before she added, "and people susceptible to this kind of thing. Like teenagers."

"You're not from New Orleans, are you?" He qualified his question. "Not originally, I mean. You live here now, have, in fact for. . ." He paused, his gaze drifting away from hers as if he was envisioning her past. "I'd say three years or so."

She faced him. Up close his eyes weren't black, but the darkest velvet brown, and now that they were focused back on her, shining with good humor. "You tell fortunes, too?"

His lips curved into his trademark stunning smile. "You'd be surprised what I could tell you."

"How did you figure that out?"

"Any New Orleanian has seen voodoo and hoodoo at work, whether he recognizes it or not. Most do recognize it, though, even if they don't believe it."

"Hoodoo?"

"A little different, but in Louisiana voodoo and hoodoo are entwined, and it's hard to tell one from the other. Gris-gris and little cloth dolls? Mostly hoodoo. But let's go back to you."

"You're serious, aren't you?" Daffy moved a little closer. He was probably just average in height and slender, too, which still made him inches taller than she was. But the height and weight were deceptive. Something about the way he stood made it clear that taking care of himself on the New Orleans streets was never a problem.

"You come from. . ." he hesitated. "You come from all over. You've lived in twenty, no twenty-one different states, and you've called every one of them home."

She tried not to show how impressed she was. She tried not to *be* impressed. "Twenty-two. You forgot Montana, but that's all right. We didn't live there long, and I was only five."

"I usually forget Montana. I don't know why."

She was hooked. "Tell me, if voodoo is so common here, why haven't I heard of it before this?"

"Before what?"

She turned away. "Before coming here."

"Ah, but you didn't just happen to come here. You're here to find out everything you can about voodoo because. . ." He stopped, then shrugged. "I don't know why."

"I'm glad to hear that."

"It must have something to do with one of your patients."

Daffy spun around, and as she did, one of the clumps of dried herbs hanging from the ceiling fell at her feet, stirring a cloud of dust. She sneezed three times before she could speak. "How do you know I have patients?"

His eyes sparkled. "My uncanny insight. My voodoo powers. Also the identification badge on your handbag."

"Duh." She looked down at her own laminated photo labeled with her name and City Hospital identification number. "Some detective I'd be."

"Was I right?"

"You got it."

"And not a medical doctor." He lifted a finger in the air. "A psychologist."

She knew when to change the subject. Jewel Martinez's story wasn't something she could discuss. And at this point she wasn't sure the Sanctuary of Voodoo was innocent in whatever was troubling the girl.

She swept her hand, encompassing the entire shop. "Tell me what all these things are used for."

"It depends." He hooked his thumbs in his pockets and let his gaze roam over her face. "The Sanctuary of Voodoo has something for everyone."

She didn't miss his appraisal or its effect. Under different circumstances she would have been captivated by her own response. Now, she was only annoyed. "Well, give me an example. What do people use these little dolls for? I'm guessing they're made in Hong Kong."

He followed her to the display of cloth dolls carefully segmented by lines, each section numbered. Included inside the plastic packaging were multi-colored pins and instructions on how to use them. Exactly where to stick the pins for a desired result seemed key.

"This is the kind of thing tourists buy," he said, opening one so she could read the directions.

Daffy scanned it before handing the paper back to him. "Doesn't this worry you?"

"Should it?"

"You can't really believe that sticking pins in a miniature Raggedy Ann doll can give anybody power. Power comes from within."

"Haven't you ever had a new dress that made you feel like a queen?"

She knew exactly where he was leading. "That's not the same thing."

"Maybe not exactly, but when you wore that dress, you probably felt powerful, and that made you act powerfully."

"Power and aggression are different. Completely different. People stick pins in these things hoping to harm others."

"No, that's the voodoo of popular culture, and, of course, Fantôme would never recommend anything like that."

"Of course." She dragged out the last word.

He grinned. "The other side of voodoo is friendlier. Take this for instance." He touched Daffy's arm and guided her across the room. "Here's something every woman might need to know one day."

She read the hand-lettered sign out loud. "Bind-A-Man: Essences of vanilla, verbena, vetiver. . . What's vetiver?"

He uncorked a vial below the sign and held it under her nose.
She almost choked. "Is that a lure or an anesthetic?" She
waved the scent away and continued reading. "Wintergreen,
lovage and follow-me-boy water. I can see how this place makes
its money."

"You're not in the spirit."

She continued reading. "Anoint a white candle with each
individual oil, then with follow-me-boy water. When properly
anointed, burn candle in a bed of white sand until it's extin-
guished. Remove wick and crumble remaining wax into the sand
in fine particles until no longer visible. In the bedroom, scrubbed
clean of dirt and hair, sprinkle the sand in concentric circles on
each side of the bed." She looked up. "After all that scrubbing,
too."

"They say love's worth working for."

"What red-blooded man would follow any woman into a
stinking room covered with sand?"

"Depends on the woman."

"Or the man." She paused. "And how desperate he is."

He grinned. "I know for a fact you don't need anything like
this yourself. I see a man in your life." He closed his eyes
momentarily.

"Daffy couldn't help but smile, too. "This ought to be good."

"A tall man with brown hair and a gentle smile. He works
with you."

The man was obviously Jeremy Miller. "What else do
you see?"

"I see you earlier in the spring, sitting side by side in St. Louis
Cathedral, holding hands like teenage lovers. I see. . ."

The truth was as spontaneous as the ray of sunshine that
finally defeated the filthy Sanctuary windows. Both had taken
their time breaking through.

"You were in Sam and Antoinette's wedding! You know, if I

weren't so jaded, I might actually have wondered if you could read my mind."

He opened his eyes, then he winked. "Admit it. You thought you'd discovered a psychological phenomenon. Something you couldn't explain."

"Listen, I can explain very little. I couldn't begin to explain the existence of this place, for instance." Daffy was delighted she'd been so thoroughly fooled. "Now I remember you. You're Sam's friend. Um. . . Scooter."

"Skeeter."

"Skeeter. You know, my instincts are usually more productive. I knew there was something about you that was bothering me. But you looked so different at the wedding." She tilted her head. "What's your real name?"

"With a name like Daffy, you can ask?"

She was surprised he'd remembered. Her nickname wasn't on her badge. She closed her eyes, the way he had. "I see a man with hair to his shoulders, and. . . a moustache? Dressed in a dark suit and a white shirt standing at the front in St. Louis Cathedral. The suit's been worn before, but the shirt's obviously new, so new that the man keeps fiddling with the collar. In fact, I predict that the shirt is now in the very back of his closet."

"So it is."

"The man stands at the back of the church afterwards, and I'm about to be introduced to him. I think, how interesting. I wonder what his name is, and then, I find out."

"And?"

She opened her eyes. "And then I wonder how such an interesting guy could have been named after the world's most annoying insect."

"Second only to a giant flying roach, another Louisiana staple."

"Your nickname says nothing about you. Everybody who knows me says mine fits perfectly."

"So I was told."

She wondered why he'd been told anything. Even more intriguing? Why had he remembered? "What else were you told?"

"That you were dating the man with the sweet smile, along with several others."

She thought she might be catching on. That he'd found her attractive on that day six weeks before was encouraging. "Sam told you that?"

"Sam and I have been friends since we were kids."

"Well, did he also tell you I wasn't serious about any of the men I was dating, and that the one with the sweet smile is a colleague and friend only?"

Interest sparked in his eyes. "Sam was a bundle of nerves. He couldn't concentrate long enough to elaborate."

"Really? Evidently he told you my life history, leaving out Montana."

"No, only that you're not from here and that you've lived all over. The number of places was a lucky guess."

The shop door creaked. Daffy glimpsed a dark-skinned man in his fifties carrying a white paper sack. Skeeter, who was between them, raised his hand in greeting. "Fantôme."

Fantôme strolled toward them. "I would have starved if you hadn't volunteered to let me slip out for a sandwich." At the sound of Fantôme's voice, the snake began to slither to the top of its branch.

Skeeter nodded in Daffy's direction. "Doctor Fantôme, meet Daffy Brookes. We're old friends." He stepped aside, giving Daffy a clear view of the other man, who was a definite disappointment in the drama department. Dressed in conservative slacks and an ivory dress shirt, he looked like any middle-aged businessman.

There was no mystery in the balding head or the bulge of his belly.

Fantôme nodded. "Welcome to my Sanctuary."

"Right. Thanks." Daffy caught Skeeter's eye. "You don't work here?"

"Disappointed?"

Fantôme had already gone to check on his snake, and Daffy leaned closer to Skeeter. "Relieved," she said softly enough that only he could hear. "What *do* you do?"

He held up his hands. "Can't you tell?"

The smudges were suddenly as ordinary as paint. She smiled at her own imagination. "You're an artist. Now I remember. When we were introduced Sam mentioned that, and I noticed what beautiful hands you have. You're a police artist."

He laughed. "No chance of that. I do portraits at Jackson Square."

"Not true. I remember what Sam said. You've helped more than once on his cases. That makes you a police artist, even if you won't claim it."

"I only do that as a favor to Sam. Believe me, the force would *never* be with me."

She groaned. Fantôme saved her from commenting. "Skeeter, you're sure I can't pay you for your time?"

Skeeter waved aside the offer. "But I do have to set up over at the Square." He nodded to Daffy. "Are you going to stay and soak up more atmosphere?"

"No, I've seen enough." She waited until he and Fantôme had said their goodbyes before she stepped out to the sidewalk. The glare of sunshine and impact of heat and humidity made her wince. "I think I almost prefer that crazy place."

"That's saying a lot."

"You don't work there at all? No connection? You just

happened to walk by, and he pulled you in to make you mind the store while he went for lunch?"

"Evidently you need to be absolutely sure I have nothing to do with the Sanctuary of Voodoo."

Daffy moved farther from the door. "Frankly, that place gives me the creeps."

"You know it's supposed to, right?"

"Fantôme has succeeded beyond all expectations."

He touched her arm. Casually, briefly, and she still felt the impact. "Which way are you walking?"

"Down to Canal to catch the streetcar back to work."

He started in that direction, too. They walked along the flagstone sidewalks under iron lace balconies that were the hallmark of the French Quarter.

Skeeter stayed close to her side. "Fantôme commissioned a portrait of Marie Laveau to hang in the shop. I delivered it this morning, so I volunteered to stay while he picked up his lunch. His assistant is out sick."

"Well, you missed your calling. You were great."

"Think so?"

"Much better than Fantôme himself. He looks like an insurance salesman."

"Insurance wouldn't be nearly as lucrative. When I told him what I was going to charge for the painting, he didn't flinch. Of course, I may find one of those little dolls in my bed. With a pin straight through its heart."

Daffy realized just how much she was enjoying their conversation. "Skeeter what?"

They crossed a narrow street, stepped past a crowd of giggling teenagers, and then another group of young men who had clearly spent some time in the Bourbon Street bars.

"Harwood," Skeeter said, once the sidewalk was clear again. She felt a return of physical awareness. Only now that she wasn't dealing with a voodoo priest or entrepreneur, the awareness had quadrupled.

"I know more about you than I said." Skeeter pulled her to one side to let a trio of tourists stomping out of a shop pass by before he continued. "I know you work with Antoinette at Psychologist Associates. You're a Gestalt psychologist."

"I use anything that works."

"An eclectic psychologist."

"That about covers it."

"What I don't know is what you were doing in the Sanctuary of Voodoo. Some people get a charge out of dabbling in the occult, but I'm guessing you're not one of them."

She debated how much she should say. She was surprised she wanted to share her reasons with Skeeter. Two of the people whose judgment she trusted knew him well, even if she didn't, and they had invited him to their very private wedding.

"I have this client," she began. "A sixteen-year-old girl who's suffering from depression. I can't get through to her."

"I'm guessing eclectic or not, you weren't planning to use voodoo as a last resort."

"Wouldn't it be terrific if we could just go down to the corner store and buy remedies for our personal problems? It's no wonder voodoo is as popular as you say."

"We could get rid of anybody we didn't like, seduce anybody we wanted to, and live in health and happiness until we died of old age."

She pushed the part about seduction out of her mind, where it had immediately started to root. "Those kinds of easy solutions have tremendous appeal, especially to people who feel they lack personal power."

Skeeter's answer sounded as if it came from personal experience. "And teenagers always feel that way."

She nodded, even though he wasn't looking at her. "Just

about. They're caught between childhood, when their parents made all the decisions, and adulthood, where they will have control over their lives."

"Sometimes adults have control," he said. "But plenty of adults have given it up. Isn't that why we have prisons and psychiatric institutions?"

"Partly maybe. Anyway, my client doesn't want to be in therapy, but her parents have insisted. We've made so little progress, but yesterday she did a strange thing. And that's what led me to the Sanctuary today."

"What was that?" He sounded genuinely interested.

"She came into her session with a small paper bag, like she'd been out shopping. When she left, she picked up her purse, but she didn't pick up the bag. She left it there. I didn't notice until she was gone."

"Doesn't that happen pretty often?"

"Maybe. But as a therapist, I have to assume that nothing that happens in a session is accidental. On some level, I think she wanted me to see what was inside that bag."

"Which was?"

"Another bag, only this one was cloth tied with string. Inside was a mixture of herbs of some kind, a rock, what looked like hair clippings. The only other thing in the paper bag was a receipt." She paused for effect. "From Doctor Fantôme's Sanctuary of Voodoo."

CHAPTER 2

Skeeter stifled a smile when Daffy frowned. The apricot-tinted perfection of her complexion was only marred by the earnest wrinkles in her forehead. When the frown disappeared, the wrinkles would, too. She had beautiful skin, translucent skin he'd never be able to capture on canvas. And her hair. Titian had made his mark painting hair like hers. With Daffy standing in front of him, Skeeter had no trouble understanding why.

He pulled himself back to the subject at hand. "So that's why you were there."

"It was just a hunch. I don't know what I expected to find. Certainly not *you*."

He wondered if her skin was as soft as it looked. Maybe the urge to find out came from the artist inside him, the sculptor, but he knew better. "I'd say it was a lucky coincidence our paths crossed."

"I'm not sure just how lucky it was for my client. I let myself get distracted. I never found out what could have been in that cloth bag."

"It does sound like a gris-gris bag. And almost anything could be in it. They're individual, made up by practitioners, depending on what's needed. Sometimes they're good luck charms, sometimes, but rarely, more sinister. Even if the contents were analyzed, only your client and the person who mixed it for her would know for sure."

Daffy began heading toward Canal Street once more. "So, how do you know so much about this?"

"I've lived in neighborhoods where voodoo and hoodoo are a way of life. A few years ago a lady three doors down, who had a certain 'mysterious' reputation, swore she was going to put a curse on her neighbor's dog if it didn't stop barking in the middle of the night. One night old Rusty started to bark, and right in the middle of a ferocious yelp, he stopped. When the owner went outside to see what had happened, she found the dog lying on his back with all four legs straight up in the air. Dead as a doornail."

"Maybe somebody poisoned him."

"I think he died of old age. In dog years he was about a hundred and two." He put his hand over his heart in false piety. "I think Rusty went mid-bark, exactly the way he wanted to."

She tried not to laugh. "Did the voodoo lady claim responsibility?"

"I doubt anybody asked her. Rusty's owner was pretty intimidated. Last time I talked to her she was sticking to cats–but not black ones."

"Maybe I should talk to your voodoo lady for more info."

"She disappeared one night. One moment she was there, sitting out on her stoop catching the breeze, and the next morning everything in the house was gone. Just like that." He snapped his fingers. "Magic."

"I love this city!" Daffy stopped, and stretched forward on her tiptoes, as if she were dancing. "This crazy, wonderful, colorful city. There's no place like it, is there?"

"No place. What brought that on?"

Daffy smiled up at him and included him in a sweep of her hand. "Here we are, and everywhere we look there's something or somebody worth looking at, and the stories! The stories told about New Orleans and its people. I just love it."

Skeeter watched her whirl as if she were dancing to music only she could hear. He bet she did that often. "My story about a dead dog inspired so much joy?"

She laughed. "All part of the milieu."

"I love women who are easy to please."

She was silent until they reached Canal Street. She turned to say goodbye. "I took you a long way from the Square, but I appreciated your company." She touched his arm. "You've been a help."

Skeeter pushed down the urge to cover her hand with his. "Have I? That's good."

"You reminded me just how easy it is to let my imagination get out of control." She nodded, as if she was trying to convince herself of something. "I'm a good therapist. I play hunches, and more often than not, they're right. But I also tend to let my right brain take over."

He knew what she meant, but he asked anyway to keep her there a moment longer. "Right brain?"

"The spontaneous, impulsive part of us. If they ever take a good look inside my head, they're going to find a left brain the size of a peanut and a right brain so heavy it'll take two technicians to cart it out of the lab."

Skeeter gave up and covered her hand briefly. Her skin was warm, and her hand fit inside his. He liked that. "And how do I figure into all this?"

"Well, less than an hour ago I could see you in my imagination writhing and chanting voodoo litanies."

"And now?"

"Now?" Her gaze locked with his. "Well, now I see someone different. I see a man with a sense of humor and keen intelligence who is comfortable with the world in a way that most people aren't. I like you, Skeeter."

Her eyes were the palest green. She was an earnest wood nymph, and he wondered if when he blinked, she would simply disappear. "I like you too, Daffy."

"Good." She turned as the stop light changed. Looking back to wave goodbye, she crossed just in time to catch the next streetcar.

Skeeter watched her go and wondered why he felt his life had just made a 360 degree turn for the better.

Two hours later Daffy's burst of exuberance had been subdued and replaced by something more professional. Professionalism wasn't something she took out of her closet and wore whenever necessary. She was a creature of many moods who trusted herself to flow with them. Now her mood was anticipatory. Something was in the air, and she was waiting to find out exactly what it might be.

"This is boring!" A gum-cracking sixteen-year-old in a short black skirt and a Goliath-sized sweatshirt got up from the small circle of chairs in the office group room and flounced to the window. Sharee claimed to be a descendant of Native Americans who had shielded runaway slaves before the Civil War, and she wore her dark curly hair in a long symbolic braid down her back. "I don't know why I have to come here. Nothing ever happens."

"Nothing ever happens because nobody cooperates with Dr. Brookes." Linda, a pretty blonde with a voice sweet enough to trigger a diabetic coma, always sided with Daffy, no matter what she really thought. "She's only trying to help."

"F---Screw you, Linda. You'd suck up to the devil if you thought it would get you a better slab of brimstone." Natalie, the third teenager, was a striking fifteen-year-old, with creamy caramel-colored skin, hazel eyes, and reddish brown corkscrew curls ending at her nape, but her anger was the most noticeable thing about her.

As usual Daffy was glad she'd established ground rules on profanity and enforced them—when she could. All the girls in this group attended the same elite private school, Riverview Academy, but she hadn't seen any sign that their mostly privileged lives had substantially moderated their vocabulary. She was determined that here, they would learn to express their emotions in more acceptable ways, no matter what they did or said on the outside.

Jewel Martinez, the fourth teenager, continued to sit quietly in her seat, her expression as blank as a rental apartment wall.

Daffy stretched her arms over her head. "I'm bored, too."

"Then do something," Sharee said. "Don't you get paid enough to do something?"

Daffy ignored the girl's tone and sneer. "What would you like me to do?"

The question was met with silence.

Finally, Linda broke it. Her tone was uneasy. "I hate this group when it gets quiet."

"The silence scares you." Daffy's tone was neutral. Linda, one of Antoinette's clients, was part of the group because at the beginning of the last school year her best friend had died after a short illness, which sent Linda's world into a spin. Her mother was worried because her daughter didn't know how to move forward or put her feelings into words. Daffy was trying to work on both fronts here.

"No. I'm not afraid of anything," Linda said with an edge to her voice that Daffy had never heard.

Natalie faked a laugh. "Bull–. You're afraid of your own shadow."

Linda whirled, and with the first display of spirit in her three months of attendance, she speared Natalie with her gaze. "What's with you, Nat? I don't need you on my case. Why don't you work on some of your own problems?"

"I don't have any problems. You and that zombie over there have problems cornered." Natalie pointed to Jewel.

Daffy watched Jewel's expression. For a moment after Natalie's remark, she'd looked terrified. As so often happened in group therapy, Daffy had to make a choice about which client to focus on. This time she chose Jewel. Linda and Natalie were on the verge of something important, but she thought that would hold.

"I wouldn't like it if someone talked to me the way Nat talks to you," she said. "How does it make you feel?"

"I don't care."

Daffy got up from her chair and stood behind Jewel. She rested her hand on the girl's shoulder to show that she was going to be speaking for her. "I don't care. If I don't care, nobody can get to me. Nothing anybody says will matter. I can be free." Daffy withdrew her hand, resumed her seat and waited.

Jewel remained silent.

Sharee challenged Daffy. "What makes you think you know how anybody in here really feels?"

"I don't. I can only guess."

"Yeah? Well, your guesses are always wrong," Natalie said. "You don't know nothing about nothing."

"Enlighten me," Daffy said. "Go ahead and tell me where my guesses are wrong. Take all the time you need."

Natalie looked surprised at Daffy's good-natured reply. She was the only girl in the group without wealthy parents, or, for that matter, parents of any kind. She lived in a crowded group home and attended Riverview on scholarship. She'd been added to the group because her grades were plummeting, and before long, if they didn't improve, she would be back in a public school with far less to offer.

A brief pause was followed by a real stream of profanity. She finished by joining Sharee at the window.

Daffy knew there was something more important going on here than forbidden words. She took the opportunity to move to Natalie's chair. "I hate living in a world where people make mistakes," she said in Natalie's voice. "I'm sick of having to put up with other people's stupidity. If they just knew what I know, if they had just gone through what I've gone through, they'd understand."

"You don't know what I've gone through!" Natalie stomped back into the circle to stand in front of Daffy. "You don't have any idea what I've gone through. Get out of my chair."

Daffy shook her head. "Go sit in my chair."

For a moment it seemed as if Natalie would resist. Then she flung herself into Daffy's chair, the opportunity to play the part of psychologist too good to pass up.

"Well, well, young ladies," Natalie said in a tone that Daffy would never use. "What do we have here? What little squabbles did you bring into the group for us to work on? Did somebody have a fight with her mommy? With her boyfriend? She rubbed her hands together gleefully. "Maybe somebody stubbed her little-bitty toe on the way to see me?"

Sharee rejoined the group. "Oh, doctor," she said in a tone that was obviously meant to imitate Linda's. "I just love being here. It's the best hour of my week. I get so much out of it."

Linda looked hurt, but she responded by pulling her skirt up to expose her knees and began to chew pretend gum in earnest. "Not me. This is boring. Bor-r-r-ing. Nothing ever happens here. Nothing ever happens anywhere. Life is boring. I am boring."

Sharee's eyes glittered with anger. "Sharee, dear," she said to Linda, "you're not boring. You're beautiful, sweet, charming. Everything and everyone on the outside are the problem."

"You're *all* the problem," Daffy said in Natalie's voice. "This stupid group is the problem. Without it, life would be so great."

Natalie as therapist interrupted. "You know, you can't say that, Nat dear. Life has never been great for you. Not since day one. And it never will be. It can't be. Not after what you've done." She stopped, realizing that she had slipped out of her role and back into herself. Her words had belonged to Natalie.

Daffy spoke in her own voice. "Why won't life ever be great, Nat? Why do you have to pay such a high price? What have you done to deserve a life filled with rage as punishment?"

"I don't have to tell you anything!"

Daffy nodded and waited.

Natalie's hand gesture was as profane as her words had been. "You and your stupid little games. You think you can trick us into telling you stuff. Well, I don't have to tell you anything! Hear me?"

"That's absolutely true. You don't have to tell me anything. It's always your right to decide if you want to share anything with me or with anybody here."

Natalie sat back and folded her arms. Her answer was clear.

Daffy's watch buzzed as a reminder that it was nearly time to end the session. A layman looking on would guess the group had been a failure, but Daffy knew the day's work was a success, a success with everyone except Jewel, unfortunately. The pretty teenager with the curling brown hair and cobalt blue eyes seemed to withdraw more every time Daffy saw her. Jewel was one step away from hospitalization. And that was something Daffy never took lightly.

"Let's just sit here quietly for a few minutes to finish up," she said. "I'd like each of you to think about something before you go." She waited nearly a minute as they reluctantly settled in. "I want you to imagine yourself on a deserted island." She ignored Sharee's groans. "You're only going to be on this island for a few minutes. A plane is going to land and take you far away. You'll never be able to get back to the island again. You have just two minutes to dig a hole, a very deep hole that no one will ever find. In the bottom of the hole you can leave anything you want, any secrets, worries, failures. When you leave the island, everything in that hole will stay behind."

Natalie broke the silence. "This is so stupid! Everything you do here is stupid."

Daffy nodded calmly, making it clear she understood. "Stupid can be another word for different. Things we've never done feel stupid at first. If this makes you too uncomfortable, you don't have to take part."

"I'm not going to."

"That's fine."

This time, except for the cracking of gum, and the restless movement of teenage limbs, the silence extended until Daffy dismissed them.

"Thank you for coming. Anybody who wants to talk about what they buried can do it next week."

"Fat chance." Natalie left the room and sucked a good portion of the air inside it with her.

Daffy watched them file out. As Jewel stood to go, she detained her with a hand on the girl's arm. "I'd like to see you for just a minute."

Jewel's expression didn't change.

"I've got something in my office for you." Daffy went to the doorway of the group room and beckoned Jewel to follow her.

Her office was only two doors away. Psychologist Associates rented most of the second story of a renovated mansion on Carrollton Avenue. The five psychologists who had joined together to form the practice shared the group room, waiting room, and the services of their motherly receptionist and secretary, Rosemarie Madison, known simply as Rosy. Daffy,

Antoinette Long and Jeremy Miller practiced full-time, so each had a private office. The other two psychologists were part-time. They saw the majority of their clients during evenings and week-ends, using whatever space was available.

The arrangement worked well for everyone. Not only could they share Rosy, they could share cases and viewpoints. Each had, at one time or another, referred clients to one of their part-ners, realizing that someone else might be able to work more effectively.

Now, looking at Jewel, who was standing stiffly in her office doorway, Daffy wondered if referring the girl to Antoinette for another evaluation might be best. Clients signed waivers to allow their cases to be discussed among the staff here for the best possible care. Jewel had been in private therapy for almost three months, and group therapy for six weeks. In all that time, Daffy has seen little or no change.

She decided to get right to the point. "Come in and close the door, Jewel. I have something here that you left yesterday."

Daffy waited until the door was shut before she pulled out the paper bag. "This is yours, isn't it?"

Jewel nodded, holding out her hand.

"I looked inside. I thought you might have wanted me to."

Jewel didn't answer. Daffy waited and finally the girl spoke. "My mother will be waiting."

Daffy handed her the bag. "Is the gris-gris bag supposed to bring you good luck?"

For a moment, feeling blazed in the girl's eyes. "No. . . yes."

"I think if I had to pick from those answers, I'd choose no."

"You won't tell my mother, will you?" The girl's tone was plaintive, not wheedling.

"Nothing that happens in here goes any further, unless you want it to." While confidentiality with teenagers was tricky, Jewel had refused to come unless Daffy promised that nothing the girl said would be relayed to the senior Martinezes.

Not that she'd said much.

"Everyone here is obligated to keep your secrets," Daffy said in reminder. "You can feel safe."

"Safe?" Jewel's voice slid up an octave as she drew out the one-syllable word. "Safe!" She began to laugh, and the sound chilled Daffy to the bone. "I'll never feel safe again!" She spun and flung open the office door, slamming it closed behind her.

Daffy listened to the echoes long after anyone else would have been able to hear them.

D affy touched her head to first one knee, and then the other. She was sitting on the Greek flokati rug in her office with heels touching and her bent legs flat against the thick wool. She had painted the walls a deep, reassuring sea green and dotted them with black and white photographs of people's faces. The plant-filled room was now perfect for almost anything, including discussing a client with a colleague.

"Something's going on with Jewel Martinez that I don't understand," she told Antoinette Long.

"I'll never understand how you do that. It's inhuman." Antoinette, on the rug beside her, tried to duplicate Daffy's movements, but her knees refused to get closer than six inches to the rug.

"Stick with it and don't overdo. You've only been stretching for a couple of weeks." Daffy adjusted the skirt of her sun dress and positioned her legs in front of her. She grasped her toes and pulled her head to her knees.

"That's one week too long." Antoinette sat back and watched

her friend contort her lithe figure. "So what's going on with Jewel Martinez?"

Daffy sat up. "I wish I knew. I can't seem to reach her." She explained about the gris-gris bag.

Antoinette frowned. Like Daffy she was thirty, but that was all they shared. Antoinette was slender, with black hair and blue eyes, assets she did very little to play up. Nor did she need to. Daffy thought that even when her friend frowned, she was remarkably beautiful.

"Did she leave the bag for you to find?" Antoinette asked.

"When I asked her, she seemed to want to talk about it, but she just couldn't. I'm worried, more worried than I've been about any client in a long time."

"It's the kids who get to you the most, isn't it?"

Antoinette understood since she had teenagers on her caseload, too, including Linda Moreda and Natalie Saizan, who Daffy only saw in group. "As if being a teenager's not hard enough," Daffy said. "Look at the world they've got to make it in."

"What do you think was the purpose of the gris-gris bag?"

"I don't know. How much do you know about voodoo?"

Antoinette shrugged. "Nothing much. Sam's cousin Leonce is married to a Cajun woman, and Didi's father is a traiteur. I gather that's a little bit like voodoo. We're such a mixture of cultures here, a little voodoo, a little Cajun black magic, a little African hoodoo, a little Creole superstition. It's hard to tell what's what."

"I wonder if Jewel knows more than we do." Daffy brightened a little. "By the way, I met a friend of yours today while I was investigating."

"Who was that?"

"Skeeter. Skeeter Harwood."

"I'm surprised you two haven't run into each other before this. He and Joshua Martane stood at the front with Sam during the wedding."

"We talked about that. He looked substantially different that day. Very Jean Lafitte."

"He'd still make an excellent pirate, wouldn't he? He said the hair and moustache brought him more customers at Jackson Square. My mother almost fainted when she realized he was going to be one of Sam's groomsmen."

"Well, he's not pretending to be Jean Lafitte now. But I bet he still has a line of women asking him to paint their portraits."

Antoinette's eyes sparkled. "You think?"

"He told me he and Sam have been friends since childhood." Daffy lifted her arms and began to twist from side to side.

"Skeeter was one of those people Sam loved before he realized he loved anybody. They grew up with Joshua, you know. The three were Irish Channel brats. I gather New Orleans has never seen the likes of that trio of walking terrors."

Daffy stopped twisting. "Well, look how well they turned out. A police officer, a psychologist—"

"Joshua's a minister, as well."

"A police officer, a psychologist-minister, and an artist. I gather Skeeter's pretty good. At least Doctor Fantôme at the Sanctuary of Voodoo liked his work well enough to commission a painting."

"No higher praise," Antoinette said wryly. "But actually, he is better than good. Skeeter can take anything, a face, a house, a landscape, and cut right to the bone. Sometimes his stuff is pretty hard to live with, because it says too much. Too much for some people to handle, I think."

"What do you mean?"

"He had a show at one of the galleries here a couple of months ago. The reviews were fabulous, but opening night hardly any of his work sold. The general feeling? Nobody wanted that much reality on their living room walls."

"He must have been hurt, or at least disappointed." Daffy realized she was feeling both for him.

"You can never tell with Skeeter. He hides a lot, although Sam disagrees. He says Skeeter shrugs off everything. Well, except once, that is."

"Once?"

They were interrupted by a rapped summons on the closed door. Before either could answer Rosy opened it and stuck her head inside. "Your intercom's off, dahlin'. How'm I supposed to tell you when you have a call?"

Daffy covered her face with her hands. "That's why it was off. You weren't supposed to tell me. I'm finished for the day."

"Then I'll tell the nice man with the beautiful voice that you don't want to have lunch with him tomorrow." Rosy began to close the door. Slowly. Very slowly.

Daffy knew full well that Rosy wasn't going anywhere. "The nice man with the beautiful voice told you he was asking me to lunch?"

"I told him you weren't taking calls. So he told me. I'd answer this one if I was you. He could be 'The Man.'"

Daffy looked at Antoinette. "She married you off. Now she's starting on me."

Rosy was unperturbed. "What'll I tell him?"

"I'll tell him myself." Daffy stood to reach for the phone. By the time she was seated again, both women were gone, and the door was closed.

"This is Daffy Brookes," she said into the receiver.

"Hi, Daffy, this is Skeeter."

He did have a beautiful voice. She'd almost forgotten because so many other things about him were beautiful, too. "Hi," she said in a warmer tone. "What's this about lunch?"

"I know a shady place at Audubon Park for a picnic. I'll supply the food and the funny stories, if you'll come."

"That's all I have to do?"

"That's it."

"Just tell me where." Daffy jotted the directions on a sticky note, then named a time the next day when she was free to meet him. "I was just talking to Antoinette about you," she said when she finished.

He hesitated just long enough for the psychologist in Daffy to register the pause and wonder. "So, now you know all about me," he said.

Daffy really knew very little other than his profession and the names of childhood friends. From his hesitation she suspected it was possible she wasn't going to like everything else she discovered. But if that were true, she wanted to hear those details from him. Whatever the mystery, she was going to find her answers under a shady tree at Audubon Park.

"I don't know all about you," she said. "I'll expect to hear everything tomorrow."

"We'll put swapping life stories on the agenda."

"Before or after we eat?"

Skeeter's answer was surprisingly serious. "Before, during and after. Mine, at least, is going to take some time to explain."

CHAPTER 3

Rain had fallen during the night, which seemed like a good thing. Unfortunately, the morning sun had zestfully converted it to steam, so that by noon, when Daffy stepped outside to get the streetcar to meet Skeeter, her shoulder-length curls kinked to chin length and her pores opened as if coaxed by an esthetician at an exclusive French Quarter salon.

She had suspected what the weather might be like, and in deference, she'd dressed in Banana Republic safari wear, like an explorer ready to tackle the farthest reaches of West Africa. Her khaki pants had enough pockets to hold three days' rations, and her extra-large cotton shirt was waterproof, bug-proof and most decidedly fantasy-proof. No one, absolutely no one, would have any exciting fantasies about her today.

The steamy atmosphere hadn't been her only reason for jungle wear. She wanted to keep her lunch date with Skeeter strictly platonic. She was impulsive; she was renowned for acting before words could form, but she was not foolish. She chose her men carefully, and she had not chosen many in her thirty years.

Skeeter was a surprise. Even when she'd thought he was

Fantôme himself, his attractions had been undeniable. He was a fantasy come to life, a voodoo doctor, a gypsy king, a buccaneer–without the eye patch–a desert sheik. And for a woman who believed that fantasies should be pursued, Skeeter was irresistible.

But there was much more than his fantasy value that appealed to her. In the final analysis, the real man, not the imaginary version, had captured her attention. Now it was that man she wanted to get to know. And she didn't want to be sidetracked by the shove-and-tug of their mutual sexual attraction.

That their attraction was mutual, she had no doubt. That it was sexual was also without question. That it was grounded in reality and capable of growth remained to be seen.

By the time Daffy walked across the lush, green length of Audubon Park, she was dripping wet from perspiration. She wasn't vain, but even a jungle explorer liked to look fresh and inviting when fighting snakes and hostile wildlife. Daffy wished she had a car. She wished she had accepted Skeeter's offer to pick her up at her office. She wished the weather would break; she wished a breeze would blow.

More than anything she wished that when she and Skeeter were finished getting to know each other, both would feel it had been worth the effort.

∾

Skeeter looked at his Mickey Mouse watch. It was quarter past twelve and hot as hell, even in the shade. Worse, it seemed he had wasted his time. The cheese he had bought at Whole Foods was melting, and the fruit salad that had looked so inviting in the store was shriveling.

Sprawled under a giant live oak, he gazed into the distance. Daffy was nowhere in sight. In fact, the only other person who had been foolish enough to venture out was a slender boy wearing jungle fatigues. For lack of anything more entertaining, Skeeter watched as he came closer. The kid was a sight. To complete the picture, he needed a machete in one hand and an elephant gun in the other. The kid looked as if he were about to succumb to the heat in spite of the oversized pith helmet shading his face.

The kid was Daffy.

When she was finally standing beside the blanket, Skeeter took one look at her perspiring face under the hat and knew that, for the first time in more years than he wanted to think about, he was probably in love.

"There are, give or take, six hundred restaurants in this city, all with air-conditioning and fabulous food, and we're having a picnic." Daffy flopped down on the blanket beside him and held out her hand.

He understood. He reached into the mini Styrofoam cooler behind him and retrieved an ice cold can of Dixie beer, popping the top before he handed it over.

"I don't know whether to drink this or pour it over my head." Before he could wonder if she was serious, Daffy took a big swallow.

He leaned back to observe her. "We could still go somewhere else."

"I'm balancing the heat with the prospect of having you completely to myself. I'd rather stay here."

Today her eyes were a deeper green. Skeeter wondered if the helmet was the reason. He reached over to remove it, using it to fan her face.

Daffy shut her eyes at the luxury. He had teased her about being easily pleased, and maybe it was true. The simple things, simple courtesies, simple gifts, simple pleasures, were the ones that made her happiest. She had never needed the attention some women craved, or the presents some believed were their due. She expected little of anyone; honesty and trustworthiness were enough. Anything else was an extra gift, or *lagniappe*, as it was called in New Orleans. Having Skeeter fan her now was definitely *lagniappe*.

He watched Daffy's red curls spring freely around her face. There was nothing artful about the way she arranged it. In fact, she probably didn't arrange it at all. Her hair was as spontaneous as she was. Lifted by his efforts and the hint of breeze that only now began to weave through the trees, it seemed to have a life of its own.

Daffy opened her eyes to take another sip before she peeled off her shirt to reveal a form-fitting knit tank top. In one heat-galvanized moment her best intentions to keep lunch friendly and platonic disappeared. Skeeter was watching her, and she returned his gaze. She had never denied the value of physical attraction; she was comfortable with her own body and its demands. But neither had she ever felt sex was the be-all and end-all of a relationship. In light of that, she wondered just exactly what her attraction to Skeeter could be called.

"I'm glad you came," he said. "I was beginning to wonder."

"There was an accident on St. Charles below Napoleon. The streetcars were backed up for a while, and I don't have your cell number. I would never stand you up."

He smiled lazily. "I thought maybe you'd had a heat stroke walking through the park. I really am sorry about this. Weather forecasters said we were supposed to get a break today."

"Where else and when else could I wear this hat?"

"I'm guessing you went on safari."

"Not me and not Africa. Somewhere on the Amazon, and my mother bought it for me." She reached for the helmet and held it out in demonstration. "She claims this very hat once belonged to a famous nineteenth-century British explorer who was eaten by a crocodile. She believes the hat is particularly resilient, since this was all that was left of him, so it will bring me good luck."

He was fascinated. "And she learned this how?"

"From the very, *very* nice man who sold it to her somewhere in the jungle."

"Do you believe it?"

"I believe anything is possible, only there's a brand-new one for sale at a store on Decatur that looks exactly like this one, minus a few dents and scratches, and *that* hat was made in Vietnam."

"Was she trying to fool you or herself?"

"She has an imagination, and she's not afraid to use it. You can never tell about Lea." She dropped the hat to the blanket. "I think I was promised lunch."

Skeeter spread out the food he had bought. "How well do you know Antoinette?" she asked, when the blanket had been covered by the contents of two shopping bags.

"I see Sam and Antoinette often. Why?"

"Did you ask her to describe my favorite foods?"

He smiled. He had considered it, but instead he had let his imagination and Whole Foods have free rein. "I'm glad you like it."

"You're going to see a physical phenomenon previously unwitnessed by the human eye. Watch closely." Daffy pretended to roll up invisible sleeves. "Lock your fingers around my arm."

"My pleasure."

"Now, both with your eyes and with your fingers, I want you to witness the additional pounds I will gain just from looking at all these calories." Daffy stared at two slices of carrot cake with cream cheese icing. "Can you see it? Can you feel it?"

Skeeter felt the soft skin of a woman without an extra ounce anywhere on her petite body. He stroked his hand down to her wrist. "Are you going to stop ogling before you swell like a Macy's parade balloon?"

"Not unless something comes between me and that carrot cake."

He leaned forward to block her view. Daffy was suddenly gazing at the mouth she'd found so sensual the day before. Today she found it both sensual and infinitely desirable. She watched as Skeeter slowly lifted her hand in the air. It stopped just short of his lips. "Back to normal," he said softly, shaking her hand back and forth.

The voice that emerged was thin and high-pitched. "Not quite." Daffy was surprised how young she sounded.

Skeeter laced his fingers through hers. "I have a feeling there's not another woman like you anywhere in the world."

She smiled to let him know she was pleased. "You'd be surprised the people who've said that in a less flattering tone of voice."

He squeezed her hand before he dropped it, then reached for a knife to slice the cheese. "So tell me about those people and you." He offered her the first piece off his fingertips.

"There's not much to tell. Basically, I march to the beat of any drummer who appeals to me. That can drive other people crazy." She bent down and took the cheese with her teeth and chewed a moment, then swallowed. "Havarti. I love it."

"Do you refuse to conform just to drive people crazy?"

"Absolutely not." She was surprised. "I'm just me. I can't be anyone else." She ate the next piece of cheese, this time lifting it from the plate where he was slicing it. "You understand. You're the same way."

Skeeter wondered if she had finally finished her talk with Antoinette. "How do you know?"

Her grin showed what she thought of his question. "Look at

you, Skeeter. You wear a Mickey Mouse watch that even I'd have to think twice about."

"A little friend gave me this for Christmas."

"You make your living in an unconventional manner. You shop-sit for voodoo doctors on request. You suggest picnics when anybody else would stay inside, and--" her grin widened "--you're attracted to *me*."

"Guilty as charged."

"What else are you going to feed me?" She watched as Skeeter reached for crackers and what looked to be a plate of several kinds of paté. He'd been hard to resist in the gloom of the Sanctuary of Voodoo. Here, in the gently filtered sunlight, he was magnificent. His white linen shirt set off his tan and the midnight black of his hair. He had rolled up his sleeves, and Daffy was fascinated by the hair-roughened stretch of arm and the broad artist's hands. She thought she could watch the masculine grace of those hands forever.

"This one's vegetarian," he said, pointing to the slice on the left. "This one's salmon and this one's—" He paused. "I have no idea."

"Delicious." Daffy was already spreading the mystery paté on a cracker. "Absolutely delicious, I bet."

"I thought you might be a vegetarian."

"I'm an anythingtarian. I'd rather eat than breathe." She popped the cracker in her mouth and groaned with pleasure.

"Then you're a good cook?"

"Cooking seems like such a waste of time when you live here." She spread another cracker. "Are you?"

"I make a seafood gumbo you wouldn't believe."

"Will I survive the description?"

"Lumps of fresh crabmeat. Succulent pink shrimp. Plump giant oysters. Crisp green okra and vine-ripened tomatoes."

"You're killing me."

"How about some fruit salad?" Skeeter filled a plastic bowl and handed it to her.

"If you make gumbo that good, you must have learned it at your mother's knee."

He understood the delicately worded probe. It was time to get down to learning about each other, only he wasn't ready. This felt too good, too special. He chose to elaborate on one of the few neutral parts of his history.

"Actually, I learned to cook in an old bar and grill on Magazine Street. It's not there anymore, but it used to be the best place in town for gumbo."

"You worked there?"

"Here, there and everywhere."

"A man who likes variety."

"A man who liked to eat. I've been fending for myself since early in high school."

She didn't ooh and ah or reach for his hand in sympathy. "Where were your parents?"

He stretched out on his side to face her, setting his fruit salad on the blanket in front of him. Daffy admired the lean poetry of his body, but she wasn't fooled. She could sense an underlying tension in his movements, and she wondered how long it would take to get to whatever was bothering him.

"My father was a one-night stand who breezed through the city when my mother was sixteen. She thought he might have been from the Canary Islands, or maybe Morocco. She didn't pay a lot of attention. After I came along she made a stab at growing up along with me. She never made it."

Illegitimacy? Was that the part of his background that caused the tension? Daffy doubted it. Skeeter didn't seem like a man who worried about society's opinions.

She spoke carefully, watching her inflection. "It wasn't an easy childhood."

"There were compensations. I lived with my great-grandfather until he died when I was nine. No finer gentleman ever walked the face of the earth." He speared a chunk of watermelon. "Tell me about you. What was it like to live in all those different places?"

"I guess you could say I had a value-packed childhood." Daffy rolled a strawberry on her tongue as she tried to think of the best way to explain her life in a few brief sentences. "My parents aren't ordinary people. Among other things they raised me to believe I was free to do entirely as I pleased, but my father, in particular, struggled to set the best example, so I'd know just how I was supposed to act." She tried to think of the most positive way to frame the next part. "We moved a lot. There were always new places to see, new friends to meet, new jobs to explore."

"And you didn't miss having roots?"

"Sometimes I missed friends, but I'm still in touch with people all over the country." She gently turned the conversation back to him. "What about you, Skeeter? I know you grew up in the Irish Channel with Sam. Have you always lived in New Orleans?"

"Just about."

She waited, but nothing more was forthcoming. Skeeter was watching her as if he were measuring responses she hadn't yet given. She filled in the gap. "Well, I suppose New Orleans is more my home than any place I've lived. I've been here three years. Except for graduate school, that's a record for me."

"Why stay so long?"

"I'm establishing myself professionally, and it's not easy for a psychologist to just pick up and move, unless she wants to work for an agency. I did a brief stint on the staff of a mental health center, but it wasn't a good fit. I like being in private practice."

They finished their fruit salad to the sounds of cars on St. Charles Avenue and the occasional quacking of ducks.

When the salad was gone Daffy spread another cracker, moving a little closer to Skeeter in the process. "I've been reading about voodoo since I saw you yesterday." She stopped, then amended her statement. "More precisely I've been trying to read about voodoo. A lot of what I found was so out of date, I'm not sure it helped much."

"I imagine most of what has been written is hearsay. The people who really believe might be reluctant to put anything on paper."

"I confronted my young patient with her gris-gris bag. I think she had it for protection. It was a way of helping her feel safe. I just wish I knew what she thinks is threatening her."

"You love what you do, don't you?"

"Does it show?"

"Everything about you shows. You're the most transparent woman I've ever met."

"I suppose that goes with spending all those hours helping clients uncover secrets. I've seen what hiding things can do."

Skeeter lay back on the blanket and put his arms under his head. The psychologist in Daffy wondered if he'd done so to avoid her eyes.

"So you love what you do," he said. "What do you love about it?"

She made a space for herself beside him and lay down, too. The legs of their pants touched companionably. "I love helping people see. I love being there when a client catches on to something that will change his life. I love seeing change happening."

"So you love it all?"

"Not all. I don't love feeling inadequate, and sometimes I feel so darned inadequate, like with the teenager I've told you about." She shifted so she was on her side looking down at him. "I did my internship in graduate school in a halfway house for drug abusers. I didn't love that. I almost quit school, but then I took a seminar in

Gestalt psychology and psychodrama, and I realized there were different ways, better ways for me to be effective. I'd found my place."

"So the druggies were hard to take."

"Still are for me. Not all, of course, but so many abusers would sell their mother's soul to buy their next hit. Addiction's a disease, but I hated not being able to make a difference. I'd hear stories from their families about what the abusers were like before they developed a dependency, and I'd cry thinking about all those ruined lives."

"And now?"

She sent him a wry smile. "I rarely cry, even though I care just as much. But I've learned to distance myself--I had to--and I've learned to examine my own expectations. Of course I'll work with abusers, if they come to me, but I don't make that a specialty. Probably most of all, I like working with troubled kids. I want to help them turn their lives around before they get involved in any of the traps they can fall into so easily."

Skeeter saw the sincerity in her eyes and the increasingly familiar wrinkle in her forehead. He wondered if her patients realized just how lucky they were to have Daffy helping them. But if he'd hoped they could move beyond his past, now he knew, after everything she'd just said, that they never would be able to. Not unless he told her a story that only Sam knew, and even then, not because Skeeter had told him.

"Skeeter, what's going on?" Daffy touched his cheek to bring his eyes back to hers. "You invited me here so we could get to know each other, but I'm doing all the talking."

"I like hearing you talk."

"And I like talking. I do it a lot, in case you haven't noticed, but I also like listening."

She'd moved her hand, but Skeeter could still feel the whisper-soft touch of her fingers on his cheek. When had he become so vulnerable to red-haired sprites with changeable green eyes and plus-sized safari shirts?

"There's not much to tell," he said. "I haven't spent my life getting ahead. I haven't collected more than the basic college degree. The jobs I've held wouldn't look good on a résumé."

"You're an artist. Antoinette says you're wonderful."

"My admiring public." His words held no bitterness. Daffy could tell that what the public thought of Skeeter's work was not nearly as important as what he thought of it himself.

"Are you good?"

"My heirs are going to make a killing."

She laughed, and the smile he shot back was the most genuine she'd seen since their conversation began.

She was encouraged to make a suggestion. "Look, I've got an idea. But you have to sit up." She held out her hand.

He took it and allowed her to tug him upright until they were facing each other.

"Now, please don't think this is silly," she said. "This is something I do when I'm starting a group and group members are resisting."

"Am I resisting?"

"You are. This is just a way for us to get to know each other better."

"Ah, but if you've done it before, you've practiced."

"Do I strike you as somebody who benefits from practice? Whatever I'm thinking about—and let's face it, my brain spins like a dervish, so I think about a lot—but whatever is there just comes out of my mouth, no matter what I've primed myself to say."

"If I was giving a Pulitzer for convoluted sentences, you would win, hands down." He couldn't help smiling again, despite the tension rising inside him. "But I know what you mean."

"Good. I'll start. This is really simple. All we're going to do is make five statements. Each one has to start with 'I am.' We'll take turns. After each sentence the other person gets to ask one question. Just one. Then after their question is answered, it's their turn to make an 'I am' statement."

"Didn't I play this game in Boy Scouts?"

"You were never in Boy Scouts. Oh, one more thing." She reached for his hands and held them firmly in hers. "Do you mind?"

He understood immediately why holding hands was part of the exercise. Touching removed the parlor game dimension and locked in something more important and intimate. He wove his fingers through hers and waited.

"I am nervous," Daffy began.

"Why?"

She sat perfectly still, trying to read her own feelings. Strangely, they weren't completely clear. "Well, because I'm not sure where this is going to lead, or what you think of me for suggesting it." She paused. "And because I'm wondering what you're hiding. And because touching you is exciting."

"Are you always that thorough? I'm up against a master."

"You're only allowed one question." She squeezed his hands slightly. "Your turn."

"I am feeling very silly."

"Do you want to stop?"

"No."

Daffy realized her question had been used up. "I am usually more subtle with men."

"Then why is today different?"

"Because *you're* different, and I don't want to waste time with you."

"I am flattered--" he paused"--and hopeful."

Daffy was quiet, then she shook her head. "No question." She held his gaze. "I am happy being who I am."

"No question." They hadn't broken eye contact. "I am happy being who *I* am."

"No question." Daffy gripped his hands a little tighter. "I am many things to many people."

"Are you going to be more specific?"

"Next time around."

He nodded. "I am not involved with enough people to play many roles."

Daffy wanted to know just why that was. "Why not, Skeeter? You don't seem like a loner to me."

"I suppose it's because I pick and choose carefully just who I'm going to trust."

Daffy wasn't satisfied, but her question had been asked. She had one more statement, and she decided to make it a doozy. "I am a woman, a psychologist, an extrovert, a friend, a daughter, a dreamer, an enthusiastic participant in life."

"Which is most important?"

"All of the above. I'm not sure I can choose," she said, after giving his question–a good one–some thought. She waited, but Skeeter remained silent. "You turn," she prompted.

His smile didn't match the bleak expression in his eyes. "I'm a man, an artist, a friend, a godfather." He stopped.

She waited because something told her he wasn't finished.

"And an ex-con," he said finally, his gaze locked with her.

The last was so unexpected that for once Daffy was at a loss for words. She sat holding his hands and staring into his eyes as she went back over the little she knew about him. He'd been an unloved boy forced on to the streets after his great-grandfather's death and most likely, his mother's poor parenting. He had supported himself when he was in high school. Was she surprised he'd served time in jail? The real surprise was that he was sitting across from her now, a well-adjusted man, a man with loyal friends and success in his chosen field.

She cleared her throat before she asked the question that she knew would solve the mystery of Skeeter Harwood's past. Then it would finally be behind them.

"What were you convicted for?" She grasped his hands tighter, and her gaze didn't flicker from his. "What was your crime?"

This time he didn't smile when he answered. The expression in his eyes was bleak. "Dealing drugs," he said. "I was arrested for selling drugs to a plainclothes cop. I got a five-year sentence."

CHAPTER 4

Daffy loved her house. Finding the quirky little shotgun with a wide gallery framed in scrolling wrought iron had felt like a miracle. Living in the French Quarter was too pricey, but the Faubourg Marigny, next door, was cheaper, and blooming with energy. She was renting on the same Royal Street that housed the Quarter's famous restaurants and shops, and she was just blocks from the Marigny's shady Washington Square and Frenchman Street, with its own stellar entertainment and food. To top it off she wasn't far from streetcar and bus lines, which had become increasingly important in the year since her vintage Volkswagen bug had been hauled away for scrap.

She still hadn't replaced her vintage baby. She wasn't simply giving in to nostalgia. For now, she didn't want to worry about finding a new car, about car-jackings, parking, or accidents in the City that Care Forgot–which often forgot to care about sobriety. She walked, took streetcars and buses and had Nelson, her favorite car service driver, on speed dial. The Marigny was perfectly situated for all three.

Counting the kitchen, her house had four rooms, which

proudly lined up back to back. Shotgun houses were plentiful in the city. According to legend, a shotgun could be discharged on the front porch–sometimes known in New Orleans as a gallery–and fly straight out the back door. The front room was her living area, and the next, with a bathroom taking up one side, was a den with a desk and television. The third room was her bedroom, and the fourth a kitchen--straight out of the fifties--that she used as rarely as she could. The side gallery, which decades ago had been chopped out of her bedroom and expanded several feet, was a welcome addition where she could read or garden.

The house didn't belong to her–nor had any house ever–so the changes she'd made were minor. Her parents had worked to make each of their temporary homes comfortable and individual, so the process felt natural. Daffy had scrubbed and painted, and immediately signed up for pest control. Finally, she had cajoled her ancient landlord to hire a professional to retile the bathroom and plug up holes.

She'd called a truce with the rest of the disrepair–which her landlord called "character." The house might not be hers, but the area rugs and furniture were, so they could be carted to her next digs for continuity. Her brightly painted walls were filled with lively, happy art she bought at fairs and local exhibitions. Myriad house plants cycled through rooms, then back out to the side gallery to recover. She was happy here, but when the house was sold out from under her some day, she could be happy elsewhere.

A week after her picnic with Skeeter she woke up and realized she'd overslept. At some point in the morning she'd opened her eyes just wide enough to see that the sun wasn't up and gone blithely back to sleep. Unfortunately, the darkness hadn't been pre-dawn but a threatening storm. To top that, even though she'd set the alarm on her clock radio, she hadn't quite tuned in a station, so the static that had arrived precisely at seven-thirty had lulled her deeper into dream land.

She dispensed with breakfast, congratulated herself on taking a shower the night before, grabbed the first thing she laid hands on in her closet, and called Nelson as she hopped on one leg and pulled on white leggings.

Ten minutes later she was on her way out the door when she skidded and stopped just short of a wide circle of wax melted into the boards of the front gallery. Teetering on the balls of her feet, she barely found her balance again.

Hands on hips, she stared down at the floor as rain swept in through the railing. The wax was pink, then white, pink, then white, like a faded ring of candy canes.

Nelson arrived and got out of his dark sedan with an umbrella to escort her. He was just past middle age, a grizzled New Orleans native whose family could trace their roots to the eighteenth century and the enslaved dancers on Congo Square—in the days when the Creole residents routinely bought and sold people the way they sold bales of cotton.

He climbed the four steps in the rain and stood looking down at the wax.

He cleared his throat. "You have a party last night, Daffy?"

"It looks like somebody did. I didn't hear a thing."

"It don't look good."

"I know. That wax is going to be great fun to scrape off the floor."

"You got any idea what this is all about?"

She'd already figured out who had probably burned candles here last night, and she was grateful that's *all* they had burned. The shotgun dated back to 1880, so it came by shabby disrepair honestly. But a careless fire, a candle knocked over in a breeze, a candle sizzling down to a nub and then toppling? The shotgun would go up in a flash, and likely with it, some of the surrounding century-plus cottages.

"We've got some kids on the street who need a stronger hand."

She glanced at Nelson and shook her head. "Troublemakers. There's a new baby next door, so I asked them not to set firecrackers off in front of that house. Let's just say they weren't happy."

"Kids like that everywhere. Kids so mad these days they don't pay attention to nothing and nobody."

"Tell me about it." She thought of the girls in her therapy group. "Anyway, I wondered if they'd do something to get even, and now I guess I know. I'm just glad they didn't burn the place down."

"Cops won't do nothing."

She knew he was right. The high crime rate in New Orleans was one of its least attractive elements. Compared to other infractions that the local police had to deal with, a little wax on her porch would be less than nothing, a joke, a pleasant moment to lighten their day.

Her cell phone rang, and she pulled it out of her handbag. It was Skeeter. She hadn't heard from him in the week since his revelation, and now she was sorry the timing was wrong—and somewhat relieved, as well.

She put the phone back in her handbag and slung it over her shoulder. "I'll have to scrape off that wax tonight. Now I've got to scoot. Thanks for picking me up so fast."

She and Nelson chatted on the trip to Psychologist Associates and she paid and tipped him, wishing him a good day. He stopped her as she slid out.

"You let me know something like that happens again." He looked serious. "I don't like anybody messing with you like that. I'll scare them right back or find somebody to do it for you."

She was afraid he just might. "It'll be okay. I'll talk to them next time I see them."

"You be careful. Kids today got guns."

"I think these kids are just armed with firecrackers and candles, but I'll be careful."

She dashed through what was now just a sprinkle and climbed the oak stairway to the second floor, doing a quick inventory of what she was wearing as she went. Everything on her body matched well enough, the turquoise tunic covered her butt and enough of the leggings, her sandals were a factory-issued pair–unlike the day last week when she'd worn a red one on her left foot and a purple on the right. She had limped all day, and no one at the office had believed her claim that mismatched sandals were a fashion statement.

Rosy, who was on the telephone, waved as Daffy strode through the empty waiting room. She had just made it to her office to open the blinds, shake off raindrops, and heat the electric kettle for her favorite herbal tea before Rosy buzzed to let her know Jewel Martinez had arrived.

As she waited for the teenager, she took deep yoga breaths and focused on paraphrasing a quote by Fritz Perls that she tried to repeat before each session as a reminder of her real role here.

"The pride of discovery makes truth palatable." Her job was to help Jewel find her own truth, so that she could then accept it. The reminder was always helpful.

Jewel arrived and closed the door behind her. She stood with her back to it, staring out the window over Daffy's shoulder. Daffy wondered what, if anything, the girl saw. The misty view of Carrollton Avenue? Something no one else could?

Today the teen was wearing denim shorts and a T-shirt printed with larger-than-life pink roses. Her brown curls were clipped on top of her head and the clip was her only adornment. Unlike the other girls in her group, who probably took an hour each morning to paint their faces and style their hair, Jewel never seemed to notice how she looked.

"Want to help me garden?" Daffy asked when Jewel didn't move or speak.

Jewel looked around. "I don't want to go outside."

"Me either. Even with the storm it's already hot as blazes out there. This is indoor gardening. I have to repot that Ficus over there." She pointed to a small tree in the corner. "Either repot it or trim the roots. And I don't really want to cut it down to size."

Jewel didn't say anything.

"Have you done any gardening?"

"I help my mom sometimes."

"What do you do?"

"She grows tomatoes. And mirliton."

Mirliton was a pear-shaped squash, a city staple that went by other names in other places. "I'd like to grow mirliton. Is it hard?"

"She's got a long vine."

"I've had mirliton stuffed with crabmeat. It's the best." Daffy's stomach rumbled, reminding her she hadn't eaten. "I'm starving. I didn't have breakfast. I'm going to see what's in the fridge. Are you hungry, too?"

"No."

The girl was as thin as a pencil, and in the weeks Daffy had been seeing her, she'd only grown more so. Daffy had referred her to a psychiatrist who had prescribed a mild antidepressant, but both he and Daffy agreed she was one step from inpatient treatment, something Daffy wanted to avoid if possible.

"Will you hold stuff while I pull it out?"

Jewel followed her to the minifridge and let Daffy pile her arms with food. Daffy took some to the counter, and Jewel followed. "String cheese, trail mix, peanut butter crackers, dates and figs. I guess I won't starve."

"We have figs. In our yard."

Encouraged that Jewel had volunteered information, Daffy added some of everything to a plate and then carried it back to the coffee table at the center of the room. "I can make tea, or I have soda in the fridge."

"Soda."

Daffy was more encouraged. She came back with Barq's root beer for Jewel and a bottle of water for herself. "We can repot after we eat."

Jewel didn't say anything, and she didn't reach for any of the food on the plate. But she did pour root beer into the glass Daffy provided and took a sip while Daffy munched string cheese with a handful of dried figs.

"Did you tell me you're taking a class this summer?"

Jewel nodded.

"I'm going to guess. Based on the summer after my own sophomore year. "Chemistry?"

Jewel didn't respond.

"Physics?"

Still no response.

"English lit?"

"Composition," she said.

"Do you like to write?"

She shrugged. "I like it better when there's nobody reading it."

"That makes sense. Some things are easier to say without an audience."

"My mother goes through my room and reads whatever I write."

Daffy liked Jewel's mother, Isabel Martinez, who was desperately worried about her daughter and probably trying too hard to find out what was bothering her. But without betraying Jewel's confidence, Daffy resolved to find a way to ask Isabel to back off. She suspected her need to know and control everything was part of her daughter's problem.

"Mothers are a special case," Daffy said. "When children are little they tell mothers everything, probably more than they want to know. Then they stop telling them anything. I think it's hard."

"Do you have children?"

"No."

"Would you go through their things?"

"Maybe. If I was worried enough."

"I wouldn't. And this is my business!"

It was the most emotion Daffy had seen from the girl in weeks. "You feel strongly about it."

"I can't do the things I have to with her looking over my shoulder."

Daffy realized she was being handed a treasure trove, and she was afraid she was going to say something to make the teenager snatch it back.

"Privacy's important to you right now." She nodded, as if she understood. "Is it just your mom who's making it hard to do what you want?"

For a moment it seemed as if Jewel wasn't going to answer. Then she looked over Daffy's shoulder. "There are others."

Daffy took a gamble. "Last week after group you said you're never going to feel safe again. Is this part of it?"

"Maybe."

"Do you want to talk about feeling safe?"

"No."

Daffy took another sip of water, and when nothing else was forthcoming, she stood. "Okay. Let's pot a tree."

"That stuff I bought at the Voodoo Sanctuary?"

"Uh-huh?"

"It didn't make me feel safe. I don't think that's really what voodoo does. I think voodoo is supposed to scare you."

And there was the mother lode. Daffy sat again. "I don't think you need anything to scare you more."

"What do you mean?"

"We're all scared of something. We just have to figure out what, why and how to overcome it. You're saying voodoo doesn't help, and I'd have to agree."

Jewel's expression smoothed into a perfect blank. "How would I know about voodoo? I just bought a stupid bag. That's all."

"I've been to the Sanctuary, and I thought it was pretty scary, just by itself. Especially the snake."

"What were you doing there? Are you trying to curse somebody?"

Daffy carefully chose her response. "No, I went after I found your gris-gris bag. I just went to see what was there. I don't believe in curses. Not the way some people might. I do think we can say things to each other, though, that make us feel bad and make us question ourselves."

"That's not a curse. That's just words."

"*Curses* are just words, but words are important. I know when I find somebody I can talk to about what's bothering me, words make me feel a lot better."

"Not me."

Daffy knew better than to lecture. Despite repeating the Perls quote to herself before Jewel arrived, she'd probably already lectured too much. Then, to prove that she didn't always do what she knew she should, she gave the subject one final try.

"Curses may seem real, but only because we give them power. That's called the power of suggestion. If I tell you that you're going to stumble and fall today, and you believe me, you'll probably stiffen up and watch every step you take. The chances you really will stumble and fall suddenly become better because you aren't walking naturally."

Jewel didn't answer. Daffy was certain the girl's silence was not because her explanation had been so brilliant.

"Let's give my theory a try." With a smile she didn't quite feel, she stood again. "I'm telling you right now that you and I are going to spill enough dirt on the floor when we repot my Ficus that we could grow another one. Now let's see what happens when we try not to."

Jewel sighed, but she stood. "Let's just dump the whole bag of dirt and get it over with."

∽

They were both dirty by the time Jewel's session was over and they went into the waiting room to see if her mother had arrived. Daffy had two regrets. That she had only cracked open the door on Jewel's problems, and that she had worn white leggings that morning.

Isabel Martinez was almost a foot shorter and a foot rounder than her daughter. She was also tactful enough not to ask why Jewel immediately took off for the office rest room to wash up.

Daffy told her anyway. "We repotted a plant in my office. It will never be the same. The office, not the plant."

Isabel managed a smile. "I guess it's easier to talk if she's busy."

A slender African-American woman with creamy skin, beautifully made-up brown eyes and intricately swirling cornrows woven with gold was standing beside Isabel, and Isabel introduced her. "Do you know Corrinda Saizan, Daffy? Her niece Natalie is in your group with Jewel."

"I would shake hands, but then you'd have to follow Jewel to the ladies' room." Daffy held up her grimy hands in demonstration. "It's nice to meet you."

"Natalie's in with that other woman who works here," Corrinda said.

"Dr. Long. Yes."

Daffy paged back through her memory. She remembered that Natalie's parents were out of the picture. One was in jail, and the other had disappeared when Natalie was little more than a toddler. Natalie lived in an overcrowded group home with at least half a dozen other teens. She recalled the girl saying that she'd had jewelry and clothing stolen, and that two of the other residents had been hauled away by the police after a fight. It wasn't a safe or happy place.

"Corrinda owns Bountiful Beauty, over on St. Claude," Isabel said. "She does my hair. And Jewel's, when I can persuade her to leave the house."

"I'm so impressed," Daffy told Corrinda. "Both Jewel and Isabel have beautiful hair, and yours is spectacular. I've tried braids, but I'm hopeless."

"Oh, baby, you can't do your own. You come to me and I'll do them for you. You won't be sorry."

"I might take you up on that."

"Natalie's letting her hair grow a little more so I can do hers. I get to spend every other weekend with her. Sometimes she helps me at the shop."

Daffy was glad Natalie still had family in her life, but she wondered why the girl wasn't living with Corrinda. She made a mental note to ask Antoinette.

Jewel emerged from the ladies' room at the same time Natalie came out of Antoinette's office. Natalie stopped, and her eyes narrowed when she saw Daffy talking to her aunt. "You better not be talking about me."

Daffy tried to defuse. "Just your hair, Nat. Corrinda says you're letting it grow."

"That's nobody's business."

Daffy's gaze flicked to Antoinette, who gave just the slightest shake of her head. Daffy had a good idea how their session had gone.

She turned back to the two women. "I'm glad I got to meet you, Corrinda." She looked up as the door closed and realized

Jewel had just exited the waiting room. "It looks like your daughter's going to beat you to the car, Isabel."

"You have a good day," Corrinda said, holding out her hand for her niece. She and a tight-lipped Natalie left right behind Isabel.

"My office or yours?" Daffy asked Antoinette.

"Mine, but only if you promise not to trail dirt in your wake."

"Foiled. Darn."

Daffy took time to wash her hands, change her leggings for black ones she kept in a drawer for emergencies, and make two cups of tea before she carried them into Antoinette's office.

She nudged the door closed with her hip. "I got some serious stink eye from Nat. Did you tell her you were going to poison her dog? Drag her down to the street and make her wash your car?"

Antoinette was removing the pins keeping her hair in a knot on top of her head. Her hair fell past her shoulders, and she shook her head to finish freeing it. "I haven't had a headache like this since I quit smoking."

"Natalie was that bad?"

"No, I think there's something going around. Sam had it last week. Headache, mild upset stomach. It's been a few days for me, so I doubt I'm contagious."

"I'll stay ten feet away, just in case." Daffy flopped down on the sofa in the corner and set both cups of tea on the table in front of it. Antoinette dragged a chair to sit across from her.

"Can I get you anything else?" Daffy asked. "Can you eat? I have crackers."

"I'll work on the tea. How did things go with Jewel?"

Daffy told her about the session. "She opened up a little. But we're still establishing trust. That could take months, and I'm not sure she has months. She's not eating. She's not spending time with friends. She's dabbling in voodoo."

"Does she have your cell phone number? Do you think she'll use it if she starts thinking about suicide?"

Daffy didn't give patients her home or cell numbers, but she did carry a pre-paid mobile phone, and every client she was particularly worried about had that number. Jewel was one of them.

"She promised she would call me if she started feeling worse. It was one of the first things we went over together."

"Did she mean it?"

Nothing was certain, but Daffy was cautiously optimistic. "I think she did. And she's never said anything to me about ending her life."

"I don't have to worry about Natalie. Nobody that out-loud angry is likely to harm herself. I just worry about the people around her."

"Seriously?"

"She hates her group home, and honestly, I can't blame her. Staff cycles through faster than she can learn their names. The newest daytime care supervisor is old enough to retire, and apparently dislikes teenagers, especially her."

"Have you spoken to her social worker?"

Antoinette sipped tea and considered. "So, here's why I haven't. Tell me what you would do. You met Corrinda. She's the only stable family Natalie has, and Corrinda seems to care about her. She says she's going to get custody herself just as soon as she can afford to stop working long hours. Apparently, she's in debt, and she works twelve hours a day to try to keep her shop open. She lives in a room above it, and she says she can't offer supervision or find a bigger apartment until she's financially secure."

"That sucks."

"At this point I hate to involve social services. If Corrinda can get custody, that might take care of things. But if they scour around for a new foster home for Natalie, her worker might not be interested in helping Corrinda any time soon."

Daffy knew better than to solve problems that weren't in her own sphere, but she also knew Antoinette would welcome input. "Sometimes there's financial help available. For Corrinda, I mean, so she could take Nat. She'd be saving the state money."

"I mentioned that. She's a proud lady. She doesn't want anybody, especially anybody in social services, involved. If I had to guess, I'd say that once she has custody, we won't see them again. She's sure all Natalie needs is a stable home with someone who loves her."

"I wish that were true. Jewel's proof it's not. And Linda."

"So. . ." Antoinette rested her head on the back of her chair and closed her eyes. "I've been waiting a week. You haven't said anything about your picnic with Skeeter. Sam says he does have another name, his real one, by the way, but everybody called him Skeeter. Even teachers. And Sam won't divulge it."

"There's probably something interesting about that, but I don't think I'll ever find out."

"You could ask him."

"I don't know if I'll see him again."

Antoinette opened her eyes. "That's too bad. I thought you two would enjoy each other's company."

Coming from Antoinette, who was always careful to phrase things without judgment or prodding, "enjoy each other's company" meant her friend had expected to get a wedding invitation no later than next week.

Daffy cut to the chase. "He sold drugs. He spent five years in prison."

"I know."

"You didn't mention that little detail."

"Should I have? I almost did. Then I decided that was up to Skeeter."

"I don't think he wanted to tell me, but he did. I'm glad and sorry, all at the same time."

"Sam says it was a terrible time in Skeeter's life. Both he and Joshua did everything they could to help, and afterwards they helped him start over."

"I believe in second chances. Third, fourth, fifth. You name it. But I hate drugs. I hate them. I saw too many young people die from overdoses when I interned at the halfway house."

"I've had clients who would willingly sell an arm, a leg, an internal organ, for the next hit." Antoinette paused. "You don't talk about your internship very often. It must have been rugged."

Daffy's phone rang. She looked down, and her heart sank. "And speaking of Skeeter."

"I'll escape to the ladies' room. Go ahead and take it here." Antoinette left, closing the door behind her. Skeeter was still on the line when Daffy answered.

"Hi Skeeter." She waited.

"How've you been?"

"Confused."

He didn't need to ask about what. "I guess I hit you with a lot."

"I'm glad you did. I know I told you I hate secrets."

"I hoped you'd be the one to call first."

"I wasn't ready."

"And now? Are you ready to talk to me?"

She considered. "I don't think so."

"Will you ever be?"

"I'm not trying to evade answering, Skeeter, but I don't have one. I'm still sorting out my feelings."

"And see? We got through that exchange without any cute little exercises. Just two adults trying to figure this out together."

She almost smiled, but not quite. "Next time I'll call you."

"Got you. Take care of yourself."

She held the phone in her hand for a long time after he'd disconnected.

Antoinette tapped on the door, then came back in and examined Daffy's expression. "I'm guessing that didn't go well."

"I don't seem to be able to get past. . ." She shrugged. "His past."

"That's not like you."

"I keep thinking of something." Daffy realized she didn't want to talk about this particular memory, so she made herself talk, to defuse it. "During my training there was a woman, talented, smart, personable. I... spent a lot of time with her, and she convinced me I was helping. In fact, she convinced me that I had what it took to move into a full and successful career."

"And she was right."

Daffy grimaced. "I didn't know as much then as I know now. One night it was my job to keep my eye on things and be available if needed. She was up making popcorn. I went in to help her, and she left for a minute and asked me to shake the pan while she went back to her room for something. I don't even remember what her excuse was. Later, when everything was quiet, and she'd left to go to bed, I went to check all the locks. We had the kind that required a key to lock and open from the inside. I found the back door standing wide open. She'd taken the door key from the desk in the living room, that I should have been guarding, and she let herself out to score more drugs. It was weeks before she turned up again. There was no question whose fault it was."

Antoinette didn't express the sympathy that was clear in her expression. "So you're angry that Skeeter sold drugs to people who used them and died. But you're also angry that abusers who don't die are liars and cons."

"You've summed it up nicely."

"He's not selling drugs. He's not a liar. He's not a con."

"But he did sell drugs and got caught."

"Daffy, he paid his dues. Several times over."

Daffy glanced up at the clock on the wall and realized she had another appointment in fifteen minutes. She stood to leave, but Antoinette stopped her.

"Your story? The woman with the popcorn? Did you say that happened at the halfway house when you were an intern?"

Daffy had known it was unlikely she would fool her friend. "No. I didn't. But you figured that out already, didn't you? It happened at home, during my first summer in graduate school. The woman was my mother."

CHAPTER 5

On Friday night as she hurried past the Marigny's gingerbread-trimmed shotguns and pastel Creole cottages, Daffy went over the events of the day, so she could put them behind her.

Two days had passed since her heart-to-heart with Antoinette, who hadn't, as expected, recovered from whatever virus had taken hold. After lunch her friend had finally admitted she needed more rest and headed home for hot soup and a nap. In addition to seeing three of her own clients, Daffy had taken Antoinette's only afternoon appointment, a man recovering from the loss of his wife of fifty years. The attractive senior was doing everything right and beginning to move on. His progress had been the high point of her day, even though she'd had nothing to do with it.

Her late afternoon group session with the teens had been less warm and fuzzy. They'd all shown up. That was the best she could say. Sharee had switched from cracking gum to crunching ice from a bottomless go-cup of cola. Linda had picked at her nail polish until she had a neat pile on her lap, which she had carefully disposed of at the end of the session. Natalie and Jewel had been themselves, only more so.

Daffy had decided to approach the subject of voodoo through a back door. She had asked each girl to think about a wish that a good fairy might bestow on them, their fondest desire. Then she had asked them to think of something a bad fairy might curse them with, their worst fear. Finally, she'd encouraged them to talk about whether real people, not fairies, could bless or curse them.

They had resisted every ploy.

After they'd left, she'd heard arguing down on the street. She had sped to the window to see Natalie gesturing and shouting at a large African-American woman in a bright red dress. Sharee was beside her, most likely egging her on, and Jewel was rapidly disappearing down the sidewalk, instead of waiting out front for her mother. Before Daffy could go down to see what was happening, the little group scattered.

Afterward, since she hadn't received a frantic phone call from Isabel Martinez, she assumed Jewel had eventually connected with her mother. But she worried about the confrontation. These days Natalie's fuse was so short anything could light it. The woman might have brushed her as she walked by or dropped a cigarette butt in her path. Maybe Natalie didn't like the color red. Whatever had happened, Daffy was glad it hadn't ended in a physical fight.

But what about next time?

To end a bad day with a bang, she'd headed to a dinner meeting at the Royal Sonesta on Bourbon Street to support a colleague who was promoting a new book. Ironically, he had droned on about eating disorders while everyone in the room devoured shrimp étouffée and bananas foster. Afterwards, instead of calling Nelson or hailing a cab at the hotel, she'd chosen to work off calories and clear her head by taking the Riverfront streetcar and walking the rest of the way.

Ordinarily she didn't walk alone this time of evening, but so far, for most of the route, plenty of people had been outside enjoying the cooler evening air. Only now, when she was only two blocks from her house, did she begin to feel alone and uncomfortable. She turned once to see if she'd really heard footsteps behind her–she hadn't–and nearly stumbled over a trash can.

Determined to arrive home safely, she sped up, walking in the street instead of along darker sidewalks where houses or shrubs of camellia or Indian hawthorn jutted nearly to their borders. When she saw her own house ahead, she was relieved and suddenly, exhausted. She trudged up the steps to her gallery, key ready.

At the top she stopped.

Yesterday she had scraped off the wax ring outside her front door until most signs were gone. Now, as a replacement, mounds of dirt were arranged in a larger circle, complete with the primitive model of a human being dead center. On closer examination she thought the figure looked as if it had been shaped from leather, clay and maybe straw. Unsure what to make of the bizarre decoration, she looked up and realized she wasn't going to need her key after all. Her front door was already open, just a crack, but it might as well have been thrown wide. She knew better than to charge inside.

She retreated to the tiny yard bordering the front sidewalk and took her cell phone out of her handbag.

"So... you don't see anything missing?"

The uniformed cop, who looked like he was riding out the final days until his pension kicked in, could not have sounded more bored.

Only ten minutes had passed since her phone call. Daffy had been stunned how quickly the policeman had showed up, until he told her he'd been down the street with his partner investigating another break-in. He'd muttered something about hurricane season and full moons and pushed his way inside the house with his gun drawn. When it was clear that whoever had broken in was gone, he'd allowed her inside to see if she could tell if anything had been disturbed.

Now she continued her quick inventory. A few books had been pulled from a bookshelf. Two of her sofa cushions lay on the floor, and one area rug was peeled back, as if the intruder had been looking for something beneath it. She opened drawers and looked to be sure her file cabinets were still locked. Nothing in the den seemed to be missing or disturbed, and as they progressed through her bedroom, she saw that her jewelry box was intact, and so was the lock on the door leading out to the side gallery. The state of the kitchen hinted that her visitor may have been hungry. A carton of milk was sitting on her kitchen counter. Bread crumbs adorned the table.

"I'd say I'm missing a cup of milk and two slices of bread. I should probably check the peanut butter. As burglaries go, I'm lucky."

The cop didn't have a sense of humor. "Ma'am I meant jewelry, money, computers, televisions. Heirlooms from your family?"

He had no idea how funny the last question was. One bad winter her mother had sold everything valuable that she or Daffy's father had inherited. Anything leftover was not worth hawking on the street.

She realized he was waiting for an answer. "I knew what you meant, Officer. I'm sorry. Nothing important seems to be gone. Nothing anybody could sell."

"And that mess on the porch?"

"It's not mine."

"Looks like voodoo nonsense to me."

"Do you see a lot of voodoo?"

"Not a lot." He was busy making notes. "But if you light that fire, you'll get burned."

"Trust me, I'm out of matches." She thought about Jewel and hoped the break-in and porch decorations were not the girl's handiwork. If they were, she was more troubled than Daffy had acknowledged.

"You have somebody who could stay with you tonight?"

"I'll be okay." Daffy had plenty of friends, but none she'd invite for a fun night of sleeping on her sofa.

They started back through the house. "Whoever it was broke that front lock good. It looks like it's as old as the house, and it's going to be hell to fix. But you got a good enough night latch on this side. You'll probably be safe tonight."

She pretended he hadn't said "probably." "Safe unless whoever broke in the first time wants another peanut butter sandwich."

"I got what I need here."

"You're not going to lift fingerprints?"

"You watch a lot of TV?"

"After tonight I'm lucky I still have one."

"Real life's not the same as TV. We're not gonna send off DNA from your milk carton, either, so don't ask."

"Last week somebody burned candles in a ring outside on the gallery. Same general area."

"I'd say somebody don't like you."

"Some teenagers down the street might fit into that category."

"Bake them brownies or something."

She walked him the rest of the way to the front door, and he checked to be sure the night latch was working. "Anything else happens, you let us know."

Closing the door firmly behind him, she slid the latch. From the other side she heard her own personal police officer rattling and twisting the knob to be sure she was locked in. Then she heard his car start, and that was that.

"I feel so much safer now." She was talking to herself, a sure sign she wasn't quite okay.

She cleaned up everything her uninvited guest had disturbed, tossing the milk and bread into the garbage, along with a suspicious looking stick of butter, which she might have left on the counter that morning. Then she gave up on the shower she'd been looking forward to, because somehow, being naked, alone and wet, didn't feel safe. She took a sponge bath, slid her most unflattering, voluminous nightgown over her damp body, and called her landlord.

Cyril Duclose was a small man who seemed to shrink an inch for every year over eighty, which meant that this year, he was about as short as a fifth grader. Cyril owned three houses in a six-block radius and saw himself as an architectural historian. He was adamantly opposed to updating property and fumed about each new round of modern conveniences. When she told him that the front door lock had been damaged, he paused so long she was afraid he might have suffered his final heart attack.

"I got a locksmith who can fix that," he said at last.

"I'm not sure it can be *fixed*, Cyril. It might need to be *replaced*." Hopefully with something less apt to provide access.

"He'll be out in the morning. You okay for now?"

"I am." But only because the last tenant had insisted on the night latch–Cyril still complained about the way it had marred the old door. She would talk to the locksmith about a state-of-the-art dead bolt, and hope he could convince Cyril.

Sleep wasn't going to come easily, so with her porch light on and a shocking pink flannel robe on the floor beside her, she crawled into bed with one of her professional journals which, unlike tonight's boring lecture, had no fabulous meal attached, and read until her eyelids grew heavy.

Half asleep, half-awake, she thought about Skeeter, as she had every time she hadn't kept her mind busy with something else. Silently she played the kind of what-if ice breaker she sometimes used in her groups. What might have happened if she'd gotten home earlier and confronted her nocturnal visitor? Most people who broke into houses were armed, and shooting deaths happened far too often. What if she'd been hurt or killed, what changes would she wish she'd made just before…?

She turned over and wadded her pillow under her cheek. She knew the answer. The time had come to let go of her past, which she had worked for years to do, and allow Skeeter to let go of his.

After that she finally drifted off to sleep, but she woke at every sound. Twice she threw on her robe and got up to peer out the door to her side gallery, once she padded to the front to see if someone was outside looking in. Finally, around two, she fell into a deeper sleep.

The next time she woke, she knew someone really was outside. She heard footsteps on the gallery and then steps going down and around the side. Heart pounding so loudly it thrummed in her ears, she bolted out of bed, slipped into the robe and turned on the floodlight that illuminated her back yard.

She caught a glimpse of gold under a baseball cap and noticeably broad shoulders. Then the man lifted his head, took off the cap, shaded his eyes and squinted up at her.

"Sam?" Hands still shaking, she fumbled with the lock on the back door and stepped into the doorway. "What are you *doing?*"

Detective Sergeant Sam Long, Antoinette's husband, was wearing jeans and a shirt covered by a jacket that probably hid his Glock. He looked up. "You always open your door to strangers, Daffy? You were sure it was me?"

"Get in here."

He came up the few steps and into the kitchen, and she closed and locked the door behind him. "I won't ask what you were doing."

"Just looking around."

"You must have seen the report."

"Are you okay? That's some display in the front."

She gestured to the tiny kitchen table. "Tea? It's too late for coffee. You're probably on your way home."

"A busy night in the city."

"Is Antoinette feeling better?"

He shrugged. "She feels like I did when I had whatever the heck this bug is. But when we talked, she said her nap helped. Thanks for covering for her."

Since he hadn't refused the tea, she plugged in the electric kettle and measured one of her favorite herbal mixtures into two tea balls, inhaling the flowery aroma as she did. She hoped the tea would help her sleep again once he left.

"You have any idea who might have broken in?" he asked.

She leaned against the fridge and related her theory about neighborhood teenagers. "Nothing I can really point to, though. Your colleague thought that might be voodoo out front." She added her story about the candle ring.

"You upset any voodoo queens?"

"I don't know any voodoo queens. But I have a client who's been dabbling, a teenager. She's scared to death of it, though. I just can't see her on my porch making mud pies and effigies, then breaking in to make herself a sandwich. Although that last part would be a good sign. She's too thin."

"You got yourself a mystery."

"Goody."

He smiled. Blond-haired Sam was as pleasing to the eye as his wife. She wondered if he and Antoinette would have children soon, and what stunning creatures that particular merging of genes might create.

He switched the subject. "Antoinette tells me you and Skeeter have spent some time together."

"She's a talker, that Antoinette."

He laughed a little. "She loves you both."

"She loves easily."

"She loved me, so we know that has to be true. I was no bargain. For all I know I'm still no bargain."

"A diamond in the rough. She has the eye."

"Skeeter and I have been friends a long time. Joshua, too. I'd do anything for either of them."

She wondered where this was going. "Sam, Skeeter can speak for himself, can't he? Does he need an interpreter?"

"He might." He thought that over, as if to be sure. "He does. There's something he'll never tell you. I'm the only one who can."

"You and Antoinette?"

"Just me. Not even Joshua."

"Then it's his secret to tell, isn't it?"

"I discovered some things about his past when I was working a case. So in that way, it is my secret to tell."

She held up her hand. "You don't have to go on. I've been thinking about my own reaction to Skeeter being in prison. Especially tonight when I couldn't sleep. I've been unfair. I have my own nasty issues with drugs and what they can do to people. I plan to call and tell him."

"That's good."

She poured the boiling water into the mugs and brought them to the table. "So we're done with that?"

"No, I'm going to tell you anyway, because somebody besides me needs to know."

She let out a long breath. "And I've been blessed with it."

"*You* need to know."

He was matchmaking, in a backward, male sort of way. Unfortunately, she couldn't call him on it. This was clearly important to Sam, and what idiot insulted a gun-toting cop sitting at her kitchen table?

"Okay." She tried a sip, realized it was still too hot, and waited.

Sam ignored his. "Nobody cut Skeeter the breaks that Joshua and I got. He was in and out of foster homes—"

"Foster homes?"

He gave a humorless snort. "When he was lucky. All the moves, the turmoil at home? His education was spotty. He graduated from high school because nobody paid enough attention. He didn't have money for college. He was interested in art, but he couldn't afford lessons or much in the way of supplies. Through all that, his talent was obvious. He made money hustling in the local pool hall, tending bar, anything he could find. One sure bet for cash were caricatures of *celebrities*." He emphasized the last word. "Local leaders mostly."

"Not unlike what he does now."

"Much crueler and cruder, especially if he didn't like someone. I imagine some of his subjects turned over their bank accounts to buy their own portraits, so they could take them home and shred them."

She could imagine this, an unloved boy turning into a man with little guidance and acres of anger. Skeeter had come a long way. "Is that when he got into selling drugs?"

He didn't answer directly. "One of his favorite subjects was a local cop, Frank Dubuisson. Dubuisson was the butt of jokes in our neighborhood. He was convinced he had all the answers, and harassing residents for no good reason was his specialty. When we were kids he used to go after Joshua and me, too, if he could catch us. The possibilities for satire were endless, and Skeeter latched on to all of them. I remember one. He drew Dubuisson issuing a parking ticket at an expired meter with bullets from a bank robbery flying all around him. He made copies and stapled it to lampposts all over the city."

"I bet that made Skeeter popular."

"Enormously. About that time he fell in love. Patty served drinks at a bar where he did caricatures. She was warm, funny and needy enough that she thought he was a prize. They drifted into a relationship before he realized she had a serious drug problem."

He stopped, as if he was thinking about how best to tell the next part. Daffy was halfway through her tea before he continued.

"Skeeter wasn't above petty mischief, but he was never involved with drugs. He'd grown up on the streets, and he knew better than to get involved with anything that had to do with gangs or organized crime. He'd seen what that did to people. And if he'd had any doubts he might be wrong, watching Patty, the first love of his life, deal drugs to feed her habit? He didn't have any doubts at all after that. He saw it was destroying her."

Daffy wasn't sure where this was going, but she wished he would finish. The story was so sad.

"She did try to stop," Sam said. "I know that for a fact, because Skeeter used whatever money he could get his hands on to find treatment. But just about the time he'd relax and think she was really getting clean, he'd find out she was using and selling again."

She thought of her mother, whose reason for using drugs had been different, but the effect had been the same. "An all-too-common story."

"One night a friend informed him the city was about to experience a huge, coordinated drug bust. Frightened Patty would get caught up in it, he went to her apartment and found her stash, which he had to scoop into a bag to dump–she blocked him from flushing it down the toilet, where it belonged. She promised she just had to make one more sale, then she'd stop for good. When he refused to listen, she grabbed the bag and ran out into the hall. He followed and grabbed it back from her. The buyer appeared and Patty made one more grab, then thrust everything at the guy."

She knew Sam wouldn't have mentioned Dubuisson unless the cop figured into this part of the story. "The bust was a set up?"

"The sweep was real, but Dubuisson had asked to be in on Patty's arrest. He wanted to get even with Skeeter for taunting him. He didn't expect to catch him in the act."

"But Patty was the one who gave the drugs to the buyer."

"True, but Skeeter had been holding them, and he was standing right there when she did it. If he'd told the cops the truth about what had happened, he might have gotten off with simple possession, and with the backlog in courts and everything else, he might even have gotten off with a slap on the wrist. Only if he'd told the truth, Patty, who already had a record, would have been buried up to her neck in charges. And he was sure she wouldn't survive a prison term. So Skeeter told Dubuisson that if he let Patty go, he would plead guilty, not only to possession but sales. He claimed Patty had just been trying to protect him."

Daffy's head was whirling as she tried to piece this together. "I don't understand. How do you know all this? You say Skeeter's never told anybody the truth?"

"Nobody expected Skeeter to get the kind of sentence he did, least of all him. But a combination of politics, Dubuisson's influences, a push to get drugs off the street? He went down hard because Dubuisson characterized him as a long-time drug dealer, even though he didn't have any evidence he didn't invent."

"But—"

He held up his hand to stave off more questions. "In all fairness to Patty, when she learned Skeeter had gotten five years for something that she'd done, she went to the station and made a statement, explaining what had happened and why. But the trial was over. Nobody believed her, and that was that. I wouldn't even have known that part, but I found her statement when I was researching something." He paused, then he shook his head. "I'm not being honest. I went looking for Skeeter's file, which strictly speaking, I shouldn't have done. But I never believed things happened the way the district attorney said they did."

"And you believed what you read." It wasn't a question.

"Everything fit. I knew he wasn't dealing. I knew he would have done anything to help her get clean. When I read Patty's account I knew everything she said was true, and Skeeter doesn't deny it."

"What happened to her?"

"About three months after he began serving time she died of an overdose."

Daffy struggled to put it all together. "He tried to protect her, and instead she killed herself."

"We've only talked about this once, Daffy. Skeeter believes if he hadn't tried to rescue her, Patty might have found help in prison."

Daffy knew that help might have been possible, but not likely. Still, she could imagine how guilty he felt.

Sam took one sip of tea, made a face and put his cup down for good. He waited until she spoke. "Why doesn't he tell his friends the truth? Why doesn't he tell the world?"

"Think about it. What good would either do? His friends love him anyway. The world doesn't care one way or the other, and besides, why would anybody believe him? But most of all? I think he feels like he deserved what happened. He should have seen how bad things were with Patty. He should have tried harder to help her. If he couldn't help her, he should have had the sense to move on."

"And in the end, he shouldn't have protected her from her own behavior."

"That's right."

"Poor Skeeter."

He smiled a little. "Have you seen his work?"

"I haven't. Not yet."

"He has a real career ahead, if he ever reaches for the brass ring. And maybe he's going to be able to put Patty and everything that happened behind him."

"You told Antoinette that Skeeter has a real name."

"Did she say that?"

"I don't suppose you want to tell me what it is?"

"Why? A new name for a new start?"

"An *old* name. The one he was born with."

"It's his to explain, but ask him sometime why he never uses it."

"You sure seem to know a lot about him."

"I love him."

She was surprised at the simple, heartfelt statement from this man. And in the end, wasn't this the most important thing she needed to know about Skeeter? That along the way he had found friends, like Sam, whose belief in him had never been shaken? His words formed into a lump in her own throat. She struggled not to cry.

Sam got to his feet. "I don't like the look of the locks on your doors."

She joined him and cleared her throat. "Locksmith is coming tomorrow."

"I'll have a squad car drive by a couple of times tonight, just to make sure nothing's out of place. You could come home with me and sleep in our guest room."

"I'll be fine."

He leaned over to kiss her cheek. "Get some sleep if you can."

She showed him to the front door, watching as he stepped

around the mud circle. "I'm going to ask around about this," he said, pointing to the gallery floor.

She watched him go, then she went inside and slid the night latch. She was crying by the time she went back into her bedroom. Sam's story had unhinged her. She'd been proud of herself for deciding to forgive Skeeter for his past. Now she wondered if he could forgive *her* for judging him so harshly. No matter what her own reasons, she had pushed him away when he hadn't deserved it. Even if he'd done what he'd been imprisoned for, he hadn't deserved her disdain. He had served his time, and nobody believed he hadn't served enough.

She heard footsteps on her gallery again, and she wondered if Sam had forgotten something. Wiping her eyes with a tissue, she went back to the front of the house. But Sam wasn't standing there looking down at the mud circle, hands on his hips.

This time the man was Skeeter.

CHAPTER 6

Daffy opened the door and stood in the doorway without saying a word.

"Sam told me you were having some issues here," he said, not looking up.

"You're my voodoo consultant. What do you think?"

He lifted his head and met her eyes. "Are you okay?"

She realized she must look like hell. "I only wear pink when I'm alone."

"You've been crying."

"For a woman who encourages everybody else to express their feelings, I seem to be wallowing in mine."

He came to stand in front of her. Then, he reached out and stroked her damp cheek with the back of his fingers. "You look pretty good to me. Puffy eyes and all."

She wove her fingers through his and held his hand still. "Skeeter, I'm so sorry for being such a jerk when you told me about your prison sentence."

"I never expected you to brush it off."

"You know all those moves I told you about when I was a kid?

I wasn't exactly honest. Not as honest as you were. They were equally divided between attempts to find help for my mother, who routinely scored whatever drugs she could find to drive away her own personal bogeymen, and--" She fell silent.

He waited, rocking back on his heels as if he would stand there all day if necessary.

She made a face. "And to get out of town before the lynch mobs descended."

"Lynch mobs?"

She spoke quickly, determined to get her life story over with so they could move on. "My mother is bipolar, which started when she became pregnant with me. My childhood and adolescence were spent helping my father try to stabilize her, and she *was* stable for significant periods of times. My father and I would think we'd found the magic bullet, and then suddenly she'd sink into depression, which was bad enough. But when she was in the manic phase of her cycles, which might last weeks, she did things nobody around us appreciated. Like sleeping off illegal drugs on our sidewalk. Running through the streets in her pajamas or worse. Trying to pay for twenty-something cartons of milk at the local grocery store with a bag of peanuts and a handful of caramels that she'd shoplifted."

He whistled softly, but he didn't interrupt.

Encouraged, she went on. "Like clockwork, at a certain phase of her illness, she always decided she was psychic. She would grab anybody who came near her and warn them of terrible things in their futures. You can imagine what that did for my standing in high school. More than once she was hauled to the police station for disturbing the peace."

"Well, doesn't that explain a lot about you?"

Somehow, she had known he would understand. "I figured I'd better cut right to the chase. You're my role model."

"So you hate drugs for good reason. Dislike psychic stuff,

which probably says something about your reaction to voodoo. And you became a psychologist because you probably felt like you'd already had the training."

"Illegal drugs were a terrible complication in the years when Mom believed they would cure her–or at least put her out of her misery. You can see where I was coming from when you told me about your past, and why my advisors assigned me to a drug rehab facility for an internship. They knew I needed to work through a lot if I was going to be a good therapist."

"Did you?"

She made a face. "Not enough, apparently."

"Where's your mother now?"

Daffy told him the happyish ending. "She struggled to be a good mother, and I love her dearly. She's on new meds, has new doctors, and she's done great for the last three years. She and my father are living in a converted bait shop in Florida. She's a poet, she writes as Lea Gantry—that's her maiden name--so she works on poetry while she sails or fishes. She says she catches words instead of grouper and snapper. My dad is an actor, and he works with–"

"Brookes. Daffy, you don't mean *Carson* Brookes, do you?"

She was impressed. Due to her mother's illness, her father's career on the New York stage had been sporadic. But people who loved theater knew his name, and Carson Brookes was still in demand. Directors continued to want him, despite his reputation as someone with a troubled home life.

"Not everybody's heard of my father," she said.

"He was here a few years ago. Willy Loman in *Death of a Salesman.* I saw it."

"I wouldn't have pegged you for a theater buff."

He sent her just a hint of a smile. "Not many people do."

"You're right. He and Mom stayed with me while they were in town. They loved New Orleans. These days he's managing a small theater outside Miami, and he can finally concentrate on himself and his own career. Mom's published two poems in literary magazines and one in an anthology. I'm optimistic."

When he didn't speak, she weighed her next words carefully. "We have something in common, Skeeter, you and me. We're both products of circumstances, things that happened to us, fair and...unfair."

He stepped back and pulled his hand from hers, hooking thumbs in his jeans. "That's never an excuse, is it?"

"Sam was here tonight. Before you arrived. He told me more about your life than you did." She paused, then decided to go ahead. "Like how you went to prison to protect someone else."

He didn't look happy. "Did he tell you why I don't talk about it?"

"He came up with some reasons."

"How about this? Because I don't want anyone to pity me. They were tough years, awful in ways I'll never talk about. But I grew up behind bars, started taking art seriously, worked toward a degree in art history, learned to read people and find the ones I could trust. Was a disintegrating correctional facility the best place for that to happen? No. But it was a lot like being a grunt in the Army. I learned discipline, respect for myself and others, how to survive. All that kept me alive and somewhat sane...."

She stepped toward him, but he took another step back, as if he wasn't done yet and had more to say.

She held up a hand to stop him. "Here's what I think..."

He cocked his head, eyebrows raised, waiting.

"I think it's a shame that the first time I kiss you, I'm wearing a hideous pink flannel robe, and you're about to launch yourself into a voodoo circle. And God knows what that nasty little doll in the middle will do to your shoes."

He stared at her, debating for a moment. Then he laughed. She smiled and slid her arms around his neck, their faces just inches apart. "I don't pity you, Skeeter. Do I wish nothing bad had ever happened to either of us? Of course, but that's not the same thing. And I think it takes an exceptional person to look at the past and find the best in it."

"Don't get carried away. That only happens on my good days."

"Is this going to be a good day?"

"It's about to be."

She brushed his lips with hers, and he put his arms around her and pulled her close. The kiss went from sweet to blazing hot in an instant. She pressed herself against him, and her lips opened under his. His were warm and clearly hungry. He trailed kisses along her cheek, and then back, deepening the next kiss. When she finally stepped away, every nerve in her body was singing hallelujah. In a matter of moments they'd moved on to something different, something new, possibly new for both of them.

"We're going inside," he said.

It wasn't a question, but she smiled and asked one instead. "Are we?"

"Don't get your hopes up. I'm going to spend the night on the sofa so you can get some sleep and stop listening for strange men on your porch."

She smiled seductively. "Is that really where you're going to sleep? You're sure about that?"

"We're going to take this slow, Daffy."

"My sofa and my bedroom have a room between them. That's slow enough for me."

"I think you and I have a lot more ground to cover before either of us is sure this is a good idea."

"After that kiss, one of us is sure already."

His eyes sparkled, but he shook his head. "I'll need a pillow and a blanket."

"There's an old-fashioned man lurking inside you."

"An extra toothbrush would be nice."

She held out her hand and he hesitated, then took it. Inside, she slid the night latch and turned off the front light. She stood with her back to the door. "It's nice of you to want to protect me. But do you really think I'll sleep better with you only one room away?"

He framed her face in his hands, surprising her. "There are all sorts of ways to stay safe, Daffy."

Then he kissed her, this time lightly, before he dropped his hands and went to check out her sofa.

The rosy rays of dawn peeked between slats of the plantation shutters covering Daffy's front windows, and Skeeter, who was already awake, got up and pulled on his jeans and slipped his shirt over his head. He could see just well enough to find his way to the bathroom that had turned Daffy's "den" into a room as narrow as a tunnel or a railroad car. He washed his face and saw that as asked, she had put out a new toothbrush in a package on the sink. He brushed his teeth, finger-combed his hair and grimaced at a day's worth of whiskers.

As a younger man he'd often wondered if the reflection in his bathroom mirror was a snapshot of the father he would never know. He looked nothing like his mother or her family, so he'd decided this was his glimpse of the man who had carelessly fathered him and never looked back.

He hadn't thought of that in years.

Leaving before Daffy woke up seemed like a good idea. No mysterious voodoo practitioner would bother her in the light of day. She would be safe now, and if he tiptoed through her room, the kitchen, and out the back, he could lock the door as he exited.

Before he could change his mind, he started silently through her room, sure he could pass by without stopping. But, of course, he had lied to himself.

Her bed was a silly affair, queen-sized with pencil-thin black posts topped with a frame draped with gossamer white fabric. She was sprawled diagonally, the way he always found Maggie and Joshua's daughter, Bridget, when he checked on her if he was babysitting for her and her baby brother Dillon, his godson.

But Daffy was no child. A nightgown nearly as puritanical as her pink robe was hiked almost to her waist, exposing much more enticing and far skimpier panties. An arm was thrown over her head, and the neck of the awful cotton gown had slipped over the other shoulder exposing the top of one breast. Her skin was pale, nearly translucent, and he could almost see her heart beating beneath it.

He closed his eyes for just a moment. Last night he'd been careful and all too aware that her reaction to him, despite everything she'd said, could be more sympathy than desire. She had been trained to question her own actions and reactions, but this was Daffy Brookes, whose spontaneity and compassion were twin lodestars guiding her through life.

Despite all that, he wanted to crawl into that ridiculous bed and do everything he'd said they shouldn't last night. Right now, in the softly spreading light of morning.

She moaned and turned to her back. As he watched, her eyes opened slowly.

He put his finger over his lips. "Go back to sleep. I'm going to let myself out. You'll be okay?"

She started to sit up, and her hands went to her head. "I–" She moaned again, this time a little louder.

She wasn't okay. That was obvious. He frowned and lowered himself to the side of the bed, resting a hand on her shoulder. His fingers dipped across her naked back under the gown, and he wished they hadn't. Her skin was soft and warm, and he had to sternly push aside his earlier thoughts. "What's going on?"

"Wow. My head..."

"Hangover? Reaction to something you took last night to get to sleep?"

"Are you–" She looked up at him and winced. "You're kidding, right? I wasn't planning to sleep at all. And I don't take–" She closed her eyes, as if the light creeping through her windows was wielding daggers.

"Okay, that's not it then. Stress? Migraine?"

"Don't have migraines. Almost never a headache."

"Anything else hurt?"

She seemed to be asking herself the same thing, then, as if she'd gotten her answer, she swung her legs over the side and took off toward the bathroom he'd just abandoned.

He was waiting outside the door when she finally emerged.

"Antoin...ette," she said, as if she'd dredged that one word from deep inside her and was now finished speaking for the day.

Skeeter remembered Sam saying that both he and his wife had been sick with an obnoxious virus. Antoinette had left work early yesterday afternoon, and Sam had been forced to take a day off the week before.

"You think you caught whatever they had?" He put his arm around Daffy's shoulders and guided her back to her room and bed.

She grunted, as if he was on the right track.

"No work for you today," he said.

"Have to. I have group...this afternoon."

"Can you cancel morning appointments?"

She slid out of his arms back down to her bed and managed to prop herself against two pillows that he quickly stacked for her.

"I...don't know."

"Shall I call your office and see if someone can cancel whatever you have?"

"Maybe bring the phone. I can leave—"

"A message. Right." He rested the palm of his hand against her forehead. "You don't feel hot. That's good."

She grasped his wrist. "You don't have to stay. I'll be..."

"Fine? I don't think so."

She managed a little smile. "You missed your chance...last night, dude."

He laughed. "Do you think you could drink some tea? Eat a slice of toast?"

"Maybe in a little while. Make yourself..." She waved her hand limply, as if that was enough information.

He brought her the phone that he'd glimpsed in the den and left her while she made a call to the office.

The kitchen needed a crowbar and a crew of three strong men. He was reminded of a trip he'd made as a small child with his great-grandfather. They'd stopped at a farmhouse museum somewhere in Mississippi, and the vintage kitchen had been more modern than this one. He'd churned butter. He remembered now the wonder of turning cream into something he could spread on bread. And he had. The bread had been freshly baked, and there had been strawberry preserves made from real strawberries. He could almost taste it.

He hadn't thought of that trip for years. Daffy had forced him to think back on his life. For better or worse, memories were pushing to the surface.

Only two narrow cabinets hugged the wall, but several open shelves perched above her sorry-ass stove, where herbs and three canisters marked tea resided. He sniffed the contents of the first and pictured a meadow with girls in sun dresses running barefoot through it. The smell was decidedly female, gaggingly floral. The second was even worse. It reminded him of hay fields after harvest. He imagined destitute farmers scooping up the remaining twigs, seeds, bugs, and selling it at a premium.

The third held grocery store black tea, plain black tea bags that everyone from the Deep South used to make iced tea so strong and sweet it could be mistaken for a life form. He poured water into her electric kettle and switched it on.

At the back of one of the cabinets he found coffee and something approximating a coffee maker, although it looked like it might predate the kitchen. When he couldn't find filters he used a paper towel, and while that brewed he toasted two slices of bread of some indeterminate age and grain. Now he knew that if Daffy drank coffee, she bought it somewhere in the neighborhood, hopefully along with something good to eat. He finished her tea, found an unopened package of crackers, and went back into the bedroom.

"You off the hook?" he asked.

"I left Rosy a message. She'll do–" She waved her hand again.

"I don't know if this will help or send you running to the bathroom again. I found black tea bags and a pack of soda crackers."

"I'll try. In a few minutes."

"What do you want to take for the headache?"

"I think–ibuprofen. In the bathroom."

He found a bottle in the medicine cabinet and shook out three, detouring to the kitchen for water which he handed her with the tablets.

He left and returned again with their breakfast, such as it was. "Want me to eat in the other room?"

"No. Sit here." She motioned to the edge of the bed.

He set her tea on the night stand with her water glass and his coffee beside it. "Your front door has to be fixed."

He listened as she worked her way through an explanation. "So the locksmith is coming today?"

"This morning."

"I'll talk to him. You need dead bolts. Front and back doors. The lock in here looks pretty secure, but more is better."

"It was weird. Nothing's gone."

"You're sure?"

She shrugged, then winced. "Nothing...obvious."

"Maybe whatever he was looking for was with you. In your car, in your purse."

"No car."

"You don't drive?"

"My car died. Hauled away. It was...indecent."

He grinned at her. "Last week? The week before? You're still in mourning?"

"A little longer."

"How much?"

"Months."

He waited.

She sighed. "A year and months."

"And you chose not to replace a car?"

"We went everywhere together. I'm a car widow."

"Tell me about it."

"Esmerelda Van Winking."

A moment passed before he realized this wasn't some sort of odd profanity. She'd named the car. "Van *Winking*?"

"VW. A vintage bug. Bright red. Green sun roof. Like a tomato." She reached for the cup of tea and took a sip. She paused, as if she were waiting for her body's reaction before she took another. He sat patiently while she drank a little more and set the cup back where it had been.

"Just Esme to me," she said.

"And you feel, I don't know, guilty about replacing her?"

"No. It's just...we fit together. When I really need another car, I'll know it when I see it. It will...speak to me."

"And if a client said that to you, your reaction would be?"

"A psychiatric evaluation." She smiled, the first of the morning.

Skeeter knew the city's bus and streetcar service were adequate. Tourist mecca that New Orleans was, cabs were easy to call or flag down. She could probably get anywhere she needed to go with a minimum of difficulty. But her devotion to something she'd loved so well was interesting.

Someone pounded on the front door, and he got up to see who it was. "If it's the locksmith, I'll let him in. We'll see what he says."

"Is this...my second strike?"

He couldn't figure out what she meant.

She saw his confusion. "Doubting you. And now, getting sick on your watch?"

"You forgot to count almost jumping my bones last night. I barely got away."

"That was a three-base run. A little more oomph and the ball would have been...over the fence."

He winked. "You have no idea how close you came to a home run, lady."

By the time Skeeter drove Daffy to her office in his dinged and battered Jeep Laredo, she felt human, if not well. She had rested and slept, and Skeeter had dealt with the locksmith. The man, a second cousin of Cyril Duclose, had gotten strict instructions to repair the original lock, no matter the cost or the hassle, and Daffy was fairly certain he was only there out of family loyalty.

While the locksmith cousin banged tools and muttered under his breath, Skeeter had tracked down Daffy's landlord, and somehow convinced Cyril that if his beloved house was going to find its way into the next century, it had to have better security.

Finally, with two dead bolts agreed to and the front door temporarily secured while the locksmith scoured for vintage parts, Skeeter had taken photos of the mud circle before removing all signs of it.

She didn't know what he'd done with the nasty little doll. She would probably never ask.

Now, as they waited at a traffic light not far from Psychologist Associates, Skeeter turned toward her. "I'm going to be out of town for a few days."

This was the first he'd mentioned leaving, but then she'd kept him pretty busy. She punched his arm lightly. "I hope you're going somewhere fun."

"New York." The light changed, someone beeped, and he started forward. "If you have any new problems, call Sam directly. He'll make sure you're taken seriously."

"I'll be fine."

"You'll call him?"

She had a feeling he wasn't going to let her off the hook. "I will. And now your turn. Are you taking in some theater?"

He seemed to debate silently before he answered. "Not this time."

"You have a sudden hankering for good pastrami? Bagels? A tour of the Statue of Liberty?"

"Do they teach you how to dig for information in grad school?"

"They do. Here's my secret weapon." She paused. "Why are you going to New York?"

He laughed. "I've only told a few friends."

"Really? Since you've made a big leap and included me, make another."

"A couple of galleries are interested in my work. An agent

wants to meet me, maybe offer representation. I made the mistake of mentioning the inquiries to Maggie, Joshua's wife. The next thing I knew she'd set up the whole schedule. Her father's an art collector. He added a few contacts, but she knows people herself."

"Skeeter, that's fabulous. What a great opportunity." Daffy liked Maggie Martane and her husband Joshua, although she didn't know them well. She did know that Maggie's father was wealthy beyond belief, and Maggie probably had lots of contacts herself. She also spent his money freely on good causes while she and Joshua lived simply.

She wished she were going to New York with Skeeter, and that surprised her. She could imagine them exploring the city together, without any of the problems they faced here. They could be young and happy. Of course, if they went to the Big Apple together, she wasn't sure they'd ever make it out of the hotel room.

"What are you laughing about?" he asked.

"Me, laughing? Definitely not at you. I'm thrilled for you. I was just thinking about how much I wish I was going to New York, too."

He rested a hand on her shoulder. "I'm going to talk to Fantôme before I go. I'll let you know if he says anything of interest about the photos I took this morning. But it might take him some time to nose around if he decides to."

"When you come back, will you show me some of your work?"

"The gallery where it was hanging put up a new show last week. So you'll have to come to my house."

"To see your etchings?"

"You got it."

Her heart sped the required extra beats. "I think I could manage that." She waited until he'd pulled up in front of her building. Then she turned before she opened her door. "You've been great. Thank you."

"You're not hard to be nice to. You're feeling well enough to do this?"

She remembered how up and down the progress of Antoinette's illness had been, so she wasn't counting on anything. "I'm hoping the girls run the session and I can just nod and smile."

"Any chance of that?"

"Absolutely none."

He leaned over and kissed her cheek, which was, under the circumstances, a wise move, since he didn't need whatever bug she had, if she hadn't given it to him already.

"I hope you don't get sick," she said. "From last night."

"It would be worth it."

She got out, smiling. But after he'd driven away she realized she was still standing in the same spot. She had to walk down the sidewalk and up the stairs. Her legs seemed unwilling. And when she was finished today, she'd have to deal with finding a way home. That thought sapped what little strength she had left. Despite what she'd told Skeeter, and whether she felt ready or not, it was probably past time to rethink her position on another car.

She looked up and saw Jewel coming toward her, with Natalie about half a block behind. She waited, as if that was her purpose for standing there. She smiled when Jewel got close enough to notice her.

"I was just going in," she said. "I'll walk with you. Let's wait for Natalie."

Jewel stopped several feet away, and for once she searched Daffy's face instead of the landscape behind her. She seemed to grow even warier.

Natalie came up to stare at Daffy. "What's wrong with you?" she demanded.

"There's some kind of bug going around, and I had a bout of it. But I'm okay. I just won't be hugging anybody today."

"You're sick?" Jewel's voice shot up an octave.

Daffy knew what was happening. She was an authority figure to the girls, to all of them, even if they would never admit it. They counted on her to be strong, both physically and emotionally, a bulwark they could push against, even pummel. Any sign of illness threatened her standing with them.

"I'm almost over whatever it was," she said, hoping it was true. "I just hope we don't pass it around the group."

"Pass what?"

"Just a headache, mostly. We can talk about this when we get inside and the others arrive." She made a mental note to swing the conversation toward a discussion of how other people's infirmities affected the teens. Linda, especially, who was still grieving the loss of her friend, would benefit.

"I don't want to be here." Jewel turned to go, but Daffy locked her fingers over the girl's shoulder.

"Jewel, I'm fine. You'll be fine. Come inside."

She could feel the girl squirm under her grip, then finally relax into resignation.

"I'm not going to say a word," Jewel mumbled.

"Wow, how different will that be?" Natalie asked.

Daffy walked between them and wished she was home in bed again.

CHAPTER 7

One week later, Daffy stared blankly into her closet. For once she was concerned about making the right fashion statement, and none of her friends or colleagues were likely to unlock this particular dress code.

She was trying to decide what to wear to a voodoo ritual.

Fantôme hadn't turned up any information about the voodoo circles on Daffy's porch, but Skeeter had convinced him to let them attend a ritual tonight, arranged by the Sanctuary of Voodoo. Apparently, the Sanctuary's proprietor and part-time voodoo doctor hadn't been thrilled at the request, particularly when Skeeter told him he'd like to bring her along. But Skeeter's painting of Marie Laveau had been a big hit with Fantôme's customers. Fantôme had probably relented because he wanted Skeeter to paint a second portrait, this time of Doctor John, another historic voodoo figure.

Whatever the reason, tonight Daffy would get her first up-close look at New Orleans voodoo, and while she didn't expect answers about Jewel Martinez to fall into place, it might be a beginning.

She'd been mulling over what to wear with little success. Her limited research had turned up photos of Haitian men and women dressed in white clothing splattered with the blood of a sacrificed animal. That probably wasn't going to work for her.

Now, as twilight thickened, she searched through her closet and decided on a dress in earth tones that might, if she were lucky, make her look like a leaf. That way she could disappear into the forest if things got crazy.

Of course, Skeeter swore that they wouldn't.

Tonight was the first time she would see Skeeter since he'd left for New York. They had talked. In fact, he had called most evenings to check on her. Each time she had assured him she was fine, even though it wasn't really true. But at least things at the house had improved. She now had dead bolts on front and back doors, a sturdier night latch on the side door, and no interesting additions on the gallery. She felt safer; she had stopped checking under her bed and inside her closet the minute she came home.

The big problem was that she might feel safe, but she didn't feel well, and today she'd been forced to cancel her afternoon group with the teens and come home to recover from another headache. If she could have stayed, she would have, but she'd realized that no matter how much she'd wanted to, she could not bear the girls' insults, anger and anxiety.

The headaches and nausea came and went, and sometimes at night the headaches were almost unbearable, making it nearly impossible to sleep. With them had come a new symptom. Twice now she'd heard voices when no one was nearby, and once she'd seen a shape moving through her bedroom when she was alone in the house.

Daffy was a psychologist with extensive training. She knew that as Lea's daughter she had a greater possibility of falling down the bipolar well herself. Inheriting mental illness wasn't close to a certainty, but still, the possibility that she might be teetering on the edge struck terror in her heart.

The good news–if it could be called good news–was that migraines could cause strange visual phenomena like hallucinations, auras, pulsing light. Patients sometimes heard noises that weren't there. This was a possible explanation, and something she'd need to have checked if they continued. But possible or not, she was still expecting whatever virus was causing her symptoms to subside, then disappear. Antoinette was only now beginning to feel like herself again. Daffy was looking forward to that day.

Tonight she hoped she would be hallucination-free, because a voodoo ceremony promised to be odd enough.

As she pulled her hair into a knot on top of her head, she heard footsteps on the gallery and then a knock on her door. Through the narrow sidelight she confirmed that Skeeter was the visitor, and she unlocked the dead bolt–the vintage lock was still a work in progress.

"Hey, stranger." For a moment she wasn't sure what to do, which rarely was the case. Then she rose awkwardly on tiptoe to give him a quick kiss before she stepped back to let him in. He looked comfortable–not to mention terrific–in a camouflage T-shirt and jeans. She guessed that like her, he didn't want to stand out tonight.

"I'm glad you made it back in time. How was your flight?"

He reached for her, which jacked up her pulse, but he only put his hand under her chin and tilted her face toward the light. "You have circles under your eyes."

"Exactly what every woman wants to hear."

He dropped his hand. "You haven't been completely honest. You're not over whatever is making you sick, are you? Have you been to a doctor?"

He was either remarkably observant or... She didn't need to

go further. Of course he was remarkably observant. He was an artist. Between her talents and his, nobody around them was safe.

"Look, don't worry," she said. "This crud seems to be the kind of thing that just hangs around. Ask Antoinette. She saw her doctor and was told to ride it out, which she did. But if I'm not over mine in a few days, I'll make an appointment."

"You really feel okay to go tonight?"

"I think the fresh air will do me good." And being with him would do her more.

"Have you eaten? We probably have time for a fast food stop."

Thinking about food made her stomach turn. She was subsisting on tea and toast. She'd lost weight, and she bet he'd noticed that, too.

"I'm fine." She smiled brightly. "But I can sit with you if you want to stop."

"I grabbed a sandwich when I got home from the airport."

"Then I guess we're set."

She locked up carefully. Then she followed him out to his Jeep. "You never said where we're going exactly."

"Deep into the middle of nowhere."

He opened the passenger door, and she slid in. Her headache seemed no worse, which was becoming the gold standard. "Are you going to tell me about your trip?" He'd said remarkably little on the phone about his meetings, and she really wanted to know. She was tired of talking about headaches and home invasions and dead bolts. She wanted to know about Skeeter.

He climbed behind the wheel and put the Jeep in gear. "Tell you what. It'll take a while to get outside the city. Why don't you close your eyes and rest, and once the driving settles down, I'll tell you all about it."

Daffy had pegged him as a typical New Orleans male, who could zoom high speed through the middle of a Mardi Gras parade without injuring himself or a bystander. But just to be agreeable, she followed his advice. The passenger seat was surprisingly comfortable.

Sometime later she woke up with stars twinkling overhead and bullfrogs croaking to their lady loves. She sat forward so fast that the seatbelt snapped hard against her chest.

"Holy cow. I fell asleep."

"You think? I thought a freight train was in the next lane trying to keep up with us."

"Oh, Skeeter, I'm sorry." Then the truth hit her. "Wait a minute. You wanted me to, didn't you?"

"You needed some sleep."

She couldn't argue. "Where are we?"

"Ever been to Wetland Watcher's Park?"

"No."

"Well, we're not going tonight, either. But we won't be far away. It's a different view of Lake Ponchartrain."

"You've been here before?"

"I used to crab not far away with my Grand-Grand."

"A good memory?"

"The best."

She imagined a portrait of the old man and the little boy Skeeter must have been. Dark eyes snapping, mischievous, ready for anything. She was so glad that someone had loved this man when he was a child.

"Grand-Grand was the first one who called me Skeeter." He rolled his window down. "We're almost there." He slowed. "Listen. . ."

She could hear the throbbing of drums, and now that she'd had a little sleep and plenty of fresh air, she was sure the pounding was not in her head. "What kind of ritual is it? I was going to ask you all this on the trip out here."

"I'm not sure it matters to Fantôme and his groupies."

"What do you mean?"

"I think you'll figure it out. Wait and see."

The drums grew louder, and now she could also hear sporadic chanting. "How many people would you guess? Did Fantôme say?"

"However many paid for the map, or booked a ticket for his bus."

"Bus? Map?"

He didn't say more. She rolled down her window. The moist air was swamp-like and sulphurous, but not unpleasant. She thought it smelled like earth's beginnings, like everything primitive and new. The drums seemed to be beating in time to her heart. For a moment she closed her eyes and let her imagination take her somewhere else, into the mind of an impressionable girl like Jewel, if she was here beside Daffy, listening.

The drums were growing louder; the chanting was growing louder, too. Without the lights of the city, the stars were an iridescent canopy, but stars and the sliver of moon rising in the east weren't the only light. As Skeeter pulled over to a grassy embankment and cut the engine, she saw torches in the distance, rimming a path along what might be a creek or a sluggish, swamp-rimmed bayou.

He came around before she could unhook her seat belt, opened her door and reached in the glove box. Then he handed her a spray can. "Mosquito protection."

"I'm glad you thought of that." She stepped down and spritzed her arms and neck, before she handed the spray back to him. "Would you do my legs?"

"Dream come true." He squatted at her feet and shook the can until it rattled. He sprayed a little on one ankle, then surprised her by smoothing it over her skin with his fingertips.

"If you do that all the way up above my knees, I'm going to throw you to the ground and have my way with you," she warned.

"Another dream come true."

She closed her eyes and swayed to the drums and the feel of his fingers inching higher and higher. Just as she thought she really might have to follow through on her threat, he stopped.

His voice sounded choked. "You have great legs. Gorgeous legs."

She was surprised those gorgeous legs could still hold her. She cleared her throat. "Do I get to do the same?"

"*I* am not wearing a dress."

"*You* have arms." She reached for the can before he could snatch it away and beckoned. "C'mere, Skeeter. A little closer."

He sidled forward, thumbs hooked in his pockets. "I could take off my shirt."

She actually debated, but the drums were louder now, as if something important might be happening. She hoped whatever it was didn't involve roosters or goats. "Rain check." She sprayed his wrist and in gentle swirls worked in the spray. The hair on his arms was softer than she'd expected. She liked the way it clung to her fingers as she moved slowly toward his upper arm.

Once there she traced the edge of what was obviously a tattoo with her forefinger. She lifted the hem of his sleeve, but it was too dark to get more than a glimpse. "One day I want to see this in its entirety. Tell me it's not prison issue."

"No, it's a design of my own."

"Maybe you could design a tattoo for me. Only I tried a tattoo and mostly proved I hate needles. Like some people hate roaches or snakes."

"I have two arms."

Reluctantly she moved to the second and finished the job, leaning as close as she could, her hip brushing his. "I guess we're ready."

He took the can and tossed it through the window on to his seat. Then he pulled her close, looking down at her. "You still want to go?"

She really wasn't sure. The idea of just standing in the moonlight with him, rubbing her mosquito-proof skin against his, seemed much more appealing. "What do you think we'll see?"

He leaned down so his breath was warm against her lips. Her eyes drifted closed. "Unbridled sex and fertility rituals," he whispered.

Her eyes flew open and she laughed. "You're kidding!"

"Absolutely." He stepped away and took her hand, pulling her toward the path. "I don't know what we'll see. Let's find out."

The path seemed to have been smoothed by countless feet, and even with the dim light of torches, they had no problem navigating side by side. Daffy was silent now, listening for movement in the bushes beside them or the slip-slop of alligators stealing out of the water for a late-night ramble.

She wasn't sure how long they walked, but the drums and the chanting beckoned. She discerned a word or two of English and something that was constantly repeated, something that sounded like "A yee bobo."

"Bobo? That's a worse nickname than Skeeter," she whispered.

"*Ayibobo*. It's the equivalent of amen. And the drums are beating to awaken the spirits."

"If I were a spirit, that would do it."

"The people at this ceremony probably believe that being here will bring them good luck. Everybody needs luck, don't they?"

"You know a lot for someone who swears he doesn't know much."

"We breathe voodoo in New Orleans. It's in the air. You'll absorb it, too, if you pay attention."

"I'm paying attention now."

The path widened, and she saw they were at the edge of a

clearing. Daffy waited as her eyes adjusted to the sudden burst of light from a bonfire and dozens of torches.

"There must be a hundred people here," she said. Of course it was hard to count bodies, since the majority of them were dressed in the same white she had carefully avoided, and dancing or swaying to the drums.

"Fantôme has a partnership with a shop in the Quarter that sells nothing but white clothing. You've probably seen the shop and didn't think anything about it."

"He sends people there before these–" She scurried through her vocabulary. "Events?"

"Imagine how much money he pulls in. There's big money in voodoo."

"See a need, fill it with merchandise and mark up the price a thousand percent. American entrepreneurship at its finest."

Skeeter was moving slowly around the edges of the circle to a spot protected by several trees and clumps of palmetto. She stayed close behind him until he suddenly stopped. A man with arms folded across his massive chest was barring the way.

"Fantôme invited us." Skeeter moved closer until he and the man were nose to nose, or rather nose to collarbone, because the man was as massive as a Bourbon Street bouncer. At least six-foot-six, even in his bare feet, white and not, apparently, a fan of daily hygiene, the man wasn't pleased to see them. Daffy could smell his body, and her stomach, which had settled down on the trip, began to clench and unclench.

"You make your offering before you come into our circle," the giant said, his voice surprisingly high. The words ended on a squeak.

Daffy guessed that the expected "offering" was money.

"Not tonight, bro," Skeeter said. "I'm just here to get ideas for a painting of Doctor John that Fantôme asked me to do."

The man scratched his scalp under a dirty white kerchief,

and Daffy tried not to think what he might dislodge. "You that artist guy?" he asked at last.

"You got it."

"I could pose. You could use me as your model."

"There's an idea. We'll talk. Catch you later." Skeeter reached for Daffy and pulled her around the man, making his way into the crowd, which was beginning to slowly circle as two men and two women flanking a trio of drummers serenaded them in a language Daffy couldn't identify. Several more women were banging the kind of handheld percussion instruments a fifth-grade teacher might pass out during general music class.

As her eyes grew more accustomed to the flickering torch light, she saw a full-figured African-American woman in the center of the clearing. The woman, dressed in layers of white with her head wrapped in a turban, was bent low over what looked like a mat, or a large rectangle of oilskin. As Daffy watched, she dripped what might be paint, or some other substance in a design on the mat, lifting her arms to the star-studded sky, stepping back, moving away, moving forward. As large as she was, perhaps nearly three hundred pounds, she moved with uncanny grace. Daffy halfway expected her to sprout wings and fly, as light as a bird.

She looked familiar.

Daffy and Skeeter were circling now. Getting into the rhythm was easy. She scanned the dancers around her and was relieved there were no children. She didn't recognize anyone, which was a bigger relief, and if any of them were teenagers, they were just on the cusp of adulthood. Some looked mesmerized, eyes closing, heads lolling, bodies swaying. Others looked as if they wished the concierge at their hotel had suggested a different evening's entertainment.

As they circled further around, she got her first glimpse of a structure that had been erected along one side.

Skeeter took her hand and pointed discreetly with his other. "The altar."

A man cracking a whip came around the other side of the circle toward them, and she winced, but he passed by without a glance. Another circled in the opposite direction carrying a slab of smoking firewood.

She and Skeeter drew closer to what she now saw was a table draped in white linen, covered with candles, shells, brightly painted pictures of saints, African masks and figurines, and because this was Southern Louisiana, plastic Mardi Gras beads hanging everywhere.

Skeeter moved beside her so he could whisper narration. "The woman in charge, in the middle, calls herself Mama Mambo. She's a local voodoo queen. Her real name is Althea Darwin. She's a cook at Jambalaya Johnny."

By now Daffy was feeling both silly and a little sick from circling the fire. She pointed to the sky. "I guess she's *moon*lighting."

Mama Mambo straightened and began a loud, fluid collection of syllables in a language Daffy didn't know. The syllables could have been gibberish or a treatise on the philosophy of Kant. Whatever they were, they were hypnotic.

The drums grew softer, and the dancing slowed. Daffy saw two women dragging a third, who had obviously fainted, out of the circle. A man waved his arms as if to say, "I've seen enough," and moved into the shadows, where he lit a cigarette.

She remembered studying crowd psychology and something called emergent norm theory. Crowds, which had no reason to be unified, often achieved unification by socializing. More important, eventually they allowed key people to determine how they should act, which then became the crowd's new normal. It happened without anyone thinking it over. She suspected the people in this crowd had never been together in one place before, and so, as they had danced and moved in the circle, they had simply followed the key leaders, Mama Mambo, the instrumentalists, several women who seemed to be demonstrating steps. The result was that they had become an entity unto themselves.

Had the girls in her therapy group become an entity? Was Jewel under the influence of key people who had convinced her to follow their norms? Had the girl somehow become involved in a voodoo cult?

The possibility seemed so far-fetched, and yet she'd learned enough about groups to try to remember exactly what differentiated a cult from a religion. Two criteria surfaced. A strong leader who knew everything and controlled everything. And fear that the outside world was evil and salvation could only be achieved from within.

The drums stopped suddenly. Now, the crowd was being led by their silence to turn and watch the spectacle that was emerging in the circle's center. For nearly a full minute only the bullfrogs and crickets entertained. Then the drums began again with renewed volume and vigor.

Swaying, Mama Mambo closed her eyes and held out her arms. Fantôme appeared through an opening near the altar. He was dressed all in white, and he wasn't alone. In his arms was the snake Daffy had seen in the Sanctuary, or at least its twin. After weaving and bobbing, holding the snake above his head and dipping in and out of the crowd, he presented the snake to Mama Mambo, and then the two of them began to sing and move together, bending and arching and calling out names and cadences unlike anything Daffy had ever heard. The snake twined between them, binding them together.

Daffy's head began to pound in earnest.

Skeeter's arms came around her. "Are you okay?"

She leaned against him, her lips near his ear. "This is a tourist orgy, isn't it?"

"Yep. But is it helpful?"

She didn't care how she was feeling. She had made her decision. "Not as much as talking to Mama Mambo will be."

T he ceremony had ended in a flurry of firecrackers and wailing. The tourists had certainly gotten their money's worth.

As she and Skeeter waited for an introduction to Mama Mambo, Daffy zipped through memories trying to remember where she'd seen the woman before. She sometimes ate lunch at Jambalaya Johnny on Oak Street not far from her office. Jeremy was a fan of New Orleans style cuisine, although Daffy was more inclined to lunch on lighter fare.

It was entirely possible she'd glimpsed Mama Mambo in the kitchen, which, as Daffy remembered, was on display through a wide window behind the bar that ran the length of the room. The menu consisted of New Orleans standards, all served with rice in one form or another, and Johnny himself had opened the restaurant decades ago during the Depression, to serve meals to men and women with limited incomes and large appetites.

So it made sense that Daffy had seen her at the restaurant. But somehow it didn't seem right.

The crowd was rapidly dwindling. When people first began to leave, Skeeter had pointed out the parking lot beyond the clearing, where two buses waited to ferry onlookers back to their hotels. Now only a handful milled around, waiting for their chance to talk to the night's star performer. Fantôme had greeted Skeeter and Daffy and then disappeared, perhaps to squeeze another few bucks from the tourists by selling bottled water or packaged pralines for the trip back.

Mama Mambo was mopping her neck and face with a thick

towel when they finally approached her. She looked tired and not particularly happy.

Daffy took the lead and stuck out her hand. "I'm Daphne Brookes, umm. . . Mama." She smiled to cover up her confusion about what to call the woman. "Fantôme gave us permission to come tonight. This is Skeeter Harwood, and he painted the portrait of Marie Laveau hanging in the Sanctuary."

Mama Mambo's gaze flicked to Skeeter and she gave him a polite nod. "It's beautiful work."

Her voice held an unfamiliar cadence. A New Orleans accent was an odd cross between the no-nonsense bustle of New York streets and the slower magnolia-scented lanes of the Deep South. Mama Mambo's was something else entirely.

The Bourbon Street Bouncer came up to stand behind Mama, his smell seeping around the big woman's body and wafting toward them. "This guy's going to paint me," he told Mama. "Aren't you?" He directed the last to Skeeter.

"You'll have to talk to Fantôme," Skeeter said. "It's up to him."

Bouncer continued to stand there, which was not what Daffy had hoped for, but she knew this was her moment.

"Mama Mambo, I know some teenagers who may be involved with voodoo. I'm worried they may not be..." She struggled to come up with the right way to phrase the end of her sentence. "They may not be old enough to handle things they don't really understand."

"What kind of things, child?"

"I think the occult–" She realized that was absolutely the wrong word to have used. "Anything that deals with a world they can't see–"

"Voudou is a religion, a religion practiced around the world. All religions deal with things we cannot see."

"Very true. Only all religions can be used for good or evil, can't they? And whether someone is using voodoo that way or not, one of my clients seems worried. I was hoping–"

"Mama's gotta go," Bouncer said. "She don't need to explain nothing. And now she needs to rest, and you know, Fantôme pays me to be sure she's left alone."

"Is there another time we could talk?" Daffy addressed Mama directly. "Another place."

"We're leaving," Bouncer said. "No more talk."

"I have to go." Mama Mambo started across the clearing toward the altar. "I have nothing helpful to tell you."

Daffy watched her go. Skeeter smiled at Bouncer, who was glaring at them now. "You have a great profile. If I painted you, that would be the way I'd pose you."

Bouncer's eyes lit up. "Like this?" He turned and lifted his arms into a boxer's stance.

Daffy restrained herself from waving the air in front of her to dispel the fumes.

"I think I need to see you in better light. Maybe by the bonfire?"

"I gotta douse it anyway." Bouncer started that way, and Skeeter inclined his head toward Mama before he followed.

She started after the other woman and caught up with her quickly, because while Mama had seemed feather-light during the ceremony, now she was trudging, clearly tired.

"I don't want to hassle you," she said, hurrying to walk beside her. "Would it be possible to meet you after a shift at Jambalaya Johnny some day? Just for a few minutes?"

"How'd you know I work there?"

"Skeeter told me. I don't work far away."

"You have a good memory?"

"Good enough."

"I live in Bucktown, on Poinsettia Street. She repeated the

house number, then shrugged. "You come tonight. I'm going right home. Better we do this sooner than later, you understand?"

"It's nice of you to help me."

"I be helping *nobody* at all if I don't like what you tell me."

"I understand. I'll be there."

Mama sped up, and Daffy, who knew there was no point in following her, went to find and rescue Skeeter.

CHAPTER 8

M ama Mambo lived in the Bucktown section of Metairie, just over the Orleans Parish line. As they headed back toward town, Daffy made bets with Skeeter about what they would find.

"A purple RV with a neon sign that says 'The Voodoo Queen is in.'" It was her third guess behind a haunted pirate ship, and a boarded-up church on a dead-end street.

"I picture a shrimp pink camelback with a magnolia in front," he said.

A camelback was a shotgun with a second-story addition on the back, and the city was filled with them. Daffy chided him in her best school marm voice. "You know, Skeeter, winning isn't the point of the game."

"You aren't by any chance doing therapy with the Saints? Because they seem to subscribe to that theory." The city's football team did seem to lose more games than it won, which never stopped New Orleans from cheering them on.

They turned off I-10 to Metairie, and she examined what little she could see of the surrounding streets as Skeeter slowed to read signs. "If I remember local history," he said, "this area was originally a string of fishing camps. Squatters, houses built on stilts. I think it was supposed to be a rocking kind of place. Speakeasies, gambling, ladies of ill repute. By the time I was a kid, it had calmed down and seafood was the major draw."

"Living this close to the lake I'd be worried about hurricanes."

"Storms change the landscape on a regular basis."

"So maybe I'll change my guess to an old seafood shack haunted by a fisherman washed overboard in the middle of a hurricane. Mama Mambo burns offerings to him every night to keep him from stealing into her bed."

"Is that how it's done? Do you burn offerings to keep men out of your bed?"

She traced a finger down his arm. "I'd be more likely to burn offerings to get a man *into* my bed."

"You have one in mind? Seems like it would work better if you could picture somebody while you're working your magic."

"If I told you, the spell would be broken. You're the voodoo expert. You should know that."

He gave a low laugh. "I'll make a run to the Sanctuary of Voodoo if you need more candles and incense."

"Considering my luck so far, I might set my house on fire before I'm finally successful."

"From my perspective? A little smoke would be a small price to pay."

He found Poinsettia and turned. For the most part the neighborhood was well-kept, and the street was lined with post-World War II one-story homes, some with iron lace grillwork over windows and doors. Hip roofs were common, and Daffy guessed the houses had attics for storage since basements were out of the question in neighborhoods that were below sea level—which far too many were.

"No sign of ghosts." Skeeter was barely pressing the gas pedal now, looking at house numbers.

"There it is." Daffy pointed to a pretty, rose-colored brick ranch with shutters that ran from the roof line to the ground. What had probably been a carport on the south side had been closed in with no windows and painted a nondescript color, tan or pale green. It was too dark to tell.

"See the addition? That's the voodoo room," Daffy said. "That's why Mama bought the house. That's where she entertains the old fisherman, or tries not to, depending on her mood and the availability of men with real bodies in Bucktown."

"Even ghosts deserve a little fun."

She fell silent. The joking had been as much to keep her mind off her physical woes as for any other reason, but it hadn't worked. He parked in front of the house and swivelled to look at her.

"You're ready for this?"

"I'm not sure what to tell her."

"As little as possible?"

"That goes without saying. But I need to know if there's anything I can do to help my client."

"Start by asking about tonight's ceremony."

That was perfect. She nodded and opened her door, and they walked up a concrete sidewalk together. His hip brushed hers, and even with a headache, she felt the impact in delicious places.

The woman who opened the door was a surprise. She was wearing a bright flowered muumuu with nothing covering her closely cropped hair. Her only adornments were gold hoop earrings that nearly touched her shoulders.

The sight of Mama Mambo in different clothing solved one problem. Daffy guessed immediately where she had first seen her. She thought this was the woman she'd seen arguing with

Natalie on Carrollton. Now she had something else she wanted
to know and couldn't ask directly.

"You are very kind to see us," Daffy said. "I'm sure you're
tired."

"You come in." Mama stepped aside, and they entered. She
hadn't really known what to expect, but this house defied imagination because it was so utterly ordinary. The wood-grained lami-
nate floor in the living area to their left was partly covered with a
sea-green area rug and dotted with simple upholstered furniture
in shades of mauve and blue. A piano sat against one wall with
music spread on the stand and the bench pulled out, as if somebody had just abandoned it. Beyond them was a walnut table
surrounded by straight-backed chairs, and beyond that a family
room paneled in dark wood and lined with bookcases and a wall
of audio equipment.

"Somebody plays the piano," Daffy said. "I always wanted to."

"It's better to start as a grown-up. No one has to remind you to
practice."

"Too many times we think what we didn't learn as children
can't be learned again."

"I didn't learn English. Perhaps you guessed?"

"Creole?" Skeeter asked. "Haitian Creole?"

"Oh, yes, you have the ear. But I have been here very long and
now speak English. Not everyone hears the Creole."

"It's a beautiful language." Skeeter smiled. "*M'ap eseye apran
kreyol.*"

She clapped. "Are you really?"

"At one time, but not lately. I only took lessons for a few
months."

"What did you say?" Daffy asked him.

"I am trying to learn Creole."

She whistled softly. Mama smiled and started toward the
family room, and Skeeter took Daffy's arm.

"Where did you take lessons?" she asked softly.

"From the guy in the next cell. Someday I'll tell you what else I learned."

She bumped his hip with hers.

Mama Mambo settled them on a comfortable sofa. Except for an ornate crucifix hanging on the wall that opened into her tidy kitchen, everything in the house was standard-issue. Daffy could just see through a doorway into what had formerly been the carport. Pillowy leather furniture faced a large-screen TV. It was a media room, with no outward signs of anything unusual.

"This house has many places to sit," Mama Mambo said. "As a child if I wanted to sit, I went outside and sat on the ground. This is why I have so many chairs and sofas."

"You grew up in Haiti?" Daffy asked.

"Yes, and I learned all I know about voudou there from a *mambo asogwe*, a high priestess, you might say."

Daffy leaned forward. "*You* seemed to be the high priestess tonight."

"You have been to other of our gatherings, then? You have seen spirits come to possess those who have gathered together?"

"No, I haven't."

"This is too bad."

"That's not what was happening tonight?"

Mama Mambo fanned herself, although the temperature inside the house was cool. "Many kinds of voudou exist, child. Many, many kinds. It's a religion, a very old one. We do good for our communities. We stress generosity and honor. We worship the supreme being who guides us all, as well as lesser gods, too, our *Loa*, who are intermediaries, like your Catholic saints."

Daffy wasn't Catholic. In fact, she'd been raised entirely without church, but she did understand. "So what we saw tonight was a kind of worship?"

"What we have here? Very different than at home, although

we share some little pieces. Marie Laveau herself was a free woman of color, but she never traveled to Haiti. What she learned, she learned here and from whom? Do we know? We do not."

Daffy had a feeling she was being led astray. "So tonight was a different kind of ritual than what you learned."

"Different from anybody's." For a moment Mama looked disturbed, then she shrugged. "But it is an introduction, yes? A popular look at something sacred that was too long banned and disregarded."

"Commercial voodoo," Skeeter said. "For tourists."

Mama smiled and didn't deny it. "You have questions for me? Because I must go to bed soon."

"I'm a psychologist," Daffy said. "I don't think I told you that. And I have a client, a teenager, who seems to be involved with voodoo. She's frightened, confused, afraid. She isn't communicating. I'm afraid she may be under the influence of someone or a group who wants to hurt her."

Mama sat up, suddenly alert. "Where is it that you work?"

Daffy named her building and the intersection. "She doesn't feel safe. I'm afraid that might cause her to do something she shouldn't."

Mama's eyes narrowed. "There is nothing I can do."

Daffy was surprised. She really hadn't asked Mama to do anything. She just wanted information. "I understand that. I can't reveal who she is. But I hoped you could help me understand what she might be thinking. She left a gris-gris bag in my office."

She waved her hand dismissively. "Gris-gris is Louisiana voodoo or hoodoo stuff. Is has nothing to do with me."

"Could someone have told her she's cursed? If I understand, then maybe I can help her see she has nothing to be afraid of?"

Mama stood. "The day has been too long. I have nothing to say that will help you."

Daffy and Skeeter stood, too, and Daffy spoke. "I think I upset you. I'm sorry. I'm just trying to find out what I can. I don't want my client to get worse, and I'm afraid she might."

"The voudou surrounding this girl is the worst kind."

Daffy didn't know what to say. The words sent a chill down her spine. As she'd told the teenagers, words had power. Mama's *statement* had enormous power. Even Daffy, who didn't believe in curses, felt it crawl along her spine. She searched the other woman's face, which had gone from pleasant to disturbed. Or possibly angry? Daffy wasn't sure. "You know this how?"

"I have said what I can."

Daffy went for broke. "I thought I saw you arguing with some teenage girls on the street under my window. Was that you? Could it have been about this?"

"I really must go to bed." Mama started through the house, which was anything but a long walk. Daffy and Skeeter followed. She turned a palm up in question, and he didn't shake his head.

"Mama Mambo," she said as Mama opened the front door to evict them. "I don't know enough to believe in voodoo. That's no secret. But sometimes, and only rarely, I do think that supporting a client's beliefs might be the best way to help them. If this girl believes she's been cursed, and I'm afraid that might be the case, it could help if you spoke to her and reassured her she's wrong. That's not the way we usually do therapy, but I want to do anything I can to help her feel safe again, to help her heal enough that I can work with her."

She'd said her piece. There was nothing else to say. But as she looked into the other woman's eyes, she knew she had failed.

"There are many things someone like you will never understand," Mama said. "Curses can be many things. This curse you speak of is as real as a show you watch on the TV," Mama said. "Do you know exactly how that show comes to you? Could you make it happen by yourself? No, but you are still sure it will be there when the time is right, when you turn a knob or press a button. And that is all I will say. Ever." She held out her hand to signal it was time, perhaps past time, for them to leave.

Daffy knew not to argue. "Thank you for talking to us." She pulled a business card out of her handbag. She'd had it ready. "If you decide you have more to tell us, will you call me?"

Mama didn't answer. Her features were as rigid as any of the African masks and idols on the voodoo altar that night, but after a few moments she took the card and crushed it against her palm. Daffy wasn't hopeful it would end up anywhere other than Mama's trash. She and Skeeter exited, and the door closed so fast behind them that she felt the breeze against her legs.

"That went well," Skeeter said, taking her arm. "Unless I'm mistaken, leaving right away would be a good idea."

"You're going to drive carefully, right? Just in case she decides to send her favorite *Loa* to escort us home."

"I'm about to win my first safe driver of the year award."

S keeter liked Daffy's house. He liked the diverse art dotting walls that she'd painted offbeat colors like tangerine and eggplant—in the same room. He liked the area rugs from Morocco and Turkey covered with symbolism like the tree of life, or the four seasons. She'd hung ferns near windows and set what looked like a citrus tree in a sunny corner. Something both herbal and spicy scented the air. The same fragrance seemed to seep from her skin, and he found it powerfully seductive. Maybe the house wasn't hers, but she'd made it her own, something he had never bothered to do.

"I like your plants," he said. "It brings everything to life."

"I have so many more. They take turns on the side gallery off the bedroom. I have a wicker loveseat where I can sit and keep them company when I have time."

"But no pets?"

"I've named the plants. That's enough for now."

"Who's this?" He fingered a leaf on the citrus tree he'd first noticed, which rested in Italian pottery adorned with lemons and olives.

She came to stand in front of him, brushing dust off a leaf with her fingertip. "That's Hope, because I hope I'll actually get enough lemons to make lemonade. Look at these." She pointed out four tiny dots at the tip of branches. "I'm encouraged. She seems happy here."

"The ferns?"

"I name my ferns after psychologists. Freud, Perls, Jung, Skinner, Rogers." She was counting on her fingers. "I think that's it. They seem very male to me, imposing and thoughtful, but they don't bear fruit or flower."

"You can tell one from the other?"

"Well, of course. How would you like it if I called you by somebody else's name?"

"You're just itching to."

She reached over and ran a finger down his cheek. "Whatever your real name is, you just have to claim it."

He glanced at his Mickey Mouse watch. "It's almost ten. I could go home, or you could offer me something to drink before I hit the road."

Her eyes lit. "Tea? Beer? The beer may be the sum total of what's in my fridge. I haven't done much shopping lately."

"Beer sounds good."

He followed her into the kitchen and sat on one of the two chairs at a table no larger than a toadstool. He tipped the chair onto its hind legs and watched as she put water into an electric kettle, then rummaged through the fridge. At some point as they'd circled the clearing tonight, her hair had come down. Now as he watched, it danced as she moved, bouncing against her neck just below her shoulders. He had tried to avoid fantasies of running his hands through Daffy's curls, of framing her face and lowering his lips to hers, and most especially of all the things that could come after.

He wanted her in the worst way and probably had since the first time he'd seen her. He wasn't sure what was stopping him. Not Daffy herself. She had told him, showed him, in numerous ways that she wanted him, too. She knew her mind, and it seemed set on having him in her bed. In the past when a woman he'd been attracted to crooked her finger, he'd never hesitated. But this was different. This felt different. He supposed it felt like a step on a journey. And the thing was? He was afraid he wanted nothing less than Daffy walking beside him the entire way.

She faced him and held up a bottle for his approval.

He laughed. "Blackened Voodoo lager?"

"I bought a six-pack before all this happened. I thought I still had one behind the shriveling lettuce and stale bread. You like?"

"Cold, dark and wet, my favorite."

She pulled down a canister, scooped tea into a ball and dropped it into a ceramic mug, which she filled with steaming water. Finally she joined him, the opened bottle in one hand, a glass in the other.

He waved away the glass and took the bottle, using it to gesture to her mug. "Does the tea help your head?"

She sat as if she was glad a chair was in reach. He knew it had been a long night for someone who was recovering. "Antoinette swore by tea while she was sick. I have different blends. Nothing seems to help all that much right now, though. I just have to plow through to the end."

"You're okay tonight?"

"I think the air did help. Of course the scene with Mama

Mambo probably didn't do me much good. But so far? Doing okay."

"I'll finish this and go."

"You still haven't told me about New York. You've managed to avoid it all night."

He wasn't sure what he wanted to say, so he had avoided the topic. "I did see a show. I had an afternoon free, so I went to the cheap tickets booth—"

"You know that's not what I want to hear about. Was it a waste of time to go? Was the agent an idiot? Did you hate the galleries?"

He tried to think of the best way to characterize his week. "It was... surprising." He rested all four legs of his chair on the floor. "I guess I'm suspicious of good news."

"You had good news?" She looked delighted.

"I guess. One of the galleries is talking about a show. They called my work invigorating and contemporary while still paying tribute to culture and tradition. How do you like that? Their only real problem is they don't think I want to be successful. They think I prove that in a number of ways, including doing caricatures at Jackson Square."

He watched her face. He wondered if her clients could see what was on her mind as clearly as he did.

"Are they right?" she asked. "Does that feel right to you?"

He saw that it felt right to her. "You agree with them, don't you?"

"Skeeter, I don't know you that well, do I? I mean, I feel like I do, but we've spent relatively little time together. I haven't even seen your work."

"Give it your best shot anyway."

"Okay. I'd guess that you think they've made a mistake singling you out for bigger things. And if you do go for the big dream, if you stop diddling around, you'll just be disappointed because you won't succeed."

He finished his beer, contemplating the fact that no matter how little they'd been together, she already understood him so well.

He finally set his bottle on the table. "So I'm that transparent?"

"I do this for a living, remember?"

"You left out the part about my being happy doing what I do. And the part where I wonder if I'd be less happy if I had more stress and self-doubt."

"You haven't had much time to think about what this might mean. And who says you have to change your entire life in a week or two? If you decide getting more serious about your work sounds right, then you could do it slowly. It wouldn't be a waste of time. You'd sell whatever you created, wouldn't you?"

He shrugged.

"What aren't you selling right now?"

"The show here wasn't a rip-roaring success."

"Would the agent and the gallery staff work with you to figure out what you do best and how to position it for the best results?" She was clearly thinking out loud.

"They claim they will," he said.

"My father believes a great actor and a bad director make a bad play. No matter how good an actor Carson Brookes is, he believes that everybody needs objective leadership to do their best. So he always listens, even when he doesn't immediately agree."

"I can't believe I'm getting advice from Carson Brookes via his beautiful daughter."

She smiled, her eyes warm. "Thanks for opening up about it. I didn't mean to nag. I'm not very good about waiting. Before every session I have to remind myself to let my clients do the work."

He knew he had to leave, or he had to put his arms around her and let the night go where it would. As much as he wanted the second, he stood. "I have to get home. And you need to rest. You're still not over this bug."

She looked as if she wanted to dispute his decision, but she stood, too. "I'll walk you to the door. You were a good sport to arrange everything tonight."

"Even if you didn't learn anything helpful."

"I'll mull it over." In the doorway leading into her bedroom she flicked a switch to light their way back to the front. She started forward but Skeeter, who had casually glanced at the other side of the room, grabbed her before she'd gone more than a few steps. He pulled her against him and turned her so she was looking at him and nowhere else.

"Daffy, don't turn around."

"What?"

"You didn't turn on the light when we came through earlier."

She was searching his face. "So?"

"There's something on your bed."

She closed her eyes. "Please tell me it's not dead." She paused. "Or alive."

His eyes flicked to the bed and back again. "Pretty dead. About as dead as it gets. At least part of it."

"Just tell me."

He tried to find words to describe the skull with the snake crawling along the top and in and out of the mouth. He couldn't. "Go into the living room and call Sam." He looked beyond the bed and saw that the door leading to the side gallery had been battered beyond repair. Whatever kind of night latch the locksmith had added had not been a success. "Tell Sam there's been another break-in, and ask him to send somebody who knows what they're doing this time, to help us figure this out."

CHAPTER 9

"This is not how I pictured your neighborhood," Daffy said, as Skeeter pulled in front of a house and turned off the Jeep's engine.

She closed her eyes, as she pretended to picture that other house, the one in her imagination. "Old New Orleans, kind of dilapidated, a neighborhood only minimally safe, and then only before dark." She opened her eyes wide, in question.

He closed *his* eyes for a moment, as if trying to picture it. "The one with the voodoo queen just down the street. I can see it clearly." He looked at her. "I used to live there. I moved last year. A friend had to leave town fast and wanted to sell his house even faster."

"One step ahead of the law?"

"Not all my friends are jailbirds, Daff."

Her head was pounding so hard she couldn't smile. "Antoinette and Sam certainly aren't."

"Ray's a cinematographer. He got a job working on a film out in L.A. He offered me a great price, so I snapped it up. The right deal for both of us, although almost everything I make goes into the mortgage. This isn't far from where I grew up, and Sam and Joshua ended up back in the neighborhood, too. Like pigeons coming home to roost."

Daffy tried to think of something else to say, but her mind whirled fruitlessly. Her heart was beating normally now, for which she was grateful. If she had seen the skull without Skeeter's introduction, the sight might have sent her into a faint, like a corseted Victorian miss. But Skeeter? Skeeter looked as calm as if absolutely nothing interesting had happened that evening, as if attending a voodoo ceremony beside a swamp, interviewing the mambo in charge, and then going home with Daffy to find voodoo on her bed, were par for the course.

Of course, as it had turned out, the skull with the snake crawling in and out of the mouth was only a latex mask. In a town that donned costumes for every occasion, masks just like it were probably sitting idly in closets or dressers on almost every block. Not all of them came stuffed with chicken bones inside, however, along with the carefully rolled skin from a snake that must have been at least five feet long before it staged a shedding party.

"Earth to Daffy?"

"I'm sorry. I'm still a little shook up."

He opened his door, but he didn't get out. "Sam's got this. And nobody's getting back inside tonight."

To make sure of that, Skeeter had nailed slats over the ruined door after Sam and a cop in uniform had investigated and taken statements. With Sam's help, he had torn the slats from a wooden lattice extending from Daffy's back steps to the ground. Somebody with patience and a crowbar might be able to pry them loose, but nobody really thought that whoever had broken in would be back right away.

Now he put his arm around her shoulder and squeezed. "A good night's sleep will help."

She hoped so, because in addition to nerves twanging in

distress and a headache that felt the way a thunderstorm sounded, she was furious. Whoever had invaded her space had also taken whatever they'd used to batter in the side door and smashed her potted garden on the gallery. She'd saved what she could, carefully placing her leafy friends and what soil she could recover in plastic bags until tomorrow, when she could buy new pots to salvage the least damaged. But the violation had been complete, which must have been the point.

She got out and stood at the curb, taking in the scene in front of her and relentlessly shoving everything else away.

Before leaving her house, Skeeter had kept watch while she grabbed a few things, then he'd driven her toward the Garden District, into a family neighborhood filled with one-of-a-kind homes, some sprawling and expensive, others smaller but well-kept. Crepe myrtle trees lined the streets, and most yards were defined by picket fences or privacy hedges. There was more space between houses here than in the Marigny, more places for children to play and even a graceful brick church on the previous block. His neighborhood was known as Touro, after the nearby Touro Infirmary. His street was close to Magazine, with its galleries, antiques and restaurants, and within walking distance of some of the best Mardi Gras parades.

Now she subtly checked out his house as they walked to the door. She thought the architectural style was Creole cottage, with a wide gallery without railings. There were two front doors that probably led to separate rooms, since the design often had no interior hallways. The doors were separated by long windows between, all with lime green shutters. The house itself was pale blue and doors a deep peach. She fell instantly in love.

"I want this house," she said, as he fished for his key. "You don't even have to show me the inside. I'll take it."

"You don't believe in owning houses."

"I may have changed my mind."

The door swung open, and she followed him inside. The two halves of the long front room were marginally separated by a free-standing brick fireplace that was open on both sides and beyond that, a staircase. One side of the room had a worn sofa, two arm chairs and a low table. The other had a dining table with four mismatched chairs and a counter separating it from the kitchen. Originally the space would have been divided by walls, and the kitchen, which was beyond them and now open to the dining area, would have been walled off.

"Did you open it yourself?"

"No, Ray did all the renovations."

"I bet he hated to leave."

"A woman was involved. He was ready to get out of town."

"My heart would have to be shattered to leave this place." She stepped farther in, and then she saw the art. Unlike her house, the walls here were a neutral tan, but everywhere she looked they were splashed with color. Without thinking she put one hand over her heart. "Oh, Skeeter!"

He didn't say anything. She walked to the nearest wall and began to examine what she saw.

"I'm . . ." She wasn't sure what to say. "I'm stunned. It's amazing."

"I'm not much for decorating," he said from behind her. "But I had to have a place to hang all these after the show."

"These are the pieces the gallery just took down?"

"Yeah. I don't normally frame my work. I have stacks upstairs in storage drawers. It takes up less room."

She faced him, but just for a moment. She didn't want to stop her examination. "I can't believe that every single piece on this wall didn't sell the first night. Why not?"

"Other than that it's probably not good enough?"

"That's not even on the list." She turned back and walked slowly to the next group. "Why? You must have some idea."

"Wrong audience. Wrong gallery. The one that handled my show mostly markets to tourists. I think they were hoping for French Quarter scenes, an edgier version of my caricatures and portraits. Little kids tap dancing, second-liners, tables at Café du Monde."

"And Mardi Gras."

"That was certainly mentioned. They thought they'd get a slightly higher- class version of what I do on the Square."

"Instead they got this." *Instead* took her breath away. She knew little to nothing about art. Despite a class or two as an undergraduate she was afraid she was in the category known as "I know what I like when I see it." But she didn't like this. Her reaction was much more intense. She was overwhelmed, saturated, immersed in Skeeter's world immediately. Strong lines, color everywhere, somehow primitive and still disciplined, educated. She didn't know what to study first. The oil painting of the roof lines of the Quarter transposed over a black and white sketch of a homeless man? Three small studies of the Mississippi at night? A series of pastels documenting the inside of a home, the family warily studying each other. Even the cat looked unsure about its future.

Every piece was signed with a tiny cartoon of a mosquito.

"Skeeter." She shook her head.

At the final wall she stopped. These pieces were entirely different, different from the art on the other walls, different from each other.

"These aren't yours, are they?" When he didn't answer, she studied them further. A series of watercolors of the French Quarter hung beside six charcoal drawings of teenagers in a courtyard. The final grouping were abstract collages using what looked like the pages of paperback novels, flower petals, placemat menus.

"My students," he said. "I teach a weekly class for some kids in the foster care system. I get more out of it than they do."

Finally, there was a sculpture, just one, in the farthest corner, an old man with his arm around a small boy formed from what looked like unfired clay.

"A prototype," he said, "in early stages. I'm not sure sculpture is my medium, but I wanted to feel this one under my fingertips."

She turned and found him right behind her. She put her arms around him and kissed him. He made a noise low in his throat, circled her with his arms and kissed her back.

Kissing him felt right, as if there was no other place where she needed to be, perhaps for a very long time. Her body seemed to melt into his, as if whatever boundaries were still between them had liquified. She opened her lips and the kiss deepened. She spread her fingers and moved her hands under his shirt to feel the heat of his skin.

Her head began to spin. The ground seemed to give way under her feet. For a moment she struggled to find it, but couldn't. Then, the world went black.

Skeeter smoothed Daffy's hair off her forehead with one hand and patted her cheek with the other. "Daffy. Open your eyes." He said her name again and then once more, patting a little harder. Just as he had decided to pull out his phone and call 911, she mumbled something and gradually her eyelids parted.

She stared at him, uncomprehending.

"You fainted."

She didn't say anything for a moment, and again, he decided to fish for his phone. Then her lips turned up just a little. "Wow, Skeeter. Some kiss."

He was so relieved she was lucid again that for a moment, he couldn't speak. Then he took her hand and squeezed it. "You went out like a light. And as much as I'd like to take credit for it, I don't think you swooned from desire."

"I would have...if I hadn't fainted from–" She seemed to consider. "I had nothing much to eat today. That...the skull..."

She didn't have to say more. Either event, on top of not feeling well for days, could do it. "Tell me how you're feeling right now."

"Head's pounding. It was better for a while. Then..."

"Listen, you need to go to the ER and get checked. Luckily we're not far away."

"No, it's just been a stressful night."

"I don't think you're a woman who faints from stress. Have you ever fainted before?"

"No. But my blood sugar must have gone kafooey."

"It's time you saw a doctor, Daffy. You've been fiddling around too long. I don't care what Antoinette's doctor told her. You need to be checked out, too."

"If I promise to call–" She lifted herself on her elbows. "Tomorrow?"

He weighed that possibility with having to carry her flailing, protesting body out of his house, and the best answer wasn't hard. He liked holding her in his arms, but she was not as light as a feather.

She relaxed against the pillow, as if she knew she'd defeated him. "Where am I?"

"My bedroom."

"Not... the way I hoped."

He gave a low laugh. "You're sure you didn't do this on purpose?"

This time she tried to sit up, then gave up the fight. Instead she managed to wiggle a few inches and patted the newly available space beside her. "You're safe tonight."

He didn't want to be safe. He wanted to have her body under his, on top of his, entwined with his. He wanted to be naked with her, in every possible way. He knew she wouldn't resist. Yet so far, he was the one who had put up all the obstacles.

He stretched out beside her, resting on one hip so he could see her face. He brushed her hair off her forehead again and smiled a little.

"Why haven't we made love?" she asked.

She'd read his mind, which didn't surprise him. "Damned if I know. It's got something to do with, I don't know, voodoo? My prison record? Break-ins at your house? Pasts we don't want to repeat?"

She closed her eyes a moment, and when she opened them, her expression was serious. "Are you afraid I'll make demands? Because I won't."

He dragged a finger along her cheek to her lips. "I'm not sure what you mean."

"I'm an adult, and you're an adult. We don't have to live up to each others' expectations. Hearts, flowers and romance aren't necessary."

"So you sleep with just anybody and get out fast before you feel anything?" he asked.

Her expression heated, and she drew in a breath to respond.

He put his finger over her lips to silence her. "I know that's not what you're saying."

"Really? Who's the psychologist here?"

He knew this wasn't the time nor place for this discussion. "While we mull that over, I'm going to heat up some soup, and you're going to eat it and take some ibuprofen. Can you do that?"

"I'll try."

She looked so serious, as if she'd just decided to finally buy a new car or a handgun to protect herself, that he leaned over and kissed her lightly on the lips. "There's an empty bedroom upstairs, but sadly only one bed in this house, Daff, and you're in it."

"I seem to be." She waved her hand toward his walls. "No art here. I may get bored."

"For the record you won't be bored. I'm sleeping in here tonight, too, but I'm just sleeping with you to make sure you're okay."

"Got it."

He slid off the bed and started toward the door, but then he turned. "Just to be perfectly clear? Here's a warning. You'll know if and when that romance you don't believe in has started. I can tell you right now, it will be very different than this."

CHAPTER 10

Skeeter pulled up in front of Psychologist Associates and left the engine running while he dropped an arm over the back of the passenger seat. "You're sure you're up for this?"

Daffy wasn't sure of anything except that she didn't want to cancel the Riverview teen group again. "Maybe not, but my doctor's not concerned, so I'm going to believe him. You need to stop worrying."

"Your doctor said he doesn't *know* what the problem is. Your doctor said you should take things easy for a few more days."

Daffy had been lucky to get an immediate appointment with her internist, a man just old enough to be seasoned and young enough to remember his training. Knowing that she might not get to see him so quickly next time, she'd thoroughly explained every symptom and the stressors she'd dealt with. She'd even told him about the hallucinations and the voices, and he'd asked all the right questions. He'd done a good if quick examination, given her an order for blood work, and told her to take ibuprofen for the headaches, drink lots of liquids and get plenty of rest.

"This is probably the same virus your friends had," he'd said as she prepared to go down to the lab on the first floor. "It's not flu season, but there's always something out there waiting to grab you if you're run down. Dehydration and exhaustion can play funny tricks in your head, so I wouldn't worry about that. You're certainly not contagious anymore, and I bet by the time your blood work comes back you'll already be feeling more like your old self."

Now she was sorry she'd been completely honest with Skeeter, because in her opinion, the absence of a diagnosis was almost as good as a clean bill of health. She leaned over and kissed his cheek before she opened her door. "You've been so good to me. Thank you."

He smiled, one eyebrow cocked, as if he knew she was trying to soften him up. "Clearly you aren't going to follow orders. You'll call tonight when you get home?"

Daffy hoped that by the time she did, Cyril's handyman would have come and gone, leaving behind a new vintage door in place of the one the intruder had smashed to bits. "I'll definitely call."

"You're sure you don't want to come back to my place?"

He had given her a house key that morning, fastened to a small paintbrush, so she wouldn't forget whose it was. He'd told her it was for emergencies, and to put it somewhere safe.

She hoped there were no more emergencies. The next time she slept beside Skeeter in a bed, she wanted to be totally exhausted, not from an annoying illness but from uninhibited sex. "I need to take care of my plants or they'll all die for sure. But if anything seems iffy, I'll ask Nelson to take me right to your house. Then maybe I can see your studio. I seem to have fainted before I made it upstairs."

His expression said he knew she was pulling a fast one.

She got out and waited until he'd pulled away, remembering the last time he'd left her here and how hard it had been to summon the energy to walk inside. At least climbing the stairs wasn't going to be any harder today, which was the only piece of good news she could dredge up.

By the time she made it to the door of the reception area, she was wet with perspiration and just weak enough to know she had to sit for a while to recover. Still, her head seemed better, so she was hopeful.

She stepped inside and realized recovery would have to wait. Jewel's parents, Isabel and Robert, were perched on the sofa, and the moment she walked in, they leapt to their feet, as if they'd choreographed their moves with great care. Rosy, who looked distressed, nodded in their direction as if to say, "they're all yours."

"Let's talk in my office," she said, without asking why they were there. Jewel wasn't with them, and that was a bad sign.

They followed her in, and Daffy closed the door behind them, motioning to the chairs bordering her rug. She took one, too, and joined them.

"Jewel's disappeared," Robert Martinez said, and the words triggered a round of sobs from his wife.

Robert, tall and muscular, owned a highly lauded construction company. He was tough, a man who could keep any crew in line, but today he, too, looked as if he was about to dissolve in tears.

"When did this happen?" Daffy was careful not to let her own reaction show. The Martinezes didn't need even a drop of added drama.

"She said she was going to bed. Last night." Isabel twisted and untwisted the handle of her purse, wiping her tears with her forearm. "When I went in to be sure she was getting ready for her summer class..." She stifled another sob.

Daffy reached for a box of tissues and set it on the table. "So she was gone this morning?"

"We called the police. They said kids run away, but they usually come home."

"They take reports and ask a few questions, but they don't actively look for sixteen-year-olds," Robert said.

Daffy knew this was true, particularly when there was no reason to suspect foul play. Police work in the city was akin to triage in an emergency room. A sixteen-year-old who just wanted to get away from her parents was thought to be mature enough to take care of herself.

Of course, the police didn't know Jewel.

"Did she talk about leaving? Was she unusually worried about something? Any clues you can think of?"

"That's why we're here," Robert said. "She did tell us something. Maybe the way we responded set her off."

"Can you tell me what it was?"

"She asked for money. Thousands. She said that you told her she needs her own car, that she needs to be independent. Back in the fall when she got her restricted license, she totaled the car we'd bought her. Even though the accident was only partly her fault, we decided to wait to replace it until next year. I know most of her friends have—"

"I never suggested a car," Daffy said, cutting him off. Since Jewel's story wasn't true, she didn't need to know Robert's rationale. "I've never talked to Jewel about a car, or suggested she ask you for money for any reason." While she couldn't tell them what she had talked about with their daughter, or even her suspicion that voodoo was somehow involved in Jewel's problems, in her opinion, she could tell them what she and Jewel had not discussed.

"She's never been a liar." Isabel sounded completely perplexed, not as if she were defending her daughter. "Why did she say that? What was she thinking, asking us for all that money and blaming you?"

Daffy stopped her. "At this point let's not worry about blame. We need to concentrate on why she felt so cornered she had to invent a story. Why would she need that kind of money?"

Robert exploded. "Drugs! You're a therapist! You haven't seen the signs?"

She understood he wanted to blame somebody, and he was right. Jewel had exhibited signs that she might be involved with drugs. Daffy had been aware of them all along, and their sessions had been designed to probe that possibility, along with others.

"I'm not saying it's impossible. But let's go over a quick list. Has she had nosebleeds? Have you noticed her eyes were blood-shot or her pupils too large? Shaking? Slurring of words? Sneaking out of the house at night?"

They listened to the rest of her list and shook their heads, again as if they'd coordinated ahead of time.

Daffy continued. "I know she's not eating or sleeping well, and I know her work at school suffered this year. When she comes back home, I think we'll need another psychiatric consult, and we'll ask the doctor to test for drugs. But honestly, I don't think drugs are the problem. I think other things are going on."

"What? Can't you tell us?"

"You remember that Jewel said she would only talk to me if I agreed our conversations would be confidential? And she particularly specified that I couldn't reveal any of them to you. We agreed to that, the four of us, right at the beginning."

Robert slammed a fist against the table beside his chair. "That was before she took off."

"And when she comes back, she needs to know she can still trust me."

Isabel put a hand on her husband's knee. "Dr. Brookes is trying to help, Robby. Don't alienate her."

Daffy leaned forward, moving into their zone, not away from it, to make sure they knew she was on their side. "You don't have to worry about upsetting me. I can only imagine how you're feeling right now. Let's make a list of what you can do to help find Jewel." She got up and went to her desk, returning with a pad for each of them and pens. "The first thing you need to do is call all her friends."

~

"Of course, they'd already called her friends," Daffy told Antoinette in their catch-up session that afternoon. They were in Daffy's office working on cups of tea that Antoinette had brought in and insisted she drink. "They're going to keep after the local police, call the sheriff's office, talk to people connected with Riverview, search her room."

"Do you have any thoughts about why she needed all that money?"

"It's possible she really did want to buy a car, so she could drive into the sunset and away from whatever she's so terrified of here."

"But they didn't give her the money."

"Thankfully, no. The request was so out of nowhere, and neither of them thought this was the right moment in her life to own a car."

"I can talk to Sam."

Daffy nodded. "Great. And Robert Martinez has a friend on the force he's going to see this afternoon. But we both know that even with his friend and Sam pushing, the police won't make Jewel a priority. They'll put out alerts, but there are a lot of missing teenagers out there."

"Do you have any new thoughts on what might be going on with her?"

"I've been reading about cults. She seems so afraid to say anything, as if she's being watched and judged, and one slip-up could bring destruction. If she's fallen in with a group that's controlling her, maybe she's fled to them for protection from the moderating influence of her parents. Judging from the gris-gris bag and her reaction when I tried to talk to her, it might even be some distorted offshoot of voodoo. And then there's all the goings-on at my house."

"I can ask Sam if he knows anything about a local voodoo cult, but it's a long shot."

"I know it sounds far-fetched. But even the woman at the ceremony Skeeter and I went to seemed afraid when I mentioned my questions had to do with teenage girls."

"How will you handle Jewel's disappearance in your group today?"

"I'm going to be truthful. It's possible one of the other girls may know something."

"Natalie dislikes her. She's pretty outspoken about it."

"Natalie's pretty outspoken about everything. Has she said anything that might be helpful?"

Antoinette shook her head, then she mimed drinking tea, lifting her own cup to her lips, then holding it out to Daffy in example. "Didn't the doctor tell you to drink lots of liquids?"

Daffy had started the conversation by reporting the happenings of the previous night, followed by her doctor's visit, although Antoinette had already heard about the second break-in from Sam.

She drank half the cup before she answered. "My head already feels better, and my stomach is only intermittently upset. I'm getting over whatever it is, like you did."

Antoinette set her cup on the table. "About that..."

Daffy sensed news in the air.

"I may have had a virus for a day or two. Sam certainly did. But as it turns out, most of my symptoms were something else." She paused, then she smiled. "I'm pregnant."

Daffy let out a whoop. "You're serious?"

"I should have figured it out before this. I did visit my doctor, but he fit me in at the end of the day, and I actually saw his nurse for most of the visit. We talked about the headaches and the fact that Sam had been sick. Since I stopped taking the pill before the wedding, my periods have been irregular. I didn't mention them and nobody asked. As it turns out, hormones in early pregnancy can cause headaches."

"Are you happy? And Sam?"

Antoinette beamed. "Ecstatic. We both want a family while we're young enough to have the energy."

Daffy rose and leaned over the table to hug her. "This is just terrific. Are you going to keep working for a while?"

"I don't plan to stop seeing clients until I have to, but I won't take new ones until I come back. After the baby arrives I'll take some time off, but I plan to keep working. My sister and I had the most wonderful nanny when we were girls, and I traced her through the internet last year. She's French, and we've had such fun catching up. I think she'll come and work for Sam and me when we need her. She loved New Orleans." She laughed a little. "She just didn't love my parents."

Antoinette's parents were rigid to a fault and obsessed with appearances. Daffy knew Antoinette and Sam wouldn't be. And what kind of parent would she be if she ever had children? The question stumped her for a moment. It wasn't one she often pondered. Now she wondered about the answer.

She sat again and picked up her own tea. "Are you going to tell your clients?"

"I'll have to soon. I'm only worried about Natalie and Linda. Everything is so fraught with meaning for both of them, especially physical things. They both asked about you after you cancelled group, and hung on my answers."

"Everything seems personal at that age."

"Linda's still so fragile, and she wants everything in her life to stay the same. You know her friend Katie died so suddenly from acute leukemia that Linda didn't have time to process it. And now Linda's sure every time somebody coughs that they'll be on their deathbed before she can even say goodbye."

"Natalie's probably a fan of deathbeds. She's so angry in group. It's like a wildfire sweeping through every conversation."

"If she doesn't make a breakthrough and some changes, she'll lose her scholarship to Riverview."

"You haven't gotten any further in your sessions?"

Antoinette shook her head. Then she got to her feet. "I hope you have better luck in group today. You feel well enough to do it? I could sit in for you."

Daffy didn't feel well enough. But another absence would be hard to explain, and the girls would begin to believe something more serious than a virus was affecting her. They needed to move forward, and she needed to be with them when they did.

She smiled her thanks. "You'll be in the office if I need you?"

"Just bang on my door. And don't overdo. Your fainting worries me."

Back in her office, Daffy finished the tea and rooted in her mini fridge for something to eat before the girls arrived. She forced herself to spread peanut butter on graham crackers and nibble on one as she cleaned up. As she was putting the peanut butter back, she glanced out the window and saw Natalie with someone on the sidewalk. She wasn't at the right angle to see who, so she moved to the farthest window. By then, she only caught sight of a woman disappearing out of view. She glimpsed a broad back clothed in bright green and the swaying of hips.

She couldn't help but wonder if those hips might belong to Mama Mambo. Of course, the only reason the voodoo priestess had come to mind was because Daffy had seen Natalie arguing with her once before. And even that hadn't been confirmed.

Was it possible that Mama had something to do with Jewel's disappearance? If she did, how could Daffy find out? She couldn't ask the police to interview her. Daffy had nothing concrete to go on, and unless she thought Jewel was a danger to herself or someone else, she couldn't bring up the voodoo connection. Jewel had never threatened suicide or made any attempt to harm herself.

She washed up, did a few useless yoga stretches that did nothing for her headache, then went into the group room to wait.

Rosy arrived before the girls did. "Sharee's mother called about a minute ago. Sharee's on a bike trip. She forgot to tell you." She stepped into the room and closed the door. "You're not better, are you, dahlin'? Why are you here today?"

"Is my life an open book?"

"You ask me, you look like you're on your final chapter."

Daffy wondered if Skeeter thought so, too. "I'll go home after group. Will that make you happy?"

"You still got that nice man taking care of you?"

"If I look as awful as you say, he's probably making a date with somebody else."

"You could try a little makeup, do up your hair?"

Daffy tried not to smile. Rosy's idea of style and her own were generations apart. If she gave Rosy permission, she'd haul out the blue eye shadow and an entire can of hair spray. "I'll give it some thought. You'll send the girls in?"

Natalie was the first to arrive. She walked through the doorway as if she expected to see dragons. Linda slipped in behind her, as if she hoped nobody would notice.

"Just the three of us today." Daffy had set up a cozier seating arrangement. Three comfortable armchairs in a circle.

Natalie squinted at the chairs, as if she expected them to attack. "Where are the others?"

"Sit and we'll talk."

"Oh, no!" Linda put her hand over her chest, as if Daffy had aimed an arrow in her direction. "Somebody died, didn't they?"

Daffy gestured to the chair at her right. "Linda, let's make a list of all possible reasons Sharee and Jewel aren't here. You start."

"Don't forget the bubonic plague." Natalie threw herself into the other chair and sprawled with her feet nearly touching Linda's chair.

Linda looked stricken. "A car accident."

"That's possible. But let's expand and list some other possibilities that might involve a car."

Linda looked stumped.

Natalie barked a laugh. "Let me demonstrate what she means, Sugar-Sweet. Dead battery. Flat tire." She paused, then winked. "Homicidal hitchhiker."

"When you do that," Daffy asked Natalie, her tone even, "when you invent a nickname or try to make things worse for someone else, how does it make you feel?"

"Oh, I don't know. Maybe I should make a list, too. Superior? Glad I have a sense of humor? Engaged?"

Linda leaned forward. "You don't feel any of those things. You just feel mean, and happy you've hurt somebody, because that's the only thing you do well."

Daffy held up both hands to silence them. "We can trade insults for an hour, or we can talk about what's really going on here, which is my choice. First, though, we do need to address the fact that there are only two of you sitting here today. Sharee's on a trip, which is why she's not here. Jewel's situation is different. Her parents don't know where she is right now. She left the house sometime before her class this morning, and her parents are looking for her."

Natalie shrugged. "Where do zombies always go? Cemeteries. That's where you'll find her."

Linda pointed her finger at Natalie. "If that was true we'd have to look for you in hell, only here you are instead!"

Daffy was surprised at Linda's comeback, and while not happy the girl was still lobbing insults, she was pleased that she was showing some backbone.

"From this moment on there will be no more comments like those." Daffy looked at Natalie first, then Linda. "I hope that's abundantly clear to you both. You are wasting time. You can be as angry as you want, but not at each other."

"And you're going to stop us, how?" Natalie asked.

"I'm not here to issue threats, Nat, although I'm guessing that's what you want. Will the group be more comfortable for you if you know ahead of time the worst thing that can happen if you screw up?"

Natalie made a dismissive noise and sat further back in her chair. Daffy moved on quickly. "I think the Martinezes could use your help. They're worried about Jewel. Do either of you ever get together with her in the summer? Do you have any ideas where she might have gone or someone she might be with?"

Natalie gave another spiteful laugh. "Like I pay attention."

"Did they check the hospitals?" Linda asked.

Daffy nodded. "I don't think she'd go to a hospital alone."

"Maybe she went for a walk and got sick along the way."

Daffy abandoned the subject of Jewel. "Are you afraid something like that might happen to you? Your friend Katie seemed to get sick out of nowhere, didn't she?"

Tears filled Linda's eyes, and she gave a slight nod. "And today is her birthday. She would be seventeen."

That explained why Linda was more fixated than ever on death, as well as her own grief. Daffy probed carefully. "So today, you must miss her even more. What did you do on her birthdays?"

"Her parents always gave a party. From the time we were in preschool."

"You knew her a long time."

"Natalie knew her, too."

Daffy looked at Natalie. "Were you friends?"

Natalie seemed to wrestle with herself. For once she had no easy comeback. "Who cares?" she asked at last.

"Were both of you at Katie's party last year?"

Neither girl answered, which surprised Daffy. "I'm not sure of the time line here. Would that birthday have been after her death?"

"No, she had a party last year," Natalie said. "I wasn't invited. I don't have any money. I don't have parents. I don't have a car to go to parties. I don't have the right clothes. Want me to go on?"

Linda defended her friend. "Katie wasn't like that. She didn't care about those things."

"Were you there?" Daffy asked Linda. She was going on a hunch triggered by the unanswered question.

Linda's eyes filled with tears, and she shook her head.

"You weren't invited either?" Daffy asked gently.

Linda was quiet for so long Daffy wasn't sure she would answer. Then she shook her head. "We had a fight."

So Linda and her best friend had fought, and despite having attended many or even all of Katie's birthday parties since preschool, she had not attended the final one. In the years to come, when Linda looked back at their friendship, the fight that had separated them would be the thing she remembered most clearly.

"Well, that sucks," Daffy said, because sometimes the best response was the completely human one.

For once Natalie had nothing cruel to say. "I didn't know that."

Linda was crying. "Well, now you do."

Daffy handed her a tissue and thought about Isabel Martinez, who had needed tissues today, as well. "Did you and Katie ever work out whatever was troubling you?"

"No, and then she died. Just like that. I thought we had all the time..."

Silence filled the room. Daffy had even more hunches. She suspected that on some level Linda felt the fight itself was responsible for her friend's death. That she believed if she'd only made amends, Katie might still be alive. That she was sure that from now on her life would be shadowed by death, in retribution for her mistakes. All that was too much to tackle today, but Daffy would pass her thoughts on to Antoinette, who could gently probe some of those possibilities in individual therapy, perhaps even have Linda talk to her dead friend, as if she were sitting across from her, and tell her all the things she hadn't had time to in life. There was healing to be had here, and she felt hopeful.

"Nat, you've lost people you love, too," she said, turning to the other girl to take the spotlight off Linda, who had so much to think about already.

"Like I care. And you know, I'm not like the others in this stupid group. I've got real problems."

"Your problems seem more important."

"No, that's not what I said! Nobody here has problems. Mine are real. And you don't see me running away because I had a bad day or got a little scared."

"Scared? You're talking about Jewel, not Linda?"

Natalie exploded. "She has everything! She has two parents, who give her everything she wants. Have you seen her house? It's, like, a mansion. And her parents love her. They take her everywhere, wait for her, pick her up. I hardly knew my mother, I could tell you all about that. But Jewel's mom and dad? They hover over her like she's a diamond from Tiffany's or something. They'd never stand her up, but that's made her weak, not strong."

"Love makes people weak?"

"Nobody has ever loved me. Not in my whole life. But I'm still here! And she's falling apart. Why is she so weak she just walks away from everything? You got a splinter, you don't cut off your toe. She's cutting off her whole foot. Well, she deserves whatever happens. Nobody's done this to her. It's her own fault!"

Daffy waited until she was sure the tirade had ended. So much had been said she wasn't sure what to go back to.

She decided and hoped she was right. "The way you see this, Jewel is to blame for everything that's happening to her. But often, when someone is as angry as you are, they feel some responsibility for whatever they're angry about. Want to talk about your part in this, if you have one?"

She had expected Natalie to leap all over that, to protest that Daffy was too stupid to be a psychologist. Maybe, even, to leave the group. Instead, for just a moment, terror completely stripped away the angry mask she hid behind and shone its eerie light through the eyes of a teenager whose life was in horrifying turmoil.

Daffy had stumbled onto something. She just didn't know what.

"I'm done talking," Natalie said. "I don't care what you say."

"I understand. Feelings are tricky things. Sometimes we just have to feel them."

"You think you know me."

Daffy sent the girl her warmest smile, knowing how badly she needed it. "I think you don't even know yourself, Nat, but I think you're definitely worth knowing. You may not want to be here, but I'm very glad you are."

CHAPTER 11

Daffy was on the final leg of the journey back home. After the group ended she'd called Nelson for a ride, but he had only an apology to offer. Two of the three cars in his private fleet were undergoing maintenance, and the third was booked until midnight. He offered to call another car service, but she'd decided to call a taxi. Unfortunately, that turned out to be a bust, too. A conference downtown had everyone tied up for at least an hour.

Since her colleagues were all in session, and she was anxious to get home, she had reluctantly taken the streetcar followed by a bus, walking between one route and the other and finally the necessary blocks from her last stop. She'd told herself that the exercise would be good, that it would clear her head and sweat out whatever virus was zinging around inside her, but she'd been wrong. Instead she'd spent long minutes resting against trees and fences.

At last, as she sagged against a live oak just blocks from her house, she watched traffic zooming up and down the street and made a decision.

A week ago she had begun to face reality. Now it stared her

in the face. It was time, past time, to buy another car. She'd been stubborn and foolish and by some people's assessment, a little bit crazy. A car was a necessity, inanimate and unfeeling and nothing at all like a living, breathing pet. She had mourned much too long. It was unhealthy.

Her mother had once lost a beloved slipper, and she'd walked barefoot everywhere, inside and out, refusing to put on so much as a sock, until Daffy and her father finally located the missing slipper in a basket of garden tools.

Daffy hadn't thought about that in years, or the fallout afterwards when Lea bought so many pairs of slippers to make up for her scare that Daffy and Carson had been forced to sneak out at night to load the excess into a charity drop box at the local strip mall.

She was sorry she'd thought about that now.

Gathering enough energy for one last push, she crossed one street, then another until she could see her house ahead in the middle of the next block. She'd spoken to Cyril before leaving the office, and he had assured her that the door to the side gallery had been replaced, and a dead bolt lock installed inside, as well.

Even Cyril must be getting tired of the break-ins, because she hadn't had to ask for the latter. She just hoped it wasn't a vintage dead bolt, first of its kind.

As tired as she was, and as anxious to collapse in her own bed, she wondered if she'd made the right decision to come home. She did have to repot what was left of her plants, but the thought exhausted her. And if the last round of locks was any indication, she'd need to clean up after the carpenter and locksmith or risk spreading sawdust and debris through the house. She probably should have spent another day recovering at Skeeter's, or taken Sam and Antoinette up on their offer to use their guest room.

And while she was being honest, she also had to admit she really didn't want to be alone tonight.

By the time she crossed the street to her block and started down her own sidewalk she was struggling not to stumble. At first, she didn't pay attention to the car parked in front of her house. Then, when she finally looked to the side and saw it, nostalgia washed over her. For a moment she wondered if deciding to buy another car had conjured Esme's ghost. The little VW sitting on the curb was Esme's vintage, painted a deep turquoise with what looked like the original sunroof. If it really was Esme's ghost, she had thoughtfully donned new clothes for the haunting.

"Java green." There'd been a time when Daffy had known all the official VW Beetle colors. Esme might have come off an assembly line years before Daffy's birth, but she had studied the little car's family tree and everything about it. She hadn't been obsessed. Not exactly.

Okay, she'd been obsessed. She'd loved the size, the way it drove, the way other vintage VW drivers always honked when they passed. Cars were just cars, but owning Esme meant she'd belonged to a secret society. And Daffy had savored their mutual membership.

"So, what do you think of her?"

She whirled, which was most surprising for the amount of energy it required. "Skeeter!"

"You walked part of the way, didn't you?"

"Guilty." She tried to stave off a lecture. "And sorry. Very sorry. Stupid, I know, but I was stuck."

Skeeter wore a black T-shirt and khakis with leather sandals and despite the heat, looked cool and comfortable. She loved his hair, glossy and black and just long enough to wave. She loved the way his expression warmed when he looked at her, the slashing brows that tilted just a little, the slightly hooked nose. The mouth... Even as exhausted as she was, something very much like lust trickled down her spine, along with whatever water she hadn't already sweated out of her system.

She turned to look at the car again. "Did you see this little beauty? It's Esme's cousin. Somebody's lucky."

"Could be you."

This time when she faced him, her heart was thumping wildly. "What do you mean?"

"My friend Larry restores old cars. It's his livelihood, but mostly he does it because he loves it. I painted Larry in his shop. More than once, because he's a great subject. I took that series to New York."

"He restored this one?"

"I asked him about VW bugs. He's been working on this baby for a while. I asked him to speed it up, and here she is, although he says he has a few things that still need work."

"He'll sell it? To me?"

"If you want it. But you don't have to jump, Daffy. Maybe you need something newer, something a bit more traditional. He has a waiting list for every car he restores. There's no obligation."

She leaped toward him, threw her arms around his neck and kissed that delicious mouth. Hard. Disheveled, sweaty, trembling with exhaustion, she was no bargain, but he laughed, then he kissed her back as if she were.

"You know, you do that a lot," he said, when he finally set her away from him. "Kiss me, I mean. When you're excited. Or grateful."

"For the record, not nearly as much as I want to. Oh, Skeeter, this is just too good to be true. On the way here I finally decided I had to have a car. Then you show up with this. You must have known I was ready."

"I thought you might be getting close."

"She's just breathtaking."

"Another Van Winking?"

She was so touched he'd remembered Esme's full name, touched that he'd gone to this kind of trouble, and touched that he'd made himself at home on her porch and waited to show her the car until she came home.

"Not sure who this little beauty is yet, but I'm already in love."

"You love easily, don't you?" He snapped his fingers. "Like that."

She sobered. She knew he'd meant his words as a compliment, but the specter of her mother made another unwelcome appearance. Lea who, in the throes of her worst manic episodes, had loved the mail carrier and grocery store clerk as much as she'd loved her husband and daughter.

"I guess I do." She tried to smile.

He pushed a strand of hair behind her ear and kept his palm against her cheek. "Hey, that's not a bad thing."

"Welcome to my world. Where it very well could be."

He waited for her to explain, but she didn't want to spoil the moment. "Can we go for a drive?"

"You look like you need a cold drink and a shower first."

She eyed the car again, yearning to get inside. "I look that bad?"

He held out his hand. "You *feel* that bad, Daff. The car's not going anywhere."

"This is New Orleans. It might."

He laughed and tugged. She was surprised when they started around the side. "Where are we going?"

"I thought you'd like to see your new door from the outside before you go in."

She really didn't care what the door looked like because she probably wouldn't be around long enough to appreciate it. While Cyril had agreed to replace the original and even install the extra lock, if anything else happened, she predicted he would find a way to break her lease and replace her with a renter less prone to crime.

She was halfway up the side gallery steps when she realized why Skeeter had really brought her here. "You did this?"

"Trust me, I didn't want to. I really didn't. I'm not much of a gardener, but even from my house I could hear your plants crying for mercy."

The porch was as neat as she'd ever seen it, with all traces of broken pottery and ravaged foliage gone. She walked to the row of plants that had been carefully salvaged, all neatly trimmed and repotted. Those damaged beyond repair were missing. Some less damaged had been trimmed to half their original size, but for somebody who claimed not to be a gardener, Skeeter had done an amazing job refurbishing and reclaiming.

She touched a split-leaf philodendron that had once filled an entire corner and now looked like an army recruit after his first day in boot camp. "You even replaced the pots."

"Not really. A lot of yours were smashed beyond repair, which is a shame, because there were some beauties."

"I picked them up at craft shows. It was kind of a hobby. I guess I can start looking again, huh?"

"I figured you'd want to shop, so I bought discount store plastic as a stopgap measure. This way you can see which plants survive and which don't, and you'll know exactly what you need."

She put her arms around his waist and leaned her head on his chest. Then she started to cry.

He stroked her hair. "Hey, you're not mad, are you?"

"You can't tell...the difference between mad...and this?"

Laughter rumbled through his chest. "Apparently I haven't had a lot of practice."

She wondered how much practice he'd had. Until now she hadn't let herself think about the women he'd known and probably loved. She knew about Patty from Sam, but her own personal play book had no room for those kinds of questions. People fell in love, they moved on, they fell in love again. She'd always operated on that assumption, and she never let herself escape into jealousy or ownership of a man's heart or his past.

But now, she wondered. She looked up. "Why haven't you?"

He laughed again, pulled up the hem of his shirt and wiped her face. "Why haven't I what?"

Her eyes drifted to his bare chest, then she forced them up again as his shirt fell back into place. "Had a lot of practice."

"Whoa! What are you asking?"

"Practice figuring out a woman's tears."

He looked surprised. "I generally don't make women cry."

"Why not?"

"Because I'm not a jerk?"

"Even non-jerks can make a woman cry if she loves the man enough."

He pushed her hair back from her forehead and brushed a light kiss across it. "Shower, big glass of water. Ride in that car you might want to buy."

"I'm not really falling apart."

He laughed softly, and his eyes shone with warmth. "I am delighted to hear that. I was worried there for a minute. You were talking about love and commitment. That's not like you at all."

Daffy looked much better after a shower, although Skeeter knew how far gone he was when he realized he liked her in all her guises. Since the black tea bags were gone, he'd made her a glass of "flowery meadow" tea on ice with honey and lemon, and she'd chugged it straight down before they went back outside to climb into the car.

"I'm shaking." Daffy turned to him and held out her hand, as if she needed to prove she really was.

"Excitement, I hope."

"This is just so darned special."

"I think you have to turn the key in the ignition for the car to move."

"It feels like Esmerelda. Sitting here. It feels the same. Although, just between us, she hadn't looked this good in years. But I still loved her. I thought about asking somebody to make a sculpture out of her, but I was pretty sure my landlord wouldn't like her sitting in the backyard. In the end, she was just hauled away. The indignity..." She turned to him. "This is like a resurrection."

"That's about as religious as we're going to get right now." He pantomimed turning the key. "And after you do that and the engine is running, you carefully use this stick to put her in reverse and you back down the curb just a bit, turn the wheel–"

"You called this car a her."

"*You* did."

"Oh no, I very carefully did not. Cars are gender-neutral until titles are signed. Everybody knows that."

"So gender first, then name?"

"You're finally on board. Hold on." She started the engine, slung her arm over his seat, looked behind her, and made a perfect exit from the curb.

"I'm going to cry again," she said, when they were on the road.

"Not while you're driving. Just no. Not done. Think about something that makes you happy."

"This makes me happy."

"Think about the day you got your Ph.D."

"It rained. Plus, my father had surgery, so my parents couldn't make the graduation."

"Think about the day you met me."

She laughed, then sniffed. "That'll work."

Twenty minutes later they parked in front of her house again. She was silent for a moment after she turned off the engine. "I don't even care what he's charging."

"Good, because it's going to give you a heart attack."

"Perfect timing. I can list that with my other symptoms next time I see my doctor."

Skeeter got out and waited for her on the sidewalk. "I'm going in just to make sure everything's still okay inside, then I'm heading out."

"Look..." She paused, as if trying to think of the best way to say something. "I can't thank you enough for everything you've done. But I'd love to really thank you for everything. We could order dinner here. Do you have to go?"

He heard the real question behind the surface one. Why not stay the night? Why not sleep in each other's arms again, only this time with no restraint?

He didn't answer, asking himself the same thing silently, aware that if he said he'd stay awhile, they'd be in her bed in minutes, doing all the things both of them had wanted to since that first scorching afternoon in the Sanctuary of Voodoo.

He waited by her front door while she opened it, then went in uninvited to be sure nothing had changed while they were gone.

Satisfied after a quick investigation, he turned, and wondered if he was crazy. She had never looked more appealing. Very clearly she wanted him to stay tonight, as much as he wanted to.

"I have to get the bug back to Larry. I promised I'd have it in his shop before dark." He smiled and tried not to notice how easy it would be to stay, to just drop all the pretenses and take her to bed–or let her take him. "And you're beat, Daff. Call out for pizza tonight and watch something stupid on TV. That's what you need, not company."

She was assessing him. "That would depend on whose company, wouldn't it?"

"I'm not going to take advantage of a lady in distress." He kissed her cheek as he did too often, like an old friend instead of the lover he wanted to be, and edged toward the door. "I know what the doctor told you. Rest, lots of liquids, rest." He shrugged. "I'll call tonight before I go to bed, just to check all's well. Don't do anything you don't have to. Just take care of yourself."

He was out on the gallery and heading down her steps before he had time to change his mind. The VW started immediately and hummed happily as he pulled onto Royal. He'd made so many mistakes in his life that now he wondered if he could tell the difference between a loss and a win. He hoped his decision had been the latter.

Daffy visited her plants on the side gallery and encouraged them to hang in and grow again. She sat on the loveseat, which had not been damaged, and spoke to them with a lump in her throat.

"You've been through a lot, I know. Nothing that happened here was your fault. Sometimes bad things happen to good plants. I know you'll miss your friends and well, your leaves..."

It all seemed enormously silly, even though she believed that plants responded to love and sound, the way people did. She finished her little pep talk quickly and went back inside.

She didn't feel well enough to fix dinner or even to make the effort to order out. She found a can of chicken noodle soup and heated it, forcing herself to eat half a bowl before her stomach rebelled. She was ready for whatever had hold of her to release its grip, and while the doctor had been optimistic that she would start feeling like herself soon, she wasn't so sure. She had a strong feeling of unease, as if someone were watching her get sicker and sicker and enjoying every minute. She could almost hear demented laughter as she turned on every light in the house, and she wondered if the sound was her imagination or worse, another auditory hallucination.

Tonight, every muscle in her body hurt, but nothing hurt as much as Skeeter's rejection. She understood how much of his time she'd stolen. And she hadn't been the best company. She didn't want to be an invalid, and she didn't want Skeeter to be her caretaker. She could understand why staying with her tonight hadn't sounded like the deal of the century. She prided herself on independence, strength and a clear head to see what was really happening around her. She was insightful--her childhood had forced her to be--and her education and training had sharpened all her best instincts.

In the past weeks, though, she'd failed everybody. Jewel was gone, and Daffy had no idea where or why, at least none that she could share with the girl's parents. Natalie was still furious at everyone and everything, and Linda was locked in a grief so deep it affected everything she encountered. Then there was Skeeter. First, she'd rejected him for his past. Then she'd dumped her crazy life on his doorstep.

As a child she'd often felt like a failure because she couldn't make her mother well. Tonight, she felt like a failure again, and the feeling was an unwelcome intrusion, a reminder of something she thought she'd thoroughly explored during her training and put behind her.

She wondered if her mother had felt the way Daffy did now at the very beginning of her illness. As if the life Lea had known and loved was slipping out of her grasp forever.

Determined to stop herself from sinking into depression, a sign she had a good reason to worry, she made a large mug of tea and took it into the den to watch TV. Nothing looked promising, but she sat there anyway, trying to concentrate. Her head was throbbing, which made sense after walking so many blocks in the heat. From now on she was going to be a good patient and do exactly what the doctor had told her she should. Tonight, she would make a point of hydrating, drink liquids, eat a little more soup, and get a good night's sleep. Tomorrow she would stay home and rest.

She woke up close to eleven, sitting straight up with television news shouting at her. At least she thought the newscaster was shouting. She didn't know why. She couldn't understand what he was saying, but the words seemed to crawl up and down her arms, stinging as they went, like an army of ants. The weather tomorrow was going to be terrible, or perfect. She couldn't figure out what the stranger on her television screen believed. As she squinted, the picture blurred and began to do cartwheels, as if something had gone terribly wrong with the set her parents had given her for Christmas.

Thinking just clearly enough to know she had to get to bed, she gathered herself to rise. But when she stood to turn off the TV, the room behaved like the moving walkway at an airport. She was carried forward without any effort on her own part, as if her legs and feet were no longer needed.

She thought she might be flying.

A ringing began far away, and she wondered if the sound was real or part of whatever nightmare she was caught up in. Because surely she was still asleep. She had to be. The noise grew louder, and as she was carried toward the television, she realized the ringing came from a telephone.

She put her hand in front of her, stretching her arm, which suddenly felt like rubber, like something that could stretch for miles if she willed it to.

She felt cold plastic under her fingertips and wrestled the phone from its cradle. She managed with effort to place it to her ear. From somewhere far away she could hear a voice, but she didn't know whose, and she didn't know why. She only knew one thing.

This was no nightmare.

She managed two words before she slid slowly to the floor.

"Help me."

CHAPTER 12

Antoinette made sure Daffy was buckled into the passenger seat before she pulled out of the circular drive in front of City Hospital. Other patients were waiting to go home, sitting in wheelchairs and smiling in the morning sun, as if it weren't ninety degrees with the temperature climbing.

"Everybody looks glad to be getting out of here," Antoinette said. "Just like you."

"Do you know nurses come into your room all night long to wake you up and find out how you're sleeping?"

"Do they really?"

"Close enough. Then Dracula swishes in before dawn in his black cape and drains your blood."

"Dracula, the phlebotomist."

"That's a disguise. I know for sure that somewhere the pale-faced one is locked in his coffin feasting on this morning's supply."

"I'm glad they let you go."

"You and me both." Daffy looked out the window and began to breathe easier now that the hospital was behind her. "Truthfully, everybody was professional and kind. I had great care."

"Tell me what the doctor said this morning before he gave you your freedom."

For her exceptionally fleeting appearance in Daffy's hospital room, the internist on staff had managed to say a lot. "I'm supposed to take it easy for a week. They'll know more when all the test results are in. In addition to draining my blood, my entire skeletal system has now been photographed and labeled."

"No theories?"

"The neurologist on call is betting on migraines, possibly caused by some sudden food intolerance. I have an appointment with an allergist next week for more tests, but in the interim I'm supposed to follow something called the migraine elimination diet, which, among other things, eliminates histamines. And that pretty much excludes anything served at any restaurant in New Orleans. All fish, unless it just came out of the water and is still flopping. Shellfish, red beans, sausage, ham, onions, tomatoes. Want me to go on?"

Antoinette made a sympathy noise low in her throat.

"You understand."

"You're going to take things easy, right?"

"I'm going to come in for the group. The girls are too fragile for me to skip it right now."

"No, you're not. I'm taking over and you're staying home. Natalie was upset at yesterday's session. Of course, she's angry at you for getting sick, but that will give me something to work on. I can do this. You rest."

Daffy knew she was right. "It must be hard to get through a day with the load of anger that's weighing Natalie down."

"One thing's come up that rang my bell. Something Linda said."

Daffy was glad to talk about something other than her health. "About Katie?" She had told Antoinette her theory that Linda felt somehow responsible for Katie's death, and they had agreed it would be worth probing.

"Yes, and it rang my bell because it had to do with voodoo. I thought of the gris-gris bag. And your voodoo visitations."

Daffy turned to her friend. "Really? Tell me."

"Linda's an evangelical Christian and very devout. Do you remember the girls had a fight, and Katie fell ill not long after and died? She had bone marrow failure before the oncologist could come up with the right treatment, and she passed away. Linda never got a chance to say goodbye."

Again, Daffy felt sad for both girls. "No wonder Katie's death haunts her, but what does it have to do with voodoo?"

"The girls fought because Katie wanted Linda to sneak away to a voodoo ceremony. Friends were going, and Katie thought it would be cool. Of course, that went against everything Linda believed in, so she said no and tried to talk her out of it. When Katie resisted, she threatened to tell Katie's mother."

Daffy whistled softly. "A cardinal sin."

"She didn't, but by then Katie was furious that she'd threatened to, and that was the end of a long friendship."

"Voodoo seems to be everywhere, doesn't it? And we still don't have anything concrete to go on. You couldn't find out more about this ceremony? Where it was? Who organized it?"

"I tried, but I couldn't push any harder. I don't think Linda knows more than she said."

"Somebody might have talked about this with a counselor or even a teacher. I'm going to call Riverview and see if there's anyone there this summer who might talk to me."

"I beat you to it. Being raised in New Orleans society has its pluses. I went to school with the headmistress, and I knew she'd talk to me. Turns out she and both high school counselors are spending the month of June in France with some of the older girls. They won't be back for two weeks, and in the meantime, only the administrative staff is holding the fort. Everybody who might know something helpful is gone. And this is something I don't want to do on a transatlantic call, even if I could find out where they are at the moment."

Daffy knew they couldn't very well call random teachers or parents. Riverview seemed to be a dead end until the appropriate faculty returned.

They were both silent until they were almost to Daffy's house.

"You have a copy of that elimination diet?" Antoinette asked. "You're going to follow it?"

"I do, and I will. But then the neurologist asked what I've been eating and drinking since I got sick and told me to make a list and not repeat anything on that list, either, until I can talk to the allergist. So I'm down to water."

"We can stop at the grocery store."

Daffy put her hand on Antoinette's arm. "No, we can't. I have to make a list first. I can have groceries delivered or haul myself a couple of blocks to the deli."

"But you're okay now? You're feeling more like yourself?"

Daffy wasn't sure which self she felt like. The self she used to be? Confident, happy, wacky-within-normal-limits. The self who wildly hallucinated? The pathetic self Skeeter had scooped off the floor before the emergency responders could get to her house two nights ago?

"Skeeter found me on the floor," she said, still astounded by the events of that night, events she couldn't even remember. "He had to break a window to get in. Cyril's going to evict me."

"It's a good thing Skeeter called to check on you when he did. And he replaced the window as soon as the hardware store opened the next morning. Cyril doesn't have to know."

"You talked to him?" Daffy had been surprised that Skeeter, who apparently had carried her to the Jeep and driven like a maniac to the hospital, hadn't visited yesterday, when she was both lucid and conscious.

"He's furious at himself, Daffy. He said you seemed shaky when he left that night, but he left anyway."

"He's not my guardian. He doesn't owe me anything, and he's already done way too much." She paused. "I've probably destroyed any chance we ever had for a–" She shrugged. "A whatever."

"A *whatever*? How old are you?"

Daffy managed a smile. "Relationship sounds so permanent, doesn't it? I need a new word."

"Affair?"

"Too back alley. Seedy kind of."

"But a relationship destined to end. Maybe a relation*quit.* Seems appropriate."

Daffy heard the edge in her friend's voice. "Am I being chastised?"

"No, but I'm trying to make sense of this. And since I happen to love you both, I don't want either of you hurt. If you can't figure out what to call what's happening, I hope he can't either, or that he doesn't want to try."

"I usually have better control over my life."

"You've had to." Both their families proved there could be many meanings to the word "dysfunctional."

"There was a lot I couldn't control growing up," Daffy said. "You, too."

"And later did you make up for it?"

"By controlling everything I could, you mean?"

"Or maybe just a portion?"

"It's no secret I've never been interested in a long-term anything."

"So you pick men accordingly? Or it's just happened that way?"

Daffy was neither happy nor sorry the discussion had led here. Antoinette was great at helping her clarify feelings. "I do choose men who probably want to move on after a while. My first serious boyfriend was already heading for a year at Oxford. He stayed in England afterwards and still sends me postcards. I have a place to stay if I ever want a tour of Westminster Abbey."

"He was typical?"

"I guess. I moved in with the second boyfriend, and a few months later I kept his apartment after he moved out to take a job on the west coast."

"Skeeter's not going anywhere. He has New Orleans in his blood. What were you thinking?"

Daffy hadn't really been thinking. She knew that now. "Maybe he just seemed like a guy who enjoys himself and moves on, somebody I could stay friends with after, well, our, you know."

"Re-la-tion-ship. Four syllables."

"You're happy with Sam. I believe it. But not everybody's cut out for what you two have. My father and mother were happy together until she got sick. From that point on..." Her voice trailed off.

"He was unhappy? He told you that? It's kind of a heavy burden to lay on a child."

"He never had to say it. I saw what he put up with."

"All the time?"

Daffy was becoming annoyed. "No, you know it wasn't all the time. My mom cycled. There were good times, too. Now they're having a long stretch of good time in Florida. I'm hopeful it may last."

"I think you should ask him, then. Someday, just ask him right out of the blue if he was unhappy."

"Our family doesn't work that way."

"Of all people, you know you have to change the way things usually work in a family to open the way for growth."

"Nobody in my family needs to grow. They're okay for now. I'm okay. I'm not rocking that boat."

Antoinette pulled in front of Daffy's house and turned off the engine. They'd been so busy talking that Daffy hadn't even realized they were already here. "This is your last chance," Antoinette said. "You can still come home with me for a few days until you're sure you're up to staying alone."

"I'll call you or somebody if the headaches come back. I promise. I know better than to tough out a recurrence by myself. Just in case...other symptoms arrive with them."

"I'll be calling regularly, and if you don't answer, I'll let myself in."

Luckily Skeeter had thought to scoop up her purse when he scooped up Daffy. Yesterday in the hospital, she had given Antoinette an extra key to get clothes and toiletries for her hospital stay. Then she had told her to keep it, just in case she ever collapsed in her own house again. "If you hear from Skeeter? You'll tell him you sprung me?"

"Why don't you just call and reassure him?"

"I left him a message thanking him yesterday. He'll probably be happier not to hear from me for a while."

"Only you can know if that's true." Antoinette leaned over to hug her. "Want me to come in and make sure everything's okay?"

Daffy knew Sam had been keeping an eye on her house. "I'm betting a certain cop made sure everything's fine."

"I'm going to sit here and wait until you check."

"I'll do hand signals from the porch. If I draw a finger across my throat, go for help."

She got the canvas bag with the things Antoinette had brought to the hospital, thanked her friend again and let herself into the house. She checked quickly and then waved Antoinette away.

The interior was as quiet as a coffin, which was a welcome change from the ranting newscaster, the last voice she'd heard before she collapsed. Mentally she checked off the other good news. Her head was quiet, too. Nothing was making noise inside it that shouldn't. No strange sounds, no unintelligible screeching. Plus, everything looked normal. No lights flashing, no ghost-like figures flitting by.

She dropped the bag on her bed along with her purse and went out the door to check on her plants. Nobody looked worse for wear, and somebody had watered because nothing was too dry. She gave them each a pep talk, calling them by name, and promised that if they grew a little she'd give each one a shot of fertilizer. Bribery and a green thumb went together.

Inside, she got out the paperwork from the hospital and removed the two page food list a hospital dietician had dropped off that morning. Then she did an inventory to see what she could eat from her cupboards and refrigerator. The news wasn't good. Technically peanut butter wasn't on the forbidden list, but since she wasn't allowed to eat anything she'd eaten recently, she had to cross it off. Nuts of any other kind were forbidden. She ended up with an unopened box of water crackers and tub of cream cheese to go with it, a bag of microwave popcorn, a pack of frozen pork chops, a new bag of rice and half a bag of baby carrots.

She struggled for a positive spin. "Well, at least I've got dinner."

She changed into leggings and a long T-shirt, coaxed her hair into a frizzy ponytail, and realized she had the rest of the day to get through.

She was lonely. She wanted to be at work. She wanted to go for a long walk. She wanted to sit in her favorite café and drink strong New Orleans coffee with chicory or one of their excellent teas. She didn't want to read or watch television–she might not watch news again as long as she lived. She knew how to knit, but she didn't want to. She could spend an hour doing yoga stretches, but she knew better than to try.

She was pathetic.

She decided to sit on the steps of her front gallery, get a little sun and observe her neighbors. She no longer believed that any of the craziness she'd experienced was due to the teenage boys down the street. A couple of times recently one had waved to her when they happened to be outside at the same time, and last week the other had come by selling chocolate bars for a soccer fundraiser. She'd bought a whole box and taken them into work, forever endearing herself to everybody.

She let her legs dangle down the steps and leaned against a post, thinking back over everything that had happened, and the tenuous connections to voodoo. Jewel's gris-gris bag. Daffy's visit to Fantôme's Sanctuary of Voodoo. Her attendance at the ceremony on the other side of Lake Ponchartrain. Her conversation with Mama Mambo. Glimpsing Natalie and quite possibly Mama on the sidewalk near her office. Voodoo cults.

None of it made sense. None of it came together. And she still wasn't feeling well enough to formulate connections.

She wanted Skeeter. She wasn't lonely on general principles. She had to admit she was lonely for him. She just couldn't make herself call him again. He'd done more than enough for her, and he'd made it clear he was reluctant to get closer.

As if she'd conjured him–a word she rejected with a shudder–his Jeep pulled up in front of her house. She watched as he got out and started toward her.

"You're out." His expression was guarded.

"That I am. Did Antoinette tell you?"

"I called the hospital." He lowered himself to the other side of the top step and leaned against the post that matched hers.

She admired his flowered tropical shirt and shorts and restrained herself from humming a Jimmy Buffett medley. He had great knees, and the shirt was unbuttoned halfway down his chest. He needed a parrot or at the very least a jigger of salt to complete the image.

She had to say something and stop ogling. "There was no reason to stay. I've got appointments with specialists next week, a diet that will cure or kill me, and meds for my migraines."

"That's the diagnosis?"

"More like a working theory. I also have strict instructions to call a friend and leave my front door unlocked if a headache comes on suddenly." She smiled at him, which was still, despite the outward tension, remarkably easy to do. "I can't thank you enough, Skeeter. I guess I wouldn't have died on the den floor, but I sure wouldn't have gotten better so fast."

He didn't smile back. "I'm so sorry."

For a moment she just stared at him. "Am I supposed to know why?"

"You didn't want to be alone that night. You made it clear. And I left anyway."

"You were free to. You don't owe me anything, and neither of us had a clue how the night would end. Here I'm so grateful for your help that I can hardly find the words to tell you, and you're apologizing. That's just crazy."

He seemed to relax a little. "I'm crazy? Am I the one who talks to her plants, who can't name her car because she won't know the gender until the title is signed? And wait. Who names her car?"

"And am I the one who babysits a shop for a fake voodoo doctor, who wears a Mickey Mouse watch, who...who turns down sex with the hottest woman he's ever met?"

He scooted closer. "How do you know you're the hottest woman I've met?"

"How do you know I'm talking about me?"

"You don't know any of the other women I've turned down. It has to be you."

She scooted across the step toward the middle but stopped a yard away from him. "Don't get excited. It's just one of the many interesting facts I've turned up about you. It's intriguing, not insulting. I don't take it personally. I—"

He covered the distance, wrapped his arms around her, and kissed her. He smelled like sunlight, like lime and maybe sandalwood. His arms around her were strong, and she leaned into them, sliding her hands around his waist. This was familiar. The feel of him lived in her memory banks now. But it wasn't going to be enough.

"Don't tease me," she said, breaking away. "We always get this far and then we stop."

"Just tell me you're sure. And while you're at it, tell me you feel well enough."

"I'm so tired of being sick. I want to feel amazing. I think we can do amazing, can't we?"

He laughed, then pushed her down so they were lying on the gallery floor, their legs trailing down the stairs. He moved to his side and slipped a hand under her head. Then he bent and brushed his lips over hers. She let her eyelids drift down so nothing would interfere with the feel of his body and lips against hers. He trailed kisses to her ear, lifted her hair and nibbled her earlobe. She sighed with pleasure. "Step one toward amazing."

"I have wanted you from the first moment I saw you," he whispered in her ear.

"But part of you must not have."

"No part of me except my head."

She turned to kiss him fully on the lips. "I'm that scary?"

"Look at me. An ex-con selling caricatures. You're a gift I don't deserve."

"Skeeter..." She held him close. "You deserve everything good in the whole wide world."

He laughed a little. "Yeah, like a more comfortable place to do this."

He pushed away from her, stood, and held out his hand. She took it, letting him pull her to her feet. "Hey, just so you know—" She shook her head, and he tilted his, waiting.

"I did change my sheets after the skull mask. In case you were worried."

He grabbed her and hugged her hard. Then he scooped her into his arms.

"You've got to stop that. You're going to ruin your back."

He hugged her tighter and carried her across the threshold. "Do you know what you said to me the other night? When I was carrying you out to my Jeep to haul you to the hospital?"

"I was talking?"

"You asked me why the only time I held you in my arms was when you were sick."

Her mood changed so suddenly she could hardly breathe. She rested her palm against his cheek. "Did I? Really?"

"You did."

"Did you answer me?"

"I told you the truth." He bumped the door closed behind them. Then he let her body slide slowly down his until she was standing. "I told you that was the only time I could trust myself."

"Skeeter..."

"Do you know what you said?"

"I wish I did."

"You told me to trust you instead."

"For that moment, at least, I made sense."

He slid his fingers into her hair, found the elastic holding it and helped it tumble to her shoulders. "I love your hair."

She sighed and closed her eyes. He smoothed her curls back from her forehead and trailed kisses along her hairline. She leaned into him, finding the bottom of his shirt and sliding her hands beneath it to his smooth, warm skin. "I love your body."

He laughed, low in his throat. "Moving right along."

She laughed, too, stepped away and took his hand.

"You want me to see those clean sheets?" he asked.

"I want you to feel them."

He let her pull him through the house into her bedroom, where she dropped his hand only long enough to grasp the canvas bag from her bed and heave it to the floor. She faced him, and while she wasn't shy, she was unexpectedly tongue-tied. She'd wanted him here, still did with a force that threatened to over-whelm her, but now she was at a loss. There was no time to silently role play, no time to ask herself why she was suddenly paralyzed, and certainly no time for a conversation.

Skeeter seemed to sense her hesitation. He smiled as he sat on the bed and pulled her down beside him. "What kind of dreams do you have in this bed?"

"Are you asking if I dream about you?"

"That would be nice."

She realized that in the weeks she'd known him she had, and often. She traced the line of his jaw with one finger. "They are nice, better than nice." She reconsidered. "Probably nice isn't the right word."

He grinned. "Want to hear about mine?"

"Oh yeah."

He moved slowly, brushing a hand across her breasts, then even more slowly down her side to the hem of her T-shirt. He brushed the bare skin at her waist as he curled his fingers to grasp the fabric. "First, I dream we're sitting here. Like this."

She could feel her breath quickening as his fingers grazed her flesh and he gently tugged the fabric skyward. "Exactly like this."

He turned so he could mirror his movements with the other side of her shirt. He slipped his hands forward so the fabric pooled over them, and with no hurry he began to slide both hands toward her breasts, his thumbs meeting to trace a line up her midriff, ending at her bra. Then, with one fluid movement he pulled the shirt up. She lifted her arms so he could slide it off and up over her head. She was glad Antoinette had brought one of her nicer bras to the hospital, because now, that was all she wore.

And after a moment, not that either.

"You're so beautiful," he said when she was naked from the waist up, bending his head to kiss her neck, her collarbone, and then, graze kisses along the tops of her breasts until she felt herself shudder with desire. "My dreams needed work."

She heard herself moan, and she was grateful his shirt was partly unbuttoned, because her fingers and her brain weren't communicating. It took far too long for her to finally spread open the shirt and slip it over his shoulders. He was muscular and tanned, and the feel of his skin against her fingertips sent more shudders through her. As he turned a little her gaze drifted to the arm farthest away and she finally saw his tattoo in its entirety. She smiled, just before she closed her eyes and fell back against the mattress, bringing him with her.

"A phoenix." Something surged through her, something more than desire. For just a moment they were connected, her heart calling to his. She felt more than saw the pictures of his life and how many miles he had traveled to become the man he was. She gave herself up to it, to the touch and caress of this exceptional human being who would probably never know just how exceptional he was.

But she knew. And she wanted nothing more than to show him that she did.

CHAPTER 13

"Now, that wasn't so tough, was it?" she asked later, snuggled against him, her leg tucked between his. "Aren't you glad I persuaded you to give this a try?"

He stroked her back. As satisfied, as replete as she felt, the motion of his fingers was beginning to make her ponder repeats and personal bests. "I just gave in so you'd stop pestering me," he said.

"You don't know pestering. I was planning strategy. It's a good thing you caved when you did."

"All you ever had to do was keep being you."

She almost purred. "You must have known you were going to give in, because you were prepared. Unless that's a leftover from high school health class."

"I slept through that one, but I'm betting that even today, they don't discuss condoms."

"If they don't, they should. But for the record, the last time I went to the drugstore, I did a little shopping, too, just in case."

"Pretty secure in your own charms, aren't you?"

She pushed herself up on one elbow and traced the whorl of hair on his chest. "Tell me about the phoenix."

He rose and kissed her before he settled back against the pillow. "I decided in prison that I would get a tattoo, just one when I got out. I spent a lot of hours imagining what it would be and creating designs. I never want my whole body to be a blank canvas for somebody else's art." He traced the tiny butterfly she had on one hip. "You, too?"

"I wanted an entire garden, but I whimpered so much with the butterfly that the tattoo artist said we were finished forever. He was a wise, wise man. Why the phoenix?"

"Why the butterfly?"

She knew that when someone answered a question with a question, the subject was usually a tender one. She decided to share her own tender memories.

"I was such a homely kid. You have no idea." She silenced his protest with a finger against his lips. "I was. Someday I'll show you photos. We moved constantly, you remember that, and every time I went into a new school I got teased, or bullied, the definition depending on degree. Eventually, as I reached my teens, the bullies left me alone, and I figured I wasn't fun to harass anymore because I'd learned to ignore them. Then one day I glanced in the mirror, and for once, I couldn't look past the real reason I was no longer a target. I was no longer homely. I was turning into a passably pretty teenager. You have no idea how grateful I was."

"The butterfly slipped out of her cocoon and didn't even notice."

"Isn't that sad? But no, at that point I wasn't ready for flight. It took more time before I began to see that we all have a butterfly waiting inside us. Looks are the smallest part of it, but what really mattered was that I was finally given a break from persecution. I was allowed to become the person I was meant to be. So now it's my mission to help other people find their butterfly."

"Nobody helped you when you were bullied? Nobody stood up for you?"

"Circumstances weren't ideal. Sometimes if a teacher or an administrator intervened, things at school improved. Then we'd move. But as painful as the teasing was, it also gave me the gift of empathy."

She waited for him to tell his story. She didn't have to tell him it was his turn. She could see it in his eyes.

"A phoenix rises from ashes," he said. "When I was locked away, my life might as well have gone up in smoke. I had nothing to show for all those years I'd already lived. Eventually I narrowed my future to two possibilities. Either I could screw up over and over and spend the rest of my life doing time, or I could be the man Grand-Grand had expected me to be."

She leaned over and traced the image with her fingertip. It was small and beautifully done. The bird's head rested against his shoulder. The tail swooped down to curl around his upper arm. "And you chose to rise. I'm so glad you had your great-grandfather."

He was quiet for a moment. When he spoke, she knew it was important. "I'm named for him."

Her hand stilled. "Are you?" She waited.

"I never felt worthy of his name."

"You've always been worthy. The phoenix flies away after it rises, doesn't it? Doubts have to fly with it."

"Was that the woman or the therapist speaking?"

"The woman."

"Seth Robertson Harwood." He smiled. "And now you're going to start calling me Seth, aren't you?"

"You knew it before you told me."

"Then you're Daphne."

"Daphne Abigail Brookes. Please tell me you won't haul out Abigail in a moment of passion."

He cupped her neck and pulled her face to his. "Are we going to have another moment of passion?"

"You can count on it...Seth."

"Any time soon, Daphne?"

She kissed him slowly, gently, knowing passion would build again quickly, and this was her chance to let him know how much he'd touched her. In every way.

By five they were both ravenous. She'd told Skeeter everything she could remember about the neurologist's pronouncements, and now she showed him the food list. She watched him try to put a good face on it.

"I might be able to make gumbo with these ingredients," he said. "Not great gumbo, but something you'd recognize."

Her mouth began to water. "Tonight?"

"With what you've got here? I couldn't even make stock. Gumbo is a process. Gumbo is a prayer. You can hurry through it and hope for the best. Or you can take your time, follow all the steps, and turn over the results to a higher power." He laughed at her expression. "After I make a major shopping trip. I promise."

They snacked on crackers, cream cheese and carrots while he sauteed pork chops and boiled rice. Then they ate at the little kitchen table.

She liked sitting across from him. He'd slipped on his shirt but left it unbuttoned. She wore the T-shirt he had so efficiently stripped off her, but this time without the leggings. There was barely enough fabric to tuck under her, and the plastic chair was cold against her thighs.

"This is the way I imagine a happy marriage." She'd eaten half her pork chop and was taking a rest before she tackled the remainder. "Sitting across a table after working together in the kitchen. Sharing silly stuff after having unforgettable sex."

"Unforgettable sex?"

"I'm not going to forget it any time soon. Are you?"

He didn't answer. "The rest seems like a small order to fulfill."

"Apparently not small enough."

"You don't think so?"

"Fifty percent of marriages in this country end up in divorce court. And judging from the people I see in my practice, a fair share of the ones that don't aren't happy."

"Hardly a fair sample. If they were happy, they wouldn't be there to see you."

She thought about her conversation with Antoinette. "I probably look for evidence that the choices I've made are the right ones."

"Choices like staying single?"

She knew she should let it go right there and move on. But she was nothing if not honest. "It's a little broader than that."

"How so?"

She looked up. "It *is* the right choice for me. I don't need more evidence."

"You seem sure."

"I've always been careful about men I spent time with. And eventually the time always came when we both needed to move on. We could, without destroying each other, because we'd both made it clear that we could, right from the start. You've felt that way, right?"

"I must have, since I seem to be alone."

"But you don't have to be alone. Alone isn't the opposite of attached."

"No, that would be *detached*. Is detachment a good way to live?"

She didn't like the word, but she pushed on. "Maybe we do

have to be a little detached, a little objective, every time we get involved with somebody. We have to be willing to take our emotional pulse, to figure out what we really need to grow and change, and what the other person needs. And we have to keep that in front of us and not be selfish if we need different things."

"And commitment?"

That was easy. "Commitment to being insightful, instead of needy. Kind instead of selfish. Thoughtful instead of complacent."

"So how close does somebody have to get to you for all this radar to go up? Is it up already, for me? Have you begun your assessment yet?"

"Skeeter..." She changed her mind. "*Seth*. I'm just trying to say that you don't have to feel hemmed in now that we've gone to bed together. I don't want you to feel like you're on the hook. I know how I feel about being with you. I just don't want you to feel like you've stepped into a trap. You've had to take care of me. A lot. That's not your job, and any time you want to walk away, I'll understand."

"And care?"

"Of course I'll care. Letting go is never easy."

"But I think it must be easier early on. Before you start to feel anything."

This conversation had gone terribly wrong, and she knew it. She shouldn't have tried to explain herself yet. Not after a perfect afternoon together. Not when she still didn't feel like herself.

"Moving on is never a sure thing," she said carefully. "It's just easier to breathe if you know you can."

He got up and took their plates to the sink. Then he turned and leaned against it. "I'm glad you're honest."

She felt no relief because his eyes said something different. "No, you're not."

He took a deep breath. "No, I am glad you're honest, but not glad it took me this long to figure out why I've hesitated to let things between us get to this point. And it wasn't just not feeling like I'm good enough for you."

"I don't see how anything I've said changes anything. It just makes it easier for you to be whoever you need to be."

"It's pretty clear I'm crazy about you, isn't it? I haven't made a secret of it. I've wanted you every bit as much as you swore you wanted me. But in the past year my life has changed so much I almost don't recognize it. And I've changed with it. I need more than freedom and psychobabble."

She felt herself go pale at his words. "Psychobabble?"

He shrugged.

"But I'm not asking you for anything," she said. "You can keep changing. I'll never stand in your way."

"But that's our problem. Hopping in and out of bed, parting friends? Moving on to the next relationship? That's your story, Daffy, but I don't think it's mine anymore. I've done that. Now I want something different. A home, maybe kids. I want to build something with a woman I love. A woman who plans to stay for the long haul. I know things can happen that destroy the best laid plans. I've seen that up close, more times than I want to think about. But I want what Maggie and Joshua found, what Sam and Antoinette found. Will their marriages last? I don't have a crystal ball, but I know they'll do everything possible."

"You can't trust that this—" She waved her hand in the air, as if to encompass everything around them. "That we can trust ourselves and each other without making demands? That we'll know when or even if it's time to move on? Without recriminations or anger?"

"I think that probably sounds enlightened on the surface, but the reality? Nobody's that mature. I'm certainly not. And if two people come at—" He waved his hand the way she had, then smiled sadly. "You couldn't even think of the right word, but there are a couple of choices. Relationship. Love affair–certainly not friendship, though, because we moved past that. So if two people come at being together from different angles, they might just pass right by each other without ever knowing it."

She put her fingertips on her forehead. "It's been a long day and I should never have started this."

"I think I'm going to head out. I need some of that freedom you're so fond of. Will you be okay here by yourself?"

She stood up. "I'll lock the door behind you."

"When Larry gets back to me, I'll call you with everything you need to know about buying the car."

"Thank you. For everything, Skeeter."

She hoped he hadn't heard that as goodbye, but he was gone before she could clarify. As she turned the lock behind him she wondered if she had finally lost her mind.

She was almost certain she had just let something special slip through her fingers. She was too good a psychologist not to ask herself why and let the possibilities bombard her.

She was still standing in the living room staring at the door when the telephone rang. She picked up the receiver and cleared her throat to answer, but no one was there. The ring she'd heard was coming from somewhere else. She hurried into the bedroom and picked up her purse. By now she realized the ring was the one for the prepaid mobile she carried everywhere, the number she gave to clients she was most worried about.

"Hello." For a moment she was afraid she'd missed whoever had been calling. Then she heard a thin, breathy voice.

"Dr. Brookes?"

"Jewel? Is that you?"

"I need help."

Daffy thought fast. "Tell me where you are. I can come and get you. Your parents can come. We'll make sure you're okay."

"Not...my parents. And you can't come here."

"Where are you?"

"I...might come there."

"Of course. But I'm not at work. I'm home. Can someone bring you?"

"I...don't know. Where are you?"

Daffy gave her the address of the house and told her the closest cross streets, knowing that giving out her home address was the best of several bad ideas. But Jewel needed help. It was clear in her voice and in the fact that she'd called Daffy in the first place.

"Please come," Daffy said. "But really, if you don't want to or can't find a way, I can come and get you in a cab. You can meet me–" The phone beeped three times, and then there was silence.

Had Jewel hung up? Had someone forced her to? She tried to pull up the number Jewel had called from, but the call list said "private."

The police wouldn't or couldn't do anything. The only new information was that Jewel was still in New Orleans and needed help. But nothing the girl had said would make it easier to find her. Daffy prayed she would find her way to the house, but she knew there was only a slim possibility.

She knew what she did have to do, and she took the land line into her den and sat before she looked up the Martinez's number.

Isabel answered on the third ring. Daffy greeted her but didn't waste time on pleasantries.

"Jewel just called," she said. "I told her I would pick her up wherever she is, but she said no. She said she might find her way here."

Isabel sounded shaken. "Your office?"

"No, my home. I gave her my address."

"Should I come?"

"I don't think it's necessary. If she does come, I'll call you immediately."

"You got my message?"

Daffy explained that she'd been in the hospital but was home now. She heard Isabel's sharp intake of breath. "I called your office. A few hours ago. Nobody told you?"

"Did you tell Rosy it was an emergency? Because they've been protecting me."

"No. No, I didn't. But it is. We haven't heard a word from Jewel, not a word. But today I realized a key to one of our safety deposit boxes is missing. Jewel is the only other person on the list to open it, other than Robert and me. It's full of her grandmother's jewelry, and we wanted her to be able to get to it to wear for a special occasion."

Daffy thought the trust that the Martinezes had placed in their daughter said everything about how much they loved her, and sadly, how much Jewel had changed in the past months.

"She didn't have a key," Isabel said, as if she could hear Daffy's thoughts. "She had to *ask* us for the key. That was our safeguard. Only now one key is missing. I went to the bank with the other one. Everything in the box is gone. It's empty. She took all of it. Every single piece."

Daffy drew a deep breath, and tried to put this together. "Maybe that's why Jewel left. She knew eventually you'd find out what she'd done, so she didn't want to face you."

"We've checked every pawn shop in the city, but without success. She didn't even pawn it. Then we might be able to get it back. She must have sold or traded it on the street. It's drugs. I know it is. She sold all that irreplaceable jewelry to buy drugs. What else would it be?"

"We can't discount anything at this point. But I don't think we can jump to conclusions, either. Let's hope she comes here, and I can find out what's really going on."

"You've let us down. You should have seen right away that she had a drug problem. You're trained and we aren't. You should have seen the signs!"

The line went dead. Daffy's head began to pound, but this time, the headache felt like stress, not the beginning of a migraine. She went into the kitchen to make herself tea before she remembered that she wasn't allowed to. She poured a glass of water instead and wondered how many hours were left in this day and how many more mistakes she would make before it ended.

She took the glass out to the porch and settled there to wait for Jewel.

CHAPTER 14

Three days had passed since Jewel's phone call, and the girl hadn't shown up at Daffy's house or called again. Daffy had stayed at home for twenty-four hours, hopeful that Jewel would come. And even when she'd finally had to leave for a doctor's appointment, she had taped a note for Jewel to her front door. Unfortunately, she'd had to peel it off, untouched.

Three days had passed since Daffy had heard from Skeeter, too, and while she felt better physically, she wasn't sleeping well. She kept replaying their final conversation and wondering what she could have done differently. Her whole life seemed to have made a turn for the worse, and she couldn't shake the feeling it was her fault.

Today she'd decided to see what she could do about Jewel by visiting Natalie's aunt. What to do about Skeeter was still a mystery.

Bountiful Beauty was nestled in the middle of a block on St. Claude Avenue. The avenue, separated by a grassy median strip, or neutral ground, as it was called in the city, was lined with businesses and graffiti-adorned privacy fences.

The salon was housed in the ground floor of a tidy building. The first story was painted royal blue and topped by a burgundy second story, with potted geraniums and petunias spilling over the upper balcony. The air was scented with deep-fried seafood and onions from the restaurant next door, and as Daffy drew closer, a young woman exited the salon, and the perfume of hair products joined the mix.

Nelson had dropped her here, so Daffy hadn't been outside his Lincoln for long. Still, she could already feel perspiration beading on her neck. The calendar claimed that today was the first day of summer, but city residents knew summer had arrived months ago.

As she stepped inside and welcomed the blast of air conditioning, a bell over the door announced her arrival. At the front counter, she searched the stations beyond her for a glimpse of Corrinda Saizan.

"We don't take walk-ins. You have an appointment?" The young woman who came to assist wore a sleek checkered tunic with the name of the salon embroidered in bright pink over one breast. She sounded skeptical.

Daffy put on her brightest smile. "Well, no, I don't. But I was hoping to speak to Corrinda. Is she here today?"

"Why don't you take a seat. Your name?"

Daffy took the closest chair while the young woman headed to the back of the shop. Several other women were waiting, too, all dark-skinned beauties with hair in up-dos or spiraling curls. Many hair salons were de facto segregated because white stylists were clueless about how to care for the hair of black women. But a quick glimpse around the room showed there was a mixture of races here, in both the women occupying the chairs and the women working on them.

The salon was larger and more updated than she'd expected, tastefully decorated in black and pink, with gleaming stainless steel counters and gold-flecked tile floors. While it was unlikely tourists ever stumbled this far from the French Quarter or Garden District to have their hair or nails done, Bountiful Beauty probably had plenty of clients in the surrounding neighborhood. Judging from the prices posted discreetly on the wall behind the front desk, and the number of stations, all filled this morning, business was good. She wondered if Corrinda, who claimed to be on the razor's edge financially, was simply overextended, and that despite the look of modest prosperity, whatever she took in went right back out.

"Dr. Brookes." Corrinda came out of the back. Today her hair swirled down her back in multiple tiny braids. She was striking but not quite beautiful. Daffy thought Natalie, who looked a little like her aunt, was destined to be both.

Corrinda walked quickly toward her, hand extended. Daffy rose and held out her own. Corrinda's grip was just firm enough, not an easy feat to pull off with long red nails.

She reached over and grasped a lock of Daffy's hair. "I bet you're here to have your hair braided, aren't you?"

"I'm sure you're too busy since I don't have an appointment. I just needed a moment—"

"Of course I'm not too busy for *you*. I'm spending my morning doing paperwork. But I can take time to do your hair." She waved one hand as Daffy protested. "Nothing complicated. That would take hours. But large braids, maybe. Your hair will hold them. Or perhaps just some rows here, on the side."

Daffy was trapped, and she knew if she stayed she'd have time to introduce the subject of Natalie and Jewel. She didn't really expect to learn much from Corrinda, but in the days since she'd spoken to Jewel, her own anxiety about the girl's safety had risen steadily.

"I'll have one of my girls start you off. Then we'll get right to it." Corrinda turned and Daffy's chance to refuse was over. She followed a young blonde wearing an identical tunic toward the row of sinks and settled in for the experience.

Half an hour later her hair had been washed, conditioned and partially blown dry. She told herself if she didn't like the finished product, she didn't have to leave the braids in, although she was afraid *un*braiding might be almost as complicated.

"Oh, so your hair is longer than it looks because of the curl. That's good," Corrinda said, coming up behind her. "Will you let me have my way with it?"

"As long as it doesn't involve scissors. Although maybe it should."

"Oh, no, your hair is lovely." Corrinda began to untangle Daffy's hair with a wide-toothed comb but switched quickly to one with smaller teeth and made a deep part on one side, spritzing it with something that smelled like roses and vanilla.

"That scent is heavenly."

"My grandmother taught me about plants, herbs, distilling scents. I use what I learned to blend many of our products myself. This is one of mine."

"What a wonderful talent."

"Next time your hair needs a trim, come to me. You should always have it cut by someone who understands curly hair."

Corrinda used her fingernails to part a small section and as Daffy watched—and felt—she divided it into three equal tails and began to twist them, pulling in more hair as the braid moved toward Daffy's opposite ear, following the hairline.

"So how is my niece?"

Daffy couldn't believe how fast Corrinda's hands flew. She'd almost reached the back of Daffy's head. "I only see her in my group." She knew she had to preserve confidentiality, so she searched for words. "I'm hoping you can tell me a bit more about her. I know she spends time with you whenever she can."

"Natalie's like a daughter. Her mother, Lissa, is my older

sister. Our poor parents couldn't control her, and Lissa left home when she was still young. She got herself in trouble over and over, and one day when that baby girl was only three, Lissa just dropped Natalie with our folks and disappeared. She could be dead for all I know. I was already gone by then, making my own life, but I tried to spend time with Natalie when I could. After my parents passed, though, I had no way to keep her with me, as much as I wanted to."

By now Corrinda was finishing the braid and fastening the bottom with a rubber band. She continued her story. "I've done what I can. I was the one responsible for getting her into Riverview Academy. One of my customers is a teacher there, and she told me how Natalie could get a scholarship. I think the school is good for her, don't you?"

Daffy couldn't tell Corrinda that Natalie felt alone at Riverview, surrounded by girls with families who had all the material possessions she lacked, girls with parents who paid attention to them. Would she be better off in one of the city's underfunded and overcrowded public schools? It was impossible to say.

"Natalie's very intelligent," Daffy said, because that was obvious. "She needs to be challenged, and I know that's what you must have seen."

Corrinda started on the opposite side of Daffy's head, but this time she separated and braided straight back, following the part. Clearly, she'd done this enough times that she didn't even have to think about her movements. She separated, spritzed, braided, tied off. Her hands were gentle, and she didn't pull harder than she had to. The rhythmic combing, twisting, braiding, was beginning to make Daffy sleepy.

"She's a smart girl." Corrinda parted more hair. "But not a happy one. That's why she's so angry. She's unhappy. She has nothing and nobody of her own, except me. And I just can't get ahead fast enough to support her and have her live with me. I do everything I can, but it's not enough."

"That has to be hard," Daffy said. "For both of you."

"Can you imagine me keeping track of a teenage girl when I'm here all day and almost every evening? Her work, her social life, her friends. And what about summers? Her mother wasn't much older than Natalie is now when she got pregnant. How could I watch her closely enough? But soon. I hope soon, I can hire more help, find a place large enough for both of us. Really get involved in her life. Every single day."

Daffy knew better than to take anything that was said at face value, and she wondered how much Corrinda really wanted Natalie. Were her standards too high? Was she reluctant to take on a troubled teen? Or was it actually impossible for her to take on her niece's care?

"It is hard to keep an eye on a teenager." Daffy tried to phrase her concerns carefully. "It's the number one concern of the parents whose children I work with."

"Yes, I know Jewel Martinez has disappeared."

Daffy was surprised it had been that easy to get to Jewel. "You've spoken to her mother?"

"Isabel? She's beside herself. She comes here because I understand her hair, not because the girls are friends. I'm not sure they are. What do you think?"

Daffy phrased her answer carefully. "I see signs they could be."

"Well, it will be impossible now, unless she goes back home. Isabel hoped Jewel might come here to talk to me. She likes me, but she hasn't come."

Daffy saw that the bulk of her hair had disappeared into wide braids close to her scalp. Her eyes looked huge, and her hair was impossibly neat. She didn't look like herself at all. "Maybe Isabel hoped Jewel might have told you something that would help."

"She didn't, but Natalie may have."

Daffy waited and hoped.

"Natalie said a woman who works over by your office might be bothering Jewel." Corrinda lowered her voice. "I know this woman, and she's a bad influence on young girls."

Daffy debated but finally nodded, or tried to. She only managed an inch since Corrinda was holding tightly to her hair. "Do you mean the woman who calls herself Mama Mambo?"

Corrinda let out a long breath. "Ah, so you know her."

"I've spoken to her once. I wanted to learn more about local voodoo. It seems important to understand it when you live here."

"Why?"

"It's part of the culture, and my clients could be influenced."

"I suppose anyone who is weak or in pain could be looking in almost any direction for answers."

"Everyone wants answers, but not everyone is able to separate good ones from bad, good role models from bad."

"If you have clients this Mama Mambo is bothering, I suggest you warn them away. She has a reputation in the community as someone to stay clear of. I've warned Natalie. She knows better, but it's possible that Jewel didn't. The Martinezes live in a different world."

"Do you have any idea what she might be doing?"

Corrinda stopped braiding long enough to cross herself. "As a good Catholic, I stay far away from that kind of mischief. I only know she has influence and uses it. And not the kind of influence children should be exposed to."

Daffy sensed nothing else about the girls would be forthcoming, and when it wasn't, she asked Corrinda about her shop. Natalie's aunt regaled her with tales of customers and styles they'd insisted on. By the time she'd pinned and sprayed and stepped away to come back with a mirror so Daffy could see the back of her head, Daffy was glad to be finished.

"So, what do you think?"

Daffy was surprised just how much she liked what Corrinda had done. The braids swirled around her head, not in slender geometric cornrows that probably took most of a day to create, but in fatter braids that still showcased a pleasing design. The ends were woven and tucked in at the back. For once her curls were tamed, not bouncing against her cheeks and jaw.

"It's great." She meant it. "How long will it last?"

"Sleep on a satin pillowcase, and maybe two days, or three. Next time make an appointment, and we'll do real cornrows. Those last for weeks."

Daffy doubted she'd ever have enough patience, but she smiled.

Corrinda walked her to the front and refused to let her pay. "You help my Natalie, and I know the state doesn't pay you what they should. It's the least I can do."

Daffy thanked her and turned to leave.

"Remember what I said about that woman." Corrinda looked worried. "I don't know enough to accuse her of hurting–" She turned up her hands, and it was clear she didn't want to say Jewel's name in front of anyone else. "You shouldn't, either. But some people are too dangerous to talk to."

Daffy knew better than to go into the office, because if Rosy didn't tackle her first, Antoinette would haul her outside into the sunshine and deposit her at the streetcar stop. So as she trudged from the bus to her house, she called Antoinette, exactly at noon. Her friend was religious about taking a break for lunch, and probably more so now that she was pregnant.

"Got a minute to talk?" she asked when Antoinette answered.

"You sound like you're panting."

Daffy rolled her eyes and veered toward the shade of a live oak hanging over the sidewalk. "I just had my hair done, and I'm walking home from the bus stop."

"You're up to that?"

"I feel a lot better. No fainting spells." And no hallucinations, which pleased her most of all.

"Your head?"

"Headaches, not migraines. Still not much of an appetite. But I feel better every day."

"Which is why you're supposed to rest."

"Yeah, yeah. Look, have you ever spoken to the staff at the group home where Natalie's living?"

"Yes. The newish daytime care worker–I think the last name is Dell–who sees her the most. The woman's not forthcoming or friendly, but we've chatted a couple of times, just to see how Natalie's doing, and whether I need to do any intervention or counseling with staff. Natalie can be trying."

"Did she mention Jewel? Has Jewel been there to visit?"

"I did ask about Natalie's friends. I didn't mention Jewel by name, but Mrs. Dell said Natalie's a loner and doesn't have friends."

"Poor kid." As trying as her own childhood had been, Daffy had always found girls she could talk to or sit with at lunch.

"She said the only thing Natalie really seems to enjoy is her art class," Antoinette said.

"With Riverview's endowment the administration probably flies in famous artists to teach finger painting to the kinder-gartners."

"No, Natalie stopped taking art at Riverview. Once her grades plummeted, all her extra periods were taken up with remedial tutoring. Mrs. Dell was talking about an art class Natalie takes with other foster kids one afternoon a week. Through the summer, too."

The shade had disappeared, but Daffy stopped in the middle of the sidewalk anyway. "Who teaches it? Do you know?"

"Teaches what?"

"The art class for foster kids."

"I think she said a man, a volunteer."

"No name?"

"Does it matter? Mrs. Dell said that she has to let Natalie go because the social worker thinks she's talented. I've tried to talk to Natalie about it, but she gets furious. She doesn't want whatever she does there mixed up in what we do together." Antoinette paused. "Or what I try to do. She's getting more and more distant."

"And group yesterday?"

Antoinette was silent.

"Antoinette?"

"I'm sorry, Daffy, but Natalie left when she realized you weren't there. She got up and walked out."

"Damn." Daffy began to walk again.

"I can call Mrs. Dell and see if she knows who's teaching the class, in case you want to get in touch with him. Is that why you wanted to know?"

"No, don't bother. I'm pretty sure I already do. In fact I'm almost sure it's Skeeter."

Two hours later Daffy found Skeeter, as she'd expected to, along the fence at Jackson Square. He had a prime spot on the corner of Decatur and St. Ann, just a stone's throw from the Café du Monde, famous for its café au lait with chicory and freshly made beignets. On a whim she backtracked and bought a bag of beignets and a cup of coffee to go before she crossed Decatur to his display.

The Square was a favorite of hers. Inside the fence, old trees swayed gracefully and flower beds and swaths of grass rimmed the walkways. The remarkable St. Louis Cathedral, where Sam and Antoinette's wedding had been held, rose at the far end.

Like other artists Skeeter had fastened his work to the wrought iron railing around the square and set up an easel to work from. The hanging art was a combination of local scenes, portraits he'd done, and insightful caricatures of people in the news and celebrities. Judging from the interest today, caricatures were his bread and butter.

"Twenty dollars?" A man with a New York accent, accompanied by three boys under twelve, was in bargaining mode, and Skeeter was listening politely. "You mean twenty each? If you did them all together, like on the same piece of paper, would it be less? It ought to be."

Skeeter had clearly done this dance before. "That's twenty for black and white only, thirty if I add color. And the price is per child, not per page. It's the same number of faces, regardless of how much paper I use. Besides, this way they'll each have their own portrait to enjoy."

"That's a lot of money."

"That's a lot of kids."

Daffy stepped forward. "While you're thinking about it, I'd sure love to have the artist do mine. I need one to send to my boyfriend. He's in the Middle East." She looked directly at Skeeter. "But I won't ask for a military discount."

"Hey, I was here first," the man said.

"Oh, I thought you were still trying to decide if you wanted to spend the money." She smiled her sweetest smile. The three boys were already chasing each other down the stone walkway and would soon split up and head in opposite directions.

The man threw up his hands. "Jeez, I'll do it. C'mere, kids!"

While he ran off to corral his expensive offspring, she handed Skeeter the coffee and set the beignets at his feet. "Can I watch?"

"Sure. Then maybe you can learn to draw something for that boyfriend in the Middle East. What branch of the service is he in, by the way?"

"The Secret Service. Very secret."

He smiled, although he looked as if he didn't want to. "Did you just happen to stop by?"

"Absolutely. And I just happened to find you, and happened to buy you coffee, etc."

"You're feeling okay?"

She wished the sun would go down and her body temperature would drop about ten degrees, but she smiled and nodded.

"Some hairstyle."

She put her hand to her head and primped. She'd showered carefully and chosen the coolest sun dress she owned before she hopped into Nelson's car for the ride to the Quarter. She'd even applied makeup, although she suspected it had already melted away. "You think?"

"It's cute."

"Just the hair?"

He raised one brow in question. "Where are you heading?"

"Here. I'm going to watch."

"I can't talk while I work."

"Can you talk afterwards?"

He didn't answer. Today he was wearing shorts and a turquoise and gold tropical shirt featuring hula girls and palm trees. A Saints cap shaded his face, which looked as if he hadn't shaved it that morning, rugged and delicious. Most significantly he looked relaxed and not particularly interested in her sudden appearance on the Square.

Dad and his three sons returned, and the tallest took the folding chair across from Skeeter. Skeeter talked to the boy as he worked, explaining that caricature was different from a portrait because it was his job to emphasize whatever aspects of the boy's face seemed most interesting.

"So by the time I'm done, you'll recognize yourself, but this won't look exactly like you."

Daffy stood back and watched. Skeeter began with what looked like a discount store magic marker and sketched the outline of the boy's head. Then he sketched his hair, which in real life was a modest swoop off his forehead, but in Skeeter's hands became a wave high enough to surf. He drew in eyebrows, one longer than the other, eyes that tilted much higher than the boy's, a nose as straight and long as the side of an Army tent, a mouth filled with oversized teeth. He didn't exaggerate more than he needed, just enough to give the right flavor.

"And there you are." He motioned the boy to come around to his side. "You like it?"

"Wow, you just did that? So fast? It's great!"

Daffy took one final peek and saw that Skeeter had signed the caricature with the same cartoon mosquito she'd seen at his house. The father muttered something about Skeeter charging two dollars a minute. Daffy nudged him and whispered: "I know. It's awful, isn't it? Here you and I barely make minimum wage, and there he is supporting himself on our hard-earned pay."

"I'm a doctor," he said stiffly, drawing himself up to his full height, which was an inch above hers.

"Isn't that funny? So am I." She waved at Skeeter and walked off to see the rest of the artists' work before she said something she really regretted.

By the time she made the entire circle, the doctor and his sons were gone, and Skeeter was on his feet, moving some of his art to more prominent positions on the fence. She loved the collection of old New Orleans houses, distorted and embellished, and noted that two had sold stickers on them, waiting to be picked up.

"It's all wonderful," she said from behind him. "Even your commercial stuff. You're so talented."

He didn't turn. "That's me. Picasso in disguise."

"Not a fan of Picasso, but I am a fan of Seth Harwood. Do you happen to know his work?"

He finished what he'd been doing and faced her. "You must have a reason for being here."

"I'm hoping you'll help me figure out something."

He waited.

"Do you teach a girl named Natalie Saizan?"

That seemed to surprise him. "How do you know Natalie?" She shrugged, and he got the reason right away. "Okay. What about her?" he asked.

"I need some clues about her life. I've talked to her aunt, and Antoinette's talked to the resident care workers at her group home. That's how I put two and two together and realized you might be her teacher."

Two young women were approaching. Daffy saw them pointing to Skeeter—the man, not his paintings—and knew she was about to have conversation competition. Man competition, too.

She moved to the chair where the boys had sat for their caricatures and perched, demurely folding her hands.

"I can't wait to see what you do with me," she said, loudly enough for the women to hear.

"I know what I'd like to do with you." He didn't sound happy.

"Perfect. Use that powerful imagination. Go all the way."

"Just surface stuff, right? You're not looking for any big insights. That doesn't seem like your style."

Her heart seemed to twist a little. "I'll leave it up to you."

"I doubt that." He sat and clipped fresh paper to his easel. "For some reason I visualize your hair down. Want it that way?"

"Whichever way you like it."

He began to draw. The young women nudged each other,

then wandered off. Daffy and Skeeter were as alone as they could be on Jackson Square.

"Does Nat show up for most of your classes?" she asked.

He made a few strokes with his marker, then a few more, changing to a thinner one housed in a Mardi Gras go-cup at his side. "She never misses."

"That's impressive. She must like you or what you teach."

"She's very talented. The most talented student I've had since I started teaching."

"When was that?"

"A couple of years ago."

"What's she like in class?"

"Absorbed. Patient. Thoughtful."

"We are talking about the same girl?"

He didn't answer.

"Does she talk about her life?"

"She draws her life. It's not an easy one, but apparently you know that."

She remembered Sam had said Skeeter had been in and out of foster care as a boy. She was silent a minute, letting him work. When he reached for a different cup filled with what looked like pastels, she tried another way to get him to open up.

"One of the teens in a group I run is missing. I have a hunch Natalie may know something about it. But that's all I have. I have all these thoughts and hunches circling around in my head, and they don't go anywhere. It's like our night across the lake. Circling and circling, and if I decide to cross to the other side, I have to walk through fire to do it. I would, too. But the only thing I'd get right now is third degree burns."

"Once upon a time, I was Natalie," he said, after more silence. "Maybe that's why I'm so fond of her. Talented, confused, abandoned. I'd like her to get through all that without ending up in jail, like I did. Or pregnant. Or abused."

"She's lucky to have you in her life."

"She's never mentioned another girl. She seems very alone to me. I don't think I can help you."

Her reason for being there had ended. She had nothing else to ask him. She sat quietly until he finally nodded.

"Done." He pulled the portrait off his easel and began to roll it, as if he was going to put it in a cardboard tube for her to carry home.

"I haven't even seen it. That's not fair." She got up and came around to stand beside him. "Put it back. Let me see."

"Maybe it's better to see at home."

"Now."

He shrugged, unrolled it, and pinned it back up.

She took a deep breath and held it. "Is this the way you see me?"

"Every bit of it."

The woman staring back at her was beautiful. Her skin glowed, her green eyes reflected some glorious inner light. Her hair was a mass of red curls pushed over her ears, and her lips looked as if they were waiting to be kissed. Nothing was exaggerated except...

"What is wrong with my feet?" He'd drawn the traditional large caricature head on a small body, but the feet were lumpy and bare, huge and brick red.

"Feet of clay." He took the drawing down again and began to roll it. "You told me to use my powerful imagination, but it didn't take much."

She rested her fingertips on his arm. "Seth, I'm sorry that I, well, talked so much, that day. You know what I mean. I really am. I just wanted you to understand—"

"Oh, I do."

"No, you don't. I don't, either. I'm... kind of a mess."

He turned to look at her. "Kind of?"

"A whole lot?"

He waited.

She sighed. "What do I owe you?"

"This one's on me."

She considered. "I can't let you do that. It's not fair, especially after the way I talked to that jerk who was trying to bargain with you. I have to pay you, too."

"No, you don't."

"Come to dinner at my house."

He faced her. "You're offering to cook for me?"

"You don't believe I can?"

"I don't believe I want to find out."

"You think I'm beautiful. It's clear you do. You can't get out of it. I have the proof. What can one dinner with a beautiful woman—"

"With feet of clay."

"Okay, with feet of clay. What can dinner hurt? Afterwards you can go your own way if you want. But please, let me do this. To thank you for everything you've done for me."

He considered. "Larry's got your car nearly done, at least until he can find one more part. But for now, he says you can drive it while he scours junkyards. I was going to bring it over tomorrow night anyway. I guess I can stay for dinner."

She lifted on tiptoe and kissed him, and not, of course, because the two young women she'd bested were walking back toward them. "I'll write Larry a check when I see you. Six o'clock? No wine for me, but bring something for yourself."

"If you don't leave before my next portraits arrive, I won't be able to afford a bottle of wine or a six-pack."

She laughed and left, but she could feel his eyes following her. Another hunch, but one she was sure of.

CHAPTER 15

D affy didn't usually split hairs when it came to the truth. Tonight was a little different. After all, there was a difference between a lie and a deception. She hadn't *lied* to Skeeter. She'd offered him dinner, but she hadn't offered to cook for him. And when he'd asked if cooking was the plan, she'd turned her answer into a question–a dubious skill she'd learned from her teenage clients.

Deception, not exactly a lie.

Of course she could cook. Anybody could boil water, use the microwave, make a sandwich or salad. Unfortunately, that's where her skills ended. Her kitchen was a postage stamp, an eight-cent stamp at that, with Eisenhower or Truman looking somber and important. And what point was there in cooking for herself in a city where every block had a chef who was more creative and skilled than she would ever be?

After leaving the Quarter she'd found one of those chefs at a local café, and after explaining how many foods she had to exclude, and promising her first-born son, they'd scrounged up a menu. Now she was warming the baked mango chicken on a platter she'd bought near her streetcar stop. She'd dumped the chef's signature salad–minus avocado and tomato–into a bowl she'd also bought, and she was heating the rice pilaf–without nuts–in her final purchase, a casserole dish. She didn't want to think about where she'd store the new pottery.

Maybe the menu had been something of a nightmare to pull together, but her health had improved so drastically that she was willing to stay on the migraine diet for the rest of her life. Of course, she was also looking forward to testing restrictions with the help of an allergist, until she knew exactly where her problems originated.

Right at six, footsteps sounded on her porch, and she went to let Skeeter in. Her new-old VW sat at the curb, preening in the diminishing light of day. She almost clapped her hands, but she decided Skeeter might take applause the wrong way.

She'd debated what to wear and had almost settled on something seductive and irresistible, but since–like the applause–that seemed too obvious, she'd changed into an oversized sparkly T-shirt over a tank top and capri length leggings. Her "feet of clay" were bare.

"I bet you're tired," she said, not sure whether to kiss him in greeting. She settled for a quick peck on the cheek and stepped back immediately. He didn't wince, which was a good sign. "I did buy Dixie beer, in case you didn't bring something for yourself, and I have bottled water."

"Water for now. Thanks."

She hoped he would follow as she made her way to the kitchen. Both chicken and rice were in the oven to stay warm. She was surprised the fragrance hadn't filled the air.

"What's on the menu?" Skeeter asked from behind her.

"Any guesses? You have no idea how hard it is to plan a meal on this diet."

"I'd make one, but I don't smell clues."

She glanced at the oven and realized she hadn't turned it on. "Whoops." She smiled brightly. "Why don't you get us each a bottle of water." She nodded to the fridge. The moment he turned his back, she flipped the oven dial and heard the whoosh of gas as it ignited. Considering how long the antique took to heat, dinner wouldn't be ready for a while.

She took her water bottle. "Dinner isn't quite finished. Would you like to go out to the side gallery and sit for a while?"

He followed her through the bedroom and out the side door, where he took the single chair in the corner instead of the loveseat. "How are the plants?"

She sat alone and wished that at the very least their hips were touching. "Traumatized. I'm working with them. A combination of role-playing and guided meditation seems to work best." She laughed at his expression. "I'm joking. Please. At this point I'm only a little crazy. The good news is that thanks to you, I haven't lost any new plants. They're all hanging in. And my lemon tree in the living room? More tiny lemons. Those I do talk to. A little encouragement does wonders."

He was staring at the house next door, as if he didn't want to look directly at her. "What'd you do with your portrait?"

"I'm going to have it framed."

"Really? You want the reminder?"

"Of you? Of my feet of clay? Of how beautiful you think I am?"

He turned so he was finally looking at her. "The feet of clay."

"Do you really think I'm weak? Not that it's my job to change your mind. Your feelings are real to you."

"Thus spake the psychologist."

She made a face. "We're going to fight again, aren't we? You'll go home with an empty stomach. I'll mope for days, examining my navel, which really isn't very interesting to me, although it might be to you. You'll start to brood, and the next time a doctor from New York tries to get something for nothing in Jackson Square, you'll hit him over the head with your easel. Sam will arrive to arrest you, and he'll call Joshua in the psych unit at City Hospital." She lifted her hands to show just how dire that would be. "All because I was trying not to argue with you."

The corners of his mouth turned up just a little, as if he was fighting hard and losing. "Why doesn't your house smell like you're cooking dinner?"

She considered the possibilities. "It's an old house. Maybe it absorbs odors. Like a box of baking soda in the fridge."

"Let's hear another theory."

"You have an inefficient sense of smell?"

"Want to hear mine?"

"I'm afraid to."

He stood and came to sit next to her. He slung his arm over the back of the loveseat and turned so he could see her. "You bought dinner and forgot to heat it up."

"You think you know me."

"Here's what else I know. You're not weak, you're scared. You don't want a serious relationship because you'd have to invest too much of yourself, and there's more to Daffy Brookes than anyone's ever discovered, even the multiple psychologists and psychiatrists you probably trained with. You've worked hard to keep that much of yourself hidden, and you're not sure you ever want anybody to take it out and look at it."

She was too good a psychologist not to wonder if he was right. "Seth–"

He shook his head. "*Skeeter*. You can call me Skeeter. I'm not Seth to you until you're Daphne to me. The real Daphne. Not that I don't love Daffy."

She melted. "You love Daffy?"

"I should have my head examined."

"I could do it."

"Fat chance."

"Are we going to kiss and make up?"

He debated, then he sighed, but lightly. "When are we going to eat?"

"The directions say to heat the chicken and rice for half an hour. I just turned on the oven."

He bent over put his arms around her and hauled her against him. Then he made sure she knew she'd been kissed, and more of the same was on the way.

The next morning she woke wrapped in Skeeter's arms, which felt so perfect she thought she might stay that way all day. She turned just enough to watch him sleep. Watching him was a pleasure and tiring of it seemed impossible. This morning he looked a little spent, but she suspected she did, too. They'd kept each other awake long into the wee hours of the morning.

She turned a little further and felt her hair tickling her cheeks and neck. The braids hadn't lasted. When it was clear the pins weren't going to stay under duress, Skeeter had patiently undone them, kissing her scalp, her cheeks, her neck as he slowly unfurled her hair. Quite possibly it was the most erotic experience of her life. By the time her curls were free and disarray reigned again, she'd been limp with desire.

He had that effect on her.

Now her stomach growled, and she smiled. At some point in the evening she'd turned off the oven. Later they'd dug into the deli's creations. She admitted she'd bought the pottery to fool him, and he admitted that she'd already made it clear on their picnic that she didn't cook. She wasn't sure which part of that pleased her the most. That he'd gone along with the gag, knowing all along dinner was arriving care of an expert, or that he'd remembered that tiny detail.

She thought back to that day and remembered his description of gumbo. More recently he'd talked about making gumbo for *her*. With luck she might be able to persuade him that today was the day. And since gumbo was a multiple stages production, he'd have to hang around. And if he hung around all day–

"Why are you smiling?"

She laughed and touched his lips. She had been so busy fantasizing she'd missed the moment he woke up. "Gumbo. I was thinking about gumbo."

"It's nice to see you hungry again."

"It's nice to be hungry. I don't have much here to eat. We have a great place not far away for brunch, though."

"Can you eat anything from their menu?"

"I'll find something."

"How hungry are you?"

"For what exactly?"

He laughed and made his plan clear.

By early afternoon they were filled with good food, and the VW was filled with all the ingredients to make a pot of gumbo–they'd stopped by his house for the pot. Skeeter had shaken his head repeatedly over Daffy's list of acceptable foods, and he'd made it clear that this gumbo would be a poor attempt next to his usual, but he'd been a good sport. Leeks would replace the forbidden onions. Chicken, the seafood. And they'd been lucky to find a fresh sausage made without preservatives that might be marginally acceptable. Daffy had been willing to take the risk.

"If I faint in your arms, it will feel familiar," she'd told him. "Let's give it a try."

Now they were in her kitchen, and she stored the perishables in her refrigerator. They'd made a quick inventory before they left, and she had more ingredients than she'd expected. She owned half a bottle of canola oil, both black pepper and cayenne, oregano and thyme, plus she'd bought lots of organic chicken broth without MSG. Omission was even less sinful than deception. She hadn't mentioned that the herbs were part of a collection her mother had sent in a Christmas basket. Lea liked to cook and had, whenever she was well enough. Now both she and Daffy's father were gaining weight because Lea was well enough all the time.

Skeeter had already poured oil into his pot and it was beginning to sizzle. He was in teacher mode.

"We start with the roux. First oil, then when it's hot enough, flour. And when that's been whisked until your arm falls off and it's turned the color of milk chocolate, we'll add the leeks, peppers, garlic. Then sausage, broth, chicken and herbs. Got it?"

"Isn't this a bit early? Does it cook that long?"

"I'm teaching this afternoon."

"Natalie's class?"

"That's the only one I have right now. I had a class of younger children, but they either moved to permanent homes or went back to their families."

She enjoyed watching him whisk the flour into the oil. She hoped he didn't remember saying that "her" arm would fall off. "You like kids, don't you?"

"I even like the ones nobody else does."

"Natalie." As always she thought of Jewel and wondered where the girl was staying. They were making the gumbo at Daffy's because she still hoped Jewel would show up. "I wonder if she knows anything about the other girl I mentioned."

"You've asked her directly?"

"When it first happened I asked all my teens. She's not my client, and I missed the last group, so I haven't had the chance to follow up. I did hear she was upset I wasn't there."

"Why don't you come with me today? You can observe the class and reassure Natalie that you're all right. She might even talk to you." He held out the whisk. "Your turn."

"Really? I love watching you do it."

"And I'll love watching *you*. If you don't grab this immediately it will burn and you'll have to start over by yourself."

She grabbed it. He put his arms around her and guided her hand until she had the motion right. "We'll make an expert of you."

"I'd rather let you make the gumbo."

"I may not always be here to do it."

His tone was light, and she wondered if she was reading more into a simple statement than was called for. She didn't want a replay of the conversation that had nearly expunged him from her life, so she didn't comment. She whisked until her arm began to go numb, watching in fascination as the color of the roux slowly changed.

Skeeter chopped while she whisked. Then, when he approved of a particular shade of brown, he dropped mounds of vegetables in and gave her a wooden spoon to mix them into the roux.

"Normally I'd make stock myself from a whole chicken, and that's what we'd stir in next. But because we're leaving the house in a little while, I don't want stock sitting on the stove. So we'll turn it off until we get back and add your canned chicken broth. Nothing in here will spoil."

"What else do you know how to make?"

She listened to a long list of New Orleans favorites. Then he transitioned to Asian, Mexican, and Italian favorites.

"You do all that just for yourself?"

"Not often. It's easier to grab something or nudge friends to invite me."

"You're invited here. Anytime. To cook, I mean."

He glanced at her, then shrugged. "Taste the gumbo first."

She left him to change for the trip to his class. She needed to look at least a bit professional, so she settled on a peach-colored knit dress and sandals. Since that was boring, she added long ropes of wooden animals from Peru and a barrette with a parrot to hold back one side of her hair. She cleaned up the kitchen while Skeeter took a quick shower.

First they stopped at Skeeter's again, where he gathered materials into bags and a portfolio. Then they left the VW at his house and took his Jeep. The art class was held in an elementary school that was now used solely for community outreach, a shabby stucco building with fading turquoise trim. Both had seen better days.

"Not much to look at," Skeeter said, parking in front. "Every time I come I wonder if the place will still be standing."

The interior was little better, but it didn't smell like mold and nothing scurried across their path. That was good news, as were the bright murals in the hallways. They could hear voices from some of the classrooms as they passed. One door was open, and the instructor was repeating sentences in English and then patiently waiting for the students to repeat them back.

Skeeter had given her a small bag to carry, but he carried everything else because there wasn't much. On the trip he'd told her that he bought supplies for the class himself, so projects had to be simple.

As they walked down the hall, Skeeter shared his plan. "We're doing crayon etching. Do you know what that is?"

She listened as he elaborated. The teens had already done a simple pencil drawing, then outlined it in black marker. Skeeter had presented examples for the students who lacked confidence and didn't know where to begin. He was proud that this time, no one had copied. Everyone had been willing to try and fail if necessary.

"Natalie never had that problem," he said, turning into a large room with work tables and plenty of sunlight. "From the beginning she's known exactly what she wants to do."

"What did she draw this time?"

"I don't know. She's kept to herself the last two classes, sitting over there, covering her work and taking it home when she left." He nodded to the farthest corner. "I collected everybody else's."

"So you don't know what she's doing?"

"It's clear it's something she thinks she might get in trouble for."

"Like?"

"Something forbidden. Something sexual? People shooting up? Kids beating or stabbing each other in the street? It's impossible to tell what these kids have seen in their short lives and what they need to say in their artwork. I gave her the space she needed. And the other kids know not to harass her or they'll pay the price."

"Where does the etching come in?"

"Last week they colored their drawings with crayons. The trick is to press hard and cover every single space except the lines. Then before they left they painted the entire paper with black ink. Today they'll etch designs over the paper, and their drawings will come to life."

"I would have loved something like that as a kid. I don't remember doing art in school."

"Cutting art programs, music, too, is just another way we make sure kids can't express themselves in acceptable ways."

She thought about that as he set out materials and carefully placed drawings in front of chairs at the tables. She counted ten.

And Natalie's, of course. She wondered if the girl would remember to bring her drawing. If she came.

As she had expected, when it was time, kids wandered through the door in groups, greeting Skeeter and finding their own art, which was tagged with their names, a good thing since every paper looked exactly the same coated with black ink.

He was introducing Daffy as a friend who'd come to watch when Natalie stormed in. She took one look at Daffy and narrowed her eyes.

"What are *you* doing here?"

Skeeter stopped mid-sentence and inclined his head. "I'll start again since I was interrupted. I'm introducing Dr. Brookes, Natalie. I saved your favorite seat in the corner." He pointed.

"Why is she here?"

Daffy answered for herself, moving closer so they could talk more privately. "Mr. Harwood and I are friends, and the class sounded like fun. I won't bother you."

Natalie's eyes were now slits. "You knew I'd be here, didn't you?"

"I thought you might like to see that I'm feeling better."

"Like I care."

"I'm still glad I came."

"Well, that makes one of us." Natalie stomped over to the table Skeeter had pointed to and flung herself into a chair.

Skeeter, ignoring the commotion, was explaining what they would do next. Apparently scratching off the ink in whatever patterns the teens chose involved nails and pointed bamboo sticks, and after the confrontation with Natalie, Daffy decided she'd be smart to keep her distance.

She spent the next hour strolling around the room, enjoying the emerging pictures. Lisa, a pretty brunette who looked to be the youngest in the room, was patiently unveiling a pink house surrounded by flowers and trees. The pattern she was scratching into the ink looked like tiny question marks.

"I like this," Daffy said. "The question marks take off just enough ink to show what's underneath, but they make an interesting statement."

"I would like to live in this house."

Daffy had guessed as much. All the kids here were in the foster care system and probably dreamed of a real home. "And you wonder when you will," she said.

"Probably never, but I can live there in my imagination."

"How old are you, Lisa?"

"Almost fourteen."

Daffy was sorry that at such a young age, the girl already knew her dreams would only come true in her fantasies.

Roy, a boy who looked to be about sixteen, had drawn and colored a flamboyant pirate. Kit, a younger boy, was scratching furiously to reveal a race car, as if he was afraid if he didn't quickly get to the picture beneath, it would disappear. Daffy bet he ate the same way and was at the head of every line. Already Kit had no faith that anything would be left for him, and she tried not to think about what kind of adult he would become.

Skeeter approached Natalie just once, but she told him to go away. He did without comment.

The class flew by. At the end of the hour Skeeter and the kids—with the exception of Natalie—opened the windows and stood beside them to spray their finished drawings with acrylic.

"All done for the day," he said, looking at his watch. "But if you don't mind, leave your work here. Next week we're going to frame everything. I'll buy frames and you can cut mats. Deal?"

The kids seemed pleased and chatted as they left. A couple made a point of saying goodbye to Daffy. Natalie stayed behind.

Skeeter gathered supplies and waited until the pictures were safely stored in his satchel before he approached Natalie again.

"You finished, Nat? We have to vacate the room. Another class comes in later."

Natalie turned her drawing so it was face down. "I'm going."

"Do you want me to spray that for you and bring it back next week?"

The girl shrugged. "Whatever." She stood. "You wait until I'm gone."

"No problem. But you don't want to show me yourself? You've worked hard."

She ignored him and turned to Daffy. "My aunt says you bothered her with questions about Jewel and me. You had no call to do that."

"I don't think I bothered her. She braided my hair."

"You leave us alone. She's going to take me soon. Then I'll be out of foster care, and I won't have to see you ever again!" She left the room so fast that the air seemed to stir for seconds after she was gone.

"I shouldn't have come," Daffy told Skeeter.

"It's not you."

"I know, but this was a safe place until I showed up."

"I don't think so. She's acted strangely the last two sessions." Skeeter folded his arms, and then he unfolded them and reached for Natalie's picture. He flipped it over for both of them to see.

Daffy couldn't stifle a gasp. The picture was of a voodoo ceremony, half-naked dancers around a bonfire and a slender woman with her head thrown back and arms raised. Her face was hidden, but there were faces of two girls in diagonal corners. Natalie had scratched off so much of the ink there that the drawing beneath was absolutely clear. One of the girls was unmistakably Natalie.

The other was Jewel Martinez.

CHAPTER 16

Natalie was nowhere in sight.

Daffy came back from searching and met Skeeter in front of his classroom. She shook her head. "This place has so many hiding places and potential exits. Looking for her is futile."

"The other girl in her picture is the one who disappeared?"

Total confidentiality seemed less important than finding Jewel. "She's the one who left the gris-gris bag for me to find."

"Any minute now you're going to start beating yourself up. I can feel it in the air."

"No, the only connection I could make between Natalie and voodoo was seeing them both on the same block with Mama Mambo. The girls certainly aren't friends."

"Natalie was one of the girls you saw Mama arguing with?"

He had remembered that from her end of their conversation with the voodoo queen. Daffy realized how carefully he listened and how much she hadn't told him directly. Confidentiality was the backbone of her practice, but confidentiality had finally become a veil keeping her from getting to the truth. "Telling you more is unethical, Skeeter, but you have just enough information now to point us in the wrong direction unless you have it all."

"You know I'll keep everything to myself."

"I need help. I'll catch you up in the car. Do you know where the group home is located?"

"I do. I'll drive, you talk."

As they circled the block and started toward the river, she told him everything she knew, including the story about Linda and Katie, omitting last names, which was her last stand.

She finished just as he slid into a parking spot across the street from the home. "You've got a little here, a little there," he said. "Too little for a conclusion."

"I've looked into voodoo cults, because this doesn't seem anything like voudou, the religion Mama talked about. I can't help but think somebody's manipulating Jewel and scaring her to death. The problem is that most of the people writing about cults are convinced that every religion except their own fits the definition."

"I haven't heard of anything like a voodoo cult, but I'd guess cults keep their activities secret unless you look like a recruit."

"The closest thing I found were news articles on fortune telling scams. Level-headed adults fall prey more often than you can imagine. They're told curses have to be lifted, psychic adjustments made, and before they know it, they've given away their life savings."

"And a teenager would be even more likely to succumb."

"It's just a theory. But Jewel was terrified by something. She took her grandmother's jewelry out of a safe deposit box and disappeared. She left the gris-gris bag where I would find it. And now we have Natalie drawing herself with Jewel at a voodoo bonfire."

They got out of the car and walked up the sidewalk to the group home together. Just as they reached the steps she touched his arm. "I've done some odd home visits, but always alone and never one like this. Thank you for doing it with me."

"You sound surprised. Why should you be?"

She didn't have time to think or answer. The door flew open and an African-American teenager pushed past them so fast Daffy didn't even get a good look at her. She only knew it wasn't Natalie.

Skeeter didn't stand on ceremony. He opened the door and gestured for her to proceed him.

In the hallway a gray-haired woman in a shapeless blue shift was yelling at two young teens. She stopped when she saw them.

"Did you knock?"

Daffy didn't smile. "Good thing we didn't. We would have pounded the girl who just flew out of here."

The woman turned back to the teens. They wore sloppy T-shirts and shorts and looked furious. "You go back upstairs and finish your chores, and don't try to leave until you're done." The woman pointed to the central stairway with a poorly manicured finger, and the girls, who hesitated, as if they were about to disobey, finally went.

"None of these kids ever learned the slightest thing about taking care of themselves." The woman turned to Daffy and Skeeter. "We're cleaning the house today. Nobody has time to visit."'

"Natalie's in a group I run at Psychologist Associates." Daffy pulled a business card out of her handbag. "We're trying to find her. Is she here?"

"She went to a class. I have to let her go, even when we have cleaning to do." She sing-songed her next words in a nasty tone. "It's re-qui-red."

"We were there. Mr. Harwood teaches the class." Daffy gestured to him. The woman hadn't given them a chance for an introduction.

"She left in a hurry, and we need to talk to her," Skeeter said.

"I can't help what she does. And she hasn't come back."

Daffy wondered how many of Natalie's problems came from having someone like this in charge of her life. No question the woman's job was difficult. No question she must have at least minimal qualifications. But it was past time for her to retire.

"When does she usually return?" Daffy asked.

"I don't know. It's not my job to keep track of everything the kids do when they're out of the house."

"Whose job is it?" Skeeter asked.

Daffy wanted to kiss him but managed a tightly controlled smile in the woman's direction. "You're Mrs. . . ?"

"Dell. And I have a million things to do right now."

"This is a tough job, I know, but we're concerned about Natalie. This may seem like a strange question." She turned up her palms, as if asking forgiveness. "But is Natalie interested in voodoo? Does she have any connection to it that you're aware of?"

"You think I would allow something like that here?" Mrs. Dell's already wrinkled face crinkled into deeper folds. Daffy wondered what she looked like when she wasn't annoyed or angry. She wondered if the kids ever saw her any other way.

"In other words, no," Skeeter said. "Is she good about staying here at the house when she's supposed to?"

"She'd better be. When I'm on duty, we run a tight ship. I can't speak to what the other staff do when they're in charge. Not my concern."

"Any chance she might be with her aunt today?" Daffy was already eyeing the front door, hoping to escape before Skeeter told the woman what he thought of her leadership style.

"I would have to go look at the schedule, and like I told you, I'm busy."

"It would be a big help," Daffy said, but the woman shook her head and started toward the stairs.

"I can tell you one thing," she said over her shoulder. "Every time Natalie comes back from being with that woman, she's twice as much trouble. I'm not her caseworker, so I can't put a stop to it. They tell me it's important for her to be with family. But it just gives the girl ideas."

"Like being loved and wanted?" Skeeter asked.

Mrs. Dell was not immune to sarcasm. "I'm done here."

"And we're all that much better because of it." Skeeter nodded, took Daffy's arm and nearly dragged her to the door.

Back at the car after he released her, Daffy hesitated and didn't get in. "Wasn't that fun?"

"Natalie can't stay there."

"I'll talk to Antoinette and tell her what we saw. But she's hoping Natalie's aunt will step up, so foster care won't even be an issue. When she braided my hair, Corrinda told me she hopes to take her soon."

Skeeter didn't answer right away, and she thought they were finished until he took her arm again as she started to open the passenger door. "Daffy, you and Antoinette are looking at this whole thing with Natalie and her aunt through rose-colored lenses."

She was surprised. He didn't sound critical. Analytical was a better interpretation. "What do you mean?"

"There's no reason good enough for Corrinda not to take Natalie right now. No agency is going to stand in the way of a family member gaining custody unless there's a serious problem. And Corrinda's been to this house, so she knows what living here is like. Natalie would sleep on a wood floor, eat cold cereal three times a day, sweep her aunt's beauty salon every day and twice on Sunday rather than live here with the Dell from Hell. Trust me. I remember how it feels to live in a place like this."

Instantly she knew he was right. Daffy couldn't believe she hadn't seen it herself. Both she and Antoinette had been taken in by Corrinda's story because they wanted to believe it. Still, why had Corrinda told everyone and especially Natalie that she wanted her, when she probably never intended to seek custody? Was she ashamed? Was it something darker?

Silently she listed the few good things she knew about the aunt-niece relationship. Corrinda spent time with Natalie each month. She'd helped get her a scholarship to Riverview Academy. But what else had she done for her niece? What else did she plan?

She finished her thoughts out loud. "I was surprised how upscale Bountiful Beauty was. We've been told Corrinda lives hand to mouth, but the shop..." She grimaced. "It was buzzing, and when I got there a staff member told me they don't bother with walk-ins. I told myself that the business probably ate all Corrinda's money, that she was probably hanging on to it by a thread."

"Did she sound like she was coming any closer to taking custody?"

Daffy shook her head. "No, she made excuses. Then we talked about Natalie, and about Jewel and Mama Mambo."

"Really? What did she say about her?"

Daffy tried to remember. "Corrinda brought her up. She said Natalie claimed Mama Mambo was bothering her and that she's a bad influence. Especially on young girls. She linked that to Jewel's disappearance." Then Daffy remembered the last thing Corrinda had said to her. "She ended by saying that some people are too dangerous to talk to."

"Corrinda brought up the subject. She warned you away. Is it possible that's why she agreed to do your hair?"

Daffy was feeling more and more foolish. What had seemed like a generous gesture may have been something else entirely. "We all see what we want to, don't we? I trained for years. I know not to take most of what I hear at face value. But that's exactly what I did."

"Do you want to confront her?"

"Right now I don't want to alienate Natalie any more than I have. But we should stop by to see if Natalie's there so we can talk to her. Corrinda claims she works day and night, so the shop is probably open."

"We'll check it out, but there's somewhere else I want to go afterwards."

"Where?"

"Where all this began."

Doctor Fantôme's Sanctuary of Voodoo was bustling. Two little boys with new crew cuts and pale scalps were staring at the snake in the corner. A woman, probably their mother, was holding up voodoo dolls in their direction, as if she was trying to decide which looked the most like her sons. Three giggling matrons wearing T-shirts with plunging necklines and naughty slogans were comparing the contents of apothecary jars, as if they had love potions in mind.

Corrinda hadn't been working at Bountiful Beauty today, and no one there had seen Natalie in some time. Without another word Skeeter had driven straight to the Quarter and parked on a side street.

Now Daffy stared at the riveting portrait of Marie Laveau, the new focal point of the shop. The young woman, wearing a tignon–a stylized head covering that all women of color had once been required to wear–looked down at them from high on the wall opposite the doorway, haughty and bold and ready to pounce.

"Your portrait's spectacular," she said. "You captured every-thing they say about her."

"Today is St. John's Eve."

In her search for information about voodoo Daffy had seen references to the eve of the official Catholic feast day of St. John, but it hadn't occurred to her that it was today, June 23rd.

Skeeter went on. "Supposedly June 23rd is the night when Marie Laveau held rituals on Bayou St. John, near Lake Pontchartrain, until dawn."

"Head washing," a male voice said behind them, and Daffy turned to see Fantôme, dressed once more like the business man he was. "Much like a Christian baptism. Offerings were accepted. Music was played and dancing. Dancing all night. It must have been quite a sight."

"New Orleans always finds an excuse to party," Skeeter said.

"I won't tell you how much I've been offered for that portrait."

"And I won't remind you that if you sell it, our contract says I get half the profit."

Fantôme laughed. "Why do you think it's still hanging here?"

"We have some questions." Skeeter lowered his voice. "The kind you might not want to answer in front of customers."

Fantôme considered, then went to the front door and turned the hanging sign to indicate the shop was closed. Ten minutes later it emptied. The matrons made their purchases, and the mother decided against hers.

"Good call," Daffy said as the young woman left without anything except her sons. She smiled tiredly, as if she and Daffy shared a secret, and pushed the little boys out the door.

The moment it closed Daffy turned to Fantôme. "I'm a psychologist." She handed him her business card. "I have a teenage client. She's missing, and I'm afraid it might have some-thing to do with voodoo. I hope you can help."

"You overestimate what I know. Before I opened the Sanctuary, I owned a pet shop on the West Bank. When the city took over the block, and I had to close, nobody wanted Dart. Either I had to keep him or turn him loose. And I couldn't make myself dump him in a marsh somewhere."

"Dart? The snake?"

"For his tongue. Darts in and out, in and out." He demonstrated.

She winced. "You opened the Sanctuary so you had a reason to keep your snake?"

"I opened the Sanctuary because I'm a good business man. I had the snake. My grandmother practiced the old ways, so I knew enough to start. Eminent domain paid enough that I took the money from the pet store and opened here. Dart and I have done well. But I have few genuine connections."

"Connections?"

"Serious voodoo practitioners go elsewhere. This shop is for tourists. Our rituals are for tourists. You must have seen that. Althea helps me because I pay her well. She's a serious practitioner, but she views our ceremonies the way the minister of a large, urban church views a country revival. People come, they listen, they may take away a little religion and their interest might be piqued for the real thing." He shrugged. "Nobody's hurt."

Daffy remembered that Althea was Mama Mambo's given name. "I've seen Althea speaking with some of my teenage clients. But she refused to help me figure out what's going on with them." She paraphrased Corrinda. "I'm worried she may be a bad influence, or even worse."

Fantôme looked puzzled.

"You trust her?" Skeeter asked.

"Althea? She does no harm and never would. For her, voudou is restoring balance in herself and the world. She takes her religion seriously. Yes, I trust her, because not to would mean I believe she's a fake. She's completely genuine."

"I need her help," Daffy said.

"If she won't help, she has her reasons."

Daffy was stumped, but Skeeter wasn't. "Fantôme, do you know a woman named Corrinda Saizan?"

Daffy could feel the air change. Fantôme drew himself from a casual slump to his full height. His sudden tension was palpable. She knew if she touched his arm it would feel like iron.

"You do," she said. All her hopes for Natalie's future curled into a little ball and quietly expired. "Please help us. She's involved in this somehow."

He was silent so long Daffy thought that again, he wasn't going to answer. Then his sigh was like the hissing of his snake. "How do you know that name?"

"I've spoken to her." Daffy couldn't say more. Confidentiality was shredded as it was. "I'm suspicious for good reason."

"Sometimes it's better to leave well enough alone. Better not to know or be involved."

"I'm afraid I am involved. And I need help."

Silence again, then another sigh. "I will deny this. You understand?"

"We have no reason to tell anyone you helped us." Skeeter sounded calm, sure of himself, even compassionate, but Daffy knew him well enough to realize he also felt angry for Natalie.

Fantôme looked away as he spoke. "Corrinda is a powerful woman with a large following. Some people call her a witch. I don't throw that word around myself, but she's rumored to use any means to establish and keep her followers, including poison, brainwashing and threats of curses and death. She does readings, works spells and then for enough money, lifts them in the rooms above her shop. She preys on the weak, and her followers earn special gris-gris if they send someone to her."

"A voodoo Ponzi scheme." Skeeter still sounded casual, as if this was merely interesting.

"Why haven't you reported her?" Daffy tried for the same tone, but she knew she hadn't succeeded when Fantôme winced.

"I have no proof. I hear rumors. I can't go to the police and tell them I heard this or that. The serious practitioners may not buy their supplies here, but they waste no time letting me know who to avoid and why, for everyone's good. And Althea has told me a little."

"Why doesn't...Althea stop her?"

"She would have to tell you, herself. But if I had to guess? Perhaps she isn't certain she's strong enough. Dark magic, evil magic." He shook his head. "Good doesn't always triumph against it."

Daffy tried to imagine fragile Jewel caught up in this. And Natalie? If she turned on her aunt, Natalie had so much to lose. Her hopes that someone loved her enough to take care of her. Her chance to leave foster care. No matter what, the girl would protect Corrinda.

Only somehow, despite everything, Natalie had created the picture they'd seen today. She had sent them a message in the only way she could. The woman with her back turned and arms raised was Corrinda. Daffy wondered why it had taken this long to make that connection.

"I don't know anything more," Fantôme said. "Except one possibility that may or may not be helpful."

"And?" Skeeter asked.

"It's St. John's Eve. She'll celebrate a ritual tonight. I can assure you she won't miss this opportunity. I don't bother because tourists don't know what this night means or care, and besides, we're done across the lake until the fall. My customers want their voodoo when it's cooler, and there are fewer bugs. But if you can find Corrinda's gathering and find *her*, you might find answers. Let me warn you, though. You have to be careful. She's dangerous. That's why nobody wants to report her. When it comes down to it? We turn away. We stay well and... alive."

Skeeter nodded toward the door, and Daffy silently agreed they were finished here. They thanked Fantôme, and he followed them to flip the sign. The store was officially open again.

Business as usual.

As they drove to Skeeter's to pick up Daffy's car, the sun was already falling slowly toward the horizon. Traffic was light, and petals from the last magnolia blossoms drifted to sidewalks in a light breeze.

"Fantôme's not a bad guy," Skeeter said. "But I can guarantee that one reason he doesn't turn in Corrinda is because she shops there. She probably shops everywhere, spreads money at every voodoo shop in town, and those who know what she's doing conveniently look the other way."

"Would the cops care, anyway? Fantôme's probably right about that. Judging from the guys who took reports after my break-ins, voodoo is so much mumbo-jumbo."

"I think Corrinda's to blame for the break-ins."

Daffy had been wondering. "Why?"

"Think about your connections to her."

"Natalie, and probably Jewel."

"Was she trying to scare you for some reason?"

That didn't make sense to Daffy. Scare her to do what? Unless Corrinda had more in store for her. "She wanted me to leave town?"

"I doubt it. She didn't put enough energy into it. She would have burned down your house, or had you jumped at a streetcar stop."

"Maybe she hoped I'd tell the girls what happened. But why?

And if she knows anything about therapy, she must realize I wouldn't share my personal life with them."

They had arrived at Skeeter's house, and both got out. "Larry's bill is inside," Skeeter said. "One-third now, and the rest when he gets the final part and gives the car a complete bill of health. I'll take your check to him on Monday."

"Am I going to faint?"

"You love the car, right?"

She did. And she was going to love owning a car again, too, although she'd have to call Nelson now and then for old time's sake.

Inside Skeeter's house she studied the invoice and didn't faint after all. "It seems perfectly fair." She dug in her handbag for her checkbook and a pen, wrote the check and left it on Skeeter's counter. She had money in savings for a car. She'd been squirreling it away since Esme's demise. She might be sentimental, but she was smart, too.

In his kitchen Skeeter was opening and closing cabinet doors. "I've got filé for the gumbo. You're sure you don't want me to bring my other herbs? Yours aren't a million years old?"

"Practically new. Possibly unopened even." Her mind was elsewhere. "Do we have time for this? We need to find out where Corrinda's whatever-you-want-to-call-it is going to be held tonight. We need to find Natalie and Jewel."

"We'll work on it at your house while we finish the gumbo. We'll think better if we take a break. I'll grab some po'boys on the way back to tide us over. I have your food list. I'll meet you there."

She considered making one more stop at Bountiful Beauty, but decided she didn't want to confront Corrinda without Skeeter, or possibly a police escort.

Back at her house, she was sorry to note there was no teenager waiting on her porch. Inside, while she waited for

Skeeter, she pondered what else she could do. And then she knew.

She couldn't exactly look up Mama Mambo under Voodoo Queens, but she did have a Metairie phone book. She tried to remember Mama's last name. "First name Althea. Last name...Edison?" There were no Althea Edisons or anything close in the phone book. As she was closing it she realized she'd remembered the wrong scientist. She looked up Darwin and found an A. Darwin on Poinsettia. She dialed the number immediately.

"Mama, this is Daphne Brookes. My friend Skeeter and I were—"

Sitting on the edge of her seat, she listened to the voice on the other end of the line. She'd expected the other woman to refuse to help, but the moment Mama Mambo drew a breath, she pressed on.

"Fantôme has nothing but complimentary things to say about you. And I desperately need your help. A girl's—no, two girls' futures are at stake. I think they've being victimized by Corrinda Saizan. I—"

The line went dead. She tried the number again, but she got a busy signal.

She was staring at the telephone when Skeeter knocked. She let him in and told him about her latest failure.

"We'll talk while I cook."

She followed him into the kitchen, where he was setting po'boys on the counter. "I just have this awful feeling we have to get this squared away tonight. St. John's Eve sounds important, and Corrinda won't waste a dramatic opportunity like this one."

"I made a couple of calls after you left. I'm putting out feelers. Right now there's nothing else we can do. We'll cook and eat. Start on your po'boy."

The first one she unwrapped was obviously hers. No seafood.

Slices of rare roast beef, plain bread, lettuce, no tomatoes–a po'boy sin–mayonnaise in a little plastic cup.

"I didn't see anything about mayo on the diet," Skeeter said.

"I think I'm supposed to use a tiny bit and monitor how I feel. Thanks for being thoughtful."

"You actually wish I'd ignored the list and bought you what I'm eating."

She opened his before she answered. It was identical to the first. Her eyes filled, and she blinked away tears and tried to remember another man, any man, who had been this thoughtful. "This isn't what you wanted, is it?"

"Do you think I'm going to eat something luscious and unforgettable in front of you? Besides, the place where I go roasts their own beef, so you're going to love it. We'll both survive."

She went to stand behind him and wrapped her arms around his waist, resting her cheek against his back. "My life isn't giving you much time for your life, is it? When was the last time you worked in your studio?"

He turned and framed her face in his hands. She thought he was going to say something profound, something to rock her world. But he only looked deep into her eyes and said, "Silly woman."

He kissed her lightly then dropped his hands. "Gumbo lesson. Get the meat, okay? We'll season and brown the chicken with the sausage before we add both to the pot."

She got both and brought them to the stove. He had assembled all the herbs. He rinsed the chicken breasts, patted them dry, then set them on a plate and began to sprinkle oregano. To her chagrin, nothing came out of the shaker top.

"Fresh, huh? It feels like cement in here." He shook harder.

"Really, they are fresh. I'm sure I've used oregano, but check anyway to see if the jar is sealed."

He flipped off the shaker top and looked inside. "Not sealed, but the holes are clogged."

"Would an herb spoil that fast? It's been sealed tight, and it's only been open maybe two months."

He didn't answer. Then, without saying anything he reached for the next herb, unscrewed the lid and tried to shake out the contents. Again, when nothing emerged he flipped off the shaker top and looked inside. He did the same thing with the remaining two jars from her shelf. He stood looking at everything, then he looked at her.

"Daffy, you haven't been using these, right? Not in the last month or so?"

She shook her head.

"And what *did* you use in this kitchen? What did you cook with? Drink? What are you avoiding because the doctor told you not to eat or drink anything you'd had recently?"

Her stomach was beginning to tie itself into a knot. She had a feeling she knew where he was going. "I ate toast. I drank a lot of tea, different kinds. The special blends I buy in the Quarter. I've drunk the same ones for ages..."

She stopped as he pulled down one of the canisters and took off the top. Then he held it out to her. "Look carefully. Do you notice anything different in here? Anything you don't normally see when you make a cup or a pot?"

She started to point out that she didn't routinely dissect tea any more than he dissected coffee grounds, but she knew better. The truth as obvious as the small brown chunks laced throughout the mixture. Chunks she never would have thought twice about because she *didn't* dissect anything, and even if she had, she wouldn't have noticed a foreign substance among all the herbs and tiny flowers. She scooped tea into a ball without thinking about it. She sprinkled herbs without considering what else might be mixed in with them.

He grabbed a spoon, dug around and lifted up one of the

larger chunks. Then he showed her the oregano, tilting it so she could see clearly. "Same stuff."

"I'm trying hard not to understand." But she was afraid she did. She needed to take time and think, but even doing a quick assessment, she realized that she'd often felt worse after drinking one of her special tea blends. She'd thought she had a virus, so she'd forced herself to hydrate. Over and over.

Skeeter was watching her expression. "We're dumping the gumbo. Don't eat or drink anything in this house until we can have this substance analyzed." He didn't say why.

He didn't have to. She said it for him. "Someone was trying to poison me. The first break-in. The food on the counter..."

"You probably interrupted whoever did it while they were adding this–" He shrugged. "This *stuff* where it wouldn't be detected. That's why food was still out."

"Milk and bread."

"Whoever did this was trying to be thorough. For all I know whatever you've been poisoned with may have been steeping all this time in the oil we used for the roux."

"That's why I've been sick."

"I'd say great chance. We're calling Sam."

"Nobody's going to believe it, Skeeter. It's so preposterous."

"The proof is in the oregano. And the tea and the pepper. We'll pay to have every bit of food analyzed if we have to. You'll need to be able to tell your doctor what you've been ingesting. He'll probably want to do more tests."

She'd felt so much better, but now she felt sick, and not from whatever they'd found. "Corrinda?" she said. "The day she braided my hair she used a rose scented spray on it. She said she makes her own products. She told me her grandmother taught her about plants and herbs."

Skeeter pulled her into his arms. "I'd say Corrinda was an A+ pupil."

CHAPTER 17

S am was down on Bayou Midnight visiting his family for the weekend. After Daffy had wasted no time asking for Sam directly, Antoinette had apologized but explained she had no way to reach him.

"He's on a fishing trip with his uncle and cousins. I'd leave a message with Leonce's wife, Didi, but she and the baby are visiting her parents in Pierre Part. I usually go along and spend the day down there because Gus is so adorable. But something about smelling fish and dirty diapers..." Antoinette's voice trailed off.

"Sit down, because you aren't going to believe this." Daffy launched into the shortest explanation she could, not deterred by what sounded like a horrified gasp on the other end of the line.

Once Daffy had finished Antoinette spoke quickly. "Sam will call when they get back, and I'll tell him immediately. It might be two hours, but it might be four. Depends on where they went and what they caught. Meantime I'm calling his partner. Either he'll come or he'll know the right person to send. This is just so hard to believe. You're feeling okay? You're not feeling sick?"

Daffy assured her that she'd been careful about what she'd eaten since the hospital stay, including, as ordered, not eating or drinking anything she'd ingested since the headaches began. She was fine. Of course, that was more evidence that her pantry had been tampered with.

"And Corrinda," Antoinette said. "I'm so ashamed. I should have been smarter."

"We're charter members of the same club. Can you think of any place Natalie might go to hide out?"

"Wherever Jewel is?"

Daffy couldn't see that. Yet wasn't it possible that all Natalie's hostility toward Jewel had simply been guilt? By now Daffy was putting more pieces together, and she had to admit that Natalie was the best possible link between Corrinda and the girls at Riverview.

Corrinda, who had been the one to help Natalie get a scholarship to the academy in the first place.

She finished the conversation and hung up to face Skeeter. "She's going to call Sam's partner."

"Don't get your hopes up. He's a new guy, young and full of himself. Sam's not enthusiastic."

An hour later Daffy left the kitchen behind Sam's partner, a young man with a shaved head and pug dog features, who had taken notes, taken samples, and taken no time at all telling them that he didn't see how they could prove their theory, even if the criminalistics unit found poison. "Anybody could have put it there," he said as he was walking out the door. "Even you."

"Sure. Because I've always wanted to die an inch at a time from my own spaghetti sauce," Daffy said.

"You can't even tell me where to find this Corrinda Saizan."

She exploded. "I tried to hang a bell around her neck, but she wouldn't cooperate."

"I'll talk to Sam when he comes back."

"Me first." She closed the door and stood with her back to it.

"A little sarcasm to lighten the mood?" Skeeter asked.

"I can't blame him, although I'm going to anyway. But he's right. Anybody could have put the poison there. Even if they search Bountiful Beauty and find the same brown stuff an inch deep on every surface, it still won't prove she was here spreading it around."

"Come here." He led her to the sofa and dropped down, pulling her beside him. He draped his arm over her shoulder. The feel of his body so close was a comfort, and the weight of his arm made her feel unexpectedly safe.

"This has to be part of a larger story," he said. "As major as it's been to you, it's only a chapter, maybe just a paragraph."

"I keep trying to work out the whole deal in my head. I realize that Natalie may be the link between Corrinda and Jewel, and possibly more girls at Riverview. I bet if we could talk to a counselor there, she might admit voodoo's come up in sessions with students."

"Maybe," Skeeter said, "but apparently not Natalie's connection to it or Corrinda's. Because if names were mentioned, Corrinda would have been asked to discuss it, maybe with the police present. And Natalie would have been sent packing."

"We don't know that Corrinda wasn't called in—" she thought before she continued "—but probably not. Most likely the other girls are as terrified to talk about what's going on as Jewel is."

"Corrinda counts on secrecy. She'd have to. The moment these girls went to their parents and admitted what they were involved in—"

She shook her head. "We don't know what they're involved in, do we?"

She could almost hear Skeeter thinking. "If secrecy is primary to Corrinda, then wouldn't your therapy group be a threat? Who's more threatening than a psychologist trained to see through people? Your purpose is to get the girls to open up to each other. It's a safe place to tell secrets. They know whatever they say will remain confidential, at least on your end."

"You think she was trying to kill me so the group would fold? Wouldn't she know that somebody else would take over?"

"Yeah, but whoever did would have to start all over building trust, learning what you already knew. It would buy her time."

"That doesn't feel right. I think you said it before. If she wanted me dead, she would have killed me or hired a thug to do it. If she's the sociopath and manipulator Fantôme says she is, she probably has followers who would do the deed for free."

"So if not dead, then sick."

"Not just sick. Sick and steadily getting sicker. She didn't drop something nasty in a Coke when I wasn't looking. Whatever she used was distributed evenly through my food, like she hoped I'd swallow it over and over, get sick, stay sick." She shrugged. "Die slowly?"

"Illness kept you away from the girls, at least a few times."

"It worried them. They were upset." Daffy thought about it. "I've assumed they were upset because I'm an authority figure, somebody who shouldn't get sick, shouldn't be absent, should take care of them no matter what."

Skeeter thumped her shoulder. "No, they were upset because Corrinda warned them you had an illness and would grow sicker if they didn't help. And she was right."

For a moment she didn't see where he was going. It was so hard to believe, and yet everything fit. "You think she told them I was, what..?"

"Cursed, Daffy. The way Katie, Linda's friend was cursed."

"You think Linda's involved?"

"No. But I'm betting that Katie went to Riverview Academy, too. We know she went to a voodoo ceremony without Linda. They fought, and for Linda that was the end of voodoo as well as

Katie's friendship. But maybe Katie attended anyway, with some of the other girls from school. And it wasn't long after that she died."

"You're not saying Corrinda killed her? Please tell me you aren't."

"No, but what if Corrinda knew Katie was sick, so she got Natalie to entice her to one of her gatherings? Let's say that somehow, Corrinda knew about Katie's illness, even before the girls did. Maybe Katie wasn't telling anybody herself. Maybe she went because she was hoping voodoo could cure her? It's the kind of thing a vulnerable teenager might try."

Daffy followed his train of thought. "If Corrinda's as powerful as Fantôme says she is, she probably has contacts all over the city. So it's not unlikely she has supporters at the hospital. They could have relayed test results, copied medical records. Or maybe it's simpler. Natalie told her aunt that Katie had missed a lot of school, or looked pale, or any number of things."

"However it happened, once they were in contact, Corrinda told the Riverview girls they had to come up with the money to help lift Katie's curse before it was too late. Of course they couldn't pay enough. So Katie died."

As far-fetched as it seemed, Daffy tried to imagine herself in Corrinda's world. "What a scam. She couldn't lose. If Katie had gotten better, Corrinda would have taken the credit. As it was she probably pretended to be devastated. Maybe she told them she had tried her best, but without the right gifts to whoever-or-whatever, there was nothing she could do. The curse was too strong. She couldn't lift it alone."

"Imagine the guilt. The girls didn't care enough. They didn't give enough. Only money would have showed the whoever-or-whatever that the girls wanted Katie to get well. So let's fast forward to Daffy Brookes, and the curse that's sapping her strength, her good health, her energy. The curse that, like Katie's, will kill her if a girl in the group doesn't come forward with enough money to lift it."

Daffy knew which girl. "Jewel. And we know Corrinda does Jewel's hair. And her mother's."

"So Jewel was the target, the reason Corrinda poisoned you. Does her family have money?"

"Tons." She remembered Natalie mentioning that in group.

"Corrinda probably showed Jewel photos of the candles she burned on your porch, the dirt mounds and the doll."

"The skull on my bed."

"Maybe even that. She would have looked helpful, worried, like she was trying her best."

"Nobody's going to believe this, Skeeter. I don't even believe it."

"No, but you don't *not* believe it, either."

As unbelievable as it seemed, everything was falling neatly into place. "What do you think will happen tonight? If there's a ritual going down somewhere? What's going to happen?"

"My guess? This isn't the only extortion racket Corrinda has going. So maybe Jewel will be at the gathering to present her offerings to lift your curse. But others will be there, too. Whatever *they've* been told, money will flow tonight, and it will flow from susceptible teenagers, and from other poor souls who are grieving or fearful."

"People who can't find answers anywhere else, or think they can't."

"Maybe Sam's partner's not excited about little brown chunks in your tea, but law enforcement might get excited about mass extortion."

"Do we get in touch again and tell him our theories?" Daffy couldn't imagine calling the same cocky newbie.

"No, we have to wait for Sam. Nobody else is going to take

this seriously fast enough. We don't have enough to go on, but he'll believe us."

"Antoinette can't even talk to him until he gets back from fishing. We're going to miss St. John's Eve. It could all be over by the time he calls her."

"We don't know where anything's happening, Daff. I know you want to find Jewel and Natalie, but we can't do anything until we know more. This woman is dangerous, and we need to let the police take over. Sam will know how to proceed."

She didn't want to wait. The girls were so vulnerable, and knowing what she thought she did, she felt duty bound to protect them from Corrinda. Jewel had been frightened enough to take her grandmother's jewelry, probably to try to block Daffy's curse. But without a destination, Daffy was powerless.

Skeeter got up and held out his hand. "Come to my house. My food's not contaminated. There's nothing we can do here that we can't do there. And you'll be safer."

She let him pull her up. "I doubt Corrinda's planning to work more black magic on me, at least not immediately. If we're right, she's done what she set out to. She scared Jewel into taking the jewelry. It's probably in a pawn shop right now, and if she hasn't given Corrinda the money yet, she'll do it tonight."

"I still think you'd be safer at my house."

"I can't go, Skeeter. Jewel has this address. Tonight is so pivotal. Maybe she'll come here first, hoping I can help her resist."

"You can leave a note on the door and tell her we'll pick her up."

Daffy had taped notes to the door every time she'd left the house, but each time she'd come home to find them unread. "I can't take the chance. That's one step too many for a girl in that kind of turmoil, too much time to change her mind. I've already been away too much. What if she's already come and gone?"

He didn't look happy. "It's your call. I'll get what I need and come back. I'm not leaving you alone until this is over. I'll bring food, too. In the meantime, I wouldn't move anything or throw away anything in your cabinets. Not yet, in case the police come back for a more thorough investigation. I'll bring basics."

"Don't worry about the diet. I think I can safely eat anything now. Nothing's off limits unless Corrinda got to it first."

"The po'boys I bought will be safe, either way. Eat if you're hungry. I'll eat mine when I get back."

She wanted to tell him she would be fine without him, that he didn't have to go to all that trouble. Dependence scared her almost as much as Corrinda Saizan. But the words wouldn't push their way out. She had to be truthful. She wanted him here. Not just because she was scared, but because he, well, he was Skeeter.

He kissed her quickly, then reminded her to lock the door behind him.

In the kitchen she got down two plates and set the sandwiches on them. Like many people in the city who didn't trust the local water supply, she had drinking water delivered. Was it possible that Corrinda had found a way to tamper with her dispenser, too? She remembered the bottles of cold water in the refrigerator, but she inspected first, before she took a bottle and her po'boy out to the side gallery to eat.

She was just settling down to start when the telephone rang. Hoping it was Antoinette with news of Sam, she raced inside and grabbed it on the fourth ring.

"Is this the psychologist Daphne Brookes?"

She recognized the voice immediately. "Mama Mambo?"

"Corrinda Saizan has nothing to do with voudou. You understand that? She represents evil. She be practicing evil."

"Teenagers can't make that kind of distinction."

"I will help you."

Daffy had to know why. Mama had been so determined not

to be involved until now. "I need your help, but why wouldn't you help me before?"

"Because I was not sure I was strong enough. And I still am not. Bad can be made worse."

"And good can be made better."

"Whatever the outcome, the answers I have sought are now clear. I can no longer sit by and do nothing. This is why I be calling you. She will be far out of the city tonight, though. If we don't leave immediately, we won't be able to find her."

"We?"

"You must drive. When we get close I will need to speak on the phone with a man who can give me exact directions and landmarks. He prefers to speak Creole and only to me. You have a car?"

"My friend Skeeter can drive."

"Then you must come immediately. You remember where I be living? I will be outside waiting. Wear white." She hung up.

Daffy called Skeeter's cell, but he didn't answer. She tried again and left a message, running into her bedroom to change. She ignored the sun dress she'd worn the first day she met Skeeter, because she bet the voodoo gathering would be outdoors and buggy. Instead she changed into a white blouse and long skirt that she usually wore as a beach covering. She screwed her hair into a knot on top of her head and grabbed a white scarf to cover it.

She took more water bottles from the refrigerator, bundled up her sandwich and Skeeter's, added insect repellant to the bag, and then called him again.

This time he answered, and she told him the basics, ending with a question. "Do you want to leave from your house or pick me up?"

He was silent so long she knew something was wrong. "We

can't do this, Daffy," he said at last. "It's suspicious, and at this point we have to involve the cops. I know you want to–"

"Skeeter! Fantôme vouched for Mama. She's going to help. She said Corrinda is evil, and she wants to stop her. We have to get there to help Natalie and Jewel. I know they'll be there, too. I feel responsible for them."

"If you show up, you could put everybody in danger, most of all yourself. It's better to wait. Please wait."

Anger blazed through her. Anger at the situation. At Corrinda for making her question her own sanity. At Sam's partner for refusing to take her story seriously. At Sam, himself, for leaving town.

But now most of all at Skeeter, for not seeing what had to be done. She had begun to depend on him, and now he had proved what she'd always known. Relationships, like revenge, were best served cold. She'd been wrong to let him so near her heart. She had forgotten how easy it was to get ensnared in someone else's life, to everyone's detriment.

She forced herself to sound calmer than she felt. "No problem. We'll go without you then. This is my battle, my mess to fix, and I knew better than to involve you. But I did, and I'm sorry."

"Daffy, please don't go."

"I am not in this world to live up to your expectations, and you are not in this world to live up to mine."

"What in the hell is that?"

She'd said it without thinking, like a meditation mantra. "Something called the Gestalt prayer, and it's the way I've chosen to live my life. We both have to do what we think is right, Skeeter. This time we just can't meet in the middle."

"You know what? I know this is all going too fast, but I love you. That should be clear by now. Doesn't loving you give me more clout than a motto that discounts both our feelings?"

"Love is never about ownership."

"You don't know me better than that? I'm not trying to own you. Love is a commitment two people make to listen to each other."

"I've listened. I don't agree. I'll let you know what happens tonight." She hung up.

She didn't want to take the VW since it didn't yet have a clean bill of health. She knew the little car would make it to Bucktown, and from there she hoped that Mama Mambo had a more dependable one Daffy could drive instead. Either way she had to take the risk.

For a long moment she stood there, paralyzed, wondering if Skeeter was right, as well as wondering how, in the heat of anger, she could have written off his advice, and by doing so, possibly written off their relationship.

Because they did have a relationship, even if she had problems with the word. And the thought of not having him in her life pierced her heart.

She reached for the telephone again to call him back, but her hand hovered over it, then clenched at her side. In a minute she had the bag she'd assembled under one arm and her handbag in the other. She was going to see this whole thing through to conclusion, no matter what price she had to pay.

CHAPTER 18

Mama Mambo had a brand-new car, but unfortunately it was still on its way from the assembly plant. Her old one had given up the ghost, and she had left it at the dealer's as a trade-in. The new one wasn't due to be delivered until next week.

"No problem, we'll take mine," Daffy offered, hoping that whatever Larry hadn't yet fixed was just pesky and minor, like a lazy windshield wiper or poor shock absorbers.

She expected to head west around the lake in the same direction she'd traveled with Skeeter to Fantôme's bonfire. Mama Mambo directed her that way at first, but then they dropped away from the lake toward bayou country. Out of urban New Orleans and its outlying communities, they drove over bridges, some vintage and some nothing more than another stretch of road. Daffy paid close attention to speed limits in small villages, then sped past refineries and rundown industrial complexes. Patches of reeds alternating with thick stands of trees separated them from stretches of water and mobile and modular homes. Pickup trucks sat under the shade of banana trees, one adorned by an egret, like a living hood ornament. The live oaks looked as if they were older than human habitation.

An hour and a half into the trip the car was still purring, so Daffy was optimistic. They had turned on to a rural road outside of Donaldsonville, and Mama had called her mysterious connection to get directions for the next leg. Daffy wished that Skeeter was with her to make sure the fluent Creole flowing from the passenger seat was actually Mama firming up where to turn rather than a plot to leave Daffy by the roadside to trudge through the thick Louisiana night back to civilization.

That was the least of the reasons she wished Skeeter was with her.

By now the sun had fallen behind cypress trees, mirrored in patches of swamp along a two-lane road. Despite eating her po'boy as she drove and passing the other to Mama Mambo, she was hungry and hoping for a rest room. Mama had been vague about how long it would take to get to their destination, but Daffy thought they were making good time.

What passed for a convenience store appeared in the distance at a crossroads with absolutely nothing else around, and she made a quick stop. The establishment had one gas pump and a wide selection of something called crankbait for bass fishermen. The boudin sausage advertised on the sign board was already gone, and while the boiled crawfish smelled delicious, Daffy couldn't very well peel it, pinch the tail and suck the head in true Louisiana style while she was driving.

She settled for a visit to a restroom carpeted with used paper towels, and after washing her hands and using sanitizer for a bonus round, she bought a pack of peanuts and a cup of thick black coffee.

Mama had been mostly silent other than giving instructions, but when Daffy pulled back on the road, she spoke. "I will tell you about Corrinda. Because you trust me and haven't asked me to prove myself."

Mama launched into a series of stories guaranteed to kink Daffy's hair–if the humidity hadn't already worked its magic. Corrinda's activities were everything she and Skeeter had guessed and worse. Extortion. Healing followers who were terrified by false visions of their death. Causing other followers to fall into actual physical decline.

"She poisoned me," Daffy said, describing her symptoms.

"You are not the first. They say she knows evil uses for many herbs and plants. Devil's cherry. Wormwood. Hen bane. Mushrooms that induce unwanted visions."

Hallucinogenic mushrooms, which might, when chopped, dry into tiny brown chunks.

"I thought I was losing my mind," Daffy said.

"But you be fortunate, child. If Corrinda had wanted you dead, it would have been easy."

Daffy shuddered as Mama continued her explanation. The women who worked for Corrinda routinely passed on information about their clients, who, in the confessional atmosphere of the salon, often chatted about troubled home lives. Corrinda then "helped" by prescribing her own oils or special candles, and promising to lift curses or soothe troubled marriages with her charms and secret rituals.

"She tells her followers they are impure, that only she can purify them, but at a great cost," Mama said. "You understand what I be saying? She promises that all the money will go to the community for good deeds, but, of course, she keeps it. It be the worst of her crimes, because she only pretends. She makes no real attempt to help, only to steal from others and hurt them. When she dies, for her crimes against the innocent, she will remain forever on earth, an evil spirit who will never make her way to heaven."

"That doesn't sound like a good thing for the rest of us."

"No, and on St. John's Eve, evil spirits be most active."

"And evil humans."

Mama made a noise of agreement. "Some people believe Corrinda killed her own sister, Lissa. She told everyone her sister was bad, and that she left her baby daughter with their parents and disappeared. But others say that cannot be true, that Lissa tried to expose Corrinda for what she be doing. Then one day she vanished. They say she would never have abandoned that little girl, that she was a good mother and loved her."

Daffy thought about Natalie, who so badly needed someone to love her now. Then she thought of everything Skeeter had said, everything Daffy had ignored.

She should have listened. Wasn't it warning enough that Corrinda had poisoned her? At what point had she left common sense behind and taken off on a fool's mission? If they found tonight's gathering, how would she stop a powerhouse like Corrinda? Daffy would be surrounded by the woman's followers, either too blindly loyal or frightened to intervene. And why had she believed she could help Natalie, who would be under the direct influence of her aunt tonight?

Asked to choose between Daffy and Corrinda, the choice would not be hard.

Why had she done it? She was a psychologist, and knowing why was important. Certainly out of fear for Jewel and Natalie. That was true. But how much of this trip was about pushing Skeeter away, about proving her independence? About closing the door on love because it frightened her so badly?

She slapped her palm against the steering wheel, furious that she had allowed her past to control her. Her job was to help others avoid exactly that. Through the years, she'd been careful to hide the depth of her own insecurities from herself and from the many supervisors who had trained her and watched her progress.

She had taken her own troubled childhood and created a secure kingdom where commitment wasn't expected, where she could feel safe and nobody would have to pretend to love her.

Or worse.

I am not in this world to live up to your expectations.

She had latched on to a motto and made it her road map.

"You're angry at what I've said?" Mama asked.

"No, I'm angry at myself. We should have waited for the police to help. What are we going to do if we find Corrinda?"

"We will find her." Mama folded her arms. "We be turning soon, and I will need to call my friend one more time. This is not the moment to change your mind. Everything is unfolding exactly the way it should. Trust me."

Daffy wasn't sure about trust, but sometimes it was too late to turn back, even when a devastating mistake hovered in the future. She could call Skeeter and throw herself on his mercy. She could give him her location and ask for his help, but she had slammed that door so tight she doubted she could pry it open again. Sam's partner was a loss, and Antoinette had Daffy's number and would call as soon as she spoke to Sam himself. They were so close, and Jewel and Natalie might well be waiting around the next bend. Despite all her qualms, Daffy kept driving.

Skeeter hadn't had time to debate whether to follow Daffy or not. He wasn't big on swooping in to rescue damsels in distress. Daffy was smart and courageous, and she could take care of herself in almost any situation.

Except a situation like this one, where anybody who was still breathing needed backup. Man, woman, soldier, spy.

Backup.

Since Daffy might recognize his car, he called Joshua and

asked if they could switch. Joshua, a big man who looked more like a prize fighter than a minister or psychologist, drove right over, swapped the Jeep keys for his Toyota Land Cruiser and didn't even ask why. He took one look at Skeeter's face and shook his head.

"Antoinette's colleague? Daffy?"

"What? You guys sit around and discuss my love life?"

"Maggie and Antoinette do. Sam and I smile and nod."

Skeeter left immediately and waited at a gas station near the interstate in Bucktown, hoping he hadn't missed her. The VW passed just moments later, and he fell in behind her on I-10, then switched to a different lane driving without incident for more than an hour. Once she exited to a smaller road, he stayed farther behind, but since the roads weren't particularly busy, he was able to keep her in sight. He pulled up and waited on the other side of the convenience store when she went inside. She was completely oblivious, and he took the time to call Antoinette and tell her what to tell Sam when she heard from him.

Now she turned again, to a two-lane road with a thick oak canopy that swallowed the VW and its rear lights. He turned, too, and thought he glimpsed her ahead. Debating whether to move closer, he decided he had to or he might lose her. He drew closer, but not so close she might wonder why his car didn't pass. By now she was slowing. He didn't know if she was looking for yet another road, or if she was just being cautious, since the sky was almost fully dark and stars had yet to appear.

Skeeter wasn't sure what he would do when he got wherever they were going. He could watch from the woods–if there were woods–and keep an eye on things, then leave when he knew everyone was safe. He figured there was maybe a one percent chance of tonight playing out that way. It was certainly too late at this point to ask her, once again, to change her mind. The best bet would be for them to strategize together, but Daffy had been clear she didn't need his help. Or him.

Not that the last part had been much of a surprise. She'd warned him more than once, but their relationship was still young. They were so good together, better than good, that he'd believed he could change her mind. He'd lied to himself before, but he'd thought by now he was smarter.

Lost in thought, he also lost sight of the car. For a moment he thought Daffy had turned off on another road. Then, slowing to a crawl so he could search both sides, he realized she hadn't turned at all. At least she hadn't turned to another road. She was just ahead, where she had pulled to a stop on the heavily wooded shoulder. He was fast coming up on her.

He debated strategy. She wouldn't recognize Joshua's Toyota. He could pass and pull off at the next drive, watch for her and follow again. But if he did, he risked losing her completely. If she had simply made a wrong turn and was planning to head back the way they'd come, he'd be too far away to see and follow.

Of course, she might be stopping to switch drivers, or get something out of the back, or clarify directions, too.

When he was nearly upon her, she stepped out and went around to the back of the car, unlatched and lifted what Larry had called the "deck lid" to view the engine. Her hands were on her hips, and she stared, as if she expected the car to say something helpful.

Car trouble.

At least now his decision had been made for him. He passed, pulled over and got out to walk back and see what he could do.

Daffy looked up when he approached. She'd been so intent on checking the engine that she'd completely ignored the passing car. She looked stunned to see him, and her smile was tentative.

"Fancy meeting you here." He went to stand beside her.

"Either you've been following me, or somebody told you where Corrinda's gathering is tonight."

"What's the problem?"

She craned her neck and looked down the road to the place he had parked. "Whose car is that?"

"Joshua's." He repeated his question. "What's the problem?"

"We stalled."

He looked up as Mama Mambo got out and came around the car. "You decided to come," she said. "Luck is with us."

"I'm no car mechanic." Skeeter stuck his head under the lid. "These things are supposed to be easy to fix, if you know what you're doing. I don't."

"Esmerelda stalled exactly the same way. Some of the time I could restart and off I'd go. More times, not. And you were right about tonight, Skeeter, and I wasn't, if that makes any difference to you."

"It's never about who's right, Daff. But that's over. Now we have to figure out what to do with this car."

She sighed. "Do you have a flashlight?"

"You know what? I would have had flashlights, lanterns, maybe even night vision goggles, if I'd had time to prepare before I had to dash out the door."

He left, opened the back of the Toyota, and lifted out a plastic box marked "emergency." He returned. "Supermom Maggie. There's probably everything from juice boxes to spare parts in here." He folded back the lid, dug around and found a flashlight the size of a ballpoint pen. He handed it to her. "I hope you know what to do with this."

"Sometimes with Esme the problem had to do with the distributor cap."

"Larry said something about a solenoid."

"Isn't that something you catch during flu season?" When he

didn't smile she ducked her head under the lid. "I'll check the distributor cap. Maybe it's loose." She leaned in, as if she knew exactly what she was doing. "I don't want to unhook anything because I could get the order wrong when I re-hook. When I had Esme I marked the lines going into the cap with nail polish because. . ." She fell silent for so long he wondered if she was meditating. Or praying.

She backed up and put her palms to her cheeks. "I don't believe it."

"Same problem?"

"Same car! This is Esme. My Esme. Esmerelda Van Winking. I marked each connection with a different color, and all the marks are still there. It's impossible somebody else would have done that exactly the same way."

"Larry rescues cars from the junkyard. Apparently, he rescued yours."

She sniffed, as if she was swallowing tears. "Same car. I love this car."

He looked away, refusing to react. "You can jump up and down another time, okay? What do you plan to do now? Can you fix the problem?"

"Probably not. I tried to restart before you showed up. A couple of times. No luck. Once Esme starts to stall, she repeats a few times, and then nothing. She might start tomorrow." She paused. "Or not." She looked at him. "Aren't you going to say I told you so?"

"*Larry* told you. I just relayed his message. Let's push the car into the trees. You can have it towed back to Larry's tomorrow, unless the car decides to play nice by then. With luck nobody will come along and steal or strip it in the meantime."

"Strip it?"

Anger flashed through him, but only for a moment. There was no point in feeling anything. He'd taken a risk, and it hadn't ended well. He'd known what he might be in for, and now he had to cut his losses as quickly as possible.

He waited until he could keep his tone even, if not friendly. "I can't help what might happen. It's reality. We can do our best to hide your car. Or we can call for a tow truck and wait what will probably be hours for somebody to show up. But if you have another place to be, you might consider my suggestion. It's totally up to you."

"If I have another place to be?"

"Do you know where you're going?" he asked Mama.

"It's not so much farther now."

"Then I'll take you. Or not. Why don't the two of you talk it over and let me know when you've made a decision. In the meantime I'll get Joshua's car in position so we can nudge the car up to the tree line. We'll have to push it by hand from that point on. If that's what you want to do."

"What do you think we should do?" Daffy asked.

He debated among several answers, none of them kind. Then he shrugged. "I'll leave you to decide. Let me know."

Mama and Skeeter sat in the front of the Toyota, and Daffy sat in the back. "Have you been to this place before?" Skeeter asked Mama.

"It is not a good place. My friend, he told me its history. At the end of the eighteenth century there was a sugar plantation here, with enslaved men and women who were badly treated. The plantation owner died mysteriously, as did the overseer who cared so little for his workers. After their deaths the wife sold every man, woman and child who had worked for her, except for three of the house servants. These women simply disappeared, although they would have been valuable. Many say they were hanged, that they had poisoned both men, and the wife demanded vengeance. After the mourning period she hired a new overseer, bought more people to do the work and treated them badly, too, but from that moment on, the plantation failed. Neither she nor her children after her could succeed. The land and the house were cursed by the hanged women. It fell to ruin."

Daffy was already on edge, and the story didn't improve her state of mind. She had no idea if anything about it was true, but she knew that simply by telling it, a mood had been set and perceptions of the simplest events changed. In the eighteenth century, food poisoning had been common, and antibiotics hadn't yet been discovered. Scarlet fever, measles, appendicitis— any number of other illnesses that were now uncommon or treatable —had felled many, and it was likely the two men had fallen prey to one or the other. Ignorance had killed the three women.

"The land's not in use today?" she asked, leaning forward to be heard.

"My friend grows the sugar cane. He says that the biologists claim their new varieties of cane will prevail over rust and smut, and so they be experimenting here. But the cane on this land is always stunted and diseased. There is talk of an archeological dig next summer, so there was activity here in the spring as they surveyed. Some people hunt on the land or fish in the small lake, but others, they be afraid to come."

"But not Corrinda," Skeeter said.

Skeeter had been so quiet, Daffy was surprised to hear him speak. She wished she was sitting beside him, that she could find a way to tell him how badly she had overreacted. But when had overreacting begun? From the moment she'd realized he was going to be more to her than she wanted him to? Had she begun pushing him away before she even opened her arms?

There was no time to look inward. Mama said something to

him that Daffy couldn't hear, and Skeeter made a sharp right turn.

Large signs reading "no trespassing" hung on both sides of the road, but a gate that should have barred their way was wide open. They drove through it.

"What are we going to do when we get there?" Daffy asked.

"We are there, child," Mama said. "And we will know when we see the situation." She pointed to an area thick with trees, palmetto and other scrub. "We should park where we can get away quickly, and where your car can be hidden."

"My thoughts exactly." Skeeter had already turned off the headlights. He pulled to the side of the road, but not into the scrub. He opened his door with the engine running and jumped down, rounded the car and disappeared a moment, then came back and began backing into the area he'd just examined, inching slowly backward until the bumper nudged a tree.

"Anyone who looks will still find it, but it won't be easily visible." He turned off the engine. "Show time."

Mama Mambo didn't open her door. "The St. John's Eve ritual is held in the old cemetery, where the enslaved workers be buried. I warn you, it may not be easy to get to. My friend told me it's on an island in the lake. They buried people there because they did not want their families to be visiting them. You understand?"

"That seems like a detail you could have shared earlier," Daffy said.

"It was the last thing my friend told me. He wanted us to come, so he spilled his information drop by drop. He lives not far away, and he knows the evil things that Corrinda be doing here on St. John's Eve. He says Assumption Parish will be best rid of her."

"And he wants us to do the dirty work."

"I have the power," Mama said, as if she was admitting she could train dogs or build houses from playing cards.

"Glad somebody does." Skeeter opened his door and got out. Daffy followed. In the brief seconds that Mama was exiting, too, she touched his arm. "I'm sorry, Skeeter."

He glanced at her. "You got yourself the adventure you wanted, Daff. Don't apologize. It may turn out fine."

"Then thank you for coming to our rescue."

Now he did look at her. "I came this far. I should at least be here for the ending."

She wondered which ending he meant.

CHAPTER 19

S keeter opened the back of Joshua's Toyota and rummaged through Maggie's box again. Then he returned, slipping a few things in his pocket first. He held out the flashlight and two plastic ponchos.

"How are we going to cross a lake to an island?" Daffy asked. "How does Corrinda get people out there?"

"She has boats and men to row them," Mama said. "But they will all be on the island by now."

Daffy realized how perfect this spot would be for Corrinda's purposes. The plantation was said to be haunted. The island held a cemetery, or had, at one time. Both easily set the scene for a voodoo ritual. Best of all, a boat was needed to get to the island, and more important, to get off. Anyone who changed their mind about being at the ritual was out of luck.

Skeeter, who was wearing dark jeans and a darker T-shirt, handed over the ponchos to cover the women's white clothing. "Let's get there and then worry. Stay with me. Daffy you hold the flashlight and stay in the middle between us. Shine it forward so

all of us can see. If you hear anything at all, shut it off immediately."

They started forward, walking in the road, which appeared
deserted. Time crawled. What seemed like ten minutes later
Daffy heard a ghostlike trill from the trees to their left. She shut
off the flashlight and stopped so suddenly Mama Mambo plowed
into her, which was not insignificant.

Mama's arms circled her and kept her from falling to her
knees. "An owl, child," Mama said in a low voice. "Screech owl."
She paused. "Some would say this be a bad sign. The owl accom-
panies Marinette, a loa who is associated with power and
violence. We must move faster."

Daffy was afraid to ask for more information. "Sorry. I'm
trying to be careful."

"Perhaps she will be on our side tonight. She is also thought
to be the freer of slaves."

They continued at a slightly faster clip. Daffy listened
closely, but the next time an owl hooted, she kept moving.

"Listen." Skeeter stopped and held his hand behind him to
warn her.

They stood still, barely breathing. And then Daffy heard
what he had. Far in the distance. The beating of drums and what
sounded like shouting.

"At least we know which way to go." Skeeter started up again,
and Daffy made sure to lift her feet all the way off the ground, to
avoid falling.

The drums grew subtly louder, but it was clear they were still
some distance away. Mosquitoes stung her arm, and she realized
she'd forgotten to use the insect repellant and hadn't offered it to the
others, either. She attracted stinging insects, as if she were home,
sweet, home. A place to rest, a place to eat. By tomorrow nobody
would doubt she'd spent St. John's Eve in the great outdoors.

Last time they had done this Skeeter had made certain both of them were protected. It was only one of many thoughtful gestures from a thoughtful man.

"I don't see cars," she whispered, quietly slapping one of the boarders feasting on her arm. "How did they get here?"

Skeeter didn't answer, but almost immediately a shape loomed in front of them, framed in pale light from something glowing behind it. They'd found the ruins of the plantation house. Against all odds, part of one wall remained, a jagged outline that was oddly foreboding. She squinted and saw that beyond the wall was a clearing. Inside that space were the cars she had wondered about. It was too dark to count them, but she thought there were at least fifteen, possibly as many as twenty, parked in two rows.

He stopped, and so did she and finally Mama, who was walking farther behind now to avoid another collision.

They listened and after a moment Skeeter pointed right. The road had ended, and the ground was uneven. They picked their way carefully around the wall and the makeshift parking lot. On the other side, the source of the light turned out to be three back-yard Tiki torches, spaced along a path.

"We can't walk near the torches or we might be seen." Skeeter carefully skirted the pool of light thrown by the first, and the women followed gingerly.

Daffy tripped once and fell against him. He stood still until she found her footing, sure and strong but not turning to help. Then he started forward again without a word. They stumbled and stopped and finally heard the lapping of water against a shore.

They followed the sound, moving as fast as they dared. The drums were louder now, and smoke spiraled toward the sky from the middle of the lake. A half moon was beginning to rise over distant trees, and the sky was brightening with stars.

Another building rose in front of them, but this one was intact, small and narrow. Daffy couldn't make out what it was, but Skeeter knew immediately. "A boathouse, if we're lucky."

"Corrinda has a boathouse?" she whispered.

"No, but maybe the university does." He took the flashlight from her hand and aimed the beam against the side. She saw a purple and gold fleur de lis with LSU above it.

She remembered that Mama had mentioned a future archaeological dig. "Do you think they leave a boat here permanently?"

"We're about to find out." Skeeter made his way to the structure, and as she shone the light on its side, he found the door. The padlock looked flimsy. She watched as he pulled a screwdriver out of his pocket, inserted it, then snapped it back. The hasp and padlock peeled off the soft wood and thumped to the ground. The door squeaked when he opened it and looked inside.

"Let's go." He motioned for her to follow and disappeared. She handed the flashlight to Mama but didn't get far. Skeeter was already sliding a small boat toward the opening, and she grabbed her end and yanked.

She knew enough to realize that this was a rowboat, not a canoe or kayak, about ten feet long and made of some lightweight man-made material. There were two bench seats, one in the rear and one between the oars and a small seat in the prow.

Skeeter viewed the boat with hands on hips. "This won't hold all of us. And I'm not dropping anybody off in the middle of whatever's happening over there and coming back for the straggler."

Mama Mambo weighed as much as Skeeter and Daffy together, but of the three, she was the most important. Daffy knew what she had to do. "I'll row, Skeeter. You stay here."

He looked at her, as if she'd crawled up from the water to feast on his toes. "You really think I'd go along with that?"

"You have a better idea?"

"We will all go. I will think light," Mama said. "I will hold myself in the air. We will not sink."

Skeeter shook his head. "There is no body of water in this part of the world without at least one resident alligator, and they're hungry this time of year. Sinking would be a bad idea."

"We will not sink," Mama repeated.

He was silent, and Daffy watched his expression change. He shook his head, but he turned and began to edge the boat toward the water. "Mama, you'll have to wade out a little to get in, or I won't be able to push us out far enough. Can you do that?"

She gave a low laugh. "Watch me, boy."

"Daffy, get in first. You'll have to perch in the front."

Until the moment they were all in the boat and moving slowly toward the island, Daffy searched for a better solution. But there was none. With all of them inside, the boat rode so low that if it sank even an inch lower, it would swamp. She watched Skeeter's face in the moonlight, but he gave nothing away, only rowed faster. She, on the other hand, was terrified.

The lake was small, and the trip short. The boat creaked, and the oars slapped the water as they approached the shore, but no one was nearby to listen. She could hear chanting now and shouting, along with drums. She saw her chance, hiked up the poncho and her skirt and jumped out, grabbing the rope attached to the bow and hauling the boat toward firm land. Skeeter stepped into the water to help, and together they pulled the boat far enough ashore that Mama could step out without sinking to her waist.

From here they could tell that the drums were coming from the other side of thick stands of tupelo gum and cypress. They tiptoed along the shore, feeling for each step since the flashlight would have given them away. Once Daffy tripped over something that moved against her foot before it chose a better route. She stifled a screech and moved faster.

Suddenly Skeeter held up his hand, and they flanked him,

staring at the scene ahead. A bonfire crackled in the middle of a clearing, sending sparks into the air. Torches–these looked authentic, as if they'd been fashioned by hand–were planted in the ground marking quadrants. Around the circle was a blurry sea of faces and bodies dressed in white, moving around the fire as a woman sang a tuneless, hypnotic song. Syllables rose and fell, each time ending on a high-pitched whine. Daffy thought she heard crying and even a scream.

"They are pretending to be possessed by the spirits of the slaves who were buried here," Mama said. "It is an act, to frighten the watchers."

"All of them?"

"No, just those closest to the fire."

Daffy's eyes were still adjusting to the blaze of light. Figures began to crystallize. She saw men and women dancing, as if they had received superior grades in a voodoo ballroom class. There were only a handful, though. Around the edges of the clearing she saw others sitting on logs, some huddled together, as if frozen in place by what they saw. There were not the hundreds of followers she had feared. She was grateful.

"Do you see Jewel?" Skeeter whispered.

She searched, straining to make her eyes focus. But between the bright light of the fire and the darkness at the edge of the clearing, she could only make out shapes.

"I can't see faces."

"Keep trying. We're going to move around the edges. Keep that poncho pulled down, and stay as far from the action as you can."

He whispered the same to Mama, who nodded. Skeeter started around the clearing, staying in the trees at the edge. She noticed two large, bare-chested men with folded arms watching the proceedings from the far side. No one had to tell her that attracting their attention would be a big mistake.

They were halfway around the circle when Skeeter grabbed her hand and pointed to the ground. They'd come to a ditch, one deep and wide enough to be taken seriously. He pantomimed what he was about to do, then jumped, landing lightly on the other side. He waited for her.

Daffy turned to show Mama Mambo what they had to do next, but the other woman was no longer behind her. Daffy squinted into the darkness, but she had disappeared.

She turned back to Skeeter, pointing behind her, but he shook his head. Then he held out his hand almost reluctantly. She had no choice but to jump. He caught her as she teetered at the edge of the ditch, which she realized was nearly filled to the top with sludge. "Thank you," she mouthed. He dropped her hand and moved on.

As they circled, she paused to view the onlookers. Faces began to appear. There were adults here, several who were old and haggard, others in the prime of a life that was apparently too difficult to manage without Corrinda's intervention. But there were teenagers, too, three girls cowering on one log. None looked familiar, and she wondered if they attended Riverview Academy. Had they arrived here courtesy of Natalie Saizan and now wished they'd never set eyes on her?

Then she saw Natalie, herself, sitting alone but not far away.

Skeeter had seen her, too. He pointed, and Daffy nodded. "Get the others," he mouthed.

She wondered how much chance she had of convincing these girls, strangers all, to come with her. But when she crept closer she realized one of the girls was not a stranger. Sharee, her long braid invisible until now under a white handkerchief, was sitting in the middle of the three. Daffy hadn't suspected her involvement. But perhaps Sharee, like Jewel, had been convinced she had to help lift Daffy's curse.

She watched Skeeter position himself in the trees behind

Natalie, and she carefully slid past him, until she was near the other girls. She could just make out his nod. Crouching, to stay hidden as long as possible, she inched forward until she was right behind them.

"Girls," she said softly. "This whole thing is a hoax, and it's dangerous. Come with me right now. I'll get you out of here."

Sharee turned, clearly startled, saw Daffy beckoning and whispered something to the others. By then they'd all turned to look at her. One of the girls, who looked younger than the others, swung her legs around and stood. Daffy signaled her to crouch, the way that she had, and run toward the trees. Sharee, who looked as vulnerable and grateful as Daffy had ever seen her, did the same, followed shortly by the third girl, a very pale blonde. But this one, who was sobbing, grabbed Daffy's hand. "Won't we die if we leave?" she asked. "She said we would."

"Absolutely not. She's a liar, and this ceremony is completely fake." Daffy tugged her hand and the girl followed, although it was clear from her hesitant steps that she wasn't sure she was doing the right thing.

Although she'd expected to be stopped any moment, no one noticed. The bonfire was bright, but the night around them was dark. There were so many other things going on, they'd simply slipped away.

Under the trees Daffy put her arm around Sharee and whispered in her ear. "Is Jewel here?"

The girl shook her head.

Daffy was stabbed by disappointment. She knew Jewel was involved in all this somehow, but Daffy had failed again. She'd been sure that she could talk sense into the girl and take her back to her parents. She felt even more of a failure when she saw that Natalie and Skeeter were standing, in full view of anyone watching, and Natalie was clearly resisting his plea to leave.

She started forward to add her plea to his, when Corrinda finally saw them. Tonight Natalie's aunt, a woman who attracted attention under any circumstances, was dressed all in white except for a red scarf wrapped around her head and a red sash at her waist. She was the personification of Marie Laveau in Skeeter's portrait, and to these people, hoodwinked and paralyzed by fear, just as commanding.

Corrinda held up her hands to stop the drums and started forward. The two men wearing nothing but white pants rolled at the knee followed close behind her.

She was halfway toward the place where Natalie was standing when a voice rang out from the other side of the clearing, and Mama Mambo stepped forward into the light.

She shouted a stream of Creole that Daffy couldn't interpret, but clearly some of those around the fire understood. They froze in place, even the two men with Corrinda. Corrinda whirled and stalked back the way she had come, going around one of the men, straight toward Mama Mambo. At the fireside she grabbed one of the lighted torches and continued on. Mama Mambo stood taller, firmer, her arms folded. Then she held out her palm and began another stream of Creole.

Some of those in the circle got to their feet and began to sway, answering Mama's words, in call and response, as if they knew what was expected. Their voices quickly became a roar.

Daffy took the moment to dash forward to the place Skeeter and Natalie stood. She clamped her hand on the girl's shoulder. There was no reason now to whisper. "Nat, you've got to come with us. You can't be part of this."

Mama Mambo raised her voice, this time speaking directly to Corrinda in English. "I am stronger than you. You will falter. You will fail. You have no power. I have the power to stop you. Your false gods will fail you. I will name mine." She began to shout in Creole now, but undeterred, Corrinda continued to move forward.

Natalie shook off Daffy's hand, but she didn't speak, and she didn't move.

Skeeter shot into the circle and headed toward Corrinda. The two men who seemed to be her bodyguards moved to intercept him, but he evaded them by leaping to one side. Corrinda raised the torch to strike Mama, who still didn't move.

"Stop!" Natalie darted after Skeeter into the circle. "Stop! It's all a lie. Corrinda's been lying to every one of you. She doesn't have power. She wants your money! That's all she wants. She's been lying, stealing, maybe doing worse. I didn't want to know, but this woman warned me." Quickly she skirted her aunt and stood in front of Mama Mambo, facing Corrinda. "Mama Mambo warned me you were evil, and you are."

Skeeter came up behind Corrinda and yanked the torch from her hands. The first bodyguard dove for him, but he swept out one leg, and the man fell to his knees, then sprawled forward like someone who had done his duty and had no intention of doing more. The second came in from the side but Skeeter held the torch in front of him with both hands, like a staff, and used it to knock him to the ground. When the second man didn't seem inclined to move again, he dropped the torch and went straight to Natalie, keeping a wary eye on both men, who still seemed content to stay where they were.

Daffy had made it to Natalie just in time to take her into her arms to comfort her. The girl collapsed against her, sobbing.

Some of the onlookers moved into the circle, making a half-hearted attempt to protect Corrinda, but Mama Mambo stopped them with another fluid stream of Creole.

More help came from an unexpected quarter.

Light emerged out of the woods from three different directions. Sam Long stepped into the circle along with three men in dark uniforms with insignias just below their shoulders. One of the two men, who seemed to be in charge, went straight to Corrinda and grasped her arm. Another went to Mama's side.

Sam, still dressed like the fisherman he'd been up to an hour ago, came to stand with Skeeter, Daffy and Natalie.

"Glad to see you haven't lost your street fighting skills," he told Skeeter. He cocked his head in question. "The sheriff can get all these folks for trespassing. Can you prove there's more to charge them with?"

"Natalie?" Skeeter asked. "Are you willing to talk to Detective Long? He's a friend, and he'll listen." He put his hand on the girl's arm and took her to one side to talk.

"There are other girls here who can help," Daffy told Sam. "Let me talk to them a moment and assure them that telling you what they've been through won't get them into worse trouble. Some of the others might help, too. They're a captive audience until somebody rows them to shore."

"Antoinette told me you may have been deliberately poisoned."

"Your partner took samples straight from my kitchen. How did you know where to find us?"

"Skeeter stayed in touch with Antoinette on his trip here. I gather he was following you? From that point on the sheriff knew exactly where to look. There have been rumors about this island for years."

She spoke her thoughts out loud. "This would have turned out very differently if Skeeter hadn't come along."

"Yeah? Well, he had a lot to protect. Anyway, it won't be easy to prove she was the one who poisoned you." Sam inclined his head to Corrinda, who was talking fast and low to a man in uniform, as if she thought she could convince him nothing had been going on except a little dancing and singing. "That's the local sheriff. He was delighted to come with me. He'll find some reason to hold her until we have more."

Skeeter came back, his arm over Natalie's shaking shoulders. "She'll talk to you," he told Sam. Then he turned Natalie to face him. "We'll stay right here until he's finished. Then Dr. Brookes and I will take you back to the city. Just let me know if this guy gets rough, and I'll wrestle him to the ground. I used to do it when we were kids."

"Did he?" Daffy asked Sam.

"More than once." Sam smiled gently at Natalie. "You ready? We can sit. If you don't mind, I'll ask one of the deputies to take a few notes."

Natalie, who looked shaken but resigned, nodded, and together she and Sam walked to the edge of the clearing.

"What did you tell her to convince her?" Daffy asked Skeeter.

"I told her that none of this was her fault, that Corrinda isn't capable of loving her or anybody else."

Daffy knew there must have been more to make Natalie decide to cooperate. "That's all?"

He met her eyes. "No, I told her that despite how hard this is going to be, when the worst is over, she will finally be able to love herself."

CHAPTER 20

By the time they finished in Assumption Parish and started back to the city, midnight was well behind them and dawn wasn't far away. Sam had taken the other Riverview girls back to New Orleans, to be picked up at the station by their stunned parents, each of whom had believed their daughter was at a sleepover.

Mama's friend, who had relayed directions to the plantation, had invited her to stay with his family before he drove her back to Bucktown in the morning. Natalie was the only passenger in the Toyota with Skeeter and Daffy. They only stopped once, to make a careful note of where the VW was hidden, so in the morning, Daffy could call whatever tow truck Larry recommended.

Skeeter had hardly spoken, and Natalie had said very little, too, as if giving her statement to the Assumption Parish sheriff had sucked all the words out of her.

"Nat, Dr. Deveraux is going to find you a better place to stay," Daffy told the girl, as they drove into the city. "Can you make it at the group home just a little longer?"

"Whatever," Natalie said, turning back to the window.

Skeeter glanced at Daffy, but she turned away to blink back tears. Natalie had been through so much. Tonight she had lost the only family she had, and now to return to a place where nobody cared about her seemed worse that cruel.

Daffy had tried to change tonight's outcome. She had called Antoinette and begged her to make an emergency call to Natalie's social worker, explain the situation, and ask if Natalie could stay with Daffy for the next few nights. But the decision had been final. Since Daffy was not a certified foster parent, that would be impossible.

Now they pulled up to the group home, and Daffy was surprised to see Antoinette waiting on the porch under a feeble street light. She stepped down and came to the door of the car, waiting for Natalie to get out. Daffy joined them.

"We're going to your new home," Antoinette told Natalie, once the girl was on the sidewalk. "Right away. I've loaded most of your things in my car. We can get the rest tomorrow."

Natalie looked as if she couldn't tolerate one more disruption in her young life, but Antoinette put her hand on the girl's shoulder. "I know these people personally. The Pattersons do emergency foster care. They don't normally take teenagers, but they want you, Nat. I trust them completely. They watched over a little girl I know, and they did it so well I'm sure they'll be just as good to you. They have lots of kids, but they never have too many. They're waiting for you right now. Can you deal with it?"

"I just want this to be over."

"Hang on a little longer. The Patterson house will be better. And we'll keep looking for just the right place for you until you're off to college."

Skeeter got out, too, and he and Daffy walked Natalie to Antoinette's car. "You've got the three of us," Daffy said, as the girl slid into the passenger seat. "We're going to be here for you. We aren't going anywhere."

Natalie closed her eyes and put her head against the back of the seat. Antoinette slid into the driver's side, and in a moment they were gone.

"You got more than you bargained for there, didn't you?" Skeeter said.

Daffy cleared her throat. "I'm not sure what you mean."

"Natalie was just a client, a kid in one of your groups, and now, no matter how much you wish it were different, she's more." He headed back to the car and climbed in, leaving her to follow.

The drive to her house only took minutes, and neither of them spoke. When he parked, she turned in her seat to try to explain what she was feeling, but he'd already opened his door. He got out and came around the side to open hers.

She stepped down, struggling to find something to say while she could. "I guess we don't need to worry about what will be waiting for me inside anymore, do we?"

"That'll be a nice change." He started up the sidewalk. "I'll wait until you're in."

"You must be dead tired. I am. But I'd like to—" She stopped, and so did he. Both of them had heard the same noise.

She started to speak, but he put his finger to his lips. He moved around the side of the house, where the noise, more than a sigh, less than a cough, had come from. She followed, because she wasn't going to let him face whatever it was alone.

On the side gallery, slumped in the loveseat and partially hidden by the potted bromeliads on the railing, was Jewel Martinez.

Skeeter stepped to one side, and Daffy climbed the steps. "Jewel?"

The girl bolted upright and blinked sleepily at her. "Dr. Brookes?"

"Do you have any idea how glad I am to see you?"

Jewel began to cry.

"I'll open the front door." Skeeter took Daffy's handbag from under her arm and left. In a few moments the side door opened. By then Jewel was wrapped in Daffy's arms, her body heaving with deep, wracking sobs.

When the sobs became less intense, Daffy guided the teen inside. She had nothing safe in the house to offer her to eat or drink but water. Skeeter had figured that out and appeared again with a bottle from the refrigerator.

"Where were you?" Jewel demanded, when she was calm enough to speak again.

Daffy almost smiled. It was very like a teenager to assume that everyone knew her plans and would act accordingly. Then she realized that Jewel had another more important reason for asking.

"I am absolutely fine," Daffy said, enunciating every word. "I know all about Corrinda Saizan and what's been going on. She's in police custody tonight, and everybody is finally safe."

Jewel began to cry again.

Skeeter gave Jewel the water, which she gulped as if she hadn't had anything to drink in years. When she calmed once more, Daffy and Jewel settled on the sofa. Skeeter offered to leave, but Daffy asked him not to.

"Can you tell us where you've been?" Daffy took Jewel's hand.

"At my friend Moira's house."

After Jewel's disappearance, the first thing the Martinezes had been told was to call all her friends. Daffy wondered how they had missed checking with Moira. "Who is Moira?"

"She's in my class. We car pool together. She doesn't live far away."

"Do your parents know her?"

"Yes, I told you. She's my friend."

"And Moira's parents kept your secret, too?"

Jewel understood. "Oh, no. Moira's not home, and neither are they. She's on our school trip. To Europe. Her parents are chaperones, but I have their house key. Moira gave it to me before she left, and she gave me their security code. I told her I'd check her fish and terrariums. She's a biology nut."

"Your parents didn't know about the key?"

"I didn't tell them." She paused. "I figured maybe I'd need a place to be alone."

"Why did you disappear?" Daffy asked. "We have a good idea what Corrinda was doing. But can you explain?"

"I don't know how all this happened." Jewel sounded as if she was still trying to figure it out. "I was having a hard time at home. My parents hover over me like I'm made out of glass, and they make all these stupid rules. At first, I thought the voodoo stuff was just lame, but I went to a couple of Corrinda's rituals with some of my friends. Natalie set it up. Do you know that?"

"I do."

"It was supposed to be fun, kind of, weird, you know? And Corrinda always cut my hair, so I trusted her. She seemed to care about us. It was exciting and wild, but I knew my parents wouldn't approve, so it felt important to be there, like I was finally making my own decisions. For once my mother wasn't in charge. Then everything changed. Katie got sick. You know about Katie?"

Daffy realized this was the most Jewel had ever said in her presence. The girl desperately needed to unburden herself. "We do."

"A couple of days after we heard Katie was in the hospital, I was at Bountiful Beauty. Corrinda told me Katie had come to her. They had prayed and discovered that Katie was cursed. Corrinda was struggling to uncross her—that means lift the curse, I guess. But she couldn't do it alone, no matter how much she wanted to. Not unless some of us got together and gave money to a special charity to show our commitment. She said Katie was too sick for us to hesitate."

"And you didn't tell your parents?"

"I was afraid to, because then they'd know I was involved with voodoo, and I'd never be let out of their sight again. And, you know, I'd seen Katie just the day before. She did look like a different person, like she was cursed. She was so thin, and she was losing her hair in clumps. It was awful, and so sudden. Corrinda told me not to speak of the curse to anyone except a couple of other Riverview girls, because only Katie's friends could help. She said Natalie was one of them and would guide us, although I'd never seen her with Katie."

"Natalie came forward tonight to stop the whole scam. Corrinda was using her most of all. She was a victim, just like the rest of you."

"How could I have been so stupid? How could all of us? But we were terrified. It all happened so fast, just the way Corrinda had predicted. It did seem like a curse. So we gave Corrinda money, but not enough. Katie died."

Daffy repeated what she hoped the girl was beginning to believe. "She had leukemia. Sadly, between the time symptoms turn serious and the cause is discovered, it can be too late to help a patient. It's rare, but that's most likely what happened."

Jewel drank a few more sips of water, as if she needed a moment to think. "I guess. I mean, I know. But everything kept getting worse. Then Corrinda found out about you and the therapy group. She said we were upsetting the spirits, that talking about our troubles made everything much worse, that the bad spirits would focus on what we said and do harm to us and our families if we continued. She talked about Catholic saints, gave us prayers to say and pictures to pray to. I'm Catholic. It got so confusing. And finally–" She swallowed, as if she couldn't get the rest of it out.

Daffy said the words for her. "And finally, she told you I was cursed, and if you didn't come up with enough money, I would die. And somehow, it became your fault."

"You know about that?"

"I do. It's okay, though. It was just another one of her lies. I was sick..." She considered how much to say, but decided the rest might come out if and when this hit the news. "If I want you to be honest, I have to be honest. Corrinda probably did things to make me sick, none of which were your fault. We're not sure how or what exactly, but she did. And it worked for a while, but now I'm fine. She did everything to scare you into paying her." She paused. "And that's why you took your grandmother's jewelry out of the safety deposit box."

"You know about that, too?"

"I know that your parents will understand when you tell them. They're worried sick about you. Pawning or selling the jewelry is nothing in comparison."

Jewel looked so tired Daffy wondered if she would make it through the rest of her explanation, but exhausted or not, the girl continued. "I didn't pawn it. I didn't sell it. I have the jewelry at Moira's house. I got it from the bank and planned to pawn it and give the money to Corrinda to stop...you know. That's why I took it. But once I got out of my house, I could think again. Without my parents asking and asking me what was wrong and trying to get into my head, I could think. And Corrinda didn't know where I was, so she couldn't keep after me. In a while I started wondering if all this was crazy, if anybody has those kinds of powers. That's when I called you."

"I wish you had come that day. I've been so worried."

"And I was worried about you." Jewel finished the rest in a rush. "But after a few more days I kind of calmed down. One night I called one of the other girls who was involved, and she told me that Corrinda said that her *mother* was cursed, and she had to come up with a lot of money to save her. I realized then that this was all wrong, that it had gotten crazier and crazier, and I had to go home again, and confess everything to my mom and dad. Moira and her parents are coming back soon. I knew the time had come."

Daffy squeezed her hand. "So you came here, hoping I'd help."

"Can you call them?"

"Darned right."

"I don't even care if they're mad at me."

"They'll be furious, but they'll be so happy you're okay, they won't notice."

Jewel shuddered, but she didn't cry. Daffy thought she was ready to face her parents.

Skeeter had been quiet through the whole explanation, but now he stood. "You don't need me for this. I'm heading home."

She wanted him to stay. "You're sure you want to go?"

"Yeah." He hesitated, then he touched her arm when she stood. Lightly. The way a casual friend might to give a little comfort. "I hope it goes well. You take care."

As much as she wanted to, she couldn't follow him. She watched him go, and then she went to the telephone.

By six a.m. Daffy knew sleep was out of the question. The Martinezes had left with their daughter about four, and Daffy had been so exhausted that she'd immediately ripped off her skirt and fallen into bed half-clothed, only to lie awake and stare at the ceiling.

She had been afraid that the reunion wouldn't go well, that

the Martinezes wouldn't be as forgiving as she'd hoped. Happily, she'd been wrong. They had listened to Jewel's story, sobbed with her, and even taken their share of the blame. Daffy had pointed out what was harder for them to see. Jewel had been under the influence of a dangerous sociopath, and despite that, despite horrifying pressure, she had still managed to protect herself.

For a while Jewel would need help dealing with everything that had happened. Daffy had offered referrals for a new therapist, but Jewel had insisted on staying with her, and the Martinezes had asked her to continue. She had agreed, but only if the family saw another therapist together, to help sort out the dynamics at home.

After everything they'd been through, she felt sure the rest of the pieces would come together.

Now her own life had changed abruptly. Corrinda was in jail, and with luck, no longer a threat. Natalie was in a better living situation, if not a perfect one. Jewel was home. Sam was sending crime scene techs to the house today for a more thorough analysis. Once the police left for good, she could toss out everything residing in her cupboards. She could buy fresh food, more plants, new pots. She could concentrate on helping her clients, call the friends she'd been neglecting, enjoy her favorite neighborhood cafés with no worries about what to eat or drink.

And she could do all of it without worrying that a relationship that was supposed to be fun, even fulfilling, for both her and Skeeter, had suddenly turned into something more threatening.

Love.

At six-thirty she gave up, got up, showered and changed into shorts and a lavender tank top her mother had given her with a rhinestone studded egret standing in a beaded marsh. Daffy always wore it when she most needed cheering up. Then she called Larry's shop and left a message asking for the name of a tow truck to rescue Esmerelda.

Afterwards she headed down the street for coffee, bagels and newspaper, but brought them home because she wasn't sure when the techs would arrive. She was just curling up on the sofa when she realized her phone was blinking. She got up to hear the message and recognized her father's voice. The call was from the night before, something she had been too preoccupied to notice before.

She took the phone back to the sofa and called her parents in Florida. Carson Brookes answered immediately.

"Good morning," he said when he heard her voice. "You're up early."

She had known he would be, too, since he always got up early to work on lines for whatever play he was involved in. As a child she'd often gotten up with him to help, and it had been their special time.

"I was out late and didn't get your message," she said. "Everything okay there?"

"Everything's great. What's up there?"

She didn't want to go into the things that had happened. She would tell her parents eventually, when she'd had time to process everything that had occurred. Instead they chatted a moment, and then Carson got to the point.

"Daffy, your mom and I have decided to get married again, a rededication ceremony here on the beach, and we hope you'll come." He named a date not too far in the future, and she realized they had chosen their wedding anniversary. "Can you take a little time off? It's been awhile since we've seen you."

She tried to remember the last time she'd flown to Florida and couldn't. Now she didn't know what to say. Her father didn't help. He waited.

"That's very romantic," she said at last.

"What's going on? You don't want to be with us?"

"Of course I do. I want to see you. It's just..." Again, she fell silent. Again, Carson didn't help. She struggled to put the right spin on his request. "I guess you want to do this because things are finally good with you and Mom. That makes sense. A celebration after..."

This time he did help. "After what, Daffy? After thirty-five years of marriage? After some tough times? After more good times than I can count?"

She was too exhausted to soften her answer. "There were more tough times than good times. I was there, remember? I'm really thrilled for both of you that the tough times finally seem to be over, but this all seems..." She stopped because she didn't know what it seemed. Wrong, she supposed.

He was quiet a moment, and then he cleared his throat. "We're not doing a rededication because the tough times are over. There are never any guarantees, and the three of us know that. But I wouldn't trade a moment with your mother, not even the hard ones. I know things weren't always easy for you growing up. It's harder for a child when someone in the family is sick. You must have felt helpless and afraid when things got bad. But don't blow that out of proportion."

Something inside her snapped. "Then don't sugarcoat, okay, Dad? You were a great husband and father, and you stayed because you're both. But can you really say that if you had it to do over, you would choose to go through it again?"

"I can."

Daffy thought he was finished, but before she could tell him she didn't believe him, he went on.

"How about you, sweetheart? Let's pretend we really can start all over, and I can give you another mother, instead of Lea. Not the one who used to stay up all night when you had a fever, or the one who hand-sewed every single costume you ever needed for school plays or concerts. Not the one who read the entire Narnia series out loud when you were home from school with pneumonia. Not the one who held your hand and made your favorite brownies when a boy you liked made fun of you, or when the girls in your gymnastics class laughed every time you got dizzy on the balance beam. Not the one who would still jump in front of a speeding car to save you. Want me to choose a mother who doesn't struggle every single day to simply be normal, to stop her life from spinning out of control? A mother who never has to show that kind of courage? Is that the one I should have given you?"

By now tears were streaming down her face. "You know I love her. I love both of you."

"Warts and all, huh? Well, me, too. All those years ago when I said 'for better or worse' I didn't know worse would come as often as it did, I'll admit that. But I also didn't know better would come just as often. And I got both because your mom and I fell in love and hung on. And now, we're going to celebrate. I hope you'll celebrate with us."

She managed to whisper a promise she would be there and hung up.

She looked down at the shirt her mother had given her, the mother who knew her tastes and preferences and often sent little gifts that were always exactly what Daffy would buy for herself.

In the space of twenty-four hours her world had shifted. Over and over and over. And now she couldn't push that aside or pretend everything was fine just the way it was.

She was the woman she was because Carson and Lea Brookes had helped her become that woman. Despite obstacles. Despite the fears that each new day must have brought with it. Because they loved her, and they had never let go of love.

Love had sustained them; it had never imprisoned them.

She was a fool for refusing to see the truth when it had been right in front of her.

She was worse than a fool. She was an emotional coward.

She, who had chosen to help other people get in touch with their feelings, had refused for much too long to be in touch with her own.

CHAPTER 21

Joshua and Maggie Martane's house was two story, with iron lace outlining first and second floor galleries. Petunias and marigolds spilled from pots lining the sidewalk, and a chalkboard easel sat beside the front door with a drawing that looked like a horse, if horses only had three legs. Skeeter had driven there after a restless afternoon nap to swap cars and keys.

He had hoped to spend a little time with Bridget and Dillon, but when Maggie answered the door she told him Joshua was off with their daughter running errands in Maggie's car, and baby Dillon had just gone down for a nap.

"Your Jeep's down the block a bit. I'll get your keys, but I'm betting you need a cup of coffee. I just made some." Maggie didn't wait for a yes, sure Skeeter would follow.

In the homey kitchen, large enough for family meals, Maggie poured a mug and held it out for him. She and Joshua had once been forced to take refuge in the house Skeeter had been living in at the time, and she knew exactly how he liked coffee. Strong, black and hot.

"We heard what happened last night," she said. "I'm glad you're okay."

Maggie was easy to be with, a small, pretty woman with brown hair waving past her shoulders and a warm smile. He nodded his thanks, wrapped his hands around the mug and sipped.

"And Daffy's okay?" she asked.

"She's had a rough time, but she'll be okay now."

Maggie joined him at the table. "Have the two of you reached a point where I can invite you to dinner to hear the whole story?"

"Afraid not."

"Oh."

He looked up. "All good things must end."

"I don't know how many times I told myself the same thing when Joshua and I were trying to figure out who we were together. Of course, you were right there, so you saw it up close."

He knew he must be tired when he didn't change the subject but admitted the truth. "When it comes down to it, Daffy and I have really only known each other for a month. But it feels longer. Like forever." He couldn't even laugh at himself.

"You went through a lot. It would feel longer."

"It's funny. I never expected to find forever. I wasn't looking. But all I seem to want now is what you and Joshua found, and what Sam and Antoinette have."

"Condensed, huh? Without the problems getting there."

He wondered if that was true, then decided it wasn't. "No. I'll take problems any time. Except when the problem is no desire to work them out together."

"I'm sorry. She's crazy if she doesn't love you."

"She may even love me, but she doesn't want to."

Maggie looked puzzled. "Really? Then she's not very self-actualized, is she?"

For some reason he had a feeling Maggie's reaction was an

act. "Self-actualized? What, you're reading *Psychology Today* at bedtime now?"

"I'm married to a psychologist. One of my best friends is a psychologist. I have almost no hope of a normal conversation with anyone except you."

"She's perceptive and smart and scared to death to commit."

"Why?"

"Because when things start to get dull or go bad, she wants to feel free to take off."

"Well, don't we all?" She got up again, and this time she poured herself a glass of water and stood at the sink sipping it.

He was surprised. "You feel that way?"

"At least once a week. Relationships, even good ones, are tough. Apparently Daffy went into the wrong business. She sees bad relationships every day. People who are problem-free don't make appointments. Are you being a bit impatient? Expecting her to snap to and start planning a future because you have? In a month?"

He didn't say anything. He finished his coffee in silence, and she let him. When he finally stood, she held out her hand for the mug. "Is she worth it? The tough parts, I mean?"

He leaned over and kissed her cheek. "Give the kids hugs from me, okay? I'll be over soon to spoil them."

Outside, he thought about all the places where he could go next, where people knew him, and friends would buy him a beer and entertain him with funny stories. But just now he'd proved beyond the shadow of a doubt that he was in no shape for company.

He decided to go home.

He hadn't been in his studio for a long time, but that was about to change. Among all his blank canvases, a painting of the Mississippi in a thunderstorm waited to be born. He envisioned a ship in distress, the crew trying desperately not to fall overboard and failing. He just had to find the right canvas and paint his darkest feelings, because right now he was on that ship with that fantasy crew, holding on for dear life.

And when the painting was finished, he would destroy it.

The drive home was short, but in the time he'd been gone, his street had come alive with activity. Someone nearby was having a party, and cars lined the street, including one in front of his narrow driveway. He parked at the end of the block and walked back.

At the front door, he hesitated. He couldn't put his finger on what was different, but something was. Then he realized he'd practically stumbled over "different." A plant sat on his porch, a tree, in fact, with what looked like tiny lemons growing on some of the branches. The pot was Italian, painted with more lemons. He knew exactly where he'd last seen it.

He unlocked the door and a smell, something acrid and unpleasant, greeted him. He hadn't cooked that morning, too tired to consider it. He'd eaten cereal and poured a glass of juice. He hadn't even had coffee until Maggie had offered him a cup.

He didn't see Daffy until he was standing in the kitchen doorway. She was perched on a stool at his counter wearing impossibly short shorts and a spangled bird on her chest. Her hair was a mop of curls piled on her head, and her legs were dangling, too short to reach the first rung. She lifted her hand in greeting.

He wasn't ready for this. He had been sure they were finished. Again. He stopped and cocked his head in question.

"This is what happens when you give somebody a key." She dangled the one he'd loaned her, hanging from the paintbrush. "I came to give it back."

"When I wasn't home."

She smiled, but tentatively. "Well, here's the thing. The crime scene techs are all over my house right now. Hopefully, that's the last Corrinda business we'll have to deal with for a long time, kind of like the exclamation point at the end of the sentence. Sam's going to lock up when they finish. But I didn't want to stay there, because, as you know, it's a shotgun. I couldn't get away from them."

"So you thought you'd come here and wait it out?" He looked away, and that's when he realized that sitting on the front burner of his stove was his stockpot.

Immediately he understood the smell. "*Newchefroux.*"

"You're speaking Creole again?"

He waved his hand, wishing he could wave away the smell. "When I cooked at the bar and grill on Magazine, that's what the owner called that smell. New chef roux. Every new chef forgets to pay attention at some point when they're making roux and burns it. Some do it more than once, especially those with short attention spans. Every time we were close to burning anything or overcooking it, he shouted *newchefroux*, and we got the point.

She saw him staring at his pot. "And my short attention span is legendary. I'm sorry. I did throw out my first attempt, and I promise your pot survived. I was about to try again. I guess you can tell I plan to make gumbo? You know you're never supposed to return an empty pot, so I just couldn't. I wanted to bring the pot filled, but my kitchen's not at its best, because there's nothing in it that might not kill us."

He felt a smile starting at his toes, but he wiggled them to keep the smile from rising. "Thank you for that."

"So I went to my local seafood market and bought everything that begged to be included. And you know what the guy behind the counter told me when I asked his advice? Well, first I had to tell him I wasn't having a party, because, well, I'd kind of over-done it on quantity, which you'll discover when you look in the fridge. But I told him this gumbo was for the man I love. And he said, gumbo is like a good relationship. And please note how easily that word just tripped off my tongue. All those syllables in exactly the right order. But anyway, he said with gumbo you take what you have, and you add new things, too. Every time you make it, it's different. But the one thing you always have to add is spice. And if two people add that, then the gumbo will sustain them forever."

Somewhere in the middle of her explanation he'd tuned out. Right at the part where she'd said, "the man I love."

"Love?" he asked. "That's something even newer than you trying to cook."

Her cheeks turned pink, and for a moment she seemed to forget to breathe. When she realized she was running out of oxygen, she sucked so much into her lungs that she started to cough.

He tilted his head the other way and waited.

"I came..." She cleared her throat. "Well, at first I was coming to apologize. But then I realized I'd done that already, and it didn't make much of a difference. And, well, it shouldn't have. Because that's not what we need to get ourselves back on the road. We need something else. So, I'm here..." She took another deep breath and blew it out forcefully. "I'm here to tell you...Skeeter, I love you. It's crazy, I think, and we both know I didn't want to. But, well, I do anyway."

When he didn't answer, she got to her feet. "I'm just making a fool of myself, aren't I? I'm kind of comfortable doing that, having had a lot of practice, but it's not really helping, is it? I'll go. But please keep the lemon tree. You need to make this beautiful house a home. You haven't even started to, and plants will do that. It would mean a lot if—"

He swept his hand across his chest to stop her. "You're not the only one who hasn't been going at this very well. I've been wrong. I fell so hard for you I wanted to be sure there was the possibility of a commitment in our future, and now I know that's not your thing. I shouldn't have pushed. I know someday you may want to leave, but if you don't mind, I'd rather it was later than sooner."

Her eyes widened. "Skeeter, no. It's never been about *me* leaving." She bit her lip. "This is the part nobody seems to understand, and to be truthful, it's taken me awhile, too. I wanted *you* to be able to leave. If you needed to. I didn't want you to chain yourself to me if things didn't work out. It wasn't fair, that's all."

"So you wanted to keep this light, so I could walk away if you —what, get a nosebleed? Miss a period? Break a leg?"

He paused and when she didn't answer, he finally understood. For the first time in their crazy month together, he realized what was driving her.

"Turn into your mother?" he asked.

Tears sprang to her eyes, and she nodded.

"Daffy. . ." He shook his head.

"That's the hard part," she said, "because, you know, I might. I'm four to six times more likely to be bipolar. It's less likely now that I'm past my mid-twenties, and so far I'm just me, which some people think is crazy enough. But it's not easy living with someone like Lea Brookes. And I just figured you shouldn't have to. But here's the truth, and I'm ashamed of it, but if that did happen?" She took another deeper breath. "I would still want you to stay. I might even ask you to, and how would that be fair?"

"So you just wanted me to know I could leave if I had to."

She nodded.

"There are never any guarantees. But just so you know, I plan to stay, no matter what." He opened his arms. "You are just too easy to love. And I do."

"That scares me to death." She jumped down from the stool and fell into his arms. She kissed him as if she'd been afraid she'd never have the chance again. He tasted salt from tears and felt her breasts flatten against his chest. His hands crept under the tank top and splayed against her bare skin.

He finally stepped away, his heart pounding, heat pooling exactly where it was supposed to. "Have you had anything to eat today?"

She shook her head and sniffed.

"Have you had any sleep?"

She shook her head again. "Food and sleep aren't all they're cracked up to be."

"Has a man who loves every curly hair on your gorgeous head swept you off your feet and taken you to his bedroom?"

"Not yet today. But you know, I worry about your back. You do this a lot."

He kissed her again, then he swept her off her feet. "Spice for the gumbo?"

"I like mine steaming hot." She kissed him as he carried her to his bedroom, and he didn't even drop her.

EPILOGUE

The first thing Daffy saw when she came home from her honeymoon was Esme, now the picture of automotive health, nose-to-nose with Skeeter's Jeep in their driveway. Inside, the first thing she saw was an oil portrait of herself, hanging on the wall opposite the door into the living room. It was far from traditional. She sparkled, like a fairy or a maybe a firefly, and she was surrounded by plants, some with faces. Skeeter had used color lavishly and behind her the sun was a halo.

She threw her arms around her new husband's neck and kissed him. "It's so beautiful. I'm so beautiful I may try my fortune in Hollywood."

"Try Broadway, so we can visit Terence Spurlock together."

Terence Spurlock, a small but renowned Manhattan gallery, had scheduled a show of Skeeter's work. It was to be held early the next summer, and even though the opening was still months away, Skeeter was working hard in his studio every day to prepare. He'd given up his gig on Jackson Square, but for now he was still doing caricatures for parties and receptions at night because he refused to let her pay the bills by herself.

Daffy went to stand under the portrait and examine it more closely. "Are you going to show this one?"

Skeeter came to stand beside her. "Nope. I'd miss it too much."

"While you were retrieving suitcases at the airport Maggie called. She and Joshua want us to drop by tonight to show off our tans. Around seven."

"Do they? To how many people?"

Daffy laughed, because she'd realized the same thing. "She thinks we'll be surprised, but I'm guessing everybody we've ever met will be there."

"The price we pay for a small wedding. An outrageous reception."

Almost immediately after the night in Assumption Parish, Daffy had given up her lease and moved in with Skeeter, painting walls colors they both loved, spreading her rugs and furniture and most of all her plants around his house to make it feel like a home. They had been happy living together, building memories, figuring out what they needed and wanted as a couple. Though they'd discussed marriage, they hadn't been in any particular hurry. Then suddenly their lives had changed and with it, their plans.

They were going to be parents.

One week ago Joshua, still ordained in his chosen faith, had performed their wedding ceremony at Audubon Park, with the Martanes and Longs in attendance, as well as Daffy's parents, who thought Skeeter was the best thing that had ever happened to her. Skeeter and Daffy had carved out enough time for a week in the Caribbean and headed for St. Thomas the same night.

And now they were back.

"You're still okay with all this, aren't you?" Daffy asked.

"How about you? The stork doesn't usually drop a bundle this soon. Not every couple starts a family just a week after they get married."

"You may not have noticed, but we don't seem to be like that mythical 'every couple.' No regrets?"

"Happiest days of my life." He pulled her close just as the doorbell rang.

Daffy kissed him quickly, then linked her arm through his. "They're early. You're ready?"

"I'd better be."

They walked to the door together. Daffy opened it. A visibly pregnant Antoinette stood on the porch, along with Natalie's social worker.

And Natalie.

Skeeter had been right. Not every marriage started with a teenage daughter.

Natalie looked uneasy, as if she wondered if she really was welcome. "Mrs. Patterson is sending over a whole basket of food tomorrow. That woman cooks and cooks." She shook her head, as if none of this mattered. "She says if I don't visit often, she'll come drag me over there. And she means it." She lifted her head and met Daffy's eyes. "I can always go back there to live if I need to. It's not so bad."

Daffy felt her eyes misting. The Pattersons had been good to Natalie, but they had a house filled with younger children who came and went with the tides of foster care. Everyone had agreed that Natalie needed a smaller, permanent family, where she could receive all the attention she'd been denied most of her life. Skeeter and Daffy hadn't come to their decision lightly, but they had come to it together. They had taken foster care training, made wedding plans, and now, Natalie was theirs.

"Your room's all ready," Daffy said, hugging the girl who, after a moment, softened in her embrace. "And guess what? There's a girl on the next block who goes to NOCCA, too."

"Yeah, she told me at school. Her name's Minna. She writes, but that's okay."

For once in her life Natalie had been lucky. The administration at the New Orleans Center for Creative Arts had listened to Daffy and Skeeter's pleas, and when a spot had unexpectedly opened in their full-day visual arts program, they had accepted her, impressed with her considerable talent. Happy to get away from Riverview Academy, where she knew that now, more than ever, she would never fit in, Natalie had been thrilled. She'd been attending the school since early in the fall and liked it.

Sharee and Jewel had gone on to other schools, too. Both were recovering and moving forward, and Linda, who had stayed at Riverview, was finally coming to terms with Katie's death. The realization that she, unlike some of Katie's other friends, hadn't gotten sucked into Corrinda's voodoo cult had given her new faith in herself.

Skeeter hefted Natalie's small suitcase, which held every single thing she owned, but wouldn't for long if Daffy had her way. "I'll show you your room," he said. "You're on the second floor next to my studio. You might want to do some work in there, too, after you settle in. I cleared a space for you."

Daffy watched them go, and said goodbye to Natalie's case worker, who looked as if she thought, for once, something good had happened for a child under her protection.

She waited until the other woman was gone, then turned to Antoinette. "Her room's a blank canvas, so now she can make it hers. We start shopping tomorrow."

"Don't overdo. Take it a little at a time. She's easily overwhelmed these days, and not sure she trusts all the good things that are happening."

Daffy knew that was sound advice. "We're bringing her with us tonight, though. I hope there'll be some other teenagers at the reception."

Antoinette laughed. "You figured out the surprise. It's going to be great."

Skeeter came down the stairs and joined them. "Natalie wanted some time alone. She's never had her own room. When I left, she was sitting on the windowsill staring at the backyard patio and your plants. She asked me if she was allowed to sit out there."

"And you told her?"

"I told her of course, she's home now. It's her patio, too." He put his arm around Daffy, and they walked Antoinette to her car and watched as she drove away.

"You know those good times and those not-so-good times we talked about, *Daphne?*" Skeeter asked, pulling her closer.

"I remember that conversation clearly, *Seth.*"

He smiled, as he always did when she called him by his real name. She knew that sharing his great-grandfather's name was finally beginning to feel comfortable. Even right.

"We're bound to have some of those not-so-good times in the near future," he said. "She's a great kid, but she's going to test us both."

"I'm ready. You're ready. Besides, there's good news. She's a teenager. She's going to be busy at school. We'll have plenty of free time to discuss our parenting skills."

"Discuss? Is that all we're going to do in our free time?" he asked.

"I'm not sure we'll need words for the rest."

"How about I love you?"

She tunneled her fingers through his hair and kissed him. "Simple is always best."

AUTHOR'S NOTE

As an avid reader, some books stand out for me, and I never forget them. Are you surprised that as an author, the same is true? If we've written dozens of books, some retreat as pleasant memories, but others remain front and center in our imaginations.

In the case of the *New Orleans Nights* series, two characters remained front and center for me, Skeeter Harwood, who was important in both *Lady of the Night* and *Bayou Midnight*, and Daphne (Daffy) Brookes, who substantially enlivened *Bayou Midnight*. It was clear to me and to the many readers who wrote at the time those books were first published, that Skeeter's story should have been next. And who else as his romantic interest than Daffy?

Unfortunately Skeeter was too much the "bad boy" for my publisher to agree. And so the word came down from on high that I couldn't write his story. With no room for argument, I moved on.

Time passed and independent publishing took off. About the same time, I got my rights back to *Lady of the Night* and *Bayou Midnight* so I could publish them again. As I readied them,

Skeeter re-emerged, the last of three men who'd grown up together in New Orleans and remained loyal friends. How could I publish the first two books without the third? It was like inviting two best friends to a wedding and telling the third he couldn't come.

I sifted through my filing cabinet and found an outline for *Night Magic*, Skeeter's story, along with three completed chapters I still loved, a folder of notes, and two research volumes. How could I resist?

The truth is, all the chapters, outlines and notes were a gift, but when it came right down to it? I wanted to tell Skeeter's story. In my heart and imagination, Skeeter had not found his happy ending. And he deserved one.

Welcome *Night Magic* and Skeeter's story at last. And welcome to *New Orleans Nights*, complete at last. Visit the seamier side of The City That Care Forgot, the bayous of Southern Louisiana and the underworld of New Orleans voodoo. Most of all welcome to the stories of three men whose friendship never wavered.

While the first two books were updated and revised, and *Night Magic* was written in the same time frame, all the books are still set before Hurricane Katrina, which changed the city so drastically in August 2005. This is the New Orleans I remember and love so well.

I hope you'll enjoy reading this series as much as I enjoyed writing it, then and now.

If you purchased the book online and would like to share your thoughts about *Night Magic*, please take a moment to post your review at the bookstore where you purchased your copy. Reviews are always appreciated by authors and other readers.

Laissez les bon temps rouler! (Let the good times roll.)

Emilie

ALSO BY EMILIE RICHARDS

If you enjoyed *Night Magic*, you'll also enjoy the other novels in the *New Orleans Nights* series, *Lady of the Night* and *Bayou Midnight*.

Have you finished them all and you're looking for more?

My four book *Tales of the Pacific* series, is also available for you to enjoy at:

http://emilierichards.com/books/tales-of-the-pacific/

And here's a peek at another favorite of mine which is back in print. *Dragonslayer* won the RITA award from Romance Writers of America as well as one of Romantic Times magazine's rare 5 star reviews. Despite the title, *Dragonslayer* is not fantasy, (not a dragon in sight) but a blend of romance and women's fiction about a man and a woman determined to make a difference in the world, no matter how many people try to stop them.

You can purchase Dragonslayer here:
http://books2read.com/dragonslayer

DRAGONSLAYER EXCERPT

CHAPTER 1

Sometime during the night, gang graffiti bled through the three coats of white paint the Reverend Thomas Stonehill and his ragtag congregation had slathered over the sanctuary walls. Sometime during the night, a homeless man picked the lock and made himself a bed under the unorthodox picture of Jesus that graced the front of the church. Sometime during the night, urban phantoms dumped trash on the steps, dug up the last chrysanthemum plant in the narrow flower bed and left a note in the mail slot complaining about the dessert at the Wednesday night sharing supper.

"More ice cream. Less talk." Thomas crumpled the two sentences in his hand and stared somberly at the old man who was gathering his belongings into a utilitarian stack honed by years of living on the street. Once he finished Thomas held out the note. "Did you write this?"

The old man shook his head.

"Do you know about our Wednesday night sharing suppers?"

The old man just stared at him.

"Every Wednesday night at six we serve a meal here for

anybody who's hungry. You're always welcome. And next time you need a place to stay, ring the bell. I'll open the door for you. No need to break in."

"Churches ain't supposed to be locked," the old man mumbled.

"And kids aren't supposed to get their kicks out of spray painting walls and smashing furniture, but sometimes they do."

The old man inclined his head toward the picture that had watched over him as he slept. "Person who painted that must have taken a kick to the head."

The grim line of Thomas's mouth relaxed a little. "Think so?"

"Jesus with four different faces." The old man shrugged. "Who'd think like that?"

"How do you know it's Jesus?"

"That face looks like him." The old man pointed to one of the four images superimposed over the edges of the others.

"The white one, you mean? Maybe if you were black, the one beside it would look like Jesus."

"What kind of church is this? What call you got to come down here to the Corners and mess with people's religion?"

"What call you got to drink yourself blind every night and wake up in a strange place every morning?" Thomas asked the question without a trace of condescension in his voice. He knew he had no right to judge. He was no better than the man in the cast-off clothing, no better than anyone.

"Ain't got much pity in your soul for a sick old man, do you? What kind of preacher are you, anyway?"

"The kind who thinks pity's a waste of time."

Thomas looked at his watch. It was gold, twenty-four carats, with a new imitation leather band that was already cracking. "We'll be having church here in less than an hour. You're welcome to stay."

"Nah." The old man scratched himself, starting at his

sparsely forested head and progressing steadily downward to places that most men didn't scratch in public. "I'll be moving on."

Thomas reached for his wallet. He pulled out three dollar bills and handed them over. "Will we see you on Wednesday?"

The man stuffed the bills in his pocket. "Don't take charity."

"Then think of it as supper with friends."

"Don't want no friends." The man strapped his belongings together with a belt and lifted the bundle to his shoulder. Without another word, he limped across the room and disappeared out the door.

The door slammed again a few seconds later behind a young woman herding two sleepy-eyed children in front of her. Her eyes were red, and her dark hair was uncombed. Her thin body seemed to fold in on itself, as if to protect the children with her shadow. Thomas didn't smile. "You're early, Ema. I haven't even set up the chairs yet."

"I'll help." She attempted a smile. It was hard, since her lip was badly swollen. "I don't mind."

"Have you had breakfast?"

"Sure."

"The kids, too?"

"They don't eat this early."

"There's cereal out on the kitchen table upstairs. Milk and juice in the refrigerator."

"I couldn't-"

"You will." Thomas hiked his thumb toward the hall and the stairs leading to his apartment. "And there's ice for your lip."

"Oh, my lip's fine. I just bumped into—"

"Wrap the ice in a dish towel. Twenty minutes on, twenty minutes off, until church starts."

She nodded. In moments she and the children had closed his apartment door behind them.

And Thomas Stonehill was alone with a painting of Jesus and his own thoughts.

He was comfortable with neither. The picture was new and disturbing in its intensity. His thoughts were old and tormented him constantly.

He stared at the picture and filled the silence with the voice that had once held a congregation of thousands of souls enthralled.

"So, J.C., there go some of your little lambs, starting Sunday morning with the wolf right behind them."

He didn't expect an answer. He had given up believing in answers the same day he resigned from one of the most prestigious Protestant churches in the Midwest.

He moved closer. The four images seemed to merge, but he hardly saw them anyway. His vision was turned inward. "One homeless lamb, one battered, and two little ones so hungry and scared they don't know how to laugh. Imagine that, J.C., kids who've forgotten how to laugh—if they ever learned how in the first place."

He stared at the picture, but in his mind he saw the front of another church. He saw an altar spread with snow-white linen, a starkly simple golden cross and polished silver cornucopias overflowing with chrysanthemums, dahlias and the fruits of the autumn harvest. All the blessings of God's good earth on God's good table. For God's good people.

"One homeless, one battered, two hungry and scared," he said softly. "And one who talks to a God he doesn't even believe in anymore. That's what passes for God's kingdom around here, J.C. Welcome to the Corners. Welcome to the Church of the Samaritan."

The silence stretched into an eternity Thomas didn't believe in, either. Then, from St. Michael's Catholic church, three blocks away, bells chimed a Sunday morning welcome.

"Sorry, J.C, but nothing doing," Thomas said, turning away. "You can't fool me. I know you too well by now. If you had a voice, it would sound like tears."

* * *

Garnet Anthony was awakened by church bells in the distance. The bells blended into the symphony of car engines, rap from somebody's stereo, and the screams of a neighbor's child.

She opened one eye and saw that it was later than it should have been. She opened the other and saw that in stumbling to bed in the dark last night she had paired a magenta satin sleep shirt with chartreuse boxer shorts.

It was the best rationale for sleeping nude that she could think of. She was just glad she didn't have company in her bed this morning to witness the mismatch.

Not that she'd had company there for a long, long time.

Garnet slowly sat up and shook the scramble of dark hair that was constant visual proof that the stereotypes people held about nurses were simply that. Her hair was long, thick and insolent— and she liked it that way. Even when it was tied back from her face, tendrils found their way into her eyes and ears, and curls bounced against her neck.

As she scrubbed sleep from her eyes, the mirror beside her bed reminded her that nothing about her called forth images of soothing voices or healing hands. She owed her outrageous face to generations of immigrant ancestors who had made the Corners their first stop in the U.S. of A. Some—the luckiest—had moved on to other, healthier places, but not before they had flooded the Corners' gene pool with a splash of this and a shower of that.

She had wide Slavic cheekbones and tilted almond eyes that she owed to a mystery country in the east—of a color green that brought to mind the hills of Ireland. Her tawny skin had been a gift from her father, who was half Egyptian, and her mother, who claimed Comanche blood. An infusion of Puerto Rican sunshine and Nordic frost had given her both a generous smile and enough caution not to use it very often. On the rare occasions when teachers had praised her during her school years, they had told her she was "striking" or "interesting." "Pretty" had been reserved for girls from more conventional backgrounds.

Garnet fought her way out of bed and crossed to the refrigerator for a long drink of milk straight out of the carton. She drank milk on waking and coffee at bedtime. She ate pasta for breakfast and pancakes at supper, and indulged in desserts any time the law allowed. She had never lived her life the way the world expected, and most of the time she didn't give the world's opinion more than a passing thought.

Except that today, considering what lay ahead of her, the world was probably right, and she was probably *loco*.

A quick shower later, and nearly dressed, Garnet noted that the child in the tiny apartment next door was still screaming.

Thirteen-month-old Chantelle probably wanted her breakfast. Her mother, Serena, no different from most sixteen-year-old girls, liked to sleep late. Of all the young mothers Garnet knew, Serena was the finest. But that didn't mean she had magically matured during childbirth into a woman who could willingly sacrifice all her own pleasures and desires for the sake of the bawling six-pound bundle of trouble that, in one supremely painful moment, had become her lifetime commitment.

In the hallway, Garnet buttoned the sleeve of her white blouse with one hand and knocked on Serena's door with the other.

"Hey, Serena, your kid's hungry. Either get up and open the door so I can take her home and feed her, or get up and feed her yourself."

"Go 'way."

Garnet switched hands to button her other sleeve and

continued to pound. "I'm not going anywhere," she said. "Open up."

The door gave way under her fist. On the other side of the doorway Serena pulled her T-shirt down so that it almost covered her panties. "You know, you oughta be somebody's mother."

"What? And be so busy with my own kids I'd miss chances to order you around?" Garnet squatted and held out her arms. Chantelle, tears dripping down her chin, came into them and wiped her face on Garnet's blouse.

Garnet rose, clutching Chantelle against her. "Thanks, runny nose," Garnet said wryly. "I probably have another clean blouse."

Serena yawned. "If you'd left us alone..."

"This was the best of two alternatives. If she'd kept on crying, I would have come over here and murdered you in your bed."

"At least I wouldn't have to get up."

"You are one lazy woman." Garnet reached out to rumple Serena's curls to take any sting out of her words. "Want me to feed her while you take a shower?"

"Nah. You feed her junk."

"Peanut butter and pancake sandwiches are not junk."

"I bought her favorite cereal yesterday." Serena held up her hands to stave off Garnet's next words. "And juice. I bought juice, too."

"You've been listening to my lectures."

"I just got a talent for self-preservation." Serena dragged Chantelle from Garnet's arms. "It's Sunday. Why are you dressed like a nurse? Don't you get a day off?"

Garnet was the administrator of Mother and Child, a unique maternal health project that struggled to provide both health care and social services to the women and children of the Corners. Garnet had carved the program and the job out of nothing, bantering and begging and threatening her way to obtaining grants from private charities and public programs so that no one in the community would have to suffer the way she once had.

She was administrator and nurse practitioner, secretary and janitor. She loved the variety, the constant challenge, the smiles on the faces of children who might not be alive if Mother and Child didn't exist.

And she despised everything and everybody who interfered with helping those children.

"I've got to go see somebody," she said.

Serena bounced her daughter on her hip, and Chantelle quieted. "Where?"

Garnet looked past Serena to the one-room apartment that was probably the nicest home the young woman had ever known. It was almost painfully clean, but Chantelle's toys cluttered the floor in colorful disarray. Garnet approved of the combination. "Wilford Heights."

"Uh-uh. That's Coroner territory."

"*People* territory."

"You're crazy, girl."

"Just doing my job." Garnet crossed her arms and prepared for battle. It would be good practice for the day to come. "And I'm not going to let a bunch of punkass kids keep me from doing it just because they think the dirt outside some housing project is worth dying for."

"You'd be the one dying."

"Better not be. These kids know me. I've delivered their girl-friends' babies, held their mamas' hands while they tried to come down off drugs. They aren't going to shoot me."

"It's Candy you're going to see, isn't it?"

Garnet turned her gaze to Serena. "She's been having cramps and she's afraid to come to the clinic tomorrow."

"It's not the Coroners you'll have to worry about, then. It's the Knights who'll shoot you. They see you going over there, they'll guess who you're going to visit."

"Let them."

"You're crazy."

"No. Sane. Somebody's got to be sane in this place. Otherwise those kids aren't going to know there's a better way to live than shooting each other over street signs and hand signs and colors."

"Candy knew what she was doing when she started kicking with Francis and his friends. She knew Demon wouldn't let her get away with it." Serena poked Garnet's chest with an index finger to make her point.

"Francis is a good man."

"That's got nothing to do with it."

Garnet was glad to see Serena was worried about her. It was always a good sign when a kid like Serena, who already had the world on her shoulders, could still worry about somebody else. "I'll be careful," she promised.

"Listen, if Hell has a zip code, it's the same as ours. You can't change that, Garnet. The Corners has been here for a hundred years, and it'll be here another hundred. Everything'll be exactly the same when Chantelle's grandkids are out playing on the sidewalk."

"If Chantelle's grandkids are *able* to play on the sidewalks, then it *won't* be the same Corners. It'll be a better place."

"I still don't think you should go."

"It could be you over there, needing me."

Serena's response wasn't fit for the baby's ears.

"You'd better hope that's not Chantelle's first word," Garnet said.

"Let me know when you get home."

"Just don't go back to bed. I don't want to have to wake you up again." Garnet leaned over and kissed Chantelle's cheek.

Half an hour later Serena's door was cracked when Garnet strode down the hall—in a fresh white blouse. As she passed she heard the clang and screech of cartoons. She wondered if Chantelle was watching them, too.

Thomas had to set up chairs and install the pulpit under the picture. With three chairs under each arm, he made his way to the front of the church. The graffiti gleamed at him as he unfolded the chairs.

There was nothing to be done about the graffiti this morning. Another coat of paint might subdue it. Then again, it might not. The MidKnights had wanted their message to last through eternity. It had been painted a deep royal blue and outlined in black enamel. The artist had talent. Their symbol, a sword, had been rendered in loving detail. The profane, mysterious message accompanying it had been carefully stroked, layer upon layer, until it seemed to leap off the wall—right through three coats of white paint.

The victorious graffiti seemed to point out the futility of everything Thomas was trying to do. But over the past year he had grown to accept the feeling that little he was doing would make a difference, anyway. He had spent two years doing nothing at all before he moved to the Corners to start the Church of the Samaritan. That had been far worse. Here, at least, he was struggling, not drifting. If he and the people of the Corners were going to drown, they were going to go down fighting. Together.

A woman's voice interrupted his thoughts.

"You could get the boy who did that, you know, get him and his friends and tell them to paint you a mural over that mess. Jesus at Gethsemane or the Last Supper. Only way it's ever gonna get covered up."

Thomas turned. For the first time that morning he smiled.

"You're early, Dorothy. Did you come to give me advice or help set up the chairs?"

"I'm on my way to Mass at St. Michael's." Dorothy Brown joined him in front of the graffiti. She was a tiny woman of indeterminate age, dark-skinned and silver-haired. This morning she was dressed in a perfectly preserved green rayon suit with padded shoulders and a pillbox hat with a short green veil. Dorothy had lived in the Corners as long as anyone could remember. She had taught in the Corners' schools, served in local government and chaired any board worth chairing. Her ruling passion was to create a community in this place that some people called a ghetto.

"Can't say those boys of ours got no talent." She cocked her head. "I'm betting Ferdinand Sanchez did that one. His mother taught him to draw like that. She was a pretty little thing. Used to spend hours with him teaching him to do stuff. Then one morning she just up and left. His father's no good."

"I've crossed Mr. Sanchez's path a time or two."

"Old Testament on this side—" Dorothy pointed to the opposite wall "—New Testament on that. Ferdinand could do it."

"Last time I saw Ferdinand, he was urinating on the front steps."

"Trying to get your attention."

"He succeeded." Thomas folded his arms. "So it's Mass this morning?"

"Your turn next week." Dorothy hiked her purse to her shoulder. "I spread myself around."

"Like icing on a cake."

"What am I missing here this morning? You gonna preach on something interesting for a change?"

"The miracle of the loaves and fishes."

"Just don't go getting down on folks like you usually do. They need some God on Sunday mornings. Get tired of hearing about how they're supposed to change the world. Most of them just sitting here wishing they'd got a little sleep last night or had something to eat for breakfast."

"And God's supposed to fill their stomachs?"

"He got a better chance at doing it than you got."

"I'll give them some God."

"Give yourself a little, too, while you're at it." She patted his arm. Before he could think of an adequate response she was gone.

Thomas stared out the window, watching Dorothy's small figure disappear into the fog of a Corners' autumn morning.

Three young men materialized out of the same fog. Two wore black hoodies left open to the elements, the other had chopped the sleeves off a denim jacket and covered it with custom patches. Underneath they wore muddy-hued plaid shirts buttoned just at the collar over black T-shirts and sagging khaki work pants. He knew that when they got closer, he would also see an array of piercings and tattoos, including the required knight's sword, tattooed on the inside of the right forearm.

Along with similarities there were differences. One wore a black watch cap pulled low over his ears, one a generic cap with the bill turned up. One wore nothing on his head except a folded bandanna tied to one side over cornrows divided and braided with military precision. Thomas knew the boys well enough to realize that the one with the watch cap was the one to worry about.

They weren't walking fast, and they weren't walking slow. They strutted as if they owned the sidewalk, the street and the neighborhood. If they had been on the other side of the street, their stride would have been jumpy and defiant. They were members of the MidKnights, often just referred to as the Knights, and the other side of the street, where the Wilford Heights housing project began, belonged to the Coroners.

And this place, where Thomas stood, where his small congregation would soon gather to try to find meaning in their existence, belonged to a God that Thomas wasn't even sure he believed in anymore.

As the young men approached the sidewalk in front of the church, Thomas watched closely. The church was nothing more than a converted storefront, the congregation nothing more than a few souls who, in giving voice to the despair that plagued their lives, spoke for a whole community. But the church and this congregation were Thomas's life.

He would be no less ruthless than any MidKnight in protecting what was his.

Despite her reassuring words to Serena, Garnet had expected trouble from the moment she promised Candy Tremira that she would go to Wilford Heights to examine her.

Garnet always expected trouble, and she was rarely disappointed. Optimism was a waste of time and pessimism a waste of energy. She was a realist, and by expecting the worst, she could always be pleasantly surprised if it didn't occur.

Today there were going to be no surprises.

"Where're you going, babe?" Andre Rollins asked as she waited for the walk sign at the corner of Twelfth and Wilford.

She turned slowly and raked him with her gaze. "Who's the babe here, Andre? I was changing your diapers when I was eight."

"I asked where you was going."

"I'm going across the street."

Andre moved in front of her, and two other young men flanked her. She sighed. "Come on. You boys got nothing better to do than hassle me this morning?"

"Don't go dissing us, babe," Andre said. "You show respect, or we'll teach you how."

"I respect you," Garnet said. "Only not as much as I used to."

She felt a hand on her arm and fingers making bruises. She forced herself not to turn her head or wince. "See, I used to think you *were* somebody," she went on. "Back when you didn't need your enforcers to make you feel like a big man."

Andre barely inclined his head, and the fingers no longer squeezed her arm. "What call you got crossing that street?"

"My job, Andre." She moved a little closer to him.

"There's no clinic 'cross the street."

"There's a woman across that street who's afraid to come to the clinic because she knows you boys are waiting for her to show her face over here."

"Candy?"

She turned to the young man who had spoken, the same young man who had probably left fingerprints on her arm. He wore a dark watch cap pulled over his ears and rolled just to his eyebrows. The pale face that leered at her was one she never wanted to glimpse on a night when she was out on the streets alone.

"Demon, let it go," she said. "So maybe Candy took off with another guy. You think you're the first man that's happened to? It doesn't matter. You've got another woman now."

Sadly, that was true. Another young woman had replaced Candy Tremira in Demon's life. Another young woman who would learn that macho posturing and smoldering good looks meant nothing next to the reality of living with his erratic temper.

He smiled, and she was chilled by it. "Candy and I are going to have a conversation," he said.

"Andre." She turned to appeal to him. "I've got a job to do. You show me where it says a nurse or doctor can only help patients who wear the right colors. Show me where it says this stupid war between you and the Coroners is going to do anything for the Corners besides make life harder here."

Andre put his fist under her chin. She didn't flinch. She felt

Demon and Ferdinand, the third MidKnight, close ranks around her.

"You go on over to Wilford Place," Andre said, "and you walking into trouble."

She looked straight into his eyes. They were the color of his skin, a deep, rich brown. "Look, I've watched you grow up. I know what you can do and who you can be. I know who you *are*. Don't do this, Andre."

There was always something flickering, simmering in Andre's eyes. Some of the kids who patrolled these blocks had eyes that were as empty as the futures they had been bequeathed. Andre's weren't. She stared into them, willing him to face the struggle going on inside himself, willing him to make the right decision.

"Get your hands off the lady."

A man's voice cut through the tension and splintered it into a thousand evil pieces. Garnet felt a hand on her shoulder, and before she could do anything, she had been flung to one side. In an instant a man's large body was wedged protectively between her and the MidKnights.

"What do you think you're doing?" the man asked.

For one confusing moment Garnet didn't know to whom the question had been addressed. Then she saw the sneer on Andre's face and knew it hadn't been addressed to her. She had been cast aside as if she no longer had a part in the confrontation. A man in a plain gray suit was facing the MidKnights for her.

"Nobody's talking to you, Padre." Andre stood taller than he had with Garnet. He and the man, who easily topped six feet, were staring eye to eye. "Don't get yourself involved in things got nothing to do with you."

"Anything that happens in this neighborhood's got something to do with me. You're standing in front of my church. I live here."

"That what you call it?" Andre reached into his T-shirt

pocket for a cigarette. His gaze didn't waver. He snapped his fingers, and Ferdinand moved around Thomas to light it for him.

"Who are you?" Garnet demanded. She tried to move, but the man continued to shield her.

"Thomas Stonehill," he said shortly.

"Padre," Andre said. He blew a puff of smoke in Thomas's face. "Got himself a real important church right over there, with at least two, three people coming of a Sunday. Got himself an idea he's gonna save the world. Starting right here on this spot."

Shock began to recede, and anger seeped into its place. Garnet couldn't fault the man, this Thomas Stonehill, for trying to protect her. Every time she had an audience she preached the gospel of people in the neighborhood watching out for each other.

But she could fault him for thrusting her aside when she had been in the midst of working out her problem with Andre. The good reverend had committed two unpardonable sins, and *she* was probably going to pay for them.

"This is between me and Andre," she said, trying to step in front of Thomas. "Thank you, but we can finish this ourselves."

Thomas hardly seemed to do more than shift his weight, but he cut off her path to Andre anyway. "I don't think the young man's intentions are the best."

"That's for me to decide."

Thomas acted as if he hadn't heard her. "The lady has a right to walk these sidewalks without you kids bothering her. Everybody has that right."

"Think so?" Andre tossed his cigarette at Thomas's feet. It bounced off his shoe. "Well, I think she don't. I think she crosses that street today, she gonna wish she never did walk these sidewalks, 'cause we be walking them right behind her."

Garnet's heart sank. Andre had committed himself now. If she ignored his warning, she would pay. She wasn't afraid; she was only sorry the chance to change things had been taken out of her hands.

Futilely, from Thomas's side, she made one last attempt to bring Andre to his senses. "Andre, taking care of Candy's my job. Even warring nations let the Red Cross come on to their battle-fields to care for the wounded."

"Candy flipped sides. She hang with the Knights first, and now she be hanging with the Coroners. She not wounded," Andre said. "Yet."

"She's dead," Demon said, with a smirk. "You're dead if you help her."

"Don't make threats, son," Thomas said. The words were mild; the tone was steel.

"You gonna stop me, Padre?" Demon stepped right up to him. He wasn't as tall as Thomas, but his adolescent body had been fired in the furnace of hot city streets. His chest was broad, and under the stretched-out hoodie, Garnet knew that his shirt bulged with muscle. And quite likely something even more sinister.

"If I have to."

Demon took a step backward and looked away, as if his bluff had been called. Then he sprang.

Garnet leaped back in horror as Thomas Stonehill came crashing toward her. It took her a second to realize that he had not been taken unaware. As she watched he twisted, using his weight to take Demon down with him. In moments Demon was pinned underneath him. Thomas had the side of one hand against Demon's Adam's apple and a knee in Demon's groin.

Demon seemed to be in shock; then he raised a fist.

Thomas slammed Demon's arm to the ground with his free hand. "Hit me, son, and I'll have to choose between cutting off your air or your chance to make babies."

Andre and Ferdinand had just looked on, used—Garnet

guessed—to Demon fighting and winning his own battles. Now they started toward Thomas.

"Leave him alone!" Garnet kicked off her shoe, a pump with a sizable heel. She grabbed it to use as a weapon.

Andre glanced at her, but he kept coming. Ferdinand backed off, not from fear, she guessed, but from a deep-seated belief that fighting with women was not masculine.

Garnet moved forward as Andre closed in, but before she could attempt to strike, Thomas's foot shot out and connected with Andre's ankle. The kick had just enough force to make him stumble backward.

A siren sounded. For a moment Garnet couldn't believe it. The Corners had inadequate police protection, as well as every other type of public service. Response time on direct calls was often longer than it took to dismantle a building brick by brick, and police patrols were few and far between. Now, for the first time in her memory, a police car was *where* it was supposed to be, *when* it was supposed to be.

She wondered if the Reverend Thomas Stonehill had somehow found time to pray for intercession.

Before her eyes, Ferdinand melted into the fog and disappeared down an alleyway. Andre started toward Thomas and Demon again, but Thomas had already rolled to the side. Demon was suddenly free. He sat up and looked around wildly, as if considering whether to go for Thomas, a gun, or to escape before the police got out of their car. Andre jerked him upright and made his decision by grasping his arm and pulling him toward the alley where Ferdinand had vanished.

The police car door opened, but for a moment Garnet and Thomas were the only ones on the sidewalk.

Thomas got easily to his feet. "Are you all right?"

Garnet stared at him. She was filled with confusing emotions. His black hair was ruffled, and his suit was dusty, but otherwise he looked as if his fight with the MidKnights had been no more taxing than a Sunday school class.

"Who in the hell do you think you are?" she exploded.

He stared at her as if she were crazy.

"You come here and think you can change this place, but you don't know a thing about it," she said. "You've just made sure that the Knights will stay on my case. Well, Reverend Stonehill, you'd better say your prayers loud and clear tonight. Because the next time those boys come looking for me, they might well *use* the guns they had tucked away today!"

ABOUT THE AUTHOR

Emilie Richards is the author of seventy plus novels, which have been published in more than twenty-one countries and sixteen languages. Emilie has won the RITA from Romance Writers of America, and multiple awards from RT Book Reviews, including one for career achievement. She regularly appears on bestseller lists, and ten of her books have been made into television movies in Germany. Emilie lives in Southwest Florida with her husband in the winter and western New York in the summer.

**Join Emilie and her readers at:
website http://emilierichards.com.**

To learn more about upcoming books, giveaways and special content for subscribers, sign up for Emilie's mailing list:
http://emilierichards.com/mailing-list/.

Made in the USA
Las Vegas, NV
20 September 2021